Ælfred's Daughter

By

H A Culley

Book one of the Birth of England

Published by

oHp

Orchard House Publishing

First Kindle Edition 2021

Text copyright © 2021 H A Culley

Cover Image: © Shutterstock-D M Cherry

Principle Characters

<u>Members of Jørren's Gesith (also called hearth warriors)</u>

Acwel – A Saxon who became a scout when he was a boy

Arne* – A Norseman, formerly Jørren's body servant

Eafer – A former outlaw pardoned by Jørren

Eomær – The Mercian son of a charcoal burner

Godric – A Dane, the son of the late Viking leader Hæsten

Lyndon* – Another Saxon who became a scout when he was a boy

Rinan – Captain of Jørren's warband

Later members of Æthelflæd's personal warband

<u>Other Characters</u>

Æbbe – The daughter of Jørren and his second wife Hilda, married to Eirik Fairhair

Ælfflæd - King Eadweard's second wife

Ælfweard –Eadweard's elder son by Ælfflæd

Ælfwynn – Daughter of Æðelred and Æthelflæd

Æscwin – Jørren's elder son, now the Abbot of Cantwareburh Monastery in Cent

Æthelflæd – Eldest daughter Ælfred and Ealhswith, later Lady of the Mercians

Æthelstan – Son of Eadweard and Ecgwynna, now Æthelflæd's ward

Æðelred – Lord of Mercia

Æðelwold – The late King Æthelred's younger son, a contestant for Ælfred's throne

Algar and Eadling – Two Northumbrian brothers who became outlaws

Almund – The captain of Æðelwold's warband

Astrid – A Danish servant girl who Wynnstan falls in love with

Beadurof – Leader of a band of young thieves in Cæstir

Beorhtric and Ceowald – Two of Ywer's hearth warriors

Bjørn Frami – Danish hersir who joined Jørren's warband with his men

Chad – One of Æthelflæd's warriors and a friend of Wynnstan's.

Cuthfleda – Jørren's eldest daughter, head of Lady Æthelflæd's household

Deorwine – One of Æðelred's gesith, later captain of Æthelflæd personal warband

Ecgwynna – First wife of King Eadweard (married in secret), now a nun

Edith – Ecgwynna's daughter, later married to King Sihtric of Northumbria

Edmund – Captain of Ywer's warband

Eadweard – King of Wessex

Edwin – Eadweard's younger son by his second wife, Ælfflæd

Eirik Fairhair – Jarl of Wirhealum (the Wirral)

Eohric – Danish King of East Anglia

Erian – Prior of Cæstir Monastery

Frode – Wynnstan's Norse companion during the time he lived in the woods

Hengist – A potboy rescued by Ywer

Hywel Dda – King of Brycheiniog

Gunnar – Ingimund's son

Gyda – Ywer's Norse wife, daughter of Jarl Harald.

Idwal the Bald – Son of King Anarawd of Gwynedd

Ingimund – Norse warlord who invaded Cæstirscīr in 902

Ingwær, Eowils and Halfdan – Joint Kings of Northumbria

Irwyn – Ywer's son

Jørren – Ealdorman of Cæstirscīr

Kjesten – Ywer's twin sister and wife of Odda, Eadred's eldest son

Leofdæg – Member of Ywer's warband, later captain of Cæstir's garrison

Niall Glúndub – Irish chieftain, later King of Ailech in north-western Ireland

Osfirth – Ealdorman of Wiltunscīr, later also Hereræswa of Wessex

Oswine - Jørren's stepson, Ealdorman of Cent

Plegmund – Archbishop of Cantwareburh

Sawin, Wardric and Tidhelm – Three of Wynnstan's scouts

Sigehelm – Shire reeve of Cent

Skarde – Half-brother of Jarl Eirik Fairhair

Swiðhun – One of Æthelflæd's scouts who joins Wynnstan

Uhtric – Physician employed by Jørren

Ywer – Jørren's second son and twin brother of Kjesten

Wilfrid – Member of Ywer's warband

Wirfrith – Bishop of Wirecestre

Wynnstan – A member of Æthelflæd's warband, later captain of Æthelstan's gesith

Place Names

Afon	River Avon
Apletune	Appleton, Cheshire
Bardenai	Bardney, Lincolnshire
Brigge	Bridgenorth, Shropshire
Britannia	The island of Britain
Brycheiniog	Brecknockshire, Wales
Cæstir	Chester, Cheshire
Cæstirscīr	Cheshire
Cantwareburh	Canterbury, Kent
Casingc Stræt (Roman road)	Watling Street
Cedde	Cheadle, Cheshire
Celelea	Chowley, Cheshire
Cent	Kent
Danmǫrk	Denmark
Dēvā	River Dee
Dofras	Dover, Kent
Dornsæte	Dorset
Dyflin (Viking name)	Dublin, Ireland
Dyfneintscīr	Devon
Ēast Seaxna Rīce	Essex
Eforwic (Saxon name)	York, North Yorkshire
Englaland	England
Fearndune	Farndon, Cheshire
Frankia	Parts of France, Belgium and Germany
Frodesham	Frodsham, Cheshire

Glowecestre	Gloucester, Gloucestershire
Grárhöfn	Near Birkenhead, Cheshire (fictional)
Herefordscīr	Herefordshire
Huntedone	Huntingdon, Cambridgeshire
Hwicce	Part of Mercia, most of Gloucestershire and Worcestershire
Íralandes Sǽ	Irish Sea
Íralond	Ireland
Licefelle	Litchfield, Staffordshire
Liedeberge	Ledbury, Hereforshire
Lincolia	Lincoln, Lincolnshire
Lindsey	Part of modern day Lincolnshire
Loncastrescīr	Lancashire
Lundenburg	London
Malberthorp	Mablethorpe, Lincolnshire
Mamecestre	Manchester
Mann	Isle of Man
Mǽresēa	River Mersey
Nestone	Neston, Cheshire
Orkneyjar	Orkney Islands
Oxenafordascīr	Oxfordshire
Sæfern	River Severn
Somersaete	Somerset
Sūð-sǽ	English Channel
Sūþrīgescīr	Surrey
Suth-Seaxe	Sussex

Tamuuordescīr	Staffordshire (then based around Tamworth)
Tatenhale	Tattenhall, Cheshire
Temes	River Thames
Tes	River Tees
Theocsbury	Tewksbury, Gloucestershire
Tiddingforde	In Bedfordshire (No longer exists)
Tomtun	Tamworth, Staffordshire
Totenhale	Tettenhall, Wolverhampton
Uisge	River Great Ouse
Waruwic	Warwick, Warwickshire
Wealas	Wales
Wōdnesfeld	Wednesfield, Wolverhampton
Winburne	Wimborne Minster, Dorset
Wintanceaster	Winchester, Hampshire
Wirecestre	Worcester, Worcestershire
Wirhealum	Wirral Peninsula, Cheshire
Yorvik (Viking name)	York, North Yorkshire
Ynys Môn	Isle of Anglesey, Wales

Glossary

ANGLO-SAXON

Ænglisc – Old English, the common language of Angles, Saxons and Jutes.

Ætheling – literally 'throne-worthy. An Anglo-Saxon prince

Avantail - a curtain of chainmail attached to a helmet to cover the throat and neck

Birlinn – a wooden ship similar to the later Scottish galleys but smaller than a Viking longship. Usually with a single mast and square rigged sail, they could also be propelled by oars with one man to each oar

Bondsman – a slave who was treated as the property of his master

Braies – underwear similar to modern undershorts. Worn only by males

Bretwalda – overlord of some or all of the Anglo-Saxon kingdoms

Bryttas – Britons, essentially the inhabitants of Cornwall (Kernow), Wales (Wealas), Cumbria and Strathclyde at this time.

Burh - fortified settlement

Byrnie - a tunic of chain mail, usually sleeveless or short sleeved

Ceorl – a freeman who worked the land or else provided a service or trade such as metal working, carpentry, weaving etc. They ranked between

10

thegns and villeins and provided the fyrd in time of war

Cyning – Old English for king and the term by which they were normally addressed

Danegeld - a tax levied in Anglo-Saxon England to bribe Danish invaders to leave

Ealdorman – The senior noble of a shire. A royal appointment, ealdormen led the men of their shire in battle, presided over law courts and levied taxation on behalf of the king

Englaland – England (meaning *Land of the Angles*)

Fyrd - Anglo-Saxon army mobilised from freemen to defend their shire, or to join a campaign led by the king

Gesith – the companions of a king, prince or noble, usually acting as his bodyguard

Hacksilver - Fragments of silver that were used as currency

Hearth Warriors - alternative term for members of a Gesith

Heræswa – military commander or general. The man who commanded the army of a nation under the king

Hersir – a landowner who could recruit enough other freemen to serve under him

Hide – a measure of the land sufficient to support the household of one ceorl

Hideage - a tax paid to the royal exchequer for every hide of land

Hundred – the unit for local government and taxation which equated to ten tithings

Pallium - an ecclesiastical vestment bestowed by the Pope upon metropolitans and primates as a symbol of their authority

Reeve - a local official including the chief magistrate of a town or district, also the person manging a landowner's estate

Sǣfyrd – Members of the fyrd (q.v.) who served at sea

Sǣ Hererǣswa – Commander of the King Ælfred's navy

Seax – a bladed weapon somewhere in size between a dagger and a sword. Mainly used for close-quarter fighting where a sword would be too long and unwieldy

Settlement – any grouping of residential buildings, usually around the king's or lord's hall. In 8th century England the term town or village had not yet come into use

Shire – an administrative area into which an Anglo-Saxon kingdom was divided

Shire Reeve – later corrupted to sheriff. A royal official responsible for implementing the king's laws within his shire

Skypfyrd – fyrd raised to man ships of war to defend the coast

Thegn – the lowest rank of noble. A man who held a certain amount of land direct from the king or from a senior nobleman, ranking between an ordinary freeman, or ceorl, and an ealdorman

Tithing - a group of ten ceorls who lived close together and were collectively responsible for each other's behaviour, also the land required to support them (i.e. ten hides)

Wergeld - the price set upon a person's life or injury and paid as compensation by the person responsible to the family of the dead or injured person. It freed the perpetrator of further punishment or obligation and prevented a blood feud

Witan – meeting or council

Witenaġemot – the council of an Anglo-Saxon kingdom. Its composition varied, depending on the matters to be debated. Usually it consisted of the ealdormen, the king's thegns, the bishops and the abbots

Villein - a peasant who ranked above a bondsman or slave but who was legally tied to his vill and who was obliged to give one or more day's service to his lord each week in payment for his land

Vill - a thegn's holding or similar area of land in Anglo-Saxon England which would later be called a parish or a manor

VIKING

Bóndi - farmers and craftsmen who were free men and enjoyed rights such as the ownership of weapons and membership of the Thing. They could be tenants or landowners. Plural bøndur

Byrnie - a tunic of chain mail, usually sleeveless or short sleeved

Hacksilver – (or Hacksilber) Fragments of silver that were used as currency

Helheim – the realm in the afterlife for those who don't die in battle

Hersir – a bóndi who was chosen to lead a band of warriors under a king or a jarl. Typically they were wealthy landowners who could recruit enough other bøndur to serve under their command

Hirdman – a member of a king's or a jarl's personal bodyguard, collectively known as the hird

Hold – Title given to a jarl with significant territorial possessions.

Jarl – a Norse or Danish chieftain; in Sweden they were regional governors appointed by the king

Konungr - King

Mjolnir – Thor's hammer, also the pendant worn around the neck by most pagan Vikings

Nailed God – pagan name for Christ, also called the White Christ

Swéoþeod – Swedes, literally Swedish people

Thing – the governing assembly made up of the free people of the community presided over by a lagman. The meeting-place of a thing was called a thingstead

Thrall – a slave. A man, woman or child in bondage to his or her owner. Thralls had no rights and could be beaten or killed with impunity

Valhalla – the hall of the slain. Where heroes who die in battle spend the afterlife feasting and fighting according to Norse mythology

LONGSHIPS

In order of size:

Knarr – also called karve or karvi. The smallest type of longship. It had 6 to 16 benches and, like their English equivalents, they were mainly used for fishing and trading, but they were occasionally commissioned for military use. They were broader in the beam and had a deeper draught than other longships.

Snekkja – (plural snekkjur) typically the smallest longship used in warfare and it was classified as a ship with at least 20 rowing benches. A typical snekkja might have a length of 17m, a width of 2.5m and a draught of only 0.5m. Norse snekkjas, designed for deep fjords and Atlantic weather, typically had more draught than the Danish type, which were intended for shallow water.

Drekar - (dragon ship) larger warships consisting of more than 30 rowing benches. Typically they could carry a crew of some 70–80 men and measured around 30m in length. These ships were more properly called skeids; the term drekar referred to the carvings of menacing beasts, such as dragons and snakes, mounted on the prow of the ship during a sea battle or when raiding. Strictly speaking drekar is the plural form, the singular being dreki or dreka, but these words don't appear to be accepted usage in English.

Introduction by the Author

Although this series of novels contains some of the characters introduced in the previous series - *The Saga of Wessex* - it is a separate quartet of novels.

The books in this series are works of fiction but I have tried to stick as closely as possible to the history as outlined in the sparse written records of the early tenth century.

The names of both people and places that I have used are, as far as possible, those in use at the time, although spelling was inconsistent at this time.

Prologue

Autumn 899

The sombre group of nobles and their wives followed King Ælfred's coffin as it was carried out of the church that served the monastery at Wintanceaster. It was colder than usual for the end of October and the late king's eldest daughter, Æthelflæd, wife of Æðelred, Lord of the Mercians, shivered despite the thick fur-lined cloak she wore. The procession was led by her mother and her brother, Eadweard, King of Cent and now heir presumptive, although his succession was far from certain. Æthelflæd glanced up at the grey clouds which scudded across the leaden sky and felt the first raindrop fall on her cheek.

Every ealdormen of Wessex was present, as were most of the senior churchmen – the bishops and abbots. The following day they would meet to choose the man who would wear Ælfred's crown. There were three possible candidates for the throne – known as æthelings, which meant *throne worthy*. The most obvious candidate was Ælfred's only son, Eadweard, but the two sons of Æthelred, Ælfred's brother and predecessor as king, were also contenders.

Æthelred's elder son had no interest in the throne and seemed content with the estates left to him by his father. However the younger son, Æðelwold, had long resented the fact that Ælfred had taken his father's throne. He'd only been a young boy at the time but, now that his uncle was dead, he was determined that the throne should be his.

Plegmund, Archbishop of Cantwareburh, led the prayers as the coffin was reverentially placed inside a simple tomb outside in the cemetery. That wouldn't be Ælfred's final resting place; an elaborate stone sarcophagus would be carved by the master masons inside the church to hold the great king's remains but it would take some time to complete. For now the humble rough-hewn slabs of limestone would have to suffice.

After the king's widow and the immediate family had each thrown a handful of earth onto the wooden coffin, four men struggled to lift the stone lid and place it on top of the tomb. Plegmund blessed the congregation and they made for the shelter of the king's hall with unseemly haste.

'Will you and Æðelred stay for the Witenaġemot tomorrow?' Eadweard asked his sister after the funeral was over.

'Why? My husband isn't a noble of Wessex,' she asked, surprised at the request.

'No, but I want to show the ealdormen and king's thegns that I have Mercia's support.'

'Our father made a mistake when he started to regard himself as King of the Anglo-Saxons in his later years; not helped by Bishop Asser who described him as such in the chronicle he wrote about our father's life,' she said. 'Mercia is fiercely proud of being an independent kingdom, not a vassal state of Wessex.'

'Mercia – even the rump that Æðelred rules over – wouldn't exist if it wasn't for Wessex,' Eadweard retorted with some heat.

It was true. The north-eastern half of the kingdom was occupied by the Danish invaders – the Great Heathen Army of four decades ago – and the south-west would have been overrun had Wessex not defeated the Danes at Ethandun and in various other battles since then.

'We depend on each other,' she replied just as fiercely. 'If we didn't, any disunity would play into the hands of the Danes.'

His father's ambition had been to unite the land of the Angles, Saxons and Jutes – who were increasingly being referred to as the Ænglisc – into one kingdom called Englaland. Eadweard's desire to do so was no less fervent. However, he was astute enough to know that was a long game and arguing with his sister served no purpose. He therefore changed the subject.

'I'm going to announce my betrothal tonight.'

'Betrothal? Who to? I've heard nothing about this,' she replied, surprised.

'No, our father wasn't in favour; now there is no obstacle to the match.'

'Who's the girl?'

'Ælfflæd, daughter of Æthelhelm.'

Æthelflæd thought for a moment. Æthelhelm was a common name but the only one with a daughter of that name was the former Ealdorman of Wiltshire who had died the previous year. Ælfflæd's elder brother, Osfirth, had become ealdorman. Presumably Eadweard intended to marry her to secure Osfirth's

19

loyalty. It was a shrewd move. Eadweard had ruled the eastern shires of Wessex but he needed to make sure the western half of the kingdom wouldn't back his cousin for the throne and none of the other ealdormen in the west had a suitable daughter or sister available.

'There is one other matter,' Eadweard continued, his voice like ice. 'Æthelstan is nearly nine, more than old enough to become a novice monk. Please oblige me by sending him to Cantwareburh as soon as you return to Glowecestre.'

Æthelflæd took a deep breath. There was one matter over which she and her brother would never agree and that was the fate of Æthelstan. Eadweard had been smitten by Jørren's niece, Ecgwynna, as a young man and he'd married her in secret. They had one child – Æthelstan – but the girl was the daughter of a minor thane and Eadweard had been forced to repudiate her by his parents. The baby had been sent to Æthelflæd to be brought up in Mercia.

Eadweard had long insisted that the boy become a novice monk so that he wouldn't constitute a threat to any future sons of his with another wife. However, his sister was vehemently opposed to the idea.

'He's not suited to the monastic life,' she retorted forcefully. 'Besides which he's your eldest, and so far only, son. He should be trained as an ætheling and, in due course, as a warrior.'

'He's a bastard and I'll decide his future,' Eadweard retorted angrily.

'We both know that's not true. You married his mother.'

'Prove it,' he sneered. 'The priest is dead and there is no deed of marriage.'

She knew that wasn't the case, even if her brother thought he'd destroyed the only copy. Another had been deposited with Æscwin, Abbot of Cantwareburh at the time, and he'd taken it with him when he moved to Cæstir. She decided that it was time that Æthelstan was moved out of his father's reach.

†††

On the same day some two hundred miles to the north Jørren, Ealdorman of Cæstirscīr, stared gloomily at another coffin as it was lowered into the earth. His elder son, Abbot Æscwin, intoned the committal prayers as the bitterly cold wind swept across the monastery's graveyard outside the walls of Cæstir.

Jørren's wife, Hilda, had been six years younger than he was and that fact depressed him as much as his grief at her loss. He couldn't help but feel that he'd outlived his allotted time on this earth.

He had always been active and had been wounded many times during the various battles and skirmishes he'd fought against the Danes. Now his joints had stiffened and his old injuries ached, especially when it was cold or wet.

When he heard about the king's death a fortnight later he became even more depressed. Eadweard had been chosen by the Witenaġemot of Wessex to succeed his father, although he had won only narrowly. His cousin, Æðelwold, had refused to accept the decision, claiming that several of his supporters hadn't been able to arrive in time. He'd sworn to take the throne from Eadweard and was mustering an army to do just that.

If he was honest, Jørren preferred Eadweard as king, despite the antipathy between the two men. Eadweard had proved himself a capable commander in the field whereas Æðelwold had no such experience. Although Wessex and the Anglian half of Mercia had been at peace ever since the death of Hæsten, the leader of the most recent Viking invasion, nearly four years ago, the threat posed by Danish Mercia, East Anglia and Northumbria remained, to say nothing of the pinprick raids by the Norse of Íralond, Mann and Orkneyjar.

Æscwin finished his prayers and Jørren's youngest daughter, Æbbe, came to comfort her father. She was the only child that he and Hilda shared; his other children were from his first marriage. Æbbe's husband, the Norseman Eirik, Jarl of nearby Wirhealum – the peninsula between the rivers Dēvā and Mǣresēa - hung back, feeling somewhat awkward. Although baptised as a Christian some years before, Eirik's people still cremated their dead and to them burial was a somewhat unusual practice.

The old Viking religion held that a person's spirit couldn't enter the various realms of the afterlife until their mortal remains had been consumed. Burning was therefore a far quicker route to the soul's final destination than the gradual decay of entombment.

On the other side of the grave Jørren's younger son, Ywer, exchanged a sympathetic look with his father.

The ealdorman wished that his other two daughters could have been there but both had left for the king's funeral in Wintanceaster before his messengers had arrived. For many years his eldest daughter Cuthfleda had been the head of Æthelflæd's household and her closest advisor. Where Æthelflæd went so did Cuthfleda. His other daughter – Kjesten – was Ywer's twin but she was married to Odda, the Ealdorman of Dyfneintscīr and it was many years since he'd last seen her or her children.

Jørren sighed. He'd been fighting Vikings since he was a boy of thirteen. Now, when peace had been established at long last, he'd been looking forward to spending his declining years with Hilda. Instead she'd been cruelly ripped from his side, leaving him alone. Even Ywer wouldn't be there to keep him company as winter drew close.

Jørren had given his son several vills along the River Mæresēa and Ywer had built a new hall for himself at Apletune over twenty miles away. It was some four miles south of the river which formed the boundary between Cæstirscīr and the wild lands to the North where Norse invaders had driven out most of the Northumbrian Angles - the previous inhabitants - in recent years.

The Norse who lived there had no single leader to unite them so Jørren didn't fear a serious invasion of his lands but they were prone to launch small scale raids across the Mæresēa. Ywer's job was to patrol the border and minimise their depredations.

He had made his task somewhat easier by falling in love with Gyda, the only child of one of the most powerful of the Norse Jarls. They had married a year ago and had recently been blessed with a baby son who they'd called Irwyn, which meant lover of the sea. The old jarl doted on his grandson and helped Ywer to keep the shire's northern boundary secure.

Unfortunately, Jørren's other borders weren't as quiet. For some time the Welsh across the River Sæfern had been his allies. Now that the threat of Hæsten's Vikings had been removed, the ancient enmity between Mercia and the Welsh kingdom of Gwynedd had resurfaced. So far trouble had been confined to the stealing of livestock but, as its king grew older and frailer, his son - Idwal the Bald - became more powerful. Unfortunately he was no friend of Mercia's.

Matters were a bit better in the east, in the area known as the Danelaw. Mercia had originally stretched from Lundenburg and the valley of the River Temes in the south along the border with East Anglia to the River Humbre and across to the River Mǣresēa in the north then down the River Sæfern in the west. Now it was bisected by the Roman road called Casingc Stræt. The vast area to the north and east of the ancient road was known as the Danelaw.

Thankfully no one overlord ruled the Danelaw. The area near East Anglia was called the Five Boroughs, each ruled by its own jarl. Although they were theoretically controlled by Eohric, the Danish King of East Anglia, in practice the jarls were virtually independent and acted as such most of the time.

The rest of the Danelaw as a hotchpotch of small jarldoms and independent Anglian vills.

24

Consequently, although there were occasion raids into the part of Mercia ruled by Æðelred, including Jørren's shire, these were small scale affairs intent on gathering a few head of livestock, some slaves and a little plunder.

In the weeks and months after the funeral Jørren sunk into despondency and, without his former diligent care, the management of his shire started to suffer. Eirik was the shire reeve and he found it necessary to take on more and more responsibility; something he resented. He was Jarl of Wirhealum and governing that took most of his time. He was on the point of going to see Jørren and giving him an ultimatum when something happened which shook the ealdorman out of his lethargy.

Æðelwold had raised the standard of rebellion. With Wessex divided into two camps it was a distinct possibility that the jarls of the Danelaw would see this as their chance to invade the western half of Mercia. Furthermore, Æðelwold had abducted a nun from the convent at Winburne in Dornsæte and forced her to marry him. The nun was Ecgwynna, Eadweard's first wife, the mother of Æthelstan and Jørren's niece.

Whilst Jørren felt no loyalty to Eadweard, any inclination he might have had to support Æðelwold was negated by the latter's treatment of Ecgwynna. He was angry and wished he could do something to avenge his niece's violation but he was far away from Wessex. Furthermore, the last thing he wanted was to get involved in the struggle for the throne that loomed on the horizon.

Chapter One

900

Four men rode into Glowecestre shortly after the news of Æðelwold's rebellion had reached Mercia. They had the look of Danish mercenaries, killers for hire, and those they encountered gave them a wide berth. They secured lodgings for the night in a tavern in one of the less salubrious areas of the settlement and, after stabling their horses, they sat down to drink and began a stilted conversation in stilted Ænglisc with the men at the next table. It wasn't so much a conversation as an interrogation and the frightened locals soon told the men what they wanted to know. The Danes left the tavern shortly afterwards and three headed towards the monastery whilst the fourth set off to hire a cart.

'What are you going to do about Æthelstan?' Cuthfleda asked Æthelflæd as she helped her to dress for the evening.

Ever since Ælfred's funeral Æthelflæd had been wracking her brains, trying to decide where to send the boy where he'd be out of reach of his father. She'd discussed it with Æðelred but her husband had been wary of upsetting the new King of Wessex. His advice was to do as Eadweard demanded. However, the boy was his wife's nephew and he therefore left the decision to her.

For now the boy was attending lessons in Latin, reading and writing with the monks in the nearby monastery but he returned to Æðelred's hall every evening. His routine was common knowledge and the men in the tavern had readily told the four strangers that the boy left the monastery just before the service of Vespers. It meant little to the pagan Danes but further questioning revealed that Vespers was held at sunset.

The monastery and the Lord of Mercia's hall were in the same complex. The gates were open during the day but closed at sunset. When the mercenaries reached the gates it was still light and the bored looking sentry was looking forward to returning to the arms of his mistress. He gave them no more than a cursory glance and made no attempt to ask their business. Warriors went to and from the hall all the time and, although he didn't recognise these three, his mind was on other things.

Æthelstan left the scriptorium when the monks and the novices with whom he studied went to attend vespers. It was only a few hundred yards from there to the hall where he lived but Lady Æthelflæd always sent one of her household and a member of her husband's gesith to escort the boy. It wasn't so much for security but Æthelstan had a habit of disappearing, either to the kitchens or the stables, if left to his own devices.

On this day Cuthfleda and a warrior called Deorwine had gone to fetch him. Cuthfleda didn't normally run this sort of errand but Æthelflæd wanted to talk to her nephew before he went back to his own chamber. Æthelstan was tall for his age, looking more like eleven or twelve than nine. He was good-looking, like his father, and he tended to be vain about his appearance. He'd been given a dagger by Æðelred on his ninth birthday and he wore this on his belt with pride. It was a handsome piece with a jewelled pommel and a gold wire binding on the handle which was meant for show rather than serious use. Nevertheless, the nine inch blade was sharp and it could be as lethal as any other dagger.

Many ladies wore a small eating knife hanging from their girdles along with their purse but not Cuthfleda. She carried a small dagger instead and knew how to use it. Training with weapons by women was frowned on but both Æthelflæd and she had practiced defending themselves for some time now. Both were proficient with dagger, seax and bow, although only small hunting bows that lacked any real power. Little did she know how useful that training in close combat was about to become.

The three mercenaries waited in the shadows of an alleyway between two huts for Æthelstan to appear. One carried a blanket to throw over the boy whilst the other two drew their swords ready to slay the boy's companions. Their quarry was late. The bell to summon the monks to vespers had already sounded but still there was no sign of him. The three abductors sweated and fidgeted, getting nervous with every passing minute.

The sun was sinking below the horizon by the time that the boy appeared walking beside a young woman and talking animatedly. A warrior who looked to be about thirty years of age walked ahead of them, his eyes darting warily from side to side. Torsten, the leader of the abductors, cursed silently. He hadn't expected the escort to be on his guard.

Instead of heading for the main door into the hall the trio suddenly turned down a side alley before they reached the abductors' hiding place. For a moment Torsten thought that they had been spotted but the three continued unhurriedly on their way, the boy still chattering to the woman. A moment later they disappeared from sight.

Torsten was in a quandary. By now the fourth member of their group would be waiting with a cart by the small postern gate nor far from where they stood. He couldn't stay there long without arousing suspicion. Torsten's plan was to kill the escort, throw a blanket over the boy and carry him to the postern through a series of narrow alleyways.

Surprise and speed were the keys to success. Now they would have to chase after the trio and the element of surprise would be lost. However, it was either that or wait another day. The latter might be have been the prudent option but the longer they delayed the greater the risk of discovery. Torsten suspected that the tavern keeper was already curious about them. He quickly made his mind up.

'We'll have to go after them, I'll take the guard whilst you deal with the woman, Gorm. Ready? Move!'

Cuthfleda was the first to hear the pounding of running feet. Thankfully Æthelstan had run out of things to tell her a second before or she might not have heard the mercenaries until it was too late.

'Run, Æthelstan!' she shouted, pushing the boy behind her as she turned, her hand already dragging her dagger from its sheath. 'Go and alert the guards.'

Gorm slashed at her head as the other two ignored her and pushed past. Had the blow landed it would have sliced deeply into her neck but Cuthfleda dropped down onto one knee and the blade whistled over her head. She thrust upwards between the man's thighs before he could recover and warm blood washed over her hand. The dagger had sunk its full length into the man's bladder, cutting into his scrotum and prostate gland en route.

He screamed in agony and, dropping his sword, clutched at his groin with both hands. Cuthfleda pulled her dagger clear, not without some difficulty, as the man fell to the ground. A second later she cut his throat and turned to see what was happening behind her.

By the time that Torsten had reached Deorwine, the Mercian had unsheathed his seax and the two engaged in a fierce sword fight. They were fairly equally matched and on any other day it would have taken time for each to explore the other's skill in search of weaknesses. However, Torsten was in a hurry and, where he would normally have probed and tested, now he tried to overcome the Mercian with speed and shear brutality. However, Deorwine was an excellent swordsman and managed to counter the Dane's attacks until he felt his opponent weaken. He also had an advantage in that the seax was more manoeuvrable than the longer blade of a sword in the confines of the alley

Torsten was tiring and became even more desperate to kill Deorwine. The Mercian turned his wrist so that the Dane's blade slid off the seax leaving him off balance. Deorwine brought his seax back into play and thrust the point into the other man's right armpit. Most men would have dropped their sword in shock but Torsten gritted his teeth against the pain and clamped his arm down, trapping Deorwine's blade.

Meanwhile the third Dane had tried to envelop the boy in the blanket but Æthelstan dashed past him. The man cursed and twisted around to try again but the boy darted away once more. The Dane gave up and dropped the blanket; he pulled his dagger from its sheath and brought the pommel down, intending to knock the boy out. Æthelstan was too quick and neatly evaded the blow. Instead of striking his head it connected with his left shoulder, numbing it.

Any other nine-year-old might have cowered away in fear; but not Æthelstan. He saw red and, pulling his own dagger out, he ducked down and darted between the man's legs. His assailant went to turn around but before he could do so the boy slashed his sharp blade across the Dane's right leg just above the knee, slicing through both hamstrings. The man cried out in pain and fell to the ground as his leg gave way.

Deorwine was frantically trying to pull his sword from its scabbard with his left hand but he couldn't do it. Torsten grinned at him, his broken teeth glinting in the faint light of the moon now that night had fallen, although the pain he was in made it more of a grimace than a grin. He pulled his own dagger free with his left hand and was about to plunge it into Deorwine's neck when he suddenly arched his back and a moment later blood spurted out of his mouth as he collapsed.

Cuthfleda stood behind him holding a bloody dagger. For a moment she looked down at the dying man and then the dagger fell from her hands and she stood there convulsed with sobs that wracked her whole body. She had trained with weapons and was especially proficient with the bow but she had never killed a man before and now she had slain two in quick succession.

Deorwine's instinct was to comfort her but his prime responsibility was Æthelstan. The boy was staring in shock at the man he'd incapacitated as he tried ineffectually to regain his feet. Giving up the attempt to stand, he started to crawl away.

'See to the boy,' Deorwine said quietly to Cuthfleda.

She nodded and, pulling herself together, went and wrapped her arms around Æthelstan. For a moment he sobbed in her arms but then he pushed her gently away and dried his tears on his sleeve.

'If I'm to be a warrior, then I must get used to using weapons against my enemies,' he said, his treble voice firm and resolute.

Deorwine had stopped the Dane's effort to escape by putting his foot on the injured leg. The man shrieked and stopped moving. The Mercian bent down and put his mouth close to the other man's ear.

'Who sent you?' he asked in Danish.

When the man didn't reply Deorwine stamped his foot down eliciting another ear piercing screech. By this time several other warriors had arrived in the alley. Deorwine looked up but ignored them.

'Come, Æthelstan,' Cuthfleda said, 'this is no place for us. You two come with me and escort us to the Lady Æthelflæd,' she told the two nearest warriors.

There probably wasn't any further danger but she wasn't about to take any chances.

Outside the postern gate the fourth member of Torsten's group was getting increasingly nervous at the delay. When he heard the sound of fighting followed by screams he didn't hesitate any longer but flicked his whip at the rump of the two horses pulling the wagon and made off.

Deorwine, failing to get a sensible response from the injured Dane, had him carried away and locked in a hut before going to report to Lord Æðelred. He found him ensconced with his wife and Cuthfleda.

'Has he said anything?' Æðelred barked at Deorwine before the warrior got a chance to open his mouth.

'No, lord, but he will. Æthelstan only cut the hamstrings of one leg so he's not in danger of dying; not yet at any rate. I'm sure we can make him talk.'

Æðelred nodded absently and dismissed Deorwine. The latter withdrew and went to drink an ale or two with his friends to celebrate surviving the attack.

'This makes it even more imperative to send my nephew somewhere where he'll be safe,' Æthelflæd said as soon as the door close behind Deorwine.

'You don't think those men were sent by Eadweard?'

'No, if he wanted to make sure that I sent his son to Cantwareburh he only had to send a letter with an escort to make sure his orders were carried out. I suspect that Æðelwold is behind this. He's already kidnapped the boy's mother and forced her to marry him. I'm not sure why Æðelwold wants to lay his hands on her son but if he'd wanted him dead the Danes would have tried to kill him, not throw a blanket over his head and abduct him.'

'Perhaps he thought that he could use him to weaken Eadweard's claim to the throne,' Æðelred said thoughtfully. 'Eadweard couldn't acknowledge his son as legitimate if he fell into Æðelwold's hands.'

'Why would he do that after refusing to acknowledge him for so long?' Cuthfleda asked, looking puzzled.

'Thing change,' he snapped, annoyed by her interruption. 'Kings always want an undisputed successor; it strengthens their position,' he replied tartly, glaring at his wife.

Her failure to give him a son, or even allow him to try for one, rankled.

'I can't see that,' his wife said, shaking her head. 'Having originally claimed that the boy was a bastard, my brother can hardly admit that he lied; especially not now that he is betrothed to Ælfflæd. It would make Æthelstan senior to any sons that she and Eadweard might have in the future and neither his new wife nor her brother and Eadweard's new ally, Ealdorman Osfirth, are likely to accept that.'

35

'That doesn't mean that Æðelwold realises that.' Æðelred pointed out. 'After all, he married Æthelstan's mother, despite the fact that she was a nun and thus imperilled his immortal soul. He must have thought that it would help his cause to do so, but without capturing Eadweard's son as well I really can't see how it has.'

The two lapsed into silence, wondering about Æðelwold's stratagem. It didn't make any sense to them but then Æðelwold's thinking was always coloured by the supposed injustice of being passed over for the crown when his father, Ælfred's predecessor as king, had died.

'Eadweard wants me to join him,' Æðelred said after a long pause. 'Æðelwold has seized Winburne and is trying to muster an army there.'

'Why Winburne? It isn't even a burh.'

'No, it may not be a defended settlement but it's where his father is buried. I suspect that it's all about symbolism.'

'Will you go?'

'I've already told Eadweard that I need to stay in Mercia in case the weakness of Wessex is seen as an opportunity by the Danes or the Welsh or, heaven forbid both, to invade. However, I have a feeling he's going to insist.'

'We are allies and both of you have promised to go to the aid of the other in times of need.'

'You're right, of course,' Æðelred admitted, 'but our alliance was intended to defend ourselves against the Danes, not get involved in an internal dispute over the crown of Wessex. Besides I'm his ally not his vassal and my loyalty is to Mercia, not Eadweard of Wessex. That said, I don't want to offend Eadweard any more than I have to. Perhaps we should do as your brother wishes and send Æthelstan to Archbishop Plegmund?'

'No,' Æthelflæd replied with some passion. 'He doesn't want to enter the Church and, as he demonstrated today, he has both courage and initiative. He will make a great warrior when he's older; but I agree that he can't stay here.'

'Harrumph,' Cuthfleda said, clearing her throat. 'May I make a suggestion? Why don't you send him to Cæstir? After all, my father is the boy's great-uncle.'

†††

Jørren re-read the letter with a sinking heart. Although it was unsigned and the seal bore no imprint he knew that it had come from his eldest daughter, no doubt written at the behest of the Lady Æthelflæd. There was no greeting or preamble.

This letter must remain anonymous in case it falls into the wrong hands. You may have heard of the attempt to abduct a young boy from here. For his safety we think it advisable that he is sent to a place out of the reach of his enemies and others who wish to decide his future for him.

I would therefore ask that you send a few men who you trust implicitly to escort him into your care. He has the makings of a warrior and I would deem it a great favour if you would train him and guard him until he is of an age to take care of himself. I realise that this is asking a lot of you as it may put you at risk if the boy's presence is discovered. I'm sure that you will understand that I wouldn't ask this if any other acceptable course of action was open to me.

If you are agreeable, please send the boy's escort back with this messenger.

Only an idiot would think that this missive could refer to anyone other than Æthelstan. It was at times like this that he wished that Hilda was still by his side so that he could ask her advice. He was tempted to go and see Ywer and discuss it with him but he knew what his son would say. Æthelstan was his cousin's son and he would no more abandon him than he would any other member of his family. If Ywer had a fault it was his loyalty, which tended to override any other considerations.

Instead he sought out his other son, Abbot Æscwin. His view was coloured by his knowledge that Æthelstan was King Eadweard's legitimate son. Others might have heard rumours to that effect but Æscwin possessed a document which proved it – the marriage certificate between Eadweard and his cousin Ecgwynna. It meant that the boy was an ætheling and a strong candidate for the throne of Wessex in due course; always provided that Eadweard managed to defeat Æðelwold.

'Surely Æthelstan is only of value if his birth can be shown to be legitimate,' Æscwin said after his father had shown him the letter.

'Perhaps not in Æðelwold's mind. If he thinks that Eadweard is about to acknowledge Æthelstan as his legitimate son to bolster his position, Æðelwold's possession of the boy would negate any advantage that Eadweard might gain by having a ready-made heir. Of course, we both know that Eadweard won't do that for fear of offending his betrothed and her family, but Æðelwold might not realise that.'

Like Æðelred and Æthelflæd, he had been puzzled about the forced marriage between his niece and Æðelwold at first. Eventually he'd come to the conclusion that Æðelwold was blinkered by his jealousy of Eadweard and coveted whatever he imagined his cousin secretly wanted. That included Eadweard's first wife and his son.

'In any case, Æðelwold's motives are not the issue here, I need to decide whether to accept Æthelstan as my ward.'

'He's your great-nephew, father. Are the ties of blood and family more important to you than upsetting Eadweard if, or rather when, he finds out?'

'The man has never made a secret of his dislike for me, although I've never really understood why.'

'Oswine has ever been jealous of you because you took his father's place as Ealdorman of Cent. Like Æðelwold, he was too young to succeed and he used his influence with the young Eadweard to poison his mind against you.'

'I'm sure you're right, although there were times when Oswine proved to be a good friend. The man is a conundrum.'

Privately Æscwin thought that on those rare occasions when Oswine had helped Jørren he was either trying to please his mother, Hilda, or else

39

inveigle his way into Jørren's confidence in order to gain information he could later use against him.

Mention of Oswine was an unwelcome reminder that Eadweard had taken Cent away from Jørren in order to give the shire to his stepson. He remembered the anger he'd felt at the time and that decided him. He would accept responsibility for Æthelstan and if that upset Eadweard, so much the better. Jørren owed him nothing and in Cæstir he was out of Eadweard's reach, or so he thought.

†††

Two days later Ywer and seven companions set off for Glowecestre. Jørren had wisely decided that he was too old for adventures of this sort and had asked his son to go and fetch Æthelstan. The mission had to be clandestine or everyone would know what had happened to the boy. Once safely at Cæstir, Æthelstan's presence needed to remain a secret.

He didn't know what story Æthelflæd would concoct to explain the boy's disappearance but that wasn't his problem. Doubtless the king would be furious with his sister and her husband for flouting his instructions, whatever excuse they came up with, but Jørren wanted to avoid an unnecessary confrontation with Eadweard. Furthermore, he needed to conceal the boy's whereabouts from Æðelwold in case he made another attempt to abduct him.

Ywer had chosen his escort carefully. He took Arne and Eomær, two long-standing members of his father's gesith, Leofdæg and Wulfric from his own warband,

Skarde the Norse half-brother of Eirik Fairhair who had married his sister, Æbbe, and Godric, who was a Dane.

Skarde and Eirik disliked each other intensely but the former had proved himself to be a staunch and loyal member of Jørren's warband. He was also an excellent scout, as was Godric.

The latter's inclusion in the group had come as something of a surprise to many at Cæstir. Godric was the son of Hæsten, the Viking leader who'd carved a path of destruction, pillage and death throughout Wessex and Mercia for over three years before he'd died in the winter of 896. However, after his father's death, Godric had been taken in by Jørren, became a Christian and seemed to have accepted his new life without a problem. Part of the reason for his inclusion was his ability to speak Danish. Many of Jørren's warriors could speak the language fluently but few could pass as a native speaker.

The final member of the group was a monk called Erian, the prior of Cæstir Monastery. He was there, not to attend to their spiritual needs and as a healer – although those attributes were useful – but as the ostensible reason for the journey. Officially the others were escorting him to Lord Æðelred's court as an emissary of Ealdorman Jørren and that's why their shields didn't display Jørren's emblem. Instead they had painted them to display that of the Bishop of Licefelle, in whose diocese Cæstir lay.

It had proved difficult to paint the five red crosses on a white background – the symbol of the diocese - on top of Jørren's red horse's head on a black background

41

and so they had to use new shields. They looked too pristine compared to the warriors' well-worn byrnies and helmets so Ywer had his men practice with sword and shield to give them a more convincingly battered appearance before they left.

The weather in early May was balmy. The trees were coming into leaf, insects and birds flew around busy collecting pollen or twigs for nests and the workers in the fields were hard at work weeding whilst small children ran around scaring birds away from the emerging crops. It was a bucolic scene but Ywer resisted the temptation to relax and enjoy the ride.

At all times he deployed two men to scout the road ahead and a third shadowed the main party, keeping concealed as much as possible, to ensure that they weren't being followed. It was probably a needless precaution on the way south but he wanted his men to get used to exercising caution; it might well save lives on the return journey if tidings about their true purpose leaked out.

The fine weather didn't last and by the time that they reached Wirecestre the weather had broken and they were soaked to the skin. Wirecestre was where the ealdorman of the surrounding shire had his hall and normally Ywer would have sought his hospitality. However, wishing to keep a low profile, they secured lodgings at the larger of the two taverns in the settlement.

There were only three rooms available so Prior Erian and Ywer took the smallest and the rest played dice to decide who would share a bed and who would have to sleep on the floor. Ywer was well aware that Erian snored loudly but it sounded far worse inside the confines of the small chamber than it did in the open air, where they'd spent the previous nights.

He was still trying to go to sleep when he heard the door cautiously open. The leather hinges creaked, however slowly you eased the door open. He listened intently as his hand closed around the hilt of the dagger under the bolster on which his head rested. When he heard the soft footfall of a shoe on the floor he gave up the pretence that he was asleep and opened his eyes.

Although it was nearly pitch black in the room, there was a torch burning in the corridor and this served to silhouette the slight figure of a child standing stock still just inside the doorway. It was difficult to tell but Ywer thought it might be the potboy who cleared away dirty tankards and washed them. He'd only noticed the boy because the tavern-keeper kept cursing him, cuffing him around the ear and calling him slow and useless. He'd felt some sympathy for the lad, who was probably no more than ten or eleven, but it wasn't his business and he certainly wasn't going to draw attention to himself by getting involved.

Now the boy had crept furtively into his room. Ywer hazarded a guess that the taverner had sent the boy to steal his purse. He cursed himself for a fool; he'd let the man glimpse the amount of hacksilver he carried when he got out a small amount to pay for the rooms and their meals.

He relaxed his grip on the dagger once he was certain that the youngster was alone. He waited until the boy had started to rummage through his pile of discarded outer clothing looking for his purse, then quietly sat up and swung his feet onto the floor.

'Is this what you're looking for?' he asked quietly, holding up the purse which, like the dagger, he'd placed under the bolster when he went to bed.

The potboy shot upright in surprise. He might have been caught off-guard but his reactions were lightning fast. He sprinted for the door a split second after Ywer had spoken. He would have made it too if Ywer hadn't stuck his leg out and tripped him. The lad went sprawling and, before he could regain his feet, Ywer put his foot on the middle of the boy's back and forced him back down onto the floor.

Ywer grabbed hold of the boy's long, greasy hair and yanked his head back, none too gently.

'You were trying to steal my purse, weren't you? Don't even try to deny it or I'll pull your hair even harder.'

'Ow, leggo, I don't know what you're talking about.'

'Let's not play games, eh? If you're honest with me I might let you go. Lie to me and I'll turn you over to the watch and you'll be tried as a thief and sold as a slave.'

'Huh, it can't be worse than working here.'

'Do you know what a spit boy does?'

The boy didn't have a reply to that. They were young slaves who turned the spit on which an animal was roasted over an open hearth. They worked as a team, each boy doing short stints, but even so the boys' flesh became hot and the boys often suffered mild burns. It was a miserable existence and spit boys didn't tend to live long lives.

Although the food in the tavern wasn't roasted – meat was a scarcity outside a noble's hall and anything served in a tavern was boiled – everyone knew about spit boys.

'It wasn't my idea,' the boy said miserably. 'My cousin makes me steal from anyone staying who looks as if they might have more than a few copper coins in their purse.'

'Your cousin is the taverner?'

'Yes, he took me in when the rest of my family died of the plague a couple of years ago.'

'I'll deal with your cousin in the morning; now get out of here before I change my mind.'

'But my cousin will beat me if I come back empty handed,' the boy wailed.

Ywer thought for a moment. He was tempted to kick the lad out anyway but then he had an idea.

'What's your name, boy?'

'Hengist, why?'

'You call me lord, Hengist. I take it that you would like to leave here?'

'More than anything, lord.'

'Right, you can sleep in the corner over there; but if I hear you move during the night I'll kill you without a moment's compunction, do you understand?'

Hengist nodded despondently.

'I'll take you with me as a servant in the morning, that is, if you're agreeable.'

Ywer couldn't make out the lad's face in the darkness but he sensed the delighted grin that lit up his grubby features.

'That's another thing. You stink. You'll need to wash and wash properly before we leave. Have you got any clean clothes?'

The boy muttered that he had and went off to the corner but he was too excited to go to sleep. He didn't drop off until just before the cocks started to crow and woke up feeling exhausted but exhilarated.

Ywer should have sent for the watch to arrest the taverner but that would have meant revealing who he was when he gave his testimony. Instead he confronted the man and told him that he was taking the boy with him as a servant. If the man didn't like it he could make a formal complaint but in that case he would find himself before the shire court accused of theft. The man wisely decided to allow the boy to leave with Ywer.

†††

The last time that Ywer had seen Æthelstan he'd been a small boy. He was still a long way from fully grown but he now came up to Ywer's shoulder. True, he was as thin as a rake but he had broad shoulders for his age and he stood straight and looked Ywer directly in the eye when they were introduced. Ywer quickly came to the conclusion that Eadweard's son was self-assured without being precocious. In that way he was unlike his father who was only too conscious of his own importance - and liked to remind everyone of it,

46

probably because at heart Eadweard was rather insecure.

The other members of the escort had gone to the warriors' hall on arrival but the prior had accompanied Ywer for his private audience with Æðelred and the Lady Æthelflæd; after all, he was the supposed emissary and the pretext for the visit. Ywer had expected the prior to remain silent and let him do the talking but Erian surprised everyone by speaking first.

'Æthelstan, are you sure that you wouldn't be happier being a monk or a priest when you are older? It is a noble calling and it's the best way you can serve God.'

'No, I love God but I can best serve my fellow Anglo-Saxons by learning the art of war,' the boy replied in a high treble voice. 'After all, I'm the king's only son and will succeed to the throne when he dies.'

'But King Eadweard is young and had recently married; he will doubtless have other sons, ones who are legitimate. You mustn't delude yourself with this arrogant nonsense.'

'That's quite enough, brother prior. It isn't for you to express opinions on matters quite outside your remit,' Æthelflæd snapped at him before anyone else could gather their wits and slap the impudent monk down.

Erian gave her a resentful glance but said nothing further. Ywer had found the prior's outburst alarming. Of course, he didn't know that Æthelstan's parents had been legally married; that was closely guarded secret. However, he had made it clear that he disapproved of the decision not to make the boy become a novice. Ywer could no longer trust him to keep his mouth shut but he didn't know what to do about him.

He rounded on him once they were alone in the guest chamber they were to share.

'What were you thinking of, arguing with the Lord of Mercia and the daughter of King Ælfred. Have you taken leave of your senses?'

'King Ælfred is dead, God rest his soul, and I'm well aware that King Eadweard has given instructions for the boy to be trained as a monk at Cantwareburh. Anyone who defies the king is a traitor,' he replied defiantly.

Ywer bit his lip in frustration. He could hardly tell Erian that the boy was Eadweard's legitimate heir. Nor could he explain that Eadweard wanted his son out of the way for political reasons. The man wouldn't believe him. After all, it was quite normal for nobly born bastards to enter the Church. They would often be given preferential treatment and rise quickly to become abbots or bishops. Erian would see that as the best future that Æthelstan could hope for. Training to become a warrior with little hope of advancement would make no sense to the prior.

'What you don't understand, brother prior, is that King Eadweard has to publically pretend that he wants his son to enter the Church but privately he has given instructions that he is to be trained by my father to prepare him for owning lands that the king will give him when he's older.'

Even to Ywer's ears that made little sense. Why keep it a secret? However, it was the best he could come up with on the spur of the moment. Then he had a flash of inspiration.

'You must remember that the traitor Æðelwold has tried once to get his hands on the boy and that he had married the boy's mother. If he were sent to a monastery the king would be unable to prevent another attempt to kidnap him. At least he will be safe behind the walls of Cæstir.'

The prior thought about this for a moment before replying.

'Yes, I can see that Lord Ywer. If you had explained that to me in the first place I would not have raised any objections. Once safely at Cæstir he can, of course, enter the monastery and I can ensure that he has the best education a novice can receive.'

The man beamed at Ywer who groaned inwardly. However, he said nothing. Let the monk think what he wanted. Once they were back at Cæstir he would let his brother deal with the troublesome prior.

Chapter Two

900 – 902

Æðelwold paced up and down in the hall at Winburne, wracked by indecision. The abducted nun, Ecgwynna, sat by the window hunched over her embroidery. Ever since Æðelwold had forced a terrified priest to marry them whilst two of his hearth warriors held his reluctant bride by his side with a gag over her mouth, she had remained silently resentful and refused to acknowledge his presence. He had raped her once in their marriage bed but she had lain there unresponsive. It was like having sex with a corpse.

He had dreamed of taking Eadweard's first love and supplanting him in her affections had turned to dust. Even his plan to abduct her son so that he could force her to his will by threatening the boy had been unsuccessful. Now Eadweard was a mere ten miles away with his army. Many of those who had promised to aid him in his bid for the throne had failed to join him and he was under no illusion that those few who had rallied to his cause could defeat Eadweard.

The wise move would be to flee before it was too late but where to? He'd been cultivating Sigfrøðr, the King of Northumbria, but he had just died and the kingdom had been divided between three brothers – Ingwær, Eowils and Halfdan. It was rumoured that each was jealous of the other and both the Danish jarls and the Anglian thegns of the kingdom feared civil war.

East Anglia was a possibility but its king, Eohric, was one of those who'd promised to come to his aid. He'd failed to keep his word and consequently Æðelwold no longer trusted him. For all he knew, Eohric could turn him over to Eadweard in order to curry favour or, more likely, in return for a chest full of silver.

When a message came from the Witenaġemot of Northumbria offering him the throne he suspected a plot. However, the messenger came from Ethelbald, the Archbishop of Yorvik, and he didn't think that he'd be party to a trick. He knew enough about Northumbria to know that many of its Danish settlers had converted to Christianity and that the original Anglian inhabitants and the Danes had learnt to live together amicably. Inter-marriage between the two races had helped unite them and most of those who called themselves Danes had actually been born in Northumbria to mixed parentage.

He re-read the letter again. The brothers had agreed to divide the kingdom into three and would rule as sub-kings under Æðelwold. However, he was no fool; he knew that he'd be no more than a figurehead. He was well aware that their real purpose in approaching him was to divide and weaken Wessex.

Northumbria had been the premier kingdom in Englaland at one time and they loathed Saxon Wessex, which had grown in power and had supplanted Anglian Northumbria in status, even before the Danes had conquered it. When Ælfred had called himself

King of the Anglo-Saxons towards the end of his life, Northumbrian animosity towards Wessex had intensified.

Æðelwold told himself that he could use the Northumbrians and, hopefully, the Anglians and Danes who inhabited East Anglia, to oust Eadweard and then build up the power of Wessex again once he had replaced Eadweard on the throne. It was flawed thinking. Wessex had teetered on the brink of defeat more than once over the past few decades and, if Northumbria and East Anglia defeated Eadweard, Wessex would be over-run with Danish settlers hungry for good farming land. The Danes would then be in the ascendency over every realm in Englaland except Western Mercia, and that wouldn't survive for long after the fall of Wessex.

That night Æðelwold and his men left Winburne and headed north. He had finally made his mind up to flee and try again another day. Not everyone went with him. Ecgwynna, her supposed usefulness at an end, had been discarded and she returned to her convent. It was only when her belly began to swell that she realised to her horror that she was pregnant and that Æðelwold was the father.

✝✝✝

'This is Hengist; he'll act as your servant on the journey.'

Æthelstan looked the other boy up and down. Now that Hengist had been washed, had his hair trimmed and been bought new clothes in the market at

Glowecestre, he looked quite presentable. His legs and arms were still stick thin – the result of malnourishment - and he was a little shorter than Æthelstan, despite being two years older. The younger boy smiled at him and Hengist relaxed before grinning back. He'd been worried that his new master would treat him with contempt and beat him as his cousin had done.

Hitherto Æthelstan had been looked after by a nurse. She couldn't keep back the tears when her young charge bade her farewell. For a moment it seemed as if Æthelstan would also cry but he hardened his heart and wished her well. It was all very awkward and Ywer was anxious to be on his way before things became emotional. Æthelstan said goodbye to his aunt and mounted the pony that had been brought for him.

It was similar to the one being ridden by Hengist and the two boys were now dressed the same, in homespun tunics, coarse woollen trousers and cheap shoes. Æthelstan had objected at first; he took a pride in his appearance and dressing like a servant boy horrified him. However, Ywer convinced him of the need for subterfuge until they reached Cæstir.

The first part of the journey was uneventful. The days alternated between bright sunshine or cloudy with occasional breaks to allow the warmth of the sun to reach them. They avoided settlements and camped in the open so the fine weather was a godsend.

Despite their very different status, Æthelstan entered into his covert role with enthusiasm. The two boys gathered firewood together and generally made themselves useful. The only noticeable difference was that Hengist washed the younger boy's clothes, dried him after bathing in a stream and kept his hair groomed – something that Æthelstan insisted upon.

The young ætheling never seemed to mind helping Hengist with his other chores and they got on well together from the start. The older boy was too much in awe of Æthelstan's status for their relationship to be called friendship but it was pretty close to it. Hengist also proved that he was a good cook.

He hadn't just been the potboy in his cousin's tavern, he'd prepared most of the meals as well. He knew something about wild herbs and Erian, who had been a herbalist as well as an infirmarian before becoming the prior, added to his knowledge during the journey. The boy also knew how to butcher a carcass and Ywer was doubly glad that he'd rescued him. Not only had he saved him from a life of abuse and drudgery but he'd found himself a much better cook than the man who was currently in charge of his kitchen at home.

On the fifth day the sky became overcast and a storm threatened. The change in the weather wasn't the only thing that Ywer had to worry about. Halfway through the morning Leofdæg, whose turn it was to watch their rear, appeared out of the trees at the side of the road.

'We're being followed, lord,' he told Ywer.

'You're certain it isn't just fellow travellers?'

'Positive; when you stopped to allow the horses to drink and graze an hour ago they waited for you to continue and then set off again.'

'Hmm, how many are there?'

'Six. They aren't wearing armour but they are armed with swords and daggers.'

'Danes?'

Leofdæg shook his head. 'They are dressed like Saxons.'

Ywer was puzzled. They were unlikely to be Æðelwold's men. The only other person interested in Æthelstan was his father, but he couldn't imagine Eadweard sending men after him surreptitiously. No, these men meant to kidnap the boy; either that or kill him. He tried to think who might have sent them. At first no-one came to mind, then he thought of Eadweard's betrothed, Ælfflæd.

She would naturally see Æthelstan as a potential rival to her own sons when they came along, despite his supposed illegitimacy. The more he thought about it, the more it seemed likely that the men shadowing them served Ælfflæd's brother, Osfirth of Wiltunscīr. If that were the case he didn't think they were aiming to abduct Æthelstan, they would want him dead and buried.

†††

Æðelwold was surprised when he reached Yorvik. He knew it had been the headquarters of the Roman army in Britannia but he'd expected it to be like Lundenburg, surrounded by crumbling stone walls patched up with timber. Instead it looked much as it must have done when it was first constructed – apart from the fact that the Romans used to whitewash their walls to make them more impressive.

He could see where the stonework had been repaired. The stone used in the new sections hadn't been hewn into blocks but left in their natural shape. However, they had been mortared in place and would no doubt be as strong as the original sections.

As with all Roman forts there had been four gateways but two of them – the eastern and western gates – had been blocked up to improve the defences. Under Roman occupation the northern and southern entrances had twin gates – one for traffic entering and one for those leaving. Now there was only one in use, again to make it easier to defend the place, and consequently there was pandemonium as traders headed for the market with their carts and people tried to leave at the same time.

The sentries were doing their best to deal with the situation but tempers were getting frayed on all sides. When two of Æðelwold's gesith rode forward to clear a passage for their master everyone turned on them and cursed them. After a minute or two Æðelwold's captain, a Saxon called Almund, forced his horse through the throng until he reached the gateway. Another of his warriors accompanied him. This one held a horn made of brass.

'Quiet,' he thundered after his companion had sounded a few blasts on his horn. 'Everyone move back and allow your king to pass or I'll start laying about me with the flat of my sword. You there,' he said, pointing to one of the harassed sentries, 'allow twenty people to leave and then halt the rest clear of the gateway before allowing a score to enter. Do you understand?'

The Dane who appeared to be in charge of the gate gave him a surly look and told him curtly to speak Danish if he wanted to be understood.

'You understand Ænglisc well enough it seems, you tell them.'

The hubbub amongst the travellers started up again and, after another couple of blasts on the horn it died down enough for the Danish sentry to explain the system. After a lot of moaning and encouragement from Almund with the flat of his sword, the gateway was cleared and those in the queue in front of Æðelwold's party entered Yorvik. It took some time as everyone had to pay a toll to the clerk sitting between two armed guards just inside the gate.

When he demanded that Almund pay a toll of ten copper pence for every man in Æðelwold's party, first in Danish and then in Ænglisc, the captain lost his temper.

'Who does the toll go to?' he demanded.

'Why the kings, of course.'

'Ingwær, Eowils and Halfdan?'

'Er, yes. Now pay up or leave the way you came.'

'And who is the King of Northumbria?'

'They are, jointly,' the clerk replied impatiently.

Almund could hear the tumult growing behind him, caused by the delay, but he ignored it.

'Wrong, the Witenaġemot have invited King Æðelwold to rule over them. He's the one sitting on the grey stallion glaring at us.'

Without another word Almund dug his heel into his horse's sides and trotted forward along the narrow street in front of him. For a fleeting second the two guards looked as if they would try and stop him but they paused uncertainly and then it was too late to do anything. Æðelwold and the sixty nobles, warriors and servants accompanying him rode past them and disappeared into the alleyways.

Æðelwold had thought that the stench that pervaded the streets of Lundenburg was bad but here it was much worse. The streets were narrower and there seemed to be more rotting matter, faeces and mud than elsewhere. Wood smoke, cooking smells and unwashed bodies added their aroma to the stench causing him to pinch his nostrils in an effort to lessen the smell. He couldn't wait to reach the king's hall and wash off the dust and grime. Unfortunately Almund had ridden off without ascertaining directions to the monastery and the hall. All he knew was that the complex lay in the north-western corner.

He quickly became lost in the myriad of narrow streets and alleyways. The local population quickly disappeared as soon as they saw the armed warriors and so there was no one to ask. When they reached a bridge he breathed a sigh of relief. This had to be the Uisge, the greater of the two rivers which ran through the city.

All he had to do now was to cross the river and continue until he reached the north gate, there he could turn left and he was sure that this would lead him to the royal complex. Unfortunately the situation at the north gate was just as chaotic as it was in the south. Losing patience, he used the flat of his sword to clear a path for Æðelwold and his entourage.

Unsurprisingly the crowd waiting impatiently to leave took umbrage and, seizing handfuls of the unpleasant slime that coated the streets, they threw handfuls of the muck at their new king and his men as they tried to ride through them. Two of the younger warriors took umbrage at this and, before Almund could intervene, they had killed two men and a young boy.

This incensed the crowd even further and they pulled one of the warriors off his horse and set about him with bare fists and sticks. Several other warriors joined in the fray and by the time that the crowd had fled in terror, the dismounted warrior had been beaten to death and half a dozen of his assailants had also perished.

Æðelwold and his men rode through the gates and into the monastery and the royal complex in a sombre mood. It wasn't the way that he had anticipated entering his new kingdom and it wouldn't have earned him many friends amongst the local populace.

†††

'What are you going to do about our shadows, lord?' Skarde asked Ywer.

The two had become good friends over the past few years but, as Ywer was a thegn and the heir to an ealdorman, he always called him lord in the presence of others.

'Find their camp tonight and eliminate them,' Ywer replied with a grin that looked almost devilish in the light given off by the campfire.

Just at that moment Godric appeared out of the darkness and came to whisper in Ywer's ear. He nodded his thanks before speaking to the rest.

'Our pursuers are camped three miles away, by the side of the same stream as we are. Arne, Eomær; I want you to take care of any sentries. The rest of us will surround their camp and move in once the other two have given the call of an owl three times to confirm the sentries are dead. Any questions?'

'What about us?' Æthelstan asked, speaking for Hengist and himself.

'You stay here and guard the horses.'

For a moment the boy thought about protesting but he knew it would do no good. Besides, Ywer was right; someone had to stay on guard. The horses were too valuable to risk and anyone could come across a deserted camp and steal them.

The seven men set off on foot with Godric in the lead, padding silently along a faint track left by animals. At first the night was pitch black but then the clouds overhead parted for a moment and silvery moonlight illuminated the treetops, some filtering down to the ground below.

An hour later the young Dane dropped to one knee and pointed towards a small clearing in the woods two hundred yards away. Ywer could just make out a line of horses tied to pegs in the ground between him and the camp. The embers of the fire cast a faint reddish glow on several rounded humps that had to be sleeping men. He started to count them when the moon went behind a cloud again.

He signalled for Arne and Eomær to move ahead and find the sentries whilst he took the rest and encircled the enemy camp. Then he waited for the signal that the sentries had been dealt with. Five minutes later he heard three hoots. He waited for the other man to signal but there was nothing. Perhaps the enemy had only put out one sentry? He decided not to wait and gave two hoots – the signal to move in.

He moved forward stealthily, careful not to snap a twig or make any other sound. Eventually he reached the first sleeping man who appeared to have covered his head with a blanket. He pulled it back to cut the sleeping man's throat only to find a pile of rocks under the cloth. They'd been tricked. The camp was deserted.

When Arne and Eomær appeared they said that there had only been one sentry and he was half asleep by the horses. Ywer's heart sank. Obviously he'd been left on guard whilst the others had gone to attack their camp. The two boys had been left alone to face five experienced Saxon warriors.

All thoughts of moving stealthily were abandoned. The priority now was to get back to their own camp with all haste. The enemy had seven horses, one for each man and one packhorse. Ywer and his men mounted without bothering with saddles and took the longer route back via the road at a gallop. Presumably that was the way taken by Osfirth's men, otherwise they would have encountered each other en route to the enemy camp. That gave Ywer a glimmer of hope. It was nearly twice as long as the path they had taken.

They rode into their camp to find Osfirth's men still there. They were on the verge of departing having loaded the horses with everything of value and were taken completely by surprise. Although there was little light to see by, the horsemen attacked anyone they could see on foot. Ywer wasn't worried that they might kill either of the two boys by mistake. He assumed that they were already dead and his rage knew no bounds.

Minutes later only two of the enemy were still alive. Ywer was in no mood for mercy and he ignored their attempt to surrender, half-severing the head of one from his body in his anger. The last one only saved himself by falling to his knees so that Ywer's blade whistled over his head. Ywer jumped from the saddle and advanced on the quivering man only to find his way blocked by Arne.

'We need to find out who sent them, lord,' he said quietly.

Ywer tried to barge past him but Leofdæg and Wulfric stepped in his way.

'Calm down, lord. You aren't thinking straight. The boys aren't here.'

'You're certain they aren't dead?'

'If so, they aren't anywhere in the camp.'

Ywer exhaled in relief and allowed his sword to droop.

'Hopefully they had the sense to hide in the woods,' Arne suggested.

'Then where are they and why didn't Osfirth's men search the woods for them instead of looting the camp?' Ywer asked.

A few minutes later Æthelstan and Hengist appeared. It turned out that they had made up the fire to illuminate the camp then moved into the trees to keep watch. When they had seen the enemy appear Æthelstan's first impulse was to attack them but Hengist had persuaded him to move deeper into the woods. It was only when they heard the sound of fighting that they had returned to find out what was going on.

'The old man refuses to talk,' Skarde said after he and Godric had tried to frighten the surviving attacker to say who had sent him. He was at least fifty years old and all he would say was they could kill him if they liked; he'd led a full life and he was ready to die.

'Take his shoes off and put his feet in the fire,' Ywer told them harshly.

His men looked at him in surprise.

'He would have killed Æthelstan, aye and Hengist too no doubt. He doesn't deserve your pity. Now do as I say!'

Within seconds the old warrior's feet started to char and the sickly smell of roasting meat filled the clearing. He endured the agony for longer than Ywer had expected but then he screamed for mercy.

'Lord Osfirth, we are Osfirth's hearth warriors,' he got out between groans after his feet had been doused in water.

'Thank you. Put him out of his misery.'

Arne nodded and thrust his seax into the old man's throat. Compared to the look of contorted agony that had distorted his face moments before, in death he looked peaceful and content.

A week later Æthelstan and his escort reached the safety of Cæstir without further incident.

Chapter Three

893 - 901

Wynnstan could hardly remember his mother. In the year of Our Lord 893 she had died of the plague, as had all the members of his family except his father and himself. At the time he was six and he was scarcely aware of what was happening. They had left the farmstead where they had been bondsmen - people who were tied to their master's land. The ceorl who owned the farm was dead, as were the rest of his family and there seemed little point in staying.

Perhaps his father should have reported to the local thegn but he didn't know who that was, nor did he know where any other settlements lay. None of his family had ever travelled outside the farmstead. Even the produce they were allowed to grow for themselves had been sold for them at the local market by the ceorl.

Furthermore, his father had heard tales of the encroaching Norsemen all along the coast. As a result, the area in which they lived was slowly crumbling into lawlessness. The two of them had ransacked the farmstead for anything that could be of use including the ceorl's leather jerkin, helmet and weapons, two hunting bows and a barrel of arrows, food and water skins. His father had dug a hole in the corner of the ceorl's hut and cried out in triumph when he unearthed a small casket containing hacksilver, a few silver and copper coins and a small gold crucifix. It wasn't exactly a hoard but it was more wealth than they could have dreamed of.

They harnessed one of the ceorl's two horses to a small cart and tied the second one to the back of it. Having loaded the cart, his father had set fire to the farmstead, thus cremating the dead, and drove the cart eastwards into the forest. Wynnstan followed driving a small assortment of livestock before him.

They had constructed a shelter in a sizeable hollow not far from a stream as well as a pen for the animals. At first they had lived on what they'd brought with them, supplemented by wild herbs, plants and various small game that they managed to snare.

His father had never used a bow and it took him a long time to learn how but eventually he became reasonably proficient, adding small deer and other animals to their larder. In their first two years in the forest they saw no other human being, but then they were well away from even the most minor of tracks.

It was the neighing of one of the horses that had awoken him. Wynnstan grabbed the knife that his father had given him for his ninth birthday – or at least a day that he thought approximated to it – and cautiously slid out from under the blankets that covered him.

Over the years they had replaced the shelter with a hut. It was a simple affair with a window covered in leather scraped thin enough to let in some light and a single door. However, they had incorporated a small escape hatch in the rear wall.

He shook his father awake and put his finger to his lips - not that the gesture was visible inside the gloomy hut – then he left via the escape hatch.

Outside visibility was better. The night was cloudless and the new moon cast a silvery light over the forest. Even under the shadow of the canopy it was possible to make out the pens holding the animals and the original shelter that now served as the stables. Wynnstan could see a shadowy figure trying to lead the better of their two horses out of the shelter but the animal was resisting, pulling back from the strange man.

Wynnstan crept up behind the stranger and was surprised to see that he was little older than he was. He brought the pommel of his knife down in the other boy's head and he collapsed in a heap.

When the boy came to he found himself inside the hut tied hand and foot. Wynnstan had built up the fire in the central hearth and the boy looked from his father to Wynnstan and back again in alarm. Wynnstan gave him several sips of water and then his father asked the boy his name. However, the lad didn't seem to understand.

'Look at the way he's dressed, father, and that thing around his neck. He's not an Angle, not even a Saxon I wager, and that's not a crucifix.'

'I think you're right. He's probably a pagan Dane or one of those Norsemen.'

✝✝✝

His father kept the boy as a slave and gradually he learned a few words of Ænglisc and Wynnstan learned some of his language. He found out that boy, whose name was Frode, was in fact Norse. He'd been separated from the rest of his companions whilst they were out raiding. They'd walked into an ambush and he thought that he might have been the only one to escape. When Wynnstan had knocked him out he'd been trying to steal a horse on which to ride back to the coast in the hope of finding his ship.

Frode seemed content with his lot working for Wynnstan and his father. He could have easily escaped but, as he told Wynnstan, where would he go? His longship would have left long since.

'I've heard about Norse settlements dotted along the coast. Why didn't you try to reach one of those?' Wynnstan asked.

'Because I don't belong and they would have made me a thrall – a slave. I would be no better off than I am here, and probably be treated a lot worse. At least you don't beat me,' he added with a grin.

As time went on Frode taught Wynnstan what he knew about fighting. He'd only just started his training at the age of twelve when he joined his longship as a ship's boy but he could perform the basic moves with sword and spear and knew how to stand in the shieldwall. In return Wynnstan taught him how to use a hunting bow.

The boys were three years apart and by the time that Wynnstan entered his twelfth summer Frode was a strapping youth of fifteen who stood six inches taller than the other boy's father. Clothing for both growing boys was a problem. Initially they had made rough tunics out of a bolt of coarse woollen material that they had brought with them from the farmstead but eventually that ran out.

After that they tanned and cured leather from animals they'd killed and made leather clothes. Wynnstan and Frode soon learnt how to use animal sinew to sew the pieces of leather together. Sinew could be broken up into separate thin fibres which were hard and stiff when dry but became supple when wet. Sinew also expands when wet and shrinks as it dries out. Wynnstan and Frode put the sinew in their mouth to wet it - except for the ends, which remained very stiff and hard.

Using a piece of sharp bone they made a series of holes in the pieces to be sewn, then threaded the sinew through the holes. The stiff end of the sinew meant that no needle was necessary and, as the wet sinew stitches dried out, they shrank and tightened, creating a very secure and strong seam. At first the clothes looked badly made and the leather was poorly prepared but as time went on both the look and the quality of the leather clothes improved. They also made fur cloaks for when the weather turned cold.

During the winter after Wynnstan had turned thirteen his father's health deteriorated. Wynnstan hoped that he might recover in the spring. He didn't; he grew worse and, on a bright sunny day when the trees were showing off their new foliage, he died.

The two boys buried him in a corner of the clearing and for some time Wynnstan became listless, relying on Frode to do most of the work and the hunting. One day his failure to return before nightfall shook Wynnstan out of his melancholic lethargy and at dawn the following day he set off in search of his friend.

His trail wasn't difficult to follow and he found Frode at noon. He lay across an animal track, covered in blood and with his guts torn out. It wasn't difficult to guess what had happened. He'd been trailing a boar but the animal had been wily. He'd hidden beside the trail that Frode was following and had gored him to death before his friend had a chance to defend himself.

Wynnstan went and fetched one of the horses to carry the body home and he buried Frode beside his father. Instead of wallowing in despair, the lack of anyone to rely one forced Wynnstan to think about the future. He could carry on living in the forest until he was a bitter, lonely and miserable old man or he could do something different. He chose the latter.

†††

Deorwine hoped that he would find more potential recruits for the Lady Æthelflæd's personal warband at the fair. There was to be an archery competition as well as bouts where men could display their prowess with sword and shield. He wasn't looking for men seeking a new lord. Such masterless men often had serious character flaws and were more trouble than they were worth. Of course, nobles died or were killed in battle and then their hearth-warriors had to find a new master but the lord who succeeded usually accepted their oaths. Otherwise the good ones quickly found employment elsewhere. The ones left seeking a master were usually those no one wanted.

What he sought were young men who were the sons of ceorls and who showed the aptitude to become good warriors with training. All those over the age of fourteen would be in the fyrd, of course, and therefore know the rudiments of fighting. However, most had neither the courage nor the talent to become true fighters.

Cuthfleda walked by his side. She could fight, after a fashion, but she wasn't there to assess a man's potential; her task was to read their character from their actions and the way they conducted themselves.

There were two categories for both bowmen and swordsmen. One for those boys who had recently completed their training and one for those who were older. The fyrd started to train a boy when he was fourteen and most were passed as competent to be included amongst the fyrd by their captains between the ages of sixteen and seventeen.

Deorwine and Cuthfleda were surprised to see a much younger boy step up to the line with the youths entered for the archery competition. It wasn't just his youth that attracted attention. He was dressed from head to foot in undyed leather, including an unusual sleeveless tunic. Although he was evidently smaller and several years younger than the rest, he had the broad shoulders and muscular arms of one who had trained with the bow for some time.

He did well in the competition but there was never any chance that he would win. Deorwine approached the three young men who had done best and, after talking to them, offered two of them the chance to join the warband he was forming. The third was too full of himself to become a good member of any group and he slunk off cursing Deorwine when he wasn't selected.

The other two were brothers, the third and fourth sons of a ceorl who had a small holding. He had more children than he could feed and he was delighted to see them find employment elsewhere, especially serving the wife of the Lord of the Mercians.

Deorwine stayed to watch the men's competition whilst Cuthfleda went over to the ring where the first bouts of the youths' competition for sword and shield would take place. She stopped to buy a pie on the way and heard an altercation coming from the ring she was headed for. When she got there she discovered that the same boy who had attracted their interest in the archery competition was arguing with the official in charge of the swordsmen.

'What seems to be the problem, Eadwig?' she asked the official, who was one of Lord Æðelred's gesith.

'This boy, lady. He's too young and he hasn't got a shield, yet he insists on entering.'

'What's your name, boy?'

'Er, Wynnstan lady.'

'And where do you come from?'

'Er, the forest.'

'The forest?'

'Yes, everyone else was killed by the plague and my father took me to live in the forest when I was a small boy. Now he's dead too.'

That explained the boy's strange attire. If he was capable of killing wild animals large enough to yield

72

the size of skins for his clothes he had to be a good hunter. Not only that, the clothes had been well made.

'Did he teach you to fight with a sword as well as train you to use a bow?'

The boy was surprised that this lady knew that he was an archer. Of course, he didn't know that she had watched the earlier competition. He became wary but decided it would be a mistake to lie.

'No, lady. A Norseman called Frode did. He's dead too now; gored by a boar.'

She knew instinctively that Wynnstan had a good heart and warmed to him. She smiled and asked him if he was hungry. It was a superfluous question. He'd been eyeing her pie ever since she'd started to talk to him. He nodded eagerly and she gave it to him. He wolfed it down hungrily and Eadwig turned away in disgust to talk to another entrant.

'How will you fight without a shield?' Cuthfleda asked.

'With this,' the boy replied, drawing both his sword and a seax, weapons he and his father had taken with them into the forest. 'With these in my hands I can match any man with a sword and a cumbersome shield.'

He'd only been in Glowecestre two days but he'd watched some of the warriors practicing and noted how they fought. He'd decided that, with his natural agility, a shield would slow him down. He could counter his opponent's moves equally well with a seax in his left hand, if not better.

'You do know you'll be given a wooden sword to fight with to stop you and your opponent doing serious damage to one another,' she asked him with a smile. 'However, the rules say that you must produce your own shield.'

'Oh, I've never trained with a shield,' he said, looking crestfallen. 'I'll just have to use a sword then,' he said, brightening.

Cuthfleda made a decision which would change Wynnstan's life.

'Eadwig, let him fight with two swords; let's see how he does.'

'Yes, lady,' the official replied doubtfully; nevertheless he did as Cuthfleda asked.

†††

Wynnstan entered the ring twirling both swords in his hands and making short jabs with them to get used to their weight. They were heavier than his steel sword and twice as heavy as his seax. He bounced on two feet, bending and flexing his arms and legs as he studied his opponent. The lad opposite him was seventeen and looked older. He stood head and shoulders above Wynnstan and had the muscles of someone who had worked the land ever since he was a small child. He stood stock still watching the antics of Wynnstan with a look of derision on his face.

When Eadwig called 'begin' he lumbered towards Wynnstan with a feral look on his face, anticipating a quick victory. When Wynnstan attacked with the sword in his right hand, the older boy blocked it with his shield, as he'd been taught, and swung his sword around to strike the younger boy in the side. However,

74

Wynnstan drove his sword down into the earth and then jumped in the air, landing on the blade. His weight was enough to pull it from the older boy's hand and he was left with just a shield with which to protect himself.

Wynnstan aimed a blow at his opponent with the sword in his right hand and the youth raised his shield to counter the blow. Instead of striking the shield, Wynnstan dropped down and jabbed his other sword up into his opponent's groin. Unbearable pain caused the other lad to drop his shield and curl up on the ground, clutching the injured area. Wynnstan placed the tip of one of his swords on the other boy's neck and invited him to yield. It was all over in less than a minute.

He won the next two bouts before someone complained to the Shire Reeve of Hwicce, who was the senior judge. He ruled that Wynnstan had an unfair advantage and that he should be disqualified. Cuthfleda thought of having a word with him but she decided against it. There was no point. Wynnstan had nothing left to prove. She had found another warrior for Æthelflæd's warband.

Chapter Four

Autumn 901 – Summer 902

'The Northumbrians have turfed Æðelwold out,' Æðelred said with satisfaction when he'd finished reading the letter from Eadweard.

Æthelflæd, who'd been sitting reading with her twelve year old daughter, Ælfwynn, looked up with interest.

'Hopefully that means he ceases to pose a threat to my brother's reign,' she said, getting up to go and join her husband.

'Not entirely, it seems that he's sailed to East Anglia in the hope of recruiting Eohric's support.'

Eohric was the Dane who ruled East Anglia. He'd always had an uncomfortable relationship with Wessex. Ælfred had allowed Eohric's predecessor, Guðrum, to become king of East Anglia after driving him and the remnants of the Great Heathen Army out of Wessex decades before. The invasion of a Viking Army led by Hæsten several years ago had relied on recruits from both Northumbria and East Anglia to replenish their numbers; something that Eohric had done little to stop. However, he hadn't openly supported Hæsten.

Now that Ælfred was dead, the situation might change. Eadweard was seen as untried and the Danes living in the Danelaw, not just East Anglia, might well be tempted to support Æðelwold if he promised them a share in the rich lands of Wessex. If that happened,

Anglian Mercia would stand alone. It wouldn't be long before it too fell to the Danes.

'You were reading with me, mother,' Ælfwynn said petulantly, annoyed at the interruption.

The girl had little interest in the politics which so concerned her parents. She had been conceived when Æðelred had raped her mother in the early years of their marriage. In those days the Lord of the Mercians saw his wife as a brood mare who should know her place and concentrate on domestic matters. Unfortunately for him, his wife didn't share his views – far from it.

His attempt to bend his wife to his will had only toughened the latter's independent streak and her determination to rule Mercia jointly with her husband. Ælfred had always encouraged his daughter to think for herself and she had inherited his intellect and enquiring mind.

After Ælfwynn's birth Æthelflæd had refused to sleep with Æðelred again and threatened him with a dagger when he tried to rape her a second time. Their relationship had deteriorated to the extent that they barely exchanged a civil word for a time but gradually Æðelred had come to realise that his wife was far cleverer than he had supposed. From that moment he came to rely on her advice more and more until the time came when they effectively ruled Anglian Mercia together. However, they continued to sleep separately and there was no prospect of another child. As a consequence, Ælfwynn had become somewhat spoiled and was used to getting her own way.

Æthelflæd smiled at her daughter but she didn't return to Ælfwynn's side. Instead she beckoned for Cuthfleda to take her place. This wasn't what Ælfwynn had wanted and she made her disappointment obvious. She disliked Cuthfleda intensely as she didn't indulge the girl and disapproved of the way she was being brought up. Ælfwynn glared at Cuthfleda as she sat down beside her and then ignored her, gazing out of the window instead of paying attention.

When Cuthfleda grabbed her chin and turned her face towards her she looked towards her mother for help but she was busy talking to her father. Ælfwynn sighed and resigned herself to spending the rest of the afternoon with Cuthfleda, a prospect which was no more appealing to Cuthfleda than it was to the girl.

'Will you answer Eadweard's summons?' Æthelflæd asked.

'I suppose there's little option. When it was just an internal dispute within Wessex I was reluctant to get involved but now Northumbria and East Anglia are aiding Æðelwold it's a different matter. I don't particularly like your brother but it would be disastrous for Mercia if Æðelwold became King of Wessex. He'd just become a puppet of the Danes.'

'Yes, I can see that you'll have to go to Eadweard's aid but what about the situation in the north?'

Æðelred's realm stretched from the border with Wessex in the south to the River Mæresēa in the north. However, Æðelred's prime concern had always been the border with the Danelaw to the north-east of his territory. Hitherto he'd been content to leave the north and its problems to Jørren.

78

Æðelred shifted uncomfortably. He didn't really want to discuss the north with his wife. He had enough to preoccupy him without that.

'Jørren is an old man and his days of leading men into battle are behind him,' she continued. 'His son, Ywer, is a good man but he is fully occupied guarding the south bank of the Mæresēa. Gwynedd can no longer be counted as an ally, thanks to the struggle for power between King Anarawd and his son, Idwal. Meanwhile, the Norse are losing ground in Íralond. More and more are looking to settle across the sea and Cæstir is a tempting target.

'Don't forget that the shire reeve and the man who controls the Wirhealum peninsula is a Norseman,' she went on. 'He may be a Christian and married to Jørren's daughter but I don't trust him not to side with his fellow Norse if they invade.'

'I've enough to do worrying about with Æðelwold and the Danes without fretting about what the Norse in Íralond may or may not do at some time in the future,' he replied irritably.

His wife looked at him speculatively for a moment. She had known that he would take that attitude and she had been busy for some time making her own plans.

'Then let me go north and see the situation for myself,' she offered.

'You? What can you do? In any case I can't spare any men to escort you,' he said as if that was an end to the matter.

'I have my own men,' Æthelflæd said, 'so you needn't worry about my safety.'

'Your own men? What do you mean?'

Æðelred hadn't been aware that Cuthfleda and Deorwine had been quietly recruiting a small warband who were pledged to Æthelflæd. They had been housed at a vill that Æthelflæd owned, far from the notice of the Mercian court. They were young and untried warriors in the beginning but what they lacked in experience they made up for in willingness to learn, and Deorwine was a good teacher. So far there was only a score or them but she had plans to expand their number with the help of Jørren once she reached Cæstir.

It took a little time for her to gain her husband's permission but her continued pestering eventually wore him down. Just over a fortnight later she rode out of Glowecestre accompanied by Cuthfleda, Deorwine, her warband, two priests and a small baggage train including enough servants to satisfy Æðelred that the proprieties were being observed.

†††

Wynnstan didn't mind being relegated to guarding the baggage train. He was the youngest member of the warband by over two years and he was aware that he was lucky to have been chosen by Cuthfleda and Deorwine. He had given his oath willingly to his new mistress and used what little wealth he had brought with him from the forest to buy more suitable clothes, a cheap helmet and byrnie and a saddle for his horse. He had sold the second horse for a pittance but it gave him enough to buy two quivers of well-made arrows and a lime wood shield suited to his size.

He'd spent the time before they set out learning how to use a shield and a spear, in addition to improving his skills with bow and sword. His companions in the warband had ridiculed him at first, partly because of his youth and partly because he was unused to other people and appeared shy.

However, they quickly learned that he had a temper and was a terror in a fist fight. Gradually they came to respect him, although he had no-one who was a particular friend.

They had set off on the road north – the same one that Wynnstan had followed south to Glowecestre the previous year - on a blustery day in late August. Lord Æðelred had left the previous week to join King Eadweard, leaving Siward, Ealdorman of Hwicce, in charge of Mercia.

The first night was spent in the relative comfort of the monastery at Wirecestre as the guests of Bishop Wirfrith. Whilst the ladies were given the guest chamber in the bishop's hall and the ten most senior of the warband shared the guest hut, the rest of the warriors and the servants had to make do with the stables.

Much to his surprise, Wynnstan was selected to stand guard in the refectory that evening. Not only did it mean that he could grab some food left over when the monks and their guests had eaten but he could listen to the conversation during the meal from his position behind the Lady Æthelflæd.

'I'm surprised that your husband allowed you to travel north accompanied by so few men,' the bishop was saying, 'especially as some of them seem to be no more than boys.'

He sniffed and waved his hand airily in Wynnstan's direction.

'We are travelling inside Mercia, lord bishop,' she pointed out, 'and my men are well trained, despite their youth.'

'You are riding north along the Sæfern, lady. There have been several raids into Shropscīr recently by the men of Powys. I urge you to turn back.'

'But Merfyn ap Rhodri has always been anxious to keep the peace between us, what has happened?'

'You haven't heard then,' the bishop said with a sigh. 'King Merfyn died a couple of weeks ago and his son, Llewellyn, has succeeded him. He's not yet twenty and he's itching to make a name for himself.'

Æthelflæd's heart sank. With Llewellyn now King of Powys and King Anarawd allowing his son Idwal to flex his muscles in Gwynedd, Mercia faced trouble all along its border from Wirecestre to Cæstir.

'I urge you to turn back. The road you are travelling is no place for a lady,' the bishop continued.

'No, it makes it even more urgent that I reach Cæstir so that I can discuss the situation with Lord Jørren as he's Mercia's hereræswa.'

'I doubt that he'll be much help,' the bishop said with a sniff. 'I hear that he's close to death.'

✝✝✝

82

Æthelflæd was annoyed that the bishop seemed so much better informed than she was but her overriding emotion was one of concern. She had been pinning her hopes on drawing on Jørren's military experience to devise a plan for defending Northern Mercia. Although she liked Ywer and knew that he would make a good Ealdorman of Cæstirscīr in due course, she wasn't convinced that he had the ability or the experience to help develop a plan for defending the north, let alone become the hereræswa.

All the other ealdorman were reasonably dependable, although some were more competent and conscientious than others, but none sprang to mind as a suitable hereræswa. Still, that would be her husband's problem; her immediate concern was getting to Cæstir and seeing the situation for herself. After all, she consoled herself, the rumours of Jørren's illness might be exaggerated.

'Wynnstan, you must have learned how to track and hunt in all those years in the forest,' Deorwine said to the boy the next day.

'Yes, Deorwine,' the boy replied warily, wondering where this was going.

'The rest are good enough warriors but only Chad has trained as a scout. I want the two of you to ride point today. Do you know what that means?'

'Yes, we ride in advance of the main body, staying out of sight of the road as much as possible and making sure we aren't riding into trouble.'

'Trouble being?'

'Coming across a Welsh raiding party unexpectedly or, worse, an ambush.'

'Good lad. You were obviously eavesdropping on the bishop and the lady last night,' he said with a grin. 'I've already spoken to Chad. Off you go.'

Wynnstan approached Chad warily. He was nearly three years older than Wynnstan and would therefore expect to take charge. However, the younger boy had no idea how good a scout he would prove to be. He knew how important their role was to the safety of the rest of the group and he wouldn't stay quiet if it was obvious that Chad didn't know what he was doing. However, he needn't have fretted.

'Deorwine says that you have been brought up as a woodsman,' the other boy said as soon as Wynnstan joined him at the front of the column. 'I've done some training as a scout but I'm hoping you know more than I do.'

Wynnstan grinned in relief.

'We need to find our way through the woods, making as little noise as possible, and keeping the road in view. Some of the time we can ride but where the foliage is dense we'll have to lead our horses. Whilst you move I'll watch for any signs of danger and vice versa.'

'Sounds sensible. We'll need a signal if we spot anything.'

'Can you make a sound like this?'

Wynnstan cupped his hand and made two different sounds like an owl hooting.

'There aren't many owls about in daylight,' he explained. 'The first sound is a male Tawny Owl calling to his mate and the second is the female responding.'

Chad practiced the two calls until Wynnstan was satisfied. By that time the column was ready to leave the monastery and the two scouts cantered off up the road before disappearing into the trees to the west of it.

The two scouts were worried that, moving cautiously off the beaten path they would have difficulty keeping ahead of the column but the carts moved so slowly it didn't prove to be a problem. The morning had started bright and sunny but as the day wore on the sky clouded over and the wind picked up. By midday the white clouds had turned a dark shade of grey and Wynnstan knew that they were in for rain. Three hours later it started; a few drops soon became a downpour and, had they not been in trees, the wind would have driven it into their faces making it difficult to see.

Suddenly Chad, who was in the lead at the time, stopped and hooted for Wynnstan to come forward. He pointed at the minor track they were about to cross. Although largely obliterated by the rain, they could still make out prints on the track heading to the east.

'Men and horses,' the younger boy muttered to the elder. 'Too many to be anything but a warband.'

'I agree. The danger is that they will be heading back to cross the river soon and our column could run into them. What do we do?'

'You go back and warn Deorwine; I'll follow the tracks and see what I can find out. I'll be as quick as I can.'

The older scout looked dubious but he eventually nodded.

'I'll be at the junction of this track and the road.'

Wynnstan mounted his horse and rode alongside the track following the few prints he could see. After a short while he could hear the sound of fighting ahead. He disappeared into the trees and made his way to the top of a rise where the trees ended. Below him lay a settlement containing a score of houses and a small hall. There was no church as far as he could see. The Welsh raiding party weren't having it all their own way. The men of the settlement were fighting back and a number of bodies littered the ground in the centre of the settlement. A score or more men and boys had formed a circle which the Welsh were attacking.

Wynnstan felt impotent; he wanted to help but he realised that would be foolhardy. Instead he mounted his horse behind the crest of the ridge and cantered back along the track to the junction with the road. Thankfully the column had halted there to wait for his report.

As soon as he explained what was happening Æthelflæd didn't hesitate but, calling for Deorwine and the rest to follow, she set off back up the track with Cuthfleda and Wynnstan following. For a moment Deorwine was nonplussed but, detailing three men to stay with the servants and the baggage train, he led the rest of the warband in pursuit.

As they crested the final ridge Wynnstan could see that three more villagers had been killed but so had five more Welshmen. The two sides had drawn apart for the moment. No doubt the leader of the raiders was regretting his decision to attack this particular settlement. He had lost far too many men but his pride wouldn't let him withdraw.

In other circumstances Æthelflæd might have decided to use arrows to whittle down the enemy numbers but in these conditions wet bowstrings would mean that arrows would lack both power and range. Instead she drew her sword and ordered her warband to charge.

Wynnstan was riding behind her and thought that she and Cuthfleda looked magnificent, sitting astride their mares, dressed in embroidered dresses divided in two to facilitate riding, their long hair streaming out behind them yelling for 'God and Mercia' as they rode into the startled Welshmen. He saw Cuthfleda cut down one man and Æthelflæd another and then he had to concentrate on his own opponent.

Unlike the rest of the Welsh, this man was mounted on a fine looking black stallion. No doubt there were other horsemen with the raiders but they must have dismounted to fight on foot. The fact that this one was still mounted meant that he was probably their leader.

The Welshman held a long sword in one hand and a small round shield with a wicked looking point in the middle of its boss in the other. Evidently he expected the Mercian boy to ride straight at him and therefore was taken by surprise when Wynnstan dug his knees into his mount's flanks to guide him wide of the

Welshman. The latter tried an ineffectual swipe with his sword but then the boy was past him. The Welshman forgot about Wynnstan and looked for a new opponent. It was a mistake.

No sooner had he passed him than Wynnstan pulled his horse around in a tight circle and rode back towards the Welsh leader. It wasn't very sporting but Wynnstan wasn't concerned about being fair. He aimed the point of his sword at the back of the man's neck and thrust it home. Such was the momentum of the blow that Wynnstan had to let go of his sword or his shoulder would have been dislocated.

He turned his horse around and watched with satisfaction as the enemy rider toppled to the ground. Shortly after that it was all over. The combined strength of Æthelflæd's warband and the remaining inhabitants of the settlement had quickly overcome the raiders and no more than three or four escaped to carry home the tale of their disastrous raid.

Both ladies were covered in blood but none was theirs. Nevertheless Deorwine scolded them for risking their lives.

'I would not ask my men to do what I'm not prepared to do myself,' Æthelflæd retorted sharply and that was the end of the matter.

It wouldn't be the last time that Æthelflæd led from the front.

✝✝✝

'You killed their leader so his possessions are now yours,' Deorwine told Wynnstan as his men stripped the bodies of anything valuable before throwing them in a common grave dug by the grateful inhabitants.

'Deorwine, half of anything my men find is to be given to the local inhabitants so that they can build a palisade around their settlement to keep them safe from future raids,' Æthelflæd told him. 'I've also told their thegn I want them to build a church.'

The captain looked at her in amazement. He thought of protesting; by tradition the effects of a dead enemy belonged to the victor. However, the look in her eye told him that she had made her mind up and it was no good arguing. His men weren't that happy about it either but they admired the two women who'd fought alongside them and they could see, albeit somewhat begrudgingly, the logic in protecting the settlement.

Wynnstan worried that the possessions of the man he'd killed would be added to the spoils to be divided up but Cuthfleda pleaded on his behalf and he was allowed to keep them. Far from feeling that he'd been treated favourably, his companions took the view that, as the killer of the enemy leader, his effects were his by right. His standing amongst his fellows markedly improved.

Three horses, in addition to the one belonging to the Welsh leader, and five mountain ponies had also been captured These were tied to the back of the baggage carts and would be sold, the proceeds being divided amongst everyone in the usual way. This went someway to mollifying the warband and they continued on their way towards Cæstir in good spirits.

The Welshman's byrnie was far too large for Wynnstan but when he reached Cæstir he'd get it made to fit him as it was of much better quality than the one he had bought in Glowecestre. He could also afford a much better helmet now. However, he was less than thrilled by the horse he'd acquired. Unlike the small mare he'd been riding this one was a black stallion with a look in its eye which warned the boy that he might be a handful.

Nevertheless, he'd look foolish in the eyes of his companions if he didn't choose to ride the much better horse. Whereas his mare was only twelve hands high the stallion was about sixteen. Wynnstan grasped the saddle horn, put his foot in the stirrup and hauled himself into the saddle. The horse tried a little buck and twisted and turned as if trying the mettle of his new owner but, when Wynnstan gripped firmly with his knees and pulled back on the reins before patting his neck and soothing him, the stallion quietened down.

The boy was amazed at how much further from the ground he seemed. Then he realised that the stirrups were too long for his short stature and he had to dismount and adjust them. This time it was more difficult for him to mount and the horse started to go around in circles. Once again Wynnstan stroked his neck, talking to him softly, and when he went to mount again the horse stood perfectly still.

Although he felt important riding the bigger horse he quickly came to the conclusion that his mare was more suitable for a scout. She was less conspicuous and he could mount and dismount much more quickly.

He and she knew each other as well and it would take time to establish the same kind of rapport with his new horse.

Therefore, when they set out the following day he chose the mare. He had nothing to prove. He'd ridden the stallion without a problem and, as he told the others, it would fetch far more money in Cæstir than the mare.

It took another three days to reach their destination by which time Wynnstan was extremely saddle sore. The others, who were more used to riding than he was, told him that it would get better as he got used to riding long distances but he wasn't sure he believed them. He wasn't the only one who walked with his inner thighs apart when he dismounted.

Æthelflæd was welcomed by Rinan, Jørren's captain, on arrival and he led her, Cuthfleda and Deorwine into the hall. Stable boys and grooms came running to take the horses whilst the servants unloaded the wagons and proceeded to carry chests into the hall. Wynnstan made haste to retrieve the armour, weapons and the small coffer containing his share of the spoils from the Welsh raiders before anyone else could lay their hands on them.

He was left wondering where to go when Chad came and found him and took him off to the warriors' hall. The garrison had taken the best spots to sleep and the new comers had to make do with the area on both sides of the doors. It was draughty, well away from the central hearth and therefore the coldest area. Thankfully that mattered less in August than it would have done in winter. Inevitably, Wynnstan, being the youngest, was relegated to the place right by the door. Not only was it draughty but he'd be woken all night long by those going out to get rid of the ale they'd drunk that evening and, in a few cases, what they'd eaten as well.

The next morning he was woken just before dawn by the slow and doleful ringing of the solitary bell hanging in a small cupola on top of the monastery's church. Lord Jørren had died during the night.

Chapter Five

Autumn 902 to Spring 903

Abbot Æscwin stood next to his father's coffin and gazed at the assembled mourners. The monastery church was too small to hold all those who wanted to pay their last respects to the man who had been not only Ealdorman of Cæstirscīr but a renowned warrior who played a large part in keeping the Danes out of Wessex. More recently, he'd been instrumental in defeating Hæsten's invasion.

All the members of Jørren's immediate family were present apart from Ywer's twin sister, Kjesten. She lived too far away to have travelled the two hundred and thirty miles from her home in Dyfneintscīr in time. The abbot's eye flickered over his only brother and his Norse wife and on to his youngest sister, Æbbe, married to another of the Norse settlers, Eirik Fairhair, Jarl of Wirhealum. The abbot's eldest sister, Cuthfleda, stood next to the Lady Æthelflæd, together with Æthelflæd's nephew, Æthelstan. The boy was eleven but looked more like thirteen or fourteen. It wouldn't be long before he was as tall as as his aunt and she stood head and shoulders over most of her gender.

The captain of the lady's warband, Deorwine, stood behind Cuthfleda and Æscwin was sure that he detected a closer relationship between them than one might normally expect from two people in the same household.

Cuthfleda was thirty three and Æscwin had long given up hope that his sister might find a husband. Now he wasn't so sure. Of course, Deorwine was much further down the social scale than Cuthfleda, being the younger brother of a minor thegn and ranking as a ceorl. As the daughter of a senior noble, Cuthfleda would be marrying far beneath her. However, he would give their union his blessing if it came to it, just so long as she was happy.

'Dearly beloved, we are gathered here in the sight of God the Father, God the Son and God the Holy Spirit to lay our brother in Christ, Jørren, to rest.'

As he spoke the words of the funeral service Æscwin's eye travelled over the congregation inside the church. Fully half were Norse jarls and their families; the rest were Mercian thegns and the senior members of his late father's household, including his gesith. Even some of them were married to Norse women.

It made him feel vulnerable. If the Norse settlers of Cæstirscīr ever rose up they could overwhelm the Mercian inhabitants, especially if they combined with the Norse and the Danes living in Northumbria to the north and east. Of course, the area along the coast on the other side of the River Mæresēa was only nominally part of Northumbria. The Danish kings in Yorvik made no attempt to impose their rule on, or extract taxes from, the jarls of the area.

Whilst his father was alive he'd felt safe. Jørren's reputation had protected Cæstirscīr from its enemies, even when he'd sunk into apathy after Hilda's death. That was one of the reasons why he was glad that

94

Æthelflæd was here. She represented her husband and brought some stability to a volatile situation. It was no secret that both Ywer and Eirik Fairhair sought to be Jørren's replacement as ealdorman; Ywer as his son and Eirik as both his son-in-law and the shire reeve.

It was true that Eirik was the one who governed the shire during Jørren's days of dark depression but Ywer was away guarding the border with Northumbria. There was no rule that said that sons should inherit the post of ealdorman from fathers but it had become common practice unless the son was too young or incompetent.

The abbot was glad that he didn't have to make the decision but he could see trouble brewing whoever was chosen.

The funeral and the feast that followed went off without incident but Æscwin noticed both Ywer and Eirik deep in conversation with Æthelflæd at different times. Just before the feast deteriorated into drunkenness and maudlin recollections about Jørren's life, Æthelflæd got to her feet and Deorwine banged the pommel of his dagger repeatedly on the table until everyone was silent.

She started with a eulogy of Jørren's life; how he set out at the age of thirteen to hunt down the Great Heathen Army and rescue his brother, his formation of a warband of boys and young men and his rise from minor thegn to ealdorman and, later, Hereræswa of Wessex. She referred to his achievement in building a navy with her father to defend the shores of Wessex and skated over her brother Eadweard's unjustified expulsion of Jørren from Cent. Instead she lauded his achievement in bringing the lawless wilderness that had been Cæstirscīr back within the Mercian fold and, finally, she touched on his part in the defeat of Hæsten's Viking horde.

Whilst she was talking about Hæsten the abbot studied Godric's face. He was Hæsten's only surviving son and he'd, somewhat surprisingly, joined Jørren's gesith after his father's death. If the young man harboured any resentment about the way that Æthelflæd referred to his father as that evil pagan, he hid it well. All the same Æscwin didn't trust Godric.

Æscwin glanced at Ywer further down the table. He too was watching Godric's reaction. Perhaps sensing his brother's gaze on him, Ywer turned and exchanged a look with the abbot. Æscwin sensed that he shared his distrust of the young Dane.

'Now we come to the matter of who should succeed Lord Jørren,' Æthelflæd said.

There was an immediate pricking of ears. Everyone wanted to know who the new ealdorman was going to be.

'The decision is, of course, a matter for Lord Æðelred and, as he's away fighting alongside my brother, King Eadweard, in Ēast Seaxna Rīce at the moment, it may be some time before the appointment is made.'

She would have had to be completely insensitive to the atmosphere if she didn't pick up the concern that permeated the hall following this statement. The lack of a leader with the authority to bring the shire together when it faced so many threats, both internal and external, was disastrous. The murmur of protest swelled until Deorwine had to bang on the table again for quiet.

'However, I fully appreciate that Cæstirscīr needs strong governorship at this difficult time, not least because of the additional threat posed by the recent Norse invasion of Ynys Môn led by a man called Ingimund.'

That statement had everyone's interest now. The arrival of Ingimund on the island where King Anarawd of Gwynedd had his base was news to practically everyone in the hall. Most were aware that the Norse Kingdom of Dyflin on the east coast of Íralond had fallen to the combined armies of Brega and Leinster but an invasion of neighbouring Wealas by some of the displaced Vikings was too close to home for comfort.

Once again she had to wait for the ensuing hubbub to die down before she could continue.

'Therefore I have decided to stay here for the winter and to rule the shire myself until such time as my husband can appoint a new ealdorman. I look to all of you to support me to the hilt in defending our land.'

She had scarcely finished speaking before the hall erupted in uproar. The concept of shield maidens – female warriors – wasn't unknown to the Norsemen present. Lagatha, the wife of the legendary Ragnar Lodbrok, whose death at the hands of the Northumbrians was said to be the catalyst for the invasion by the Great Heathen Army nearly forty years ago, had been a legendary shield maiden. However, that was quite different to being governed by a woman.

It wasn't even as if Æthelflæd was well known this far north. She was regarded as a Saxon – age old enemies of the Angles of Mercia. The fact that she had a Mercian mother and was married to the Lord of Mercia counted for little. Of course, Jørren himself was a Jute but his reputation preceded him. The idea of being ordered about by a Saxon woman was anathema to most of those present.

Deorwine banged the table once more until quiet was eventually restored.

'What most of you don't know is that the Lady Æthelflæd is Lord Æðelred's closest advisor on matters both political and military. On the way here we came across a settlement being attacked by the Welsh. Æthelflæd led the attack herself and was the first to kill one of the raiders. Don't let the dress and the pretty face fool you. She and Lord Jørren's daughter, the Lady Cuthfleda, are as good at fighting as most men here and she has a wiser head on her shoulders than any of you.'

In the stunned silence that followed Ywer got to his feet and raised his tankard.

'I give you a toast – the prettiest ealdorman in Mercia and, by the sound of it, the most able; the Lady Æthelflæd.'

He looked directly at Eirik, urging him to support him. After a pause, the shire reeve echoed Ywer's toast, albeit without great enthusiasm. That was enough for most of the men present and they clambered to their feet and toasted their new leader.

98

✝✝✝

Æthelflæd came into the hall and took the chair at the head of the table. Cuthfleda sat to her right and Deorwine to her left. The other people in her inner council were Ywer, Eirik, Abbot Æscwin and Rinan, the former captain of Jørren's warband who was now in command of the garrison at Cæstir.

Most of Jørren's gesith had transferred their oaths to Ywer but he already had his own captain, a Mercian named Edmund. In addition to his personal hearth warriors – his gesith - Lord Jørren had had maintained a warband of over sixty warriors. Another thirty older men formed the garrison of Cæstir and its night watch. The rest of the shire's fighting force consisted of the thegns and jarls together with their own hearth warriors and the fyrd.

The latter was found from every ceorl over the age of fourteen. Officially boys between the ages of fourteen and sixteen or seventeen were trainees but in an emergency they took their place in the shieldwall, usually at the back.

Rinan was not a happy man and it showed. From being one of Jørren's senior warriors he'd been relegated to commanding those too old to go on patrol or fight in the shieldwall. Ywer was also resentful; he'd fully expected to be appointed as ealdorman in his father's place. Now it seemed as if he would have to wait for an unspecified period and serve under a woman; one he didn't know well and about whose abilities he was sceptical, despite what Deorwine had said.

Even Eirik was disgruntled. He had carried out many of the duties of ealdorman as well as his own during Jørren's declining years. Now it seemed as if he was to answer to Æthelflæd who wanted to play at being Queen of the North. He shared Ywer's cynicism about her abilities as a leader, especially as a warlord.

Æthelflæd was well aware of the magnitude of the task that lay before her. There was nothing she could say to alter the opinion of her that Eirik and Ywer evidently held. The only thing she could do was to demonstrate her abilities. The first thing she said took them all aback.

'Where is my nephew? Æthelstan should be here to listen to our deliberations.'

'Why, lady?' Eirik asked, looking somewhat bewildered. 'He's just a young boy, and a bastard at that.'

'Nevertheless he's Eadweard's eldest son. It's time he started to learn how to be an ætheling.'

'I thought Eadweard had disowned him?'

Æthelflæd didn't reply; it was too early in her nephew's life for her to disclose that he was the king's legitimate heir. Once he was older she fully intended to reveal that Eadweard and the boy's mother were married but not whilst he was vulnerable and Eadweard's own position was far from secure.

'Never mind. He can join us next time,' she said with a forced smile. 'Our immediate problem would seem to be the expulsion of most of the Vikings from

Dyflin. As a result more than thirty longships led by a man called Ingimund have landed on Ynys Mon.'

'Surely that's a problem for Gwynedd, not us?' Rinan asked, adding 'lady' after a pause that was long enough to be insulting.

Cuthfleda gave him a sharp look. He may have been her father's captain and his close friend but he was behaving like a sulky boy at the moment. She noticed that she wasn't the only person to glare at Rinan; Ywer had also given him a warning look.

'I understand that King Anarawd and his son were away when the Vikings landed. They are hardly likely to take the invasion lying down. My worry is that they will muster enough men to drive Ingimund out of Ynys Mon.'

'And the next place they will land will be here?' Ywer concluded. 'Probably somewhere on the Wirhealum Peninsula.'

'Yes, either there or possibly on the north bank of the Mӕresēa,' she said.

'If they land in Loncastrescīr they would face the Norse who have already settled there. They are hardly likely to welcome so many new arrivals who want to share their land,' Eirik mused. 'Nor would my fellow jarls and I be prepared to allow them to settle on Wirhealum. I foresee trouble - and soon, lady.'

'Thirty or more longships means well over a thousand Vikings, does it not?' Cuthfleda asked.

Ywer nodded. 'They will have their women, children and thralls with them, of course, and they will take up room on the ships but a thousand isn't a bad estimate.'

'The danger, and here I must be blunt, is that other Norsemen already here might be tempted to join this Ingimund,' Deorwine said morosely. 'We saw it often enough with Hæsten a few years ago. We defeated him time and time again and yet young Viking warriors kept flooding to replace those of his men who we'd killed.'

'Are you doubting my loyalty and that of all the other jarls in Cæstirscīr?' Eirik asked, his tone low and ominous.

'Not at all, Eirik, but can you swear that some of your young warriors mightn't be tempted to join him? Becoming Viking raiders may have more appeal than farming the land.'

'They are faithful to me. Neither Eohric of East Anglia nor the various kings who have claimed to rule Northumbria in recent years inspire much loyalty in their subjects. Certainly not Æðelwold, the so-called King of Yorvik. His people hate him,' he said with a sneer.

'This isn't getting us very far,' Æthelflæd said. 'Our safest course is to assume that Ingimund will come here. If he does, we have two options. We defeat him and drive him out or we negotiate with him and come to some sort of agreement.'

'You would negotiate with him, lady?' Abbot Æscwin asked, sounding horrified. 'How can you trust him; and what could we offer him and his pagan horde?'

'Land,' she replied simply. 'There is still a lot of wilderness out there which needs to be cultivated. As to trust, I don't trust him one little bit. However, I do

102

need time to build up our military strength and to construct burhs and forts to defend the shire. It's how my father finally secured Wessex and it's what Lord Æðelred and I intend to do all over Mercia in due course. Why not start here in Cæstirscīr?'

Her statement wasn't quite true. Æthelflæd was convinced that a series of strongly garrisoned burghs interlinked by good roads was the only way that Mercia could be defended but, whilst he agreed with the principle, Æðelred maintained that Mercia couldn't afford the cost.

†††

King Eadweard paced up and down trying hard to keep his frustration in check. Æðelwold had landed on the coast of East Anglia with a small fleet of Northumbrians in September. Having linked up with a much larger local army commanded by King Eohric, their combined force had raided along the south bank of the River Temes before crossing it at Merlaue and entering Mercia. The fortified burhs along the Temes had withstood attack but the surrounding countryside had been pillaged and laid waste.

Eadweard and Æðelred kept on finding themselves one day's march behind the enemy and their failure to bring the foe to battle was taking its toll on the fyrd's morale.

'I've had enough of this. They must suffer for what they've done to Wessex,' Eadweard said bitterly. 'Æðelred, this is your land; you stay here and pursue them. I'm heading to East Anglia to give Eohric a taste of his own medicine.'

'I haven't got enough men to defeat Æðelwold and Eohric on my own,' the other man protested.

'You won't need to. They're not to know that I'm not with you; that is, until reports start to reach them of the devastation I intend to wreak on Eohric's domain.'

'What happens then? They'll realise that we've split our forces.'

'I'm willing to gamble that Eohric will march back as fast as he can to protect his own kingdom. Either my cousin plus the small number of Northumbrians that he's managed to recruit will go with him or he'll stay in Mercia. If he stays you'll easily outnumber him.'

Æðelred looked dubious but Eadweard's assessment proved to be correct. As soon as word reached Eohric that Eadweard was pillaging his kingdom he abandoned his raid on Mercia and rapidly headed eastwards. Æðelwold went with him. They skirted Lundenburg to the north and eventually arrived at a place called Huntedone.

'The Saxons are camped three miles away at a farmstead called the Holme,' Eohric's chief scout told him.

'Good. We'll attack at dawn tomorrow,' Eohric said without bothering to consult Æðelwold.

However, Eadweard had no intention of offering battle now that he'd achieved his objective of enticing the Eohric back to defend his kingdom. He gave orders for the army to withdraw but it wasn't a popular command.

'Why are we retreating,' Oswine wanted to know.

'You call me cyning and it's not your place to question my decisions,' Eadweard snapped at him.

'I'm the Ealdorman of Cent and my men make up a large part of your army,' Oswine replied and then added 'cyning' after a pause.

'Yes, and who made you ealdorman? I'm beginning to think that replacing Jørren by you was a mistake.'

One of Eadweard's first actions on being made King of Cent – a sub-kingdom of Wessex which also included the shires of Sūþrīgescīr and Suth-Seaxe – by Ælfred was to dismiss Jørren and replace him with the latter's stepson, Oswine. At the time the two were very close but over time Eadweard and Oswine had fallen out several times and now they were barely on speaking terms.

Oswine left the king's presence feeling more than a little disgruntled. They had been given the run around by Æðelwold and Eohric for months and now that they had the opportunity to face them in battle Eadweard wanted to turn tail and find a more suitable site on which to face the Danes. Well, Oswine decided, he was damned if he was going to flee like a coward. He therefore went in search of his shire reeve, Sigehelm.

'Lord, we can't take on the combined armies of East Anglia and Northumbria,' Sigehelm objected, appalled by Oswine's suggestion.

'Why not? According to our scouts their army totals no more than fifteen hundred men and we have roughly the same number.'

'No doubt a lot of their men have gone home, satisfied with the plunder they seized from Wessex and Mercia but even so the Danes are all trained warriors whilst the majority of our strength is made up of the fyrd.'

'Are you as cowardly as Eadweard then?' Oswine asked derisively.

'I don't believe that the king is afraid, merely that he wants to choose the ground on which to face the enemy,' Sigehelm replied stiffly, 'and I don't think it's wise to call Eadweard a coward. That's treason.'

'Just think of the treasure that will fall into our hands when we defeat the Danes on our own,' Oswine urged.

Both men were greedy and Sigehelm was tempted by the thought of not having to share the spoils with the rest of the army.

'Very well,' he said reluctantly. 'What's your plan?'

†††

Oswine had drawn his men up in a shieldwall four deep on firm level ground some two hundred yards back from a small stream which ran from east to west across his front. Either side of the stream the ground was boggy. There was a wood which protected his left flank and he had stationed his archers on the right flank.

Mist lay low on the ground as the Danes advanced shortly after dawn on the thirteenth of December 902. It would take the weak sun some time to burn it off but Oswine was content. The mist was only a few feet in height and so his men could still see the helmets of the enemy warriors as they advanced. He prayed quietly that the sight of the disembodied heads coming towards them didn't unnerve the fyrd. The Danes had a bigger problem; they couldn't see the ground beneath their feet and they struggled in the marshy terrain.

By the time they came to the stream many of them were exhausted from having to wade through mud and slime that came halfway up to their knees. Unaware of the stream many fell down the bank into the water and emerged soaking wet and chilled to the bone. However, this didn't depress them; it merely made them angry and even more eager to slay the men of Cent.

Once clear of the bog there was little or no mist clinging to the ground. As the Danes rushed towards the Centish shieldwall a cloud of arrows descended on their left flank, killing and wounding scores. Undeterred they rushed at the enemy shieldwall expecting it to give way. Once they had broken the line of shields the fate of the men of Cent would be sealed.

The front rank of Oswine's army were made up of thegns, experienced warriors and men of the fyrd who had fought the Danes before. Many of them had faced Hæsten's Viking horde when they'd invaded Cent a decade ago. The job of the second rank was to use their spears to stab at any exposed Danish flesh they could see. The last two ranks were there to push their shields against the first two ranks and keep the line in place.

The youngest boys crouched down between the legs of the second rank. Each held a sharp knife or a dagger and had orders to stab at the legs of the Danes as they tried to force the shieldwall back. Some even managed to hamstring a few of the enemy.

The Danes were surprised by the resilience of their foes. They had expected a quick victory once they'd struggled through the morass around the stream. Instead it quickly became apparent that they were suffering more casualties than they were managing to inflict on the Jutes and Saxons of Cent. They drew back to regroup.

Both Eohric and Æðelwold were infuriated by this reversal and forced their way through the ranks ready to lead the next attack and press it home. It was a mistake. A lucky arrow found Æðelwold's exposed neck as he advanced and he fell, mortally wounded. The point of the arrow had nicked one of his carotid arteries and he lay there bleeding to death; not that this bothered the East Anglian Danes much.

The Northumbrians were a different matter. They were reluctant followers of Æðelwold in the first place and it was only his promise of rich rewards that induced them to join him. With his death they quickly left the field and headed for the coast where their longships lay ready to take them back north. Æðelwold's gesith tried to stop them but they were too few in number and, after the Northumbrians had killed half a dozen of those who stood in their way, the rest joined the retreat.

Oswine stood in the front rank alongside Sigehelm. The Dane coming towards him was a giant, standing at least head and shoulders above his comrades. He had no shield but carried a double-headed battleaxe with a haft some four feet long. He swung the axe to and fro as he walked like some sort of murderous pendulum. The axe must have weighed a great deal but in his hands it appeared to be as light as a feather.

Sigehelm held his shield ready to take the blow from the axe with his sword ready to slice into the axeman's neck. However, he never had the chance. The heavy axe blade cut through the stout lime wood shield as if it was made of paper, breaking Sigehelm's arm and then cutting through the flesh down to the severed bone.

The giant dragged the axe clear and swung it back the other way just as Oswine plunged his sword into the Dane's right thigh. At the same time a boy overcame his awe and fear of the giant and slashed his blade across the back of the man's left knee. His leg collapsed under him and Oswine stabbed down into his neck. The giant Dane was dead but in killing him Oswine had left himself exposed, especially as Sigehelm, who was guarding his right hand side, was badly injured.

The Dane behind the fallen giant seized his opportunity and thrust his spear into Oswine's chest, breaking asunder the links of chain mail and piercing his heart. He fell on top of the boy who was trying to stab this new opponent in the leg. The boy was trapped and the Dane tried to kill him by forcing his face into the mixture of mud and gore with his foot in an effort to suffocate him. At the same time he thrust his spear at the man who had stepped forward to take Oswine's place. The Dane's opponent batted it aside with his shield and thrust his own spear into the Dane's left eye, killing him instantly.

With the pressure removed from his head, the boy started to get up, spitting out muck and blowing his nose to clear it. He didn't have time to thank his saviour before another Dane stepped forward and thrust his sword into the boy's neck.

Sigehelm might be wounded and have a broken arm but he gritted his teeth against the pain. He'd sunk into a kneeling position and from there he stabbed upwards under the hem of the byrnie worn by the boy's killer and into his groin. With a howl the man collapsed clutching his crotch and the man standing behind Sigehelm stepped forward and used his spear to finish him off.

Sigehelm was helped to his feet and men tried to take him to the rear where his wound and broken bone could be attended to. However, he was having none of it and, once his broken arm had been strapped to his chest and the cut roughly bandaged, he stepped back into the front rank. He managed to cut down two more of the enemy before the pain and loss of blood took their toll and he was too slow to counter another Danish axeman. The blade sliced through Sigehelm's neck and his head struck the ground just before his body did.

The loss of both their ealdorman and their shire reeve took the heart out of the men of Cent and they fled the field fully expecting the Danes to pursue them and cut them down in droves. They didn't. They had also lost both their leaders in addition to several prominent jarls. Moreover their losses had been even greater than those of the Centish army. They were content to be left in possession of the battlefield.

The threat to Eadweard's throne had disappeared. Moreover, Eohric had no living relatives and no-one tried to seize his throne. Those who might have done had died at the Battle of the Holme. Like the rest of the Danelaw, East Anglia now dissolved into a patchwork of independent jarldoms.

Chapter Six

Spring 903

'What I am I to do, Cuthfleda?' Æthelflæd asked her oldest friend as they sat together.

It might have been the beginning of April but it was still cold and so a brazier burned in one corner of the chamber, its smoke leaving through the hole in the roof above it and lazily drifting around the ceiling above them in equal measure.

Æðelred had returned to Glowecestre after the death of Æðelwold at the Battle of the Holme and had sent several messengers north insisting that his wife returned to his side.

Æthelflæd had replied, using Jørren's death and the threat posed by Ingimund as her excuse to delay her return. It was only part of the reason for staying at Cæstir. She was enjoying being the shire's ruler too much to want to return to her secondary role as counsellor to her husband. She also was enjoying the reunion with her nephew far from Eadweard's reach.

In her initial reply she informed Æðelred about Jørren – although he was bound to have heard the news from elsewhere – and somewhat exaggerated the threat from the Irish Vikings. In his reply Æðelred appointed Ywer as ealdorman in his father's stead and told her that she could safely leave the problems of the north in his hands.

She demurred, pointing out that by choosing Ywer now, he risked alienating Eirik, who also had ambitions in that direction. She pointed out the risk that Eirik and the other Norse jarls in Cæstirscīr might unite with the countrymen from Íralond and drive Ywer and the Mercians out. Finally she asked that the matter be deferred until she could speak to the Witenaġemot, who had to formally confirm the appointment, once she had sorted out the problems that Cæstirscīr currently faced.

Æthelflæd read through the latest missive from her husband again before throwing it on the fire in disgust.

My dearest wife, it began.

I fully appreciate the danger that Northern Mercia faces from the Norsemen from Íralond; indeed, there have been reports that they have fled to Mann and the west coast of Northumbria, boosting the pagan populations of these places as well. However, that is not my problem. Leave Cæstirscīr to Ywer to sort out and return to my side. This isn't a request; it's an instruction.

Quite apart from the fact that I need your advice, I won't have you putting yourself in danger.

Your loving husband,

Æðelred

'I wonder what he'd say if he knew you'd led a charge against Vikings and killed one yourself?' Cuthfleda asked with an amused twinkle in her eye.

'That's not helping,' she retorted. 'Now that Anarawd and his son have driven Ingimund out of

113

Ynys Môn, we need to find out where they've gone. I won't leave here until I know that he's no threat to us.'

Cuthfleda knew that she wasn't only worried about losing Cæstirscīr to the Norse, although that would be bad enough, she was also concerned about Æthelstan's safety. Her nephew and Wynnstan were the same height, despite the age difference between them, and the two had become good friends. Normally she would have discouraged a friendship between her most junior warrior and her nephew but Wynnstan was training Æthelstan to fight with sword and shield and to use a bow and her nephew was flourishing under his instruction.

Perhaps she should have appointed one of her more senior warriors as the boy's tutor but they would have regarded Æthelstan as too young to commence weapon training. They would have done as they were told, of course, but their heart wouldn't have been in it. If she went south now she could leave Wynnstan behind, of course, but that would have meant formally acknowledging Wynnstan as her nephew's mentor; something many would have frowned on.

In any case, quite apart from her desire to stay in Cæstir for now, she couldn't abandon Æthelstan to Ywer's care when the situation was so volatile. It would have made her ill with worry. The other option was to take her nephew with her but she was well aware that would mean turning him over to Eadweard and the Church. That could be putting him in danger as Eadweard's wife, Ælfflæd, was said to be pregnant. She didn't think for one minute that her brother would kill his son to eliminate a rival to his new baby but she wouldn't put it past Ælfflæd's family.

In the end she wrote to her husband to say that she was unwell; nothing serious but she was unable to travel for the moment. Instead of buying her more time it had the one effect she didn't want. Æðelred wrote back to say that he was heading north.

✝✝✝

Wynnstan and Æthelstan were racing each other across the sands at the northern end of the Wirhealum peninsula when they spotted the sails out to sea. The two boys weren't alone. Skarde, Arne and Lyndon had been detailed by Cuthfleda to keep an eye on Æthelstan but they were riding some way behind the two boys and as yet they hadn't seen the fleet heading inshore.

Of the two, Æthelstan had the sharpest eyesight and it was he who first saw that the red sails were emblazoned with a black disc with strange white curves inside it.

'I make it sixteen ships. I wonder who they are,' Æthelstan pondered.

'Possibly Ingimund, but he is said to have thirty longships or more,' the other boy replied. 'Can you make out the device yet? It looks like swirling curves.'

'Why have you halted?' Skarde asked as he joined them.

Instead of answering Wynnstan pointed westwards and Skarde swore in Norse.

'I know that device; it's the triple horn of Odin.'

'Then those longships must belong to Ingimund or some other pagan Norse fleeing from Íralond,' Æthelstan said. 'We must warn my aunt.'

'Wynnstan, you and Arne go with Æthelstan to Cæstir and tell the Lady Æthelflæd,' Skarde ordered. 'Lyndon, ride to Apletune and warn Lord Ywer. I'll head for Grárhöfn and inform Eirik.'

Although Eirik and Skarde were half-brothers they hated the sight of each other. Eirik and Skarde shared the same father but the former's mother had been a thrall. When the father died the local thing – the Norse equivalent of a witan - had elected Eirik to succeed as jarl, despite being of illegitimate birth. Skarde was only a young boy at the time but it didn't stop him feeling deprived of his inheritance, in much the same way as Æðelwold had felt cheated out of the throne of Wessex by Ælfred and then Eadweard. However, despite his antipathy towards his half-brother, the Norse inhabitants of Wirhealum were still his people.

'What do you want here, Skarde,' Eirik demanded angrily when he was told of his brother's arrival.

'I wouldn't be here unless the matter was urgent, Eirik. There are sixteen longships approaching the north coast of Wirhealum; they have the triple horn of Odin embroidered on their sails and so it's probable that they are Ingimund's warband or some other Viking horde.'

Eirik's attitude changed immediately.

'How far offshore were they and are they heading for the mouth of the River Dēvā or the Mæresēa?'

'The sails had just cleared the horizon so they were several miles offshore but that was twenty minutes

116

ago. It wasn't clear which river they were heading for and I wasn't about to waste time waiting to find out.'

He glared at his brother, who scowled back at him. Eirik was about to say something in response but he bit his tongue and yelled for his warriors to mount up instead. It took ten minutes for them to clamber into byrnies or leather jerkins and arm themselves whilst boys ran to saddle their horses. Eirik led half his warband along the west bank of the Mǣresē towards the open sea whilst the other half headed across the peninsula to check the Dēvā and the approaches to Cæstir.

Eirik had said nothing further to Skarde and so he took it upon himself to ride and inform the other jarls and thegns who lived in the south-eastern part of the peninsula. Most had a palisade around their settlements but not all. Even so, it wouldn't take the newcomers long to capture each individual place. They needed to muster every man capable of bearing arms in one place if they were to stand any chance of defeating the invaders.

When he eventually returned to Cæstir he found that Eirik was there before him and a meeting of Æthelflæd's council was in progress. He was shown in straight away when he said that he needed to make his report.

'Lady,' he said without preamble, 'I have taken it upon myself to call a muster of all those who live between Jarl Eirik's lands and here. The muster point is Cæstir where the women and children can take refuge within the walls.'

'Excellent, you are to be congratulated on taking the initiative in doing so. I have just persuaded your brother to do the same. Even the defences of Grárhöfn aren't sufficient to keep out hundreds of Vikings.'

'Do we know how many they have and where they've landed, Lady?' Skarde asked.

Both Eirik and Deorwine glared at him for his impudence. He had no business questioning Æthelflæd. He had joined Ywer's gesith when Jørren had died but he held no position of importance within it. However, Æthelflæd didn't seem to mind his boldness and answered him.

'Jarl Eirik's estimate is that there are between five and seven hundred warriors and the same number of women, young children and thralls. They have landed near Nestone and have set up camp in and around the settlement.'

'Then I'm glad I managed to warn Thegn Pybba in time. He and his people were leaving as I rode on to warn the rest.'

'Night isn't far off,' Cuthfleda pointed out. 'I think it's safe to assume that they won't start raiding the hinterland until dawn. We need to minimise the destruction they can wreak on the morrow.'

'You think we should move to confront them during the hours of darkness?' Rinan asked, sounding appalled at the idea.

'Not confront, no,' she replied. 'I'm not so foolish as to think we can gather an army together and march it cross country to Nestone in the dark. I merely suggest that it might be sensible to meet him and discover Ingimund's intentions, if indeed it is him.'

'And why would he be interested in negotiating?' Rinan asked, sounding scornful.

Deorwine scowled at him but Rinan ignored him. He was still feeling hard done by and, although he knew he was being churlish, he couldn't stop himself.

'Because we know he landed on Ynys Môn with more than double the number of warriors he has now. He will have lost some when he was driven off the island and he must have tried his luck elsewhere, probably along the coast of Wealas somewhere. Evidently he was defeated again or he wouldn't have arrived here with so few warriors compared to the number he left Íralond with,' Cuthfleda replied in the sort of patient tone one used when explaining something to a child.

'I think that is the most likely explanation, thank you Cuthfleda,' Æthelflæd cut in before Rinan could reply.

The last thing she wanted was members of her council falling out at a time of crisis.

'If that is the case, he won't be too popular with his men at the moment. He won't want to risk another pitched battle and further losses, not to mention the loss of reputation that would entail,' she continued.

'Do we know it's definitely Ingimund?' Abbot Æscwin asked.

'Yes, his symbol is the three horns of Odin; it's him alright,' Eirik confirmed.

'Very well, we leave here an hour before dawn,' Æthelflæd decided. 'I'll take all those who've already answered the muster and who are mounted in addition to my own warband. Rinan, I leave you to

119

defend Cæstir with your own men and all those members of the fyrd encamped outside the walls who are on foot. Hopefully, Lord Ywer will arrive with his men during the night but, whether he does or not, we leave on time.'

✝✝✝

The sky lightened in the east, bathing the column of horsemen in golden light as they approached Nestone with the sun behind them. It was a deliberate ploy so that the enemy couldn't see how many men accompanied Æthelflæd. Ywer hadn't arrived and so her escort numbered less than two hundred. Apart from her warband - which had risen to thirty five with those warriors recruited in Cæstirscīr – there were another eighty made up of local Norse jarls, Mercian thegns and their hearth warriors and a further fifty mounted ceorls, some of whom were archers.

Deorwine had thrown out a screen of a dozen scouts to the front and flanks to make sure that the column wasn't ambushed. However, Wynnstan could see that those encamped around the settlement at Nestone were only just stirring. One man came out of a small leather tent and dropped his trousers to urinate directly in front of the screen of scouts. He was wearing nothing but a linen tunic and the baggy trousers favoured by most Vikings and stood there barelegged and gaping at the oncoming cavalcade.

The approaching column was led by the Lady of Mercia, Cuthfleda, Deorwine, Abbot Æscwin and Eirik Fairhair with the banners of Mercia, Cæstirscīr, the diocese of Licefelle and that of Eirik – a red hawk on a black background. The banners of other Norse jarls fluttered further down the column. It made for a brave show and Æthelflæd only hoped that it made up for her lack of numbers.

The man stopped urinating and squinted into the sun trying to make out the details of the approaching riders. Suddenly he turned and yelled something. There was an immediate flurry of activity and men, women and children emerged from their tents amidst what seemed like chaotic activity. However, within ten minutes the men had armed themselves and formed a shieldwall between the tents and the approaching cavalcade. At the same time the women, children and other men - who were presumably thralls – hastened through the gates into the settlement before they clanged shut.

Æthelflæd held up her hand and the cavalcade came to a slightly shambolic halt behind her. Meanwhile Wynnstan and the other scouts closed in to form a protective screen between her and the Norsemen.

For five minutes or so nothing happened then the gates opened and half a dozen men rode through them on horses that they had presumably brought with them on board the knarr tied up alongside the settlement's short jetty. The other fifteen ships were either beached or anchored in the inlet that ran into the main channel of the Dēvā.

The shieldwall parted to allow the six riders through and then closed again behind them. The horsemen stopped a hundred yards short of the line of scouts and Æthelflæd let her gaze sweep over them. The one in the most expensive byrnie with a helmet inlaid with runic designs in gold had to be Ingimund. She thought that he might be in his late twenties but the haughty looking boy sitting beside him couldn't have been more than ten or eleven. If he was the Norse leader's son, as she supposed, Ingimund must have sired him when he was sixteen or seventeen.

The other four men were presumably minor leaders or his hearth warriors. One carried a banner with a red flag embroidered with the strange design that Eirik had called the triple horns of Odin.

Æthelflæd rode forward accompanied by Cuthfleda, Deorwine, Æscwin, Eirik and two of her warriors. As the little group came to halt a hundred yards from the Norse delegation, Æthelstan arrived to join his aunt from where he'd been sent back to the rear for safety. She frowned at him but didn't send him away.

'I am Lady Æthelflæd, wife of Æðelred, the Lord of Mercia, whose territory you seem to have invaded,' she said in Ænglisc.

Eirik started to translate what she had said into Norse but the man in the expensive helmet held up his hand.

'I speak Ænglisc in addition to Norse, Danish and Gaelic – the language of the natives of Íralond. I have no need for translators,' he said arrogantly. 'My name is Ingimund and I have a large enough warband to go where I please, lady.'

'Then why are you here instead of staying on Ynys Môn? Or perhaps one of the other places along the coast of Wealas where you tried to land?'

Ingimund's face flushed with anger before he composed himself and his arrogant expression re-established itself.

'Those other places weren't suitable,' he replied airily, 'but we like the look of this land; it is fertile and close to the sea for raiding.'

'It is also my land,' Eirik replied curtly.

'No one settles in Mercia without the agreement of Lord Æðelred,' Æthelflæd replied, giving the jarl a warning look not to interrupt again. 'However, it may be possible to find a suitable area near here where you can settle.'

'And if I don't like this other area?'

'Then we'll push you back into the sea where you came from, just as our allies, the men of Gwynedd, did.'

Ingimund looked at Æthelflæd speculatively for a moment, then let his eyes wander over the warriors she had brought with her. The latter had spread out into two lines and, as all were mounted, they made an impressive sight despite being inferior in numbers to the horde of Vikings who had gathered a couple of hundred yards behind Ingimund's group.

'Come, let's talk in more civilised surroundings. If you leave twenty suitable hostages with my men I'll come to your hall to discuss matters with you.'

'So you can inspect Cæstir's defences? I think not, Lord Ingimund. I'll have a tent erected here so that we can take refreshments and conduct our discussions in more comfort.'

Half an hour later a large tent had been fetched from the baggage train and chairs brought for both sides to sit on. Servants produced ale and mead as well as platters of venison and various cheeses.

'Please introduce me to your companions,' she said as the negotiators took their seats.

'This is my son, Gunnar,' he said, indicating the young boy who stood behind his chair. 'These two are Jarls Hakon and Leif, my chief advisors. The others are three of my senior hearth warriors.'

Æthelflæd introduced Cuthfleda, Deorwine, Æscwin and Eirik before calling forward Æthelstan from the back of the tent.

'This is my nephew, Æthelstan, the son of King Eadweard of Wessex.'

Both Ingimund and his son studied the boy with interest; the father because he wondered what he was doing so far from Wessex whilst his son dismissed him as beneath his regard. Æthelstan was nearly thirteen and was already as tall as most men. As yet he had no sign of a beard and his long brown hair hung down to his shoulders. He was a handsome boy; if he'd been a girl he might even have been described as pretty. This gave those who didn't know him the impression that he was effeminate, which was far from the case.

'Are you sure he's his son; he looks more like a girl,' Gunnar said derisively.

The two jarls and the other Norse warriors laughed but Ingimund rebuked his son for his rudeness and the laughter immediately ceased.

'Æthelstan defeated a Danish warrior when he was nine,' Deorwine said quietly. 'Can you boast the same, boy?'

Gunnar went red in the face, not because of what Deorwine had said, although that was bad enough, but because of his father's reprimand in front of everyone. He determined to take his revenge on the other boy.

The negotiations dragged on. Ingimund wanted enough land to settle his people and, although there were still areas of Cæstirscīr that were virtually uninhabited, especially in the east near the border where Northumbria met the Danelaw, the Norseman insisted that he wanted to settle on the coast so that his warband could still raid Wealas, the coast of Loncastrescīr north of the River Mæresēa and Íralond. The fact that two of these places had been settled by other Norsemen and their families didn't seem to bother him.

Ideally he wanted to stay where they had landed but unsurprisingly that was unacceptable to both Eirik and Æthelflæd. It seemed that the talks were deadlocked when Bjørn Frami stepped forward and whispered in Æthelflæd's ear.

Bjørn was a Danish hersir who had joined Hæsten's Viking horde but who had subsequently been captured by Jørren together with his ship's crew. Faced with a choice of death or changing sides, he had opted for the latter and he and his men had served Jørren faithfully until his death. In his will Jørren had given him a vill on the coast near Cæstir. Like other landholders he had answered the muster and had been chosen as one of the men to guard Æthelflæd during the negotiations.

She thanked Bjørn and held a whispered conversation with Cuthfleda and Deorwine before turning her attention back to the Norse warlord.

'Perhaps we have a solution, Lord Ingimund. There is a settlement called Frodesham. It's part of Mercia but it has been taken by Northumbrian Danes. It's a problem that I need to confront because it is a port on the River Mæresēa with good access to the sea. It is especially important because it stands at the confluence of the Mæresēa and another river down which salt is brought from several settlements in eastern Cæstirscīr. Not only do we need the salt for preserving meat for the winter but the sale of the excess is quite lucrative.

'If you can recapture Frodesham you can become its new lord. There is good farmland around it and several farmsteads to the west of it that I'll give you as well.'

'It might be suitable,' Ingimund replied after conferring with Hakon and Leif, 'but naturally I want to see it for myself. By the sound of it, it lies near the border with Northumbria so it will need to be a good defensive location.'

'As you say, Northumbria lies across the river. However, that part is called Loncastrescīr and the kings in Yorvik have little or no control there. The area is mainly settled by other Norse invaders but there is no overall leader. There is an old hill fort on top of the ridge overlooking the settlement which would make a good defensive position for you.'

126

'You say that the area is occupied by Norsemen and yet this place, Frodesham, has been captured by Danes?'

'Yes, I understand that they sailed east along the river network from an old Roman fort at a place called Mamecestre. It's one of the few remaining outposts of the Kingdom of Yorvik in Loncastrescīr.'

'Very well, if Frodesham proved suitable I will hold it for you and swear allegiance to your husband, the Lord of Mercia.'

'Excellent. Your immediate lord will be the Ealdorman of Cæstirscīr and in due course you will need to give your oath to him as well.'

'Which of you is the ealdorman,' he asked looking around.

'Lord Jørren was the last ealdorman but unfortunately he died recently,' she said. 'Lord Æðelred has chosen a replacement but the appointment has to be approved by the Witenaġemot. Until that happens, I've taken charge of the shire.'

She ignored the sour look that Eirik gave her. The fact that he'd been passed over rankled and she had left Ywer at Apletune until he'd been formally confirmed to avoid any acrimony between the two men. She knew that Ywer would be on his way here now but prayed that the negotiations would be satisfactorily concluded before he arrived. It was vital that Ingimund detected no signs of disunity amongst her nobles.

'Forgive me, lady,' Ingimund replied. 'You are obviously an exceptional woman but my warriors would think me weak if I gave my oath to you.'

'I understand,' she replied a trifle frostily. 'My husband is on his way north. You can come and pledge your fealty to him and then to the new ealdorman when he is confirmed. One other thing, I expect you to convert to Christianity. Abbot Æscwin will appoint two monks to instruct you in the true faith ready for your baptism and those of your jarls and your families.'

Ingimund stiffened and clutched the mjolnir hanging around his neck. He glanced at Eirik who was wearing a gold crucifix where he had expected to see a mjolnir. Most of the Irish were Christians and he and his men despised them and their religion. It was a condition he couldn't possibly agree to if he expected to retain the loyalty of his men. Already the reverses he'd suffered in Wealas had damaged his reputation. Not all his losses had been the result of casualties in battle; several jarls and hersirs had deserted him because of his failure to find a place where they could settle. He decided to compromise.

'By all means send us monks to teach us about the Nailed God but it is up to each individual to make up their own mind about baptism.'

Æthelflæd felt the abbot stiffen and she hurriedly replied before he could protest.

'That seems fair but I expect you and your family as a minimum to become Christians before the year is out. Hopefully, others will follow your example.'

She was well aware that there was little chance that Ingimund would abide by this and, once he was in possession of Frodesham, there was nothing she could do to compel him to be baptised. It was a necessary artifice to resolve the situation and they both knew that.

Three days later Ingimund's fleet sailed around the Wirhealum peninsula and into the wide estuary of the Mæresēa. They were accompanied by two Mercian ships sent by Æthelflæd to guide them and help them to capture Frodesham. One was the longship belonging to Bjørn Frami and the other was a birlinn captained by Rinan. Wynnstan had been chosen to be one of the archers on Rinan's ship and he was thrilled by the prospect of taking part in his first battle.

Chapter Seven

June 903

Wynnstan had never been on a ship before and initially he found its motion at sea unnerving. However, he soon got used to it and found the way it cut through the waves exhilarating. The birlinn was rowed up the Dēvā but, as soon as it turned north-east at the end of the Wirhealum peninsula, the ship's boys hoisted the sail and they sped almost silently through the water powered by a stiff breeze coming beam on from the north-west.

The birlinn had a deeper keel than a longship but she was narrower in the beam. Consequently she heeled over even more. On her current course the larboard gunwale rode much higher than the starboard one and Wynnstan wondered how he was meant to send an arrow with any accuracy into an enemy vessel from such an unstable platform. However, the old hands amongst the archers taught him how to brace his feet and anticipate the movement of the ship. After a while he found that he could aim his bow at one of the other longships and move with his knees bent so as to keep an arrow trained upon it.

Thankfully he wasn't called upon to test his new found skill against an enemy and after an hour the fleet turned south-east to enter the mouth of the Mǣresēa. Now the motion changed. With a following wind the ship rolled from side to side instead of heeling but, as the river narrowed to a mile and a half wide, the surface became calmer and the ship rode upright.

The day had started sunny but as the hours passed the clouds in the sky increased and got darker. Soon it was ominously overcast and the wind increased to gale force. The sail on every ship was reefed just as the heavens opened and rain lashed down, reducing visibility considerably.

The river had gradually grown wider until it was perhaps three miles wide. When the storm hit them it became impossible to see either bank. The sails were lowered and the crew unshipped their oars. Once the mast was lowered into the cradle on deck the force of the wind propelling the ships onwards lessened. The rowers edged their craft forward slowly in the murk.

'Land dead ahead.'

The cry came from the oldest of the ship's boys who was stationed in the bows as lookout. The steersman leant on his steering oar and, with the larboard rowers resting, the longship came around to head due west. Shortly afterwards they reached the confluence of the Mæresēa and the tributary on which Frodesham lay. The birlinn led the other ships into the smaller river and all seventeen ships headed prow first into the right hand bank.

Wynnstan followed the other warriors over the bows and sank up to his ankles in soft mud. Cursing the filth which now clung to his expensive new boots he struggled up onto the grassy bank. All told, nearly seven hundred warriors formed up ready to attack Frodesham. Probably thanks to the torrential rain which still beat down on them and the wind, their landing seemed to have gone unobserved.

The settlement and port of Frodesham lay a thousand yards to the south-east but that wasn't Ingimund's first objective. He needed to capture the old fort on top of the hill which dominated the surrounding countryside. He therefore set off due south.

Rinan's men, supported by Bjørn Frami's crew, were designated as the vanguard and Wynnstan was sent out with three others as scouts ahead of the rest. Unlike the others, he was unfamiliar with the Frodesham area but he was chosen because he was the most skilled tracker and woodsman.

The rain stung his face as he made his way carefully across the stretch of meadow between the river and the trees which covered the lower slopes of the escarpment looming above him. He made use of dead ground as much as he could but anyone looking down from the fort, which he was told stood on top of the ridge, wouldn't be able to see far in the prevailing conditions in any case.

Behind him the rest of the vanguard made their way over the meadow in an extended line. Wynnstan wondered why he and the other scouts were being so careful when the rest looked as if they were out for a stroll. When he reached the trees he became even more vigilant. If their landing had been spotted the obvious place to ambush them was in the wood. He and the other scouts advanced two at a time whilst the other two hid in the undergrowth scouring the area ahead for any sign of movement, then swopped over.

Suddenly he heard singing coming from somewhere ahead. The voice sounded like a young girl's. A few yards further on Wynnstan spotted her in a small glade picking mushrooms and putting them in a basket. She didn't look older than twelve but he remained cautious all the same. It was unlikely that she was the bait in a trap but he wasn't taking any chances. He waved to the other three to keep watch whilst he silently crept up behind her.

She didn't realise that she wasn't alone until he grabbed her, putting one stout arm around her and using his other hand to cover her mouth. The girl stiffened in alarm and then started thrashing wildly, biting his hand at the same time. Wynnstan cursed at the unexpected pain from the bite and threw the girl to the ground, knocking the breath out of her. He drew his dagger and pricked her throat with it before she could recover enough to scream. Her eyes grew wide with fear and she lay perfectly still.

'What's your name, girl, and where have you come from?' he asked quietly in Ænglisc.

She looked bewildered and he told himself he was a fool. His Danish was poor but he spoke Norse fairly well and the languages were similar enough for him to make himself understood. He tried again in the language that he'd learnt from Arne.

'Astrid,' she stuttered fearfully. 'What do you want with me?'

'You haven't told me where you live.'

'In the fort up there,' she said, nodding her head in the direction of the top of the ridge.

133

'Tell me about it if you want to live,' Wynnstan demanded, trying to sound fierce.

In truth he felt sorry for the girl. She was a pretty little thing with an elfin face framed by long blonde hair. As he gazed down at her he felt the stirrings of sexual attraction. He felt confused by his reaction and then ashamed. She was barely on the verge of puberty. If she had any breasts to speak of they weren't apparent in her coarse woollen strap-dress. No, she was too young for him to be having such thoughts about her he told himself; in any case, she was the enemy.

'What do you want to know?' she said, interrupting the bewildering thoughts racing through his head.

'Er, describe the fort, especially its gates and defences.'

'Why, are the four of you going to attack it?' she asked derisively, regaining some of her courage.

Just at that moment the leading ranks of the vanguard appeared.

'No, we have a few friends with us,' he replied with a grin.

He helped the girl to her feet and took her to meet Rinan and the captain of the other ship – Bjørn Frami. In less than five minutes they learned from her what they wanted to know. She couldn't have been more cooperative. She said that the defences consisted of three concentric mounds, the last of which was surmounted by a palisade. There was only one gate which was left open during the day with two men guarding it. There was also a sentry in a watchtower.

The jarl in charge was a Dane called Vígmarr. He had built himself a hall and there was another for the unmarried warriors. The rest of them lived with their families and thralls in various huts. The huts varied in size, depending on the wealth and status of the warrior living there. The merchants, artisans and other bondi lived in the settlement down by the river. When asked about the size of the garrison she said that she thought it was about a hundred and fifty strong.

Rinan seemed satisfied with her answers but Wynnstan asked her about herself.

'I'm a servant, as was my mother before she died. The jarl likes to have servants in his hall as well as thralls.'

'In more ways than one, I bet,' one of the listening men said with a laugh, thrusting his hips to and fro.

'Keep quiet you idiot,' Rinan hissed at him.

The exchange had been in Ænglisc and Wynnstan hoped that the girl hadn't understood. Although he wasn't quite sure why, it was important to him that she was still unsullied. Unfortunately the man's actions needed no interpretation and he saw Astrid blush.

'He's right,' she whispered to Wynnstan. 'But I'm too young for Vígmarr or any of his hearth warriors to be interested.'

He felt relieved and wondered how he could keep the girl safe during the attack. He hoped against hope that somehow he could take her with him when they returned to Cæstir. He knew it was a long shot. Ingimund would want to retain the women and children they captured, either as thralls or to be sold

135

in various slave markets. He would regard them in the same way as any other plunder.

'Do you want to be a thrall?' he said quietly.

Astrid looked at him in dismay. 'Why?' she asked. 'I may be a servant but I'm free.'

'Not any more. Ingimund has six hundred warriors, quite apart from our two ship's crews. He has been given Frodesham and he will either keep the Danes he captures as thralls or sell them; do you understand?'

She nodded miserably.

'What can I do? Will you help me?'

'Stay close to me for now. When you get a chance run and hide in the bushes near where our ship is beached. It's called the Holy Saviour and has the carved figure of Christ hanging on the cross on its prow. Make sure you hide near the right one; there's a longship next to ours with a cross but there is no figure on it. The other longships are all pagan with carved serpents, dragons or other beasts on the prow. I'll come and find you but it may take some time.'

'How do you know you can trust me?'

He didn't reply but took her gently by the shoulders and kissed her on the lips. She pulled away initially but then relaxed and returned the kiss before he pulled away and looked her in the eye.

'I want to take care of you,' he said with a smile. 'Now wait for my signal and then slip away.'

He became aware that Rinan was looking at him impatiently and he slipped into the trees with the other scouts, taking Astrid with him on the pretext that she knew the local area.

✝✝✝

Astrid led Wynnstan and the other scouts to a spot in the trees closest to the only gates into the fort. He wondered why she was being so cooperative and worried that she might be leading them into a trap. However, she had no way of letting the Danes know of their presence and he dismissed his concerns as foolish. What he hadn't appreciated was how depressing her current life was; filled with drudgery only enlivened when she was allowed into the woods to collect firewood or mushrooms. Her capture promised a change to her life which gave her hope for the future. Furthermore, she was as attracted to the young Mercian as he was to her.

The stronghold had been built on the site of an ancient hill fort. Three concentric ditches defended the approach to the palisade which would make it nigh on impossible to storm the walls using scaling ladders. The only feasible ways of capturing the place without a siege or filling in the ditches was either to secure the gates in a surprise attack or use a battering ram to breach them. The latter would be expensive in terms of casualties as the men wielding the ram would be exposed to arrows, spears, rocks or anything else the defenders rained down on them.

'We need to capture the gate,' Rinan said when he and Bjørn Frami joined them. 'The problem is how to cross the one hundred and fifty yards between the trees and the fort before they can slam the gates shut.'

'There are only two sentries on the gates,' Astrid told them. 'They do shifts, as does the man in the watchtower, changing when each daymark is reached.'

Rinan knew that Vikings had a different system for measuring time than the Anglo-Saxons. They divided the day into eight equal parts and used the position of the sun to tell them when the end of each part, called a daymark, had been reached. Normally they would identify prominent features on the ground which coincided with each daymark. When the sun was over the feature they knew that that daymark had been reached. Unfortunately it didn't work on days when the sun wasn't visible.

'The rest of the guards on duty will be resting, or more likely gambling, in a hut twenty five yards from the entrance. Often they are late in relieving their comrades and one of those on duty has to go and fetch them.'

'Leaving only one man who can't shut both gates at the same time,' Rinan said with a grin.

'Especially if he has a knife in his neck,' the girl added pulling out a small kitchen knife from the pouch at her waist.

'You can't take that risk!' Wynnstan said in alarm.

'Why not?' Rinan asked, his eyes narrowing. 'Keep your mouth shut unless you have anything helpful to say.'

He didn't particularly like the boy and, more importantly, he could see that he had a soft spot for the young Danish girl which was clouding his judgement.

'When do they next change watch?'

She shrugged.

'They'll have to estimate when the daymark is reached on a day like this. We'll just have to wait until one of the sentries disappears inside the fort.'

It seemed like an eternity before the younger of the two Danes went inside the fort. Thankfully the rain had stopped by then but the sky was still overcast. With any luck those due to go on watch would argue that it wasn't yet time, so delaying the arrival of the relief guards.

Astrid walked towards the entrance to the fort as quickly as she could whilst trying to appear as if she wasn't hurrying. Normally she would be reluctant to leave the freedom of the woods and return to the jarl's hall where she worked. She was surprised that the Mercians had trusted her so readily but she was well aware that someone was probably training an arrow on her back just in case she betrayed them.

'Did you get a good crop of mushrooms, Astrid?' the remaining sentry asked as she approached.

'Yes, look,' she replied with a smile, removing the cloth over the few she had managed to gather before she was captured.

The man looked down and was about to ask what she had been doing all this time when the girl pulled out her knife and stabbed him in the neck. It wasn't a lethal blow but the pain and the suddenness of her attack meant that he was slow in responding. She pulled out her knife and went to stab him again but he blocked the blow with his arm and pushed her away. She fell to the ground and lay there looking up at the furious warrior, too paralysed by fear to move.

His shield and spear were propped up by the gate; he grabbed the latter and was about to thrust the point into Astrid's body when an arrow struck him in the back. He wasn't wearing a byrnie and the arrow penetrated his flesh before being deflected by his rear ribs and ending up piercing a lung. He wasn't dead but he soon would be. More importantly to Wynnstan, whose arrow had saved Astrid, the man was no longer a danger to her.

The three men who emerged from the hut to go on shift stood there dumbfounded as a horde of yelling warriors ran into the fort. A second or two later the man in the watchtower was belatedly ringing the alarm bell for all he was worth.

Rinan's and Bjørn's crews made short work of those on watch and then fell back to form a shieldwall in front of the gates. With the men he had he would be hard pressed to keep the Danes from regaining it. He prayed that Ingimund and his Norsemen wouldn't take too long to join him and sent a man back to tell him what had happened.

Wynnstan watched him go, wondering where Astrid was. He breathed a sigh of relief when he saw her disappear into the trees a hundred yards in front of the messenger. He was still thinking about her when he realised that Rinan was yelling at him. He quickly followed twenty other men – all good archers – up onto the walkway around the inside of the ramparts. From there they could do some damage to the Danes when they attacked but, without any protection, they would be vulnerable to any enemy bowmen.

There was a great deal of noise coming from the centre of the fort but it soon died away. Minutes later fully armed Danes began appearing from the alleyways and formed their own shieldwall fifty yards from Rinan's men. Astrid had said that there were a hundred and fifty warriors in the fort but, from where he stood, it looked to Wynnstan as if there were many more than that. As he pulled his bowstring back and took aim at a giant axeman in the front rank of the enemy he hoped that it wouldn't be long before Ingimund arrived.

✝✝✝

Astrid ran through the trees heading to where Wynnstan said his longship was beached. Although she had helped Rinan to capture the gates she was under no illusion that this would be of any help to her if she ran into a group of Norsemen. She therefore took a circuitous route to the west, down the steepest part of the escarpment.

However, unbeknownst to either Rinan or Bjørn, Ingimund hadn't immediately followed the vanguard up the hill. Instead he'd spread his warriors around the fort to make sure that no one escaped. By the time that Astrid left the fort the cordon was already in place.

It wasn't until the last man was in position that Ingimund led the rest of his men to support those already inside. He was still several hundred yards from the entrance when Rinan's messenger found him. Even then Ingimund didn't seem to be in any particular hurry. The messenger Rinan had sent to urge the Norsemen to hasten formed the distinct impression that the Norse war lord wouldn't be too bothered if most of the Mercians died, just so long as the gates were still open by the time he got there.

Astrid paused as she made her way downhill and took cover in a nearby bush when she heard the unmistakable clash of metal on metal followed by a hushed but profane rebuke directed at the man responsible. He had hit his helmet with his spear point when the other end got tangled in some undergrowth. The young girl blessed the miscreant; without his mistake she would have walked right into the cordon.

She picked up the rear hem of her under-dress and pulled it - and the strap-dress she wore over it - between her legs and tucked it into the rope that served her as a belt. She climbed up a nearby oak tree keeping hidden as much as possible within the foliage and trying not to shake the leaves on the thinner branches. Normally she could swarm up a tree such as this but trying to do so stealthily took time. From the top she had a good view of the Norseman who had made the noise and his closest companions. They were spaced several yards apart and standing holding their spears or axes ready. However, they had rested their heavy circular shields against nearby trees and, encouragingly, they looked bored.

Astrid was in a quandary. She couldn't see any way of sneaking past the men below her but if she stayed where she was then Wynnstan might leave without her. It didn't occur to her that the young Mercian wouldn't be leaving until sometime after the place had been captured and by then the men in the cordon would have moved up to the fort. She only had to stay where she was and wait for them to leave. Instead she decided to try and divert the attention of the warriors and run past them. She climbed down the tree as quietly as she had ascended.

Once at ground level she picked up a stone and threw it against the trunk of a tree. The man standing not ten yards away jerked his head round and peered towards where the sound had come from. Astrid sprinted for the gap between him and the next man whilst he was distracted. She felt a surge of exhilaration as she made it past them before they could react.

However, her triumphant feeling didn't last long. The cordon was staggered and she ran headlong into another of the Norse warriors standing fifteen yards further back in the trees. He dropped the axe he was holding and grabbed her long fair hair as she tried to elude him. He yanked hard and she fell backwards, screaming at the pain in her head.

'What have we here? My my, aren't you the pretty one?' the man said as he leered down at her.

✝✝✝

Wynnstan released the bowstring and yelled in triumph when the arrow hit the axeman in the middle of his chest, punching through his leather jerkin, tunic, flesh and ribcage to enter his heart. The Dane fell to the ground just as other men in the first rank of the enemy shieldwall were hit. The axeman hadn't been protected by a shield but most of the others were. Nevertheless, several arrows from the archers on the walkway found the gap between helmet and shield rim or else struck the Danes' exposed legs.

The archers had time for another volley before the enraged Danes charged the Mercians inside the gate. At the same time Danish archers standing in the rear of their comrades sent arrow after arrow skywards against those standing on the parapet. Wynnstan saw the man to his right hit in the shoulder. It wasn't a fatal wound but he toppled forwards and fell to the ground fifteen feet below, breaking his neck.

Wynnstan had never felt so vulnerable. The archer to his other side dropped to the parapet and lay there. In that position the walkway itself protected his body from the Danish arrows so Wynnstan did the same.

The Danes were firing together and so there was a gap of twenty seconds or so between volleys. As soon as their arrows had flown overhead Wynnstan scrambled into a kneeling position and took aim at one of the enemy bowmen. There wasn't room to hold his bow vertically so he had to tilt it to one side. Nevertheless, his arrow took one of the Danish archers in the throat, not that he saw it. As soon as he released his bowstring he dropped to the prone position again.

Others saw what Wynnstan had done and copied him. Although they had lost several of their own men, the Danes were now suffering many more casualties until whoever was in charge of the archers below had the sense to order his men to fire at will. Now the attrition rate was more even as the Mercians couldn't expose themselves without risk.

Wynnstan crawled to the edge of the wooden walkway. From there he could look down at the enemy with only his head exposed. An arrow struck his helmet but it ricocheted away, doing no more damage than making a ringing noise in his ears. The rate of fire from the enemy decreased and, without a target to aim at, eventually ceased.

'Ready lads,' Wynnstan called out. 'Now!'

Almost as one the Mercian bowmen rose to a kneeling position and sent a volley down into the opposing archers. The sudden attack was unexpected and the Mercians managed to get another arrow away in the confusion before dropping back out of sight.

The Danes tended to use bows mainly for hunting, despising them as a coward's way of fighting. A warrior fought face to face, not from a distance, and so relatively few used a bow. Of the fort's garrison of nearly two hundred, less than a score possessed a bow and were prepared to use it in battle. The Mercians had suffered seven casualties but they had inflicted more than a dozen on the enemy.

'There's only seven of them left,' Wynnstan called out after he'd risked another peek over the edge of the walkway.

No one had been designated as the leader of the archers on the walkway in the confusion at the start of the fight. Wynnstan was the youngest of them but somehow he appeared to have taken charge and now the others looked to him.

'If we all stand at once we should be able to eliminate them before they can do much damage to us. Are we agreed?'

Several looked dubious but no one voiced an objection and a few nodded.

'Right, get ready.' He waited for the right moment and then yelled 'now!'

They rose and sent two dozen shafts into the remaining Danes before they could respond. Wynnstan nocked a third arrow to his bowstring but it wasn't necessary. All seven were dead or badly wounded. The Mercian bowmen cheered and several clapped the boy on the shoulder to congratulate him. He looked towards the gate and his face fell. They might have won the battle of the bowmen but the men led by Rinan and Bjørn Frami were in danger of being driven out of the fort.

†††

Astrid looked up at the man standing over her. He was in the process of unbuckling his belt and lowering his trousers. It didn't take a genius to work out what his intentions were. The girl fumbled for her knife but fear made her clumsy and the Norseman grabbed her dress and was about to rip it from her body when her frantic hand closed on the hilt. Pulling it out of its sheath she stabbed wildly upwards in the direction of the man's groin.

The blade missed its target but panic lent her strength and she carved a deep cut in his inner thigh before the knife came to a halt at the top of his leg. Blood spurted out and the man cried out, both in pain and in rage. At the rate he was losing blood Astrid

146

guessed that he had no more than a few minutes to live but he still had the strength to grab her hair again and force the knife out of her hand. He picked it up and thrust towards her neck.

She just managed to jerk her head to one side and the blade did no more than make a shallow cut to her shoulder. He was growing weaker and when he made another attempt to stab her she sunk her teeth into his wrist, ignoring the pain as his other hand threatened to pull her hair out by its roots.

His hand slackened its grip on her hair and she managed to pull free just as she heard a voice asking her assailant something. Norse and Danish were similar languages and she gathered that he'd asked the dead man if he was alright. She heard twigs snap as someone came in her direction and, pausing only to retrieve her knife and slice through the straps attaching her attacker's purse to his belt, she darted away into the trees. As soon as she was clear she cleaned her gory knife and shoved the dead Norseman's purse into her bodice.

As she headed downhill the incline grew steeper and she lost her footing. She tumbled downhill until her progress was halted by the base of a large tree. Her head hit something and everything went black.

††††

'Shoot into their backs,' Wynnstan yelled, sending an arrow into a man in the rearmost rank of the Danes below.

Shaft after shaft struck the vulnerable backs of the enemy. Even those wearing byrnies weren't safe; the narrow points of the arrows forced the welded iron rings apart and, although their momentum was reduced in doing so, there was still sufficient force for the point to penetrate the clothing underneath and enter their flesh.

It didn't take the Danes long to realise what was happening and the rear ranks turned around to face the new threat. In doing so they stopped pushing at the backs of those in front and the reduced pressure allowed the Mercian shieldwall to regain a foot or so of the ground it had lost.

Less than a minute later thirty or so of the Danes broke away from the rest and headed for the steps leading up to the walkway.

'What do we do, they'll slaughter us!' one of the younger archers called out in panic.

'Quiet,' Wynnstan growled at him. 'Three of us can hold the top of the steps whilst the rest pepper them with arrows.'

He pointed at three of the largest archers, each of whom had a seax hanging from his belt.

'You three hold them off; the rest of you hit them as they mount the steps.'

'I've only two shafts left,' one of the archers pointed out as the three raced off.

'Then make each one count. Chad, you and two others recover as many arrows as you can from the walkway.'

Chad nodded and strode away to pull Danish shafts from where they had struck the top of the palisade and, unsavoury as it was, from the archers who'd been killed. Some were so damaged as to be unusable and none was perfect but the latter were better than nothing.

By the time that a dozen shafts had struck those trying to climb and get at the three Mercians holding the top of the steps even the most resolute of the Danes realised that they were losing men for no good reason. They quickly retreated back down again and joined the others at the rear of the main body who were using their shields to protect their comrades from the archers.

Wynnstan and his fellow archers kept up a desultory fire with the few arrows that Chad had managed to gather to keep them occupied but once again the Danes were pressing forward. He estimated that perhaps half of Rinan and Bjørn's men had fallen. It was some consolation that they had taken many more Danes with them but they were still outnumbered three to one.

They had been forced back into the gateway itself but at least that meant that the Danes could only bring the same number of men to bear as there were in the Mercian front rank. However, the press of men behind the Danish shieldwall was far greater and gradually the Mercians were being forced back a pace at a time.

'Where the hell is Ingimund,' Wynnstan wondered and he wasn't alone.

He and his fellow archers were now out of arrows and he pondered what they could do to help. He knew that going down and attacking the rear of the Danes with just a dozen men was tantamount to suicide but he couldn't see any other way of helping.

Just at the moment he'd decided it was the only honourable thing to do, a horn sounded from outside the fort. He and the others rushed to the palisade and peered down at a glorious sight. A couple of hundred Norse warriors were charging across the open ground between the edge of the trees and the gate.

†††

Wynnstan stumbled out of the fort sickened by what he'd experienced. It hadn't taken long after the Norsemen had joined the fray before the Danes were pushed back into the fort and then the slaughter began. Outnumbered, they had fought on until only a score or so were left. They had tried to surrender but they were still cut down where they stood. The Mercian contingent hadn't taken part in the execution of the surviving warriors; they stood by and watched, dismayed by the ferocity of Ingimund and his men.

That was only the beginning. With the Danish men dead, the Norsemen went in search of their women and children; the former to rape and the latter for sale in the slave markets. Rinan and Bjørn let them get on with it. There was nothing they could do to stop them. Out of the eighty warriors who had charged into the fort only thirty nine had emerged unscathed or with only minor flesh wounds. Another six had more serious wounds but they should survive once they had been treated by the monks, who had remained with the ships. Rinan's men had sustained most of the casualties but Bjørn's Norse crew had also suffered losses.

They might not have been guilty of the atrocities committed by the pagan Norsemen but the Mercians felt that they were due a share of the plunder. They therefore joined in the pillaging of the hall and the huts looking for anything valuable.

Wynnstan joined them, not because he was avaricious but because he wanted to find better clothes for Astrid. Initially all he managed to find was a quiver full of arrows. Most of the chests belonging to the wealthier Danes contained clothing for adults or smaller children. At last he found a chest in one of the larger huts in which there were two ankle length linen under-dresses which looked to be the right size for Astrid. Under them he discovered several dresses made of fine wool and dyed various colours. Each had embroidered straps fastened by a broach at the front. He seemed to recall that the coarse strap-dress that Astrid had been wearing was fastened using cheap bone pins.

He searched for something better to give her and eventually found a small coffer containing jewellery including several pairs of silver and bronze broaches. Finally he found a pair of ankle length leather boots that he thought might fit her.

He bundled everything into a leather sack and was about to leave when two Norsemen entered the hut. The larger of the two spoke with a guttural accent that made what he was saying difficult to understand but the general gist was clear enough. They wanted him to give up what he'd found.

There was no doubt in Wynnstan's mind that the two would kill him without a second's hesitation if he failed to comply. Therefore he acted first. He drew his seax and leaped forward, chopping at the neck of the first man as he did so. The blade cut halfway through the thick neck and the man dropped like a stone. Unfortunately for Wynnstan, the blade remained embedded in his neck and it was dragged out of his hand as the man collapsed.

The second warrior roared with rage as his hand went to the sword at his waist. For an instant Wynnstan thought of reaching for the axe the dead man carried on his back but he wouldn't be able to get it free of its fastenings in time. Instead he ran for the ladder which led up to the sleeping platform. He scrambled up it, hoping he would make it before the Norseman could grab his legs. Panting he threw himself onto the platform, landing on a bed of furs. He heard the second man climbing the ladder still cursing volubly and, without looking over the edge, he kicked the ladder away.

He heard the Norseman crash onto the beaten earth floor but didn't waste time looking. Instead he quickly strung his bow and pulled one of the arrows he'd retrieved earlier from his quiver. He stood and took a step forward so that he could look down. Evidently the man was winded but he grasped the ladder and put it back in place. As he started to climb it again he looked up. It was a mistake. Wynnstan let fly the arrow which entered the man's open mouth and exited the back of his neck. It didn't kill him but he let go of the ladder and fell back to the hard-packed earth.

Wynnstan sent a second arrow into his chest and then climbed down. Having checked that both men were dead he had the presence of mind to retrieve the arrows and his seax before hurrying out of the house. Now there was nothing to say that the two Norse hadn't been killed by Danes hiding in the hut.

He passed one of Ingimund's men raping a girl even younger than Astrid and he thought of interfering but common sense prevailed and he ignored him. Others were nearby and he couldn't take them all on. All the same he felt sick and a few minutes later his stomach heaved and he spewed its contents all over the ground. A passing man made some comment about boys not being able to hold their drink and his companions laughed.

Eventually he made it back to the gate and set off back down to the ships, praying fervently that Astrid had made it safely.

†††

His relief when he found her was profound. They hugged each other and smiled into each other's eyes. He wanted to kiss her but, after what he'd witnessed in the fort, he couldn't bring himself to do it. His desire for her made him feel like the pagan rapists. Instead he showed Astrid the clothes and the silver broaches he'd found and her eyes lit up. She gave him another hug and then told him to turn around whilst she changed out of her bloodstained clothes.

To his surprise he heard water splashing and he glanced behind him. Astrid was swimming in the river but all he could see was her head and a pink area under water that had to be her bottom. Hastily he looked away and waited for her to emerge, dry herself on her old clothes before discarding them, and dress in her new finery. To his surprise she saw that she had chosen the two brass broaches to pin the shoulder straps to the front of her dress and not the silver ones he'd given her.

He had thought her enchanting before but, with a clean face and in her new clothes, she looked like no other girl he'd ever seen. She grinned at his awestruck expression and when he asked why she wasn't wearing the silver broaches, she replied that the valuable jewellery was his to sell. It would make him modestly wealthy. She then produced the purse she'd taken from the Norseman in the woods and when he peeked inside he gasped. There had to be the equivalent of four or five hundred shillings there. It had taken her precious time to find it after her fall but, knowing she had it – and was therefore not entirely dependent on the charity of others - emboldened her to ask her next question.

'Will you let me live with you?' she asked anxiously.

He shook his head. 'I'd love that but not yet. We're too young. However, I have an idea.'

She was disappointed by his reply but he wouldn't say any more. He took her onto Rinan's birlinn where the ships' boys pestered him to tell them about the fight; they were naturally curious about Astrid as well and more than one gave her a speculative glance. Wynnstan was happy enough to tell them what had happened but he didn't say anything about what had followed after the fort had fallen. He doubted if he would ever speak about it to anyone.

Chapter Eight

June/July 903

'What is she doing on my ship?' Rinan thundered at Wynnstan.

The boy nervously chewed his lip, frightened that Rinan would put her ashore, but he stood his ground.

'Astrid was instrumental in allowing us to capture the fortress, we can't leave her here at the mercy of the Norse pagans,' he replied quietly.

He knew that if he appeared defiant Rinan would refuse to listen to him.

'She's a Dane, she'll have to take her chances like the rest of them.'

'She helped us,' Wynnstan protested, 'we don't owe the rest of the Danes anything but we are indebted to her.'

'I don't like women on my ship,' Rinan said after a pause. 'See if Bjørn will take you back to Cæstir; but be quick about it, we're leaving.'

Wynnstan gave Rinan an angry look but jumped over the bows and ran to where Bjørn's crew were already pushing his longship off the mud and into the water.

'Rinan says he won't take Astrid back with him; he doesn't like women,' he yelled up at the Norse captain in the bows.

The crew of the longship laughed and he realised what he'd said.

'On board his birlinn I mean,' he added lamely.

'We'll take her,' Bjørn told him with a grin. 'We like women.'

For a moment Wynnstan wondered if he'd made a mistake asking to go with them; after all he hardly knew the Norse jarl and his men; all he knew was that they'd served Lord Jørren and they'd sworn allegiance to his son, Ywer, after he died. Their task was to patrol the coast off Wirhealum and the estuaries of the two rivers that flowed either side of the peninsula.

'I'll be coming with her,' he added.

'Her virginity will be safe enough without you acting as her chaperone,' Bjørn said with a frown. 'You impugn my honour, boy.'

'I don't mean to; I just don't want to sail with Rinan.'

The Norseman nodded in understanding. Rinan had been a good man when he was captain of Jørren's hearth warriors but he'd taken his lord's death hard and his demotion to commander of the garrison of Cæstir had embittered him.

'Be quick about it then. If you're not back with the girl by the time we've floated my ship we'll go without you.'

Wynnstan ran back towards the birlinn and was relieved to see that Astrid had already been put ashore. When he saw that his sea chest and weapons had also been offloaded his relief changed to anger. If Bjørn had refused to take them, he and Astrid would have been stranded at Frodesham. He swore to make Rinan pay when he saw him again. He owed both of them a debt of gratitude for their part in the success of the mission. Even if he had no time for Astrid, to abandon him like this when he didn't know whether Bjørn would have taken them was unforgivable.

†††

When they docked at Cæstir Wynnstan lifted Astrid down onto the jetty, his hands lingering around her slim waist for slightly longer than was necessary, and she helped him carry his chest in through the sea gate.

'Why have you stopped?' she asked him as he stood indecisively at the cross roads just inside the walls of the old Roman city.

'I can't leave you in the warriors' hall on your own but I need to see Lady Cuthfleda. However, I need an appointment first.'

'You said that Deorwine is your captain, I think?'

'Yes; I could ask his advice but he is also living in the royal complex and I don't want to arrive carrying all I own with me.'

'Then let's go to where you live and leave your chest and weapons there, then we can go and find this Deorwine.'

He looked at her in relief and he set off towards the warriors' hall. The sentry on duty made ribald suggestions about the two of them until Wynnstan threatened to cut off his manhood. The boy went inside whilst the sentry muttered something about being surprised he couldn't take a joke. Astrid stood looking uncomfortable when the sentry leered at her as soon as Wynnstan was out of sight. The warriors' hall certainly wasn't a suitable place for her to stay, even temporarily, and she was vastly relieved when Wynnstan reappeared.

His nervousness grew as he approached the royal enclosure. The two men on guard at the gate looked bored but they suddenly became alert as the couple drew near. Thankfully one of those on duty was Lyndon, one of Jørren's former hearth warriors who had now joined the Lady Æthelflæd's warband.

'How did it go,' he asked, 'and where did you find such a pretty girl?'

Unlike the leering sentry at the warriors' hall, Lyndon gave her a friendly smile which put her at her ease.

'Hasn't Rinan reported back yet?'

'No, you're the first one we've seen who was at Frodesham. I take it that you were successful?'

'Yes, I've come to make my report to Deorwine.'

It wasn't true, of course; it wasn't really his place to tell Æthelflæd and her advisers about the success of the mission but it provided him with an excellent opportunity to ask about Astrid's future.

'Wait here. I'll go and find him.'

With that Lyndon left them, reappearing shortly afterwards with Deorwine in tow.

'Wynnstan? Why are you here? Where's Rinan?'

'We lost a lot of men taking the fort at Frodesham. Rinan has less than half his crew to man his birlinn and, as we had to row against the wind to get clear of the Mǣresēa, Rinan dropped further and further behind us.'

'So you were successful? Good! But I don't understand why you're not with Rinan.'

159

'I came back with Bjørn's longship.'

'Why?'

Suddenly Deorwine noticed the pretty young girl standing just behind Wynnstan.

'And who's the girl?' he added.

'This is Astrid. She helped us to capture the gates.'

A small crowd had gathered around them and were eagerly listening to every word, much to Deorwine's annoyance.

'You had better come up to the hall,' he said, glaring at the eavesdroppers. 'Bring the girl,' he added when Wynnstan hesitated.

The pair followed him in silence until they entered the complex that comprised the main hall, various bed chambers and other buildings. Hall really wasn't an appropriate term anymore and some people now referred to it as a palace, derived from the Frankish word paleis. Instead of taking them to the hall Deorwine, took them to a nearby door that led into the private area occupied by Lady Æthelflæd.

The sentry on guard outside asked them to wait and disappeared inside, returning a minute later. He didn't say anything, just nodded and held the door open for them. They found Æthelflæd sitting with Cuthfleda and Abbot Æscwin in the ante-chamber as they listened to Æthelstan recite the Creed. Deorwine waited for the boy to finish and then coughed discretely.

'Lady, forgive the intrusion but Wynnstan has news of the attack on Frodesham.'

He stood back and Wynnstan took a hesitant step forward and bowed his head.

160

'Lady, the attack was successful but we suffered a lot of casualties,' he began hesitantly. 'We Mercians were sent forward as the vanguard with three others and myself as scouts.'

As he recounted what had happened he grew more confident and his voice strengthened.

'Rinan refused to allow Astrid on board and so we returned on Bjørn Frami's ship. He lost fewer men and so we arrived back first. I thought I should come and report to Deorwine.'

He hesitated before continuing.

'I also wanted to find Astrid a place of safety. I could hardly take her back to the warriors' hall with me,' he finished lamely.

'Do you speak Ænglisc, child?' Æthelflæd asked her.

The girl looked to Wynnstan for help and he told Æthelflæd that she only spoke Danish but understood Norse well enough.

'Tell me about yourself, Astrid,' Æthelflæd said in fluent Danish.

'I was a servant in Jarl Vígmarr's hall, lady,' she replied with a worried look. 'Not a thrall, you understand. I'm the granddaughter of a bondi who owned a farmstead in Danmǫrk but he had four sons and the land couldn't support all of them. My father was the youngest and he took service with Jarl Vígmarr as a hearth warrior when he was seventeen. My mother was a servant in Vígmarr's hall and the two fell in love. When she was pregnant with me they married but my father was killed when Vígmarr attacked Frodesham.'

161

'How old are you, Astrid,' Cuthfleda asked in Danish.

'This is my twelfth summer.'

Cuthfleda looked at Æthelflæd who smiled and nodded.

'Deorwine and I are to be married soon and I will need servants for the hall we plan to build when we return to Glowecestre. Would you like to join our household?'

'Yes, lady,' she replied, beaming with pleasure. 'I'd like that very much.'

She didn't know Cuthfleda, of course, but she seemed sympathetic to her plight and furthermore she was extremely relieved to have secured a place in which to live and work. Wynnstan had also told her that he would be returning to Glowecestre – a place she had never heard of but which she'd been told was far to the south – and she'd been worried that he'd leave and she'd be abandoned to fend for herself in Cæstir.

Wynnstan sensed that the audience was over and he bowed and left, leaving Astrid with her new mistress. On his way out he passed an impatient Rinan who was pacing up and down waiting to be admitted to make his report. He scowled at Wynnstan and was about to ask him what he was doing there when, thankfully, the sentry told him he could go in.

The boy knew that he'd made an enemy of him but he wasn't overly concerned. By the sound of it they would shortly be returning south and, in any case, he was in love and nothing could be allowed to trouble him on such a day.

✝✝✝

Rinan had little to add to the report that Wynnstan had already made and he was furious that his thunder had been stolen by the wretched boy. However, he was also asked why he thought that Ingimund had taken so long to come to his support.

'My feeling is that he wanted us to lose as many men as possible and only joined in when he felt that the Danes might recapture the gate,' he said bluntly.

What he said only confirmed what Wynnstan had hinted at. Ingimund obviously wanted to weaken the garrison of Cæstir. As soon as Rinan had left the others began to speculate on Ingimund's motives.

'I don't trust him,' Deorwine said bluntly. 'He won't be satisfied with Frodesham; he wants Cæstir and the whole shire.'

'However, he's not strong enough to try anything of the sort at the moment,' Æthelflæd surmised. 'If only I could stay here I could keep an eye on him. As it is, I daren't delay heading south any longer. I suspect that my husband has already set off for Cæstir and I need to meet him on the road. At least that way I can claim that I was obeying him just as soon as I'd neutralised the threat from the Norse invaders.'

'He'll still be angry with you,' Cuthfleda said with a sigh, 'but that can't be helped. The important question now is who do you put in charge here? Ywer is the obvious choice but we mustn't alienate Eirik Fairhair. If he and Ingimund combine, the other Norse jarls will join them and we won't be able to hang on to Cæstirscīr.'

'I agree. However, I think that Ingimund will be preoccupied with the danger posed by the Danes around Mamecestre for the immediate future; they're not going to take kindly to the loss of Frodesham and the slaughter of their compatriots.'

'May I make a suggestion?' Æthelstan asked.

He'd been quiet ever since his recitation of the Creed and everyone had forgotten he was there.

'There's no reason why Cæstirscīr has to remain as a single shire. If you make Eirik Ealdorman of Wirhealum and give Ywer the rest of the shire, they may not be as happy as they would be to have the whole of Cæstirscīr but it doesn't put them at each other's throats.'

The others looked at Eadweard's son with new respect. It was a neat solution and one that was probably the most sensible course of action in the circumstances. It also showed that Æthelstan had a wise head on his shoulders, especially for one who was barely thirteen years of age.

'Of course, it isn't ideal to split the leadership of the north in this way but any other solution would no doubt produce an even bigger rift between Ywer and Eirik,' Deorwine pointed out.

'And at least they are brothers-in-law, united by Holy matrimony, so that will bind them together,' Æscwin added brightly.

Privately everyone else thought that Eirik's marriage to Ywer's sister would count for little if the two men fell out but no one disabused the abbot of his pious hope.

'Of course, Lord Æðelred will have to agree and the Witenaġemot of Mercia will have to confirm it,' Æthelflæd reminded them.

'You can't think that he would reverse your decision?' Cuthfleda asked, appalled at the possibility. 'That would result in chaos up here and who knows what the outcome might be.'

'He is not best pleased with me at the moment and he might well reverse my decision just to teach me a lesson,' Æthelflæd replied gloomily.

Neither Ywer nor Eirik were best pleased with the solution that Æthelstan had proposed when it was put to them but they reluctantly accepted Æthelflæd's decision. Ywer moved into the hall in Cæstir and Rinan was given the role of guarding the northern border: the task that had previously been Ywer's. He was pleased by the appointment and it lifted the depression he'd suffered ever since Jørren's death and his demotion from captain of the latter's gesith. However, he still bore a grudge against Wynnstan and vowed that one day he would make the boy pay.

Chapter Nine

Summer / Autumn 906

Astrid grimaced in pain when Cuthfleda squeezed her hand tightly as another contraction wracked her body. At the ripe age of thirty seven she had thought that she and Deorwine were too old to have children but it seemed that the Lord had answered their prayers after all. It had been two and a half years since Deorwine and Cuthfleda had wed just after their return to Glowecestre. During that time life had been peaceful. The threatened trouble in the north had failed to materialise and both borders – that with Wealas in the west and with the Danelaw in the east – had been quiet, apart from the inevitable small scale raids from time to time, that is.

Astrid had become Cuthfleda's principle maid and the two had grown quite close. At fifteen the Danish girl had changed from a pretty young girl into a beautiful young woman. Wynnstan, who was now eighteen, was no longer one of the junior members of Lady Æthelflæd's personal guards; he had risen to become both chief scout and trainer of her archers. However, the continued existence of the Lady's warband had seemed unlikely at one time.

As she had anticipated, Æthelflæd's husband had been furious with her when they met at Wirecestre on the return journey south. He'd publicly berated her for her tardiness in obeying his summons and had sworn never to allow her to leave his side again.

'You won't need your warriors,' he had sneered, 'as you will have me and my gesith to protect you. Without them you won't be able to go wandering around Mercia again.'

'Lord, many of these men have given their lives to protect me and to serve Mercia. You cannot just cast them out after their loyal service to you as well as to me.'

'Very well,' he'd agreed after a long pause for thought. 'But they will join my warband, not my hearth warriors you understand, but the garrison of Glowecestre.'

She had to be satisfied with that and Deorwine had become deputy to the captain of the watch who guarded Mercia's capital. Instead of the hall he'd planned to build for Cuthfleda and himself, they had rented a modest hut with just Astrid and an eleven year old boy to look after them. To make matters worse, the captain under whom Deorwine now served was slothful and self-opinionated. He regarded Deorwine with suspicion, convinced he'd been put there to spy on his incompetence, and made his life as difficult as he could.

However, the situation didn't last long. Two months after Æthelflæd's return her husband had a seizure and was paralysed down his left side. During his incapacity she took over the reins of government and one of her first acts was to reinstate her personal guard. The inept captain of the garrison was dismissed and Lyndon took his place. Wynnstan re-joined her warriors and was given the task of recruiting and training more scouts.

167

That had been over two years ago. Æðelred had made a slow recovery but his speech remained slurred and he could only walk with assistance. He was lucid some of the time but lapsed into incoherence quite frequently. He became a shadow of his former self and seemed content to leave the government of Mercia in his wife's hands – at least for now.

Deorwine had built his hall and more servants were recruited. Although most were older than Astrid, she remained in charge of them and those who challenged her soon regretted it. The timid Danish girl had become a strong young woman.

Many young men sought her hand but there was only room for one in her heart. Her love for Wynnstan had remained steadfast but it had changed over time. They had been attracted to one another when she first arrived in Glowecestre but it could so easily have been infatuation which didn't stand the test of time. Slowly they got to know one another and the more they did so, the more their love deepened.

However, there was little time when they could be together. She was busy running the hall and he was on guard duty, training others or away on patrol. Finally he'd decided that they were now old enough to marry and he'd accumulated enough money to afford a hut of their own with a servant to look after them when Cuthfleda had become pregnant.

Astrid was adamant that she couldn't leave Cuthfleda's service at a time like this. They would have to wait until the baby was born, a wet nurse had been found and a suitable replacement had been trained before they could think about a wedding.

Wynnstan hadn't been at all happy at the prospect of waiting for the best part of a year but he didn't have a lot of choice. When he heard that Cuthfleda was in labour he rejoiced; now at last the end must be in sight. What he hadn't considered was that many women died in childbirth and Cuthfleda was a lot older than normal. Most mothers had their first baby long before they were twenty; a few no more than a year or so after reaching puberty.

Astrid knew it wasn't going to be an easy birth, even before the goodwife told her that there was a problem. The birth took hours and all three – mother, goodwife and Astrid were exhausted by the time that a baby's cries rent the air.

'It's a beautiful boy,' Astrid told Cuthfleda, holding the bawling infant up for her to see. However, Cuthfleda was past caring and had slipped away into unconsciousness.

She hung between life and death for two days before the fever broke and she began to recover. When Wynnstan heard the news he was ecstatic.

'Now we can wed at last,' he said happily.

Astrid looked at him in amazement.

'Lady Cuthfleda has a long way to go to complete recovery,' she admonished him. 'I couldn't possibly think of leaving her at a time like this.'

'I'm beginning to think you don't want to marry me,' he shot back angrily.

'If that's your attitude, then perhaps I won't.'

She stormed off but she hadn't gone far when she regretted what she'd said and burst into tears. He was stunned by what had just happened and for some time couldn't work out what had gone wrong. Then he too broke down. He felt as if a horse had just kicked him in the stomach but at the same time deep resentment burned within him. The sensible thing to do was to go and find her and make it up but he just couldn't bring himself to do it.

†††

Æthelflæd would have been the first person to visit Cuthfleda had she been in Glowecestre at the time but as it was she was visiting Bishop Wirfrith in Wirecestre with her daughter, Ælfwynn. The girl was now seventeen and should have been married before now. The choice of a suitable husband hadn't been easy; whoever it was would effectively succeed Æðelred in due course as Lord of the Mercians.

Eventually they had decided on the only son of the Siward, the Ealdorman of Hwicce. Siward was elderly and when he died his son would become the most powerful nobleman in Mercia after Æðelred. Unfortunately, and most inconveniently, the young man had been gored to death whilst out hunting a few months after their betrothal.

Ælfwynn hadn't bothered to hide her delight at the news. She disliked her arrogant fiancé intensely and had refused to marry him. Even the threat of banishing her to a convent had failed to make her change her mind. Her parents had received the news of the youth's death with mixed feelings. At least now they wouldn't have to call off the betrothal and incur the family's wrath.

After the young man's death, Æthelflæd's brother, Eadweard, had suggested that Ælfwynn should be betrothed to his son Ælfweard, Æthelstan's half-brother. The fact that he was Ælfwynn's cousin and was less than two years old at that time didn't appear to be any sort of impediment as far as the King of Wessex was concerned. Æthelflæd had replied to the offer diplomatically, pointing out that the Pope would never agree to the match between first cousins and the matter had been quietly dropped.

Æthelflæd wasn't as keen on finding a husband for their daughter as Æðelred was. He was getting on in years and he was intent on finding a suitable man as his successor. His wife, on the other hand, was quite content to rule alone and presumed that their daughter could do likewise. It was a false assumption. Unlike her mother, Ælfwynn was capricious and superficial. She was more interested in a new dress than she was in politics.

Her mother had hoped that, by taking her on her annual tour of Mercian territory, she could encourage her daughter to take an interest in the art of government. However, even she was now coming to accept that Ælfwynn was quite unlike her.

Æthelstan on the other hand was developing into a promising leader of men who was both clever and cunning, according to the reports she'd received over the past few years. When she had returned from Cæstir she had left him there with instructions that Abbot Æscwin should complete his education and

Ealdorman Ywer should train him both as a warrior and in the tactical and strategic skills he would need when he became king.

Despite the fact that Eadweard continued to disown his eldest son and had designated Ælfweard, now four, as his successor, Æthelflæd had every confidence that her nephew would one day sit on the throne of Wessex.

Her family weren't the only thing on her mind, however. Siward of Hwicce was ill and reportedly close to death. As there was no son to follow him, she would need to find a replacement soon. Whoever she chose would have to be approved by the Witenaġemot and thus he would need to be selected with some care.

Furthermore Bishop Wirfrith was ill and might well die as well. There were only two dioceses in Anglian Mercia at the time - the other being based at Licefelle and covering the shires to the north of Hwicce – so Wirfrith's replacement would wield significant power, secular as well as ecclesiastical. Both the new appointees would need to support her if she was to retain the power she currently wielded when Æðelred eventually died.

At one time that event had looked likely but, although her husband was still incapacitated, he was slowly getting better. He continued to drool and talked incoherently much of the time but his periods of lucidity were on the increase, as was his mobility. He could now walk unaided, although only slowly and with a pronounced limp. She knew it was wrong to pray for a relapse but the thought of giving up even some of the authority she currently wielded was anathema to her.

She also missed Cuthfleda's companionship. She had relied on her for advice, comfort and support ever since she had wed Æðelred and - although the two women remained close - since her marriage Cuthfleda's duties as a wife had kept her from her side much of the time. Her daughter wasn't much of a replacement for Cuthfleda and Ælfwynn's incessant chatter about trivial things drove her mother to distraction.

It was after her visit to Wirfrith's sickbed that inspiration came to her. Æscwin had a good reputation amongst the clergy as a pious and righteous man. No one could object to his elevation to bishop. With him leading the Church in Mercia and his brother Ywer's support in the north her own position would be strengthened.

Then she had a further thought. Cuthfleda was Ywer's sister and her support was naturally unequivocal. She could consolidate her power base further if she could somehow give Cuthfleda's husband, Deorwine, a more powerful position. Æðelred hadn't bothered to find a new hereræswa after Jørren's death. He'd been the last holder of the post although he hadn't been called upon to act as the commander of Mercia's army in the years after his defeat of Hæsten's Vikings.

If she could get the Witenaġemot to appoint Deorwine to the position, his standing would be enhanced to the extent that he might be acceptable as

Ealdorman of Hwicce after the present incumbent's death.

She went to bed that night pleased with the decisions she had reached. However the morning was to bring news that drove all other considerations from her mind.

✝✝✝

'You're certain about this?' Ywer asked his youngest sister as he paced up and down the chamber that served as his office at Cæstir.

'Of course I'm sure. I'd have hardly fled from Grárhöfn with my children if it wasn't true,' Æbbe replied scornfully.

She had arrived just after dawn bringing her four year old son and two year old daughter with her. Her only companions had been the children's nurse and a stable boy who was besotted with his jarl's wife. They were the only people she trusted and she wouldn't have involved the lovelorn boy if she hadn't needed him to saddle the horses and take them around to the postern gate. Even then she had worried that they would be spotted by the sentries as they crept out of Grárhöfn under cover of darkness.

The conversation she had inadvertently overheard between Eirik and an unknown Norseman had alarmed her sufficiently to cause her flight. The stranger was evidently an emissary from Ingimund and what they were plotting was no less than the capture of Cæstir.

This was only the first step of the Norseman's plan. Once they had secured Cæstir the next step would be to conquer the whole shire and evict or kill every Mercian family so that the Norse could take their land. Worse still, Ingimund had managed to broker a treaty with the jarl who led the Danes living on the borders of Cæstirscīr. In exchange for some of the land, he would support the revolt.

Ywer wondered inconsequentially whether his father-in-law was part of the conspiracy. If so, he was confident that his wife didn't know about it. They were very much in love and he would have been well aware of any change in Gyda's attitude towards him. Furthermore, their sons, Irwyn and the infant Eadwyn, would be at risk if the settlement fell to the Norse. The more he thought about it he doubted if Gyda's father, Jarl Harald, was party to the plot. He was too fond of his daughter and his grandsons to risk their safety.

No, he decided, Harald must be unaware of what was planned. If so, he too could be in danger. Ingimund wouldn't want to leave a potential enemy in his rear. The same went for Rinan and the warriors that guarded the south bank of the River Mæresēa. Ingimund would need to eliminate them before he attacked Cæstir.

He strode to the door and told the sentry outside to fetch Edmund, the captain of his gesith. He needed to send messengers immediately to warn Harald and Rinan as well as call out the fyrd. He would also need to get word to Æthelflæd so that she could organise an army to come to their rescue. He was confident that he could hold Cæstir now that he'd been warned but only for a time. Refugees would flock into the place once word got out and there weren't enough supplies laid in this close to harvest time for a prolonged siege.

He wondered who to send to Æthelflæd and eventually decided to send Æthelstan with a small escort. The boy was resourceful and sending him would also remove him from immediate danger, or so Ywer thought.

Once Edmund had joined him the two sat down to make preparations for the war to come.

†††

Jarl Harald found himself in something of a quandary. Although his daughter and grandsons were in Cæstir, Ingimund and his Norse neighbours in western Northumbria were insistent that he threw in his lot with them. He was tempted to warn Gyda what was afoot but, if he was found out, he would be killed and his people slaughtered or enslaved.

He'd tried to persuade the other Norse jarls who lived north of the River Mæresēa to remain neutral but they pointed out that their young warriors would join Ingimund whatever they said; the prospect of raiding and pillaging instead of leading a peaceful life as farmers was just too tempting.

Matters had come to a head in mid-September when the harvest was in. Ingimund himself arrived together with fifty mounted warriors. Harald threw a feast for the visitors, even though it would eat into the provisions laid by for the coming winter. To do otherwise would look suspicious.

'Well, Harald, I trust I can count on your support when we attack Cæstir in the spring?' Ingimund said as he sat between the jarl and his wife.

'I think your plan is flawed,' Harald said bluntly. 'You have no siege engines and you'd have to wait a long time before the starving Mercians would be forced to surrender. By that time Æthelflæd would have gathered the Mercian army and you'd be trapped between them and the walls of Cæstir.'

'I won't need to lay siege to the place,' Ingimund said smugly. 'There are those inside who will open the gates to us.'

Harald's heart sank. If that was the case he might have to take the risk and warn Ywer but, even if he did so, how would his son-in-law discover who the traitors were?

'It's a clever plan, Ingimund. In that case you have my support.' Harald promised him, although he didn't mean a word of it.

Harald felt that he had no alternative but to pretend to join the rebels. His one hope was that he could find out enough to identify the collaborators within Cæstir. If he failed to do so and it subsequently fell, then at least he and his warriors might be able to reach Gyda and her children before the rest of the rebels and protect them.

✝✝✝

To Ywer's surprise, Æthelstan declined the offer of a dozen men to escort him to Glowecestre.

'So many riders will attract attention, Lord Ywer,' the boy explained. 'For all we know Ingimund, or more likely his Danish allies, will be watching the roads south. I propose to travel cross country using forest trails as much as possible. All I need are two or three good scouts and a couple of good archers in case we run into trouble.'

What the young ætheling said made sense but Ywer wasn't happy about it. In the end he chose Acwel, Eafer and Eomær as the scouts. All three had been members of his father's gesith and had been trained as scouts when they were boys. That was many years ago now but they were still the best available. He also chose two of his best archers – a youth called Ceowald and an older man named Beorhtric.

The only other member of the group was Hengist, the potboy Ywer had rescued six years ago from a tavern in Wirecestre. He had served as Æthelstan's servant at first but had then joined Ywer's household. In addition to being a good body servant, he was an excellent cook and he had other qualities such as resourcefulness and a clever head on his shoulders. Furthermore he and Æthelstan got on well together.

All seven members of the group rode the best horses that Ywer could find. Hengist led a packhorse laden with provisions, a cooking pot, spare arrows and the like. There were no tents or other luxuries. They would be sleeping rough and living off the land as much as possible. It was a hundred and forty miles to Glowecestre and Æthelstan aimed to reach there in three days. Covering some fifty miles a day through rough terrain was ambitious - even on horseback - and the riders expected to arrive with their inner thighs chafed raw.

The weather was warm for the start of autumn and the sun shone throughout the first day. It passed uneventfully and Eafer and Eomær, who were scouting ahead as the day drew to a close, found a hollow near a stream in which to camp. Æthelstan decided they could risk a fire; the hollow was deep enough to hide the glow at ground level and the smoke wouldn't be discernible after the sun had set.

Hengist might be a servant but he had trained as a member of the fyrd since the age of fourteen. He was on watch with Ceowald when he heard a twig snap not that far away from him. He was standing with his back to a tree near the lip of the hollow scouring the woods ahead of him. The darkness was intense under the clouds which had formed overhead during the night but just at that moment they parted and the ground was illuminated by the faint silvery light of the new moon. Although they had frozen the moment the cloud cover had parted he could make out several figures crouching no more than a hundred feet away.

Ceowald was guarding the far side of the hollow where the horses were tethered. There was no time to reach him and so Hengist hooted like an owl calling its mate and then imitated the return call. Hoping that Ceowald was alert enough to recognise the warning call, he slid down the bank and ran to where the rest were fast asleep.

He knelt by Æthelstan's side and put his hand over the boy's mouth before shaking his shoulder gently. The ætheling's eyes opened wide and Hengist whispered 'attackers in the wood to the north' before removing his hand and going to wake the next man.

By the time that the strangers had reached the rim of the hollow everyone had gathered their weapons and had moved south to join Ceowald near the horses. The moon went behind another cloud and Æthelstan quietly cursed. Now the only illumination was the faint red glow given off by the dying embers of the fire.

He whispered to the men next to him and they passed on the message. His men silently spread out and crept down into the hollow. After a few minutes they could hear the sound of men stabbing the empty blankets laid out around the fire. Without being told what to do they moved forward as one and closed in on the enemy.

'Now,' Æthelstan yelled and plunged his sword into the back of the man standing in front of him. His men yelled 'Mercia', not as a war cry but to identify themselves to their comrades in the darkness. They continued to yell 'Mercia' until they couldn't find anyone else to kill. Hengist threw an armful of brushwood onto the red embers and blew on the fire until it sprang into life. He then added more kindling and a few logs to the blazing pile of twigs.

By the light of the rejuvenated fire they could see the bodies of their attackers. Some might have escaped in the darkness but Æthelstan counted eight bodies. Someone was sobbing in pain somewhere in the darkness. Acwel went in search of the wounded man and returned a few moments later hauling someone along the ground by his feet. The Norseman had been wounded in the stomach and would soon be dead. Nevertheless Acwel promised him he would push his guts back into his body and sew him up if he would tell him who he was and who had sent him to kill Æthelstan.

The man was scarcely more than a boy. His beard was thin and straggling and he was plainly terrified of dying. He evidently believed Acwel's lie and promised him that he would tell him what he knew if only they would deal with his wounds. Acwel promised and he kept his word. After the man was dead he stuffed his innards back into his body and roughly closed the cut with catgut and a needle. Having done what he'd pledged he left the body where it lay. It would make a splendid feast for the crows and wolves, along with the other corpses.

Before he died told them that his name was Gorm and he confirmed that he was one of Ingimund's warriors. He and the several other groups of Ingimund's warriors had been tasked to watch the gates of Cæstir from the wood on top of a nearby hill and kill any messengers who left. It confirmed what Æthelstan had thought but his next question prompted an interesting reply.

'How many other groups are watching the gates?'

'Two but they will have remained to watch for others trying to summon help.'

Æthelstan wondered how Ingimund knew that Ywer was aware of the impending attack but then he realised that Æbbe's flight to Cæstir would have warned him.

The young man grimaced in pain before muttering that Ingimund's Danish allies were watching every route south; they would all be dead before another day was out. He said nothing further and died in agony shortly afterwards.

'There's another few hours before dawn,' Æthelstan observed. 'I suggest you two get back on watch. Everyone else, drag the bodies into the wood and douse the fire; then try and snatch a little more sleep.'

When they set off just after dawn the next day drizzle had set in which reduced visibility to a couple of hundred yards. This time Æthelstan decided to abandon the need for speed in favour of caution. Acwel and Eomær were sent ahead whilst Eafer brought up the rear to ensure that they weren't being followed this time. All were mounted except for the two scouts. Hengist was left to cope with their horses as well as the packhorse. Acwel and Eomær could move undetected more easily on foot but it slowed progress down considerably.

The drizzle petered out by noon but by that time everyone was soaked to the skin and their byrnies and helmets had started to rust. In the six hours since they had set out they had only managed to cover twenty miles. Although the scouts had been rotated they were all tired by the time that they paused to allow the horses to drink at a stream.

The good news was that they had seen no sign of any Danish patrols and by now they were only twenty miles away from Wirecestre. The whole time they had been travelling the Roman road known as Casingc Stræt, which was the accepted border with the

Danelaw, ran further and further to the east of them. At Wirecestre it was around fifty miles away; far enough for the likelihood of penetration by a sizeable force of Danes to be remote.

When they moved on everyone was more relaxed and, whilst a pair of scouts continued to check the road ahead, they did so on horseback. Consequently they expected to reach Wirecestre well before night fell.

This time the pair in the lead were Eomær and Eafer who were both in their forties. Eomær was the elder by several years. He'd been the son of a charcoal burner who had sheltered Jørren when he'd been a fugitive from the Danes in Mercia thirty years before. He'd left with him and eventually the pair made it back to Wessex. Eafer had been a feral boy who had joined a band of outlaws. The gang had attacked Jørren and had paid with their temerity with their lives – all except Eafer who Jørren had spared. He had become his body servant and eventually had joined his warband as a scout.

They might have been elderly – Eomær was nearing fifty – but there was nothing wrong with either their eyesight or their hearing. They had just entered a stretch of woodland and were moving through the undergrowth on foot leading their horses a few feet from the track the others were following when they heard a noise ahead. It sounded like a man hawking and spitting and was followed by a quiet voice uttering a profane expletive in Danish and telling him to shut up.

The two scouts dismounted and, whilst Eomær held the horses, Eafer climbed a nearby oak tree. After five minutes he climbed down again and the two men moved back along the track until they were sure that they were out of earshot.

'It looks like there are fifteen of them. Three are archers and the rest are spearmen or axemen – all Danes,' Eafer said.

'So much for thinking we were safe this far from the Danelaw.'

At that moment the rest came into sight and halted before dismounting when they saw the two scouts.

'What's happening?' Æthelstan asked after he'd joined them.

'Ambush ahead, lord. Fifteen Danes in all. They're a few yards back from the track in the undergrowth, about the same number on each side. Only three archers as far as I could see,' Eafer told him succinctly.

'Right, I want you two, Acwel and Ceowald up in the trees where you can see the ambushers. When I whistle send as many arrows into them as fast as you can. I don't need to tell you to kill the archers first. I expect those who survive to run; Beorhtric and I will chase them and cut down as many as we can but I want at least one as a prisoner I can question. Clear? Very well, off you go.'

The four archers managed to get three volleys away in quick succession before the surviving Danes broke cover and hared away down the track to where they'd left their horses. As Beorhtric and Æthelstan rode after them they saw that only six were left. They cut down four of them before they reached the two boys who'd been left holding their horses. The first of the fleeing Danes to reach them climbed into the saddle and galloped away, scattering the other horses as he did so.

When the Mercians reached them the one remaining man threw down his sword and the two boys knelt on the earth pleading for mercy. A few minutes later the rest of Æthelstan's men arrived and he began to question them. Evidently the Danes took courage from the presence of their comrades and refused to answer him. It was only when Æthelstan ordered his men to hang the younger of the two boys – a lad who looked to be no older than twelve – from the nearest tree that the man caved in.

It transpired that the boys were brothers and the man was their uncle; their father having been killed back at the ambush site. They were followers of a Danish jarl called Rikwin who had allied himself with Ingimund. Rikwin's warriors had been divided into four groups, each watching one of the likely approaches to Wirecestre. They had assumed that was where the Mercians were heading as the Lady Æthelflæd was there at the moment. This was news to Æthelstan but it was very welcome; it meant that he wouldn't have to go all the way to Glowecestre.

There was nothing else that the man could tell them and the two boys knew even less than their uncle.

'What are you going to do with them? Hang them as a warning to others?' Acwel asked.

'No, we'll take them with us; my aunt may want to question the man and I'm not about to slaughter two young boys needlessly. Round up the Danes' horses and tie the three of them on the worst of the nags.'

However, when they reached Wirecestre early the next day it was only to discover that Æthelflæd had left for Glowecestre as soon as she had heard the news about Cuthfleda.

†††

Æthelflæd was getting frustrated. She had travelled north with an escort of forty of her personal guards and the usual plethora of advisors, clerks, clergy and servants appropriate to her status as de facto ruler of Mercia. The baggage train necessary for her mobile court stretched for half a mile and moved at a snail's pace. In her impatience to visit Cuthfleda and see for herself how ill she was she decided to abandon the majority of her entourage and her daughter. She took ten of her warriors and set off for Glowecestre.

When Æthelstan finally caught up with the slow moving convoy he was dismayed to find that his aunt was no longer with them. He cursed her foolhardiness. He didn't think that she risked encountering any Danes but then he hadn't expected them to try and ambush him so far into Mercia. Furthermore, there was always the danger of running into Welsh raiders who had crossed the River Sæfern. The road from Wirecestre to Glowecestre ran close to the river for much of the way.

At one point it went through the settlement of Theocsbury at the confluence of the Sæfern and the River Afon where there was a bridge. There was a small garrison to guard the crossing as well as a priory, a daughter house of the monastery at Glowecestre. It was here that he finally caught up with Æthelflæd.

She had stopped to rest and water the horses and snatch a quick meal of bread and cheese brought to her party by the monks. Æthelstan and his men had ridden fast all the way and they would have probably killed some of their horses had they not had the remounts taken from the Danish ambushers.

At first Æthelflæd looked at her dishevelled nephew in incomprehension. Not only had she thought him over a hundred miles away but he appeared to be exhausted.

'Aunt, I came as quickly as I could,' he told her once he'd dismounted and bent the knee to her. 'I need to speak to you urgently and in private.'

The prior led them to the hut in which he lived and left them alone. Once the door was shut with two of Æthelflæd's warriors on guard outside to ensure no one tried to eavesdrop, he told her why he was there,

'The Norse under Ingimund are planning to seize Cæstir and take over the shire, slaughtering its Mercian inhabitants. The Norse and some of the Danes in Northumbria have agreed to join him and, even worse, Eirik Fairhair and many of the Norsemen in Cæstirscīr have betrayed us and will join him.'

She took a minute to take this in and then she asked him how he knew of the plot.

'Æbbe, Eirik Fairhair's wife, got wind of it and fled with her children to warn her brothers in Cæstir.'

'Do we know when they plan to attack?' she asked, biting her lip in concern.

'No, but now that Ingimund is aware that Ywer has been warned, I doubt that he'll delay any longer than he has to. However, nothing is certain. Ywer has ordered the mobilisation of the fyrd as a precaution and is sending out messengers to encourage all Mercians living in the countryside to take refuge within his walls. The problem is that the Norse have patrols waiting to intercept the messengers.'

'So the people who live in the vills and farmsteads are likely to be at the mercy of the Norsemen and Ywer will only have those already in Cæstir to defend it. They could all be slaughtered and that will leave the shire in Norse hands whether or not we defeat Ingimund. I think we need to take the initiative here and strike before he can make his move,' she said decisively. 'We need to get back to Glowecestre and call a meeting of my war council.'

She smiled and embraced him, despite the way he stank. 'Thank you for bringing me warning so quickly.'

However, when she reached Glowecestre she found that Æðelred had seized back power in her absence. He seemed to have recovered all his mental faculties and had shaken off the apathy that had him in its grip ever since he'd collapsed. Her heart sank. She had relished the time she had been the ruler of Mercia and to be relegated to the role of consort again at this time of crisis was a bitter blow.

Moreover, Æðelred was less than pleased with some of the decisions she had made during his illness and now excluded her from his council. Having been his closest confident before he'd been taken ill, this was the hardest blow of all.

Chapter Ten

Autumn 906

'You can't mean to leave me behind!'

Æthelflæd was furious with Æðelred when he told her that she wouldn't be accompanying the army north.

'Why not? Surely you want to stay and look after your friend Cuthfleda?' he sneered.

'She is well on the road to full recovery, as you know very well. Who else knows Cæstirscīr and the people involved better than I do?'

'Oh yes, especially Ingimund,' he said sarcastically. 'It was your decision to allow him to stay and to give him Frodesham that has caused me all this trouble. Besides, I'll have Æthelstan with me; he knows the area as well as anyone.'

'You can't mean to take him,' she said, appalled at the idea. 'He's barely thirteen and too young to go to war.'

'He didn't do so badly on the journey here though, did he? The boy's a born fighter.'

'You can't blame me for Ingimund's rebellion,' she said, changing tack. 'What choice did I have? His Vikings outnumbered the force I had at my disposal and they were far more experienced as warriors than the fyrd who made up most of my army. It was the pragmatic solution at the time. Now we can bring all of Mercia against him.'

'There is no *we* about it. You are staying here and that's the end of the matter.'

Æthelflæd knew when she was defeated and nodded her acceptance.

'I'm leaving Lord Siward in charge whilst I'm away,' he added, not without a certain malicious pleasure, knowing how upset his wife would be that he had taken even that responsibility away from her.

She stormed out of his chamber, knocking a surprised page against the wall as she swept past him. It was doubtful if she was even aware of him, so great was her fury.

She managed to hold back her tears until she was with Cuthfleda. Deorwine was back as captain of the watch, which now included all those who had previously served in Æthelflæd's bodyguard. He was out training his men so only Astrid and the baby's wet nurse were with her when she burst in and they quickly made themselves scarce, taking the baby with them. She poured out her frustration to Cuthfleda who was sympathetic but she realised that her role was to listen until Æthelflæd had got it all off her chest.

The two sat in silence when she'd finished. Words were unnecessary; Æthelflæd just needed the comfort of sitting in companionable silence for a while.

'From what I hear Siward is no more capable of governing Mercia than Lord Æðelred was when he was ill,' Cuthflada said eventually. 'The man is living on borrowed time. Your husband has done this to spite you. You are going to have to step in and take over as soon as Æðelred leaves.'

'He'll have an apoplectic fit if I do that.'

'Good, perhaps this time he'll have the grace not to recover!'

Æthelflæd was shocked by what Cuthfleda had said but she knew she had merely voiced what she herself was thinking.

'No, what I'll do is to go and see Siward and offer my help should he need it. That way Æðelred can't complain that I usurped his authority.'

The army left two days later and Æthelflæd waited one more day before going to the ealdorman's hall. She was too late to offer her help; Lord Siward had died in his sleep the previous night.

†††

The portion of Mercia under Anglian rule consisted of Hwicce and four other shires – Oxenaforsascīr, Lundenburg, Cæstirscīr and Shropscīr. The men from Hwicce and Shropscīr had joined Æðelred on his way north. Some of the fyrd had been left behind under the command of the shire reeves in case either the Welsh or the Danes took advantage of the situation and raided Mercia. Nevertheless a total of two and a half thousand men had answered the muster.

Most of them were members of the fyrd but four hundred were trained warriors who served in the warbands of Æðelred, the ealdormen and those thegns who could afford to keep hearth warriors. Cæstirscīr could probably field another five or six hundred Mercians but if their fyrd had been unable to reach Cæstir in time, Ywer might have as few as two hundred with which to man the walls.

Ingimund was known to have a warband of over six hundred and the Norse jarls, including Eirik, probably had another eight hundred. His Danish allies might contribute another three hundred, which brought their probable total to around fifteen hundred. Although this was fewer than the Mercian army, the rebels were experienced warriors in the main and most of the fyrd wouldn't be anywhere near the same quality.

By early October the army had reached Shropscīr where the last of the shire contingents joined them. The weather was still mild but that was about to change. They marched north in pelting rain for the next few days. Everyone was soaked to the skin, cold and miserable. Morale was low and the prospect of having to fight hundreds upon hundreds of fierce Vikings when they reached their destination didn't help. Two nights later over two hundred men deserted and returned home.

Part of the problem was one of leadership. Æðelred was relatively elderly and he'd been ill for so long that many Mercians had nearly forgotten about him. He wasn't an inspiring commander and few felt any great loyalty to him. His bad temper made things worse and everyone resented his treatment of the Lady Æthelflæd who was much more popular now than her husband.

By the time that they reached the settlement of Celelea some seven miles from Cæstir even more of the fyrd had gone home. The ealdormen insisted that Æðelred do something to stem the desertions or they would stand no chance against the rebels. However, he seemed to be at a loss. The desertions had shaken his confidence and he wished now that he had brought Æthelflæd to advise and comfort him.

†††

'Come quickly, lord. The heathens are at the gates,' Skarde said, shaking Ywer's shoulder none too gently to wake him from a deep slumber.

It was just after dawn and the first rays of sunshine showed as pink and orange reflections off the clouds to the east.

Brogan, Ywer's body servant, stood by the door carrying fresh woollen trousers, linen under-tunic and a thick woven tunic in shades of red and blue. It was cold outside at this hour of the day. Ywer shook his head to clear it of the cobwebs of sleep and dunked his head in the bucket of water in one corner of his bedchamber. Gyda stirred in the bed recently vacated by Ywer and asked sleepily what was amiss. As her husband dressed, Skarde explained that the walls had been surrounded by a horde of Vikings during the night.

'Ingimund?' she asked but she already knew the answer. 'Is my father's banner there?'

'I'm afraid so, lady.'

She couldn't believe that her father would willingly side with Ingimund.

'He must have been coerced,' Ywer told her, although he had a sinking feeling in his stomach that might not be true. He wanted to believe it but it was

194

possible that Harald might have seen the rebellion as an opportunity to seize more land.

He waved away the byrnie and helmet that Brogan offered him, asking instead for his cloak.

'There'll come a time when I'll need my armour,' he told his servant. 'Neither the Norse nor the Danes have siege machines. They will either launch an assault using ladders or sit down to starve us out. If the former they won't have bothered to bring them with them; they'll need to make them first. In which case they won't attack for a day or so yet.'

Normally Ywer would have been correct in his assumption but what he didn't know was that Ingimund had collaborators inside the old city who planned to open the gates.

When he reached the walls he looked down on the Vikings besieging Cæstir. The Romans had laid it out in the same design as every other fort they'd built: a rectangle with a tower at each corner. There were four sets of gates, one in the centre of each of the walls. Two of the gates faced the river which looped around the fortifications from the south-west to the south-east.

Not all buildings were inside the walls; the port with its warehouses, taverns and dock labourers' hovels lay between the gates and the jetty. The other river gate, to the south-east, led to the bridge over the Dēvā. Originally this had been constructed in stone but this had fallen into disrepair over the centuries and the only vestiges of its existence were two crumbling piers in the middle of the river.

Ywer's father, Jørren, had built a new timber bridge alongside the ruins of the old one. He had the foresight to design the final span so that it could be raised by chains attached to windlasses in the two towers at the end of the bridge nearest the settlement. Not only did this allow access to the far bank, whilst still allowing river traffic to travel upstream, but it also prevented an enemy using the bridge to cross the river. The nearest alternative crossing place was many miles away.

The settlement had been allowed to expand between the bridge and the walls to house many of the poorer inhabitants. When word of Ingimund's intentions reached Ywer the folk who lived there fled inside the walls and found shelter wherever they could – in stables, in outbuildings and under makeshift shelters. Ywer then had the hovels flattened to deny the enemy cover near the defensive walls.

The only other buildings outside the walls were the huge amphitheatre and the old Roman baths. Both had been built near the north east tower and, like the bridge, they had been ruins for a long time. However, they could still offer shelter to the besiegers near the walls and so Ywer had repaired the amphitheatre and blocked up three of its four gates. Stone had been taken from the baths to do this but he'd also carted a quantity of it inside the walled settlement.

He was short of men to defend the walls properly but nevertheless he manned the amphitheatre with fifty men including thirty archers. He hoped that this redoubt would deter any attack on the north-eastern and south-eastern perimeter so that he could concentrate his men on the other two walls.

His main worry was the port area to the south west. If the enemy came by sea this was where they would land and the buildings would hide them from his archers until the last minute. However, he was confident that Ingimund and his allies didn't have enough longships to transport more than a fraction of his warriors. Any attack from the port would have to run the gauntlet of the open area to the west. He therefore sowed this area with pits full of sharp stakes hidden under grass turves laid over thin willow hurdles.

On the assumption that the Vikings would confine their main assault to the north-western walls, it was here that he placed large pots full of oil, small boulders and most of the spare spears. The walls here would be manned by those least able to wield a weapon – the women, boys and the old men. Their job would be to hurl down the oil, flaming torches, the stones and the spears. He also deployed all those archers he could spare there. The rest manned the four towers and the walkways above each gateway.

Having done what he could he sat back and waited for the first attack.

It was early afternoon before anything happened. The alarm bell from the west tower rang out. Ywer raced up the steps and onto the platform at the top of the tower closely followed by his captain, Edmund.

'Ships to the west coming up the river, lord,' Leofdæg told him pointing unnecessarily towards the five craft which had just come into sight.

One was a birlinn followed by three knarrs and the final ship in the first group was unmistakably the longship belonging to Bjørn Frami. Ywer breathed a sigh of relief. He was willing to bet that the birlinn was the one that Rinan used to patrol the River Mæresēa and hopefully the knarrs contained the inhabitants of the vills along the south bank of the river. If so, it would add another hundred fighting men to the garrison.

As the five ships sailed down towards the jetty half a dozen longships came into view. These were Norse and Danish drekkar and snekkjur; longships carrying between forty and eighty men each. As the Mercian ships reached the jetty the crews tied them up and those on board hurriedly disembarked. The Vikings besieging Cæstir were camped on the far bank from the bridge and in another two camps a few hundred yards to the north and west. Thankfully there was no way that they could attack the new arrivals before they reached the safety of the walls.

The longships gave up the chase when they saw that they were too late and moored along the north bank of the Dēvā near the Vikings' western camp.

Ywer hastened down to greet Rinan and embraced him.

'You are an extremely welcome sight,' he told the older man. 'Come, you must tell me what you know.'

'Yes, lord,' Rinan replied with a smile, pleased at the warmth of his reception, but it quickly faded. 'But you should know that there is a traitor in your ranks who plans to open one of the gates and let Ingimund in.'

✝✝✝

Æthelflæd was both pleased and surprised to receive the summons from her husband. The message was as terse as it was uninformative. He merely told her to come north and join him with all speed and to bring as many reinforcements as she could raise quickly.

'What do you think?' she asked Cuthfleda and Deorwine.

'Well, obviously he misses your counsel,' Cuthfleda replied after a moment's thought.

'I think it's more than that,' Deorwine cut in. 'The gossip in the warriors' hall is that the fyrd are deserting him in droves. I'm sure that he now recognises your worth in terms of morale as well as your value as an adviser. The mere fact that he needs more men, and quickly, lends credence to the rumours.'

'Very well; how many men can you let me have from the garrison here?'

'I'm to stay behind then?' Deorwine asked, sounding disappointed.

'I'm going to propose that you should be the next Ealdorman of Hwicce. I've no idea whether Æðelred will heed my advice or not but someone has to govern the rest of Mercia whilst I'm away. Much as I would like to take Cuthfleda with me, her place is here with you and the baby now.'

'I assume that you will be reforming your personal guard?' Deorwine asked and she nodded.

He was gratified by the trust that Æthelflæd evidently put in him and, provided Æðelred and the Witenaġemot agreed, becoming the premier ealdorman would give him a status suitable for the husband of Cuthfleda. He was conscious that, as the eldest daughter of the late Lord Jørren, she had married beneath her. His elevation to the nobility would rectify that. Nevertheless, he would have much rather he and his wife had continued to serve in Æthelflæd's household. Life was going to be much more boring from now on.

'Who will take my place as captain of your warband?' he asked once he had gathered his thoughts.

'Who would you recommend?'

He looked at Cuthfleda and knew immediately who she would have chosen, however Wynnstan was still very young for such responsibility.

'Well, Lyndon is the captain of the garrison,' he began but Æthelflæd shook her head.

'You will have other concerns and Lyndon is a good man. You need him to remain in charge of the defences of Glowecestre.'

'Well then Arne?'

'Yes, I agree. He's both experienced and respected, despite his humble origins.'

Arne was in his thirties. He was a Viking who'd been captured at the age of eleven. As a slave he'd become Jørren's body servant before being freed and allowed to train as a scout and a warrior. Since then he'd proved his loyalty and his courage many times over.

'Very well, Arne it is; but I'll make Wynnstan his deputy,' she added, knowing that it would please Cuthfleda who had a soft spot for the young man.

At the mention of Wynnstan's name a sob had escaped from Astrid's lips. She had accompanied Cuthfleda and Deorwine to the meeting with Æthelflæd and the mention of her former lover's name had driven the knife of remorse a little deeper into her heart.

'Really, I've no patience with you, Astrid,' Cuthfleda snapped at her. 'You may never see the lad again; war isn't a game. Go and make it up with him before he leaves.'

For a moment Astrid's face hardened into a scowl. She was damned if she was going to make the first move. Then she thought how she'd feel if he was killed and she ran from the room to compose herself before going to find him.

†††

'Do you know who this traitor is?'

Rinan shook his head.

'Bjørn may know more than I do. It was one of his men who infiltrated Ingimund's stronghold at Fordesham,' he told Ywer.

The captain of the longship jumped from the gunwale onto the jetty without waiting for the gangplank to be run out and strode towards where Ywer and Rinan were standing.

'I never trusted Ingimund,' he said as he joined them. 'When I heard rumours of secret meetings between him and the Norse jarls across the Mǣresēa I sent a couple of men to watch Fordesham. They confirmed that he crossed the river several times, presumably to convince the Northumbrian Norse to support him. When they also reported that Danes had been seen coming to his hall I was convinced that a serious revolt was in the offing.'

'When Bjørn came to report to me I was all for collecting as many loyal men as I could and coming straight to Cæstir but he convinced me to wait whilst he sent a spy into the fortress to see if he could learn any details about Ingimund's plans,' Rinan explained.

'Ingimund's warriors were boasting about what they'd do when they sack Cæstir,' Bjørn said, taking up the story again. 'He overhead one of them say that it was good job that Ingimund had men inside Cæstir who would open the gates for them. I'm afraid that's all he managed to learn.'

Later Ywer racked his brains trying to think who the traitors might be. There were several former Vikings amongst his men, the two most notable being Eirik's half-brother Skarde and the Dane Godric. The latter had been the son of Hæsten, the leader of the last serious invasion of Wessex and Mercia a decade before. When Hæsten died and his Vikings had dispersed, Jørren took Godric into his household. Now he was a member of Ywer's gesith and one of his closest companions. He couldn't believe that he would betray him.

Skarde also seemed an unlikely traitor. He had always resented Eirik because he had become jarl after their father's death. He had been the legitimate heir but the Thing had opted for Eirik because they considered Skarde too young. It seemed very unlikely that he would now join his half-brother and, by extension, Ingimund.

Time wasn't on his side. With Cæstir now under siege the gates could be opened to the enemy at any time, although in the middle of the night would seem the most likely time. It could even be tonight.

Telling Rinan and Bjørn to follow him he set off back to the hall to call a meeting of his war council.

✝✝✝

Wynnstan's promotion to deputy commander of Lady Æthelflæd's warband – her personal guard - meant that he now led the vanguard of the relief army heading north. His one regret was that Cuthfleda and - more importantly - Astrid hadn't accompanied them.

Æthelflæd hadn't risked mustering too many men for the relief force; the threat from Wealas and the Danelaw remained. In the end she took a mere one hundred men from Glowecestre in addition to her warband, and another two hundred from the rest of Hwicce. She hoped to gather more on her way north but, at best, she doubted if she'd be able to gather more than seven or eight hundred in total. Even that number might leave the rest of Mercia vulnerable to a concerted attack.

There were other warriors available in Lundenburg, where there was a large garrison in addition to a sizeable population, and in

Oxenaforsascīr, but there wasn't enough time to muster them.

They camped for the first night beside the River Sæfern. It was a pleasant enough spot: a large, flat meadow in the curve of the river backed by trees and shrubs which would provide firewood and somewhere to defecate in privacy.

Wynnstan, being the first to arrive with the vanguard, secured the best spot for the Lady Æthelflæd's tent and had his own pitched nearby. Æthelflæd would have wished to travel as unencumbered as possible but inevitably she was accompanied by clerics, secretaries and their servants so other tents soon sprang up nearby.

She wasn't alone in having a large entourage; the nobles and officials who accompanied her had brought along their own cooks and other servants. Consequently the baggage train stretched for over half a mile back down the road and, in order to allow for its arrival and the setting up of the camp, Wynnstan had been forced to call a halt for the day two hours before sunset.

Although they had set out just after dawn, it meant that they had only managed to travel forty miles in the eleven hours of daylight available. At that rate it would take them another three days to reach Celelea where Æðelred was encamped. It frustrated him but he nothing could dampen his happy mood. When Astrid had come to find him before he'd left Glowecestre they'd been reconciled. His euphoria was somewhat tempered by her warning that her first duty was to her mistress but he thought he could accept coming second best if it meant that she would still marry him.

That feeling didn't last. The more he thought it over as they made their way north the more resentment built up within him. He wanted Astrid as a wife and mother to their children, not someone who'd spend a few moments with him when Cuthfleda could spare her. He was realistic enough to realise that he'd have to accept Astrid's conditions for now - after all it was better than remaining estranged – but he would somehow have to make her see that her first priority should be her husband.

'Let me take a few men and ride to inform Lord Æðelred that we will join him shortly,' he suggested to Arne on the evening of the third day. 'As far as I know, he isn't even aware that we are on our way.'

Arne scowled. He should have suggested it to Æthelflæd himself. It was an oversight on his part but, instead of chiding himself, he took his anger out on Wynnstan.

'No, you've been appointed to command the vanguard,' the new captain of Æthelflæd's personal guards snarled.

'There's hardly any danger,' Wynnstan pointed out. 'The enemy is busy besieging Cæstir.'

'Æthelstan Ætheling said that there are Danes watching the roads between here and Cæstir.'

'Yes, there were a handful, but that was to intercept any messengers trying to get word to the rest of Mercia; that's hardly the case now. In any case,' he added, 'there are plenty of other warriors who can lead the vanguard.'

'If you don't want the job, then I agree that there are others who'll be only too happy to replace you; but as my deputy as well, just so we understand one another.'

It was only then that Wynnstan became aware of the dislike with which Arne regarded him. Like some others, he evidently thought that, at nineteen, Wynnstan was too inexperienced for such responsibility.

'You think I'm too young?'

'Bluntly, yes I do. I wasn't consulted about your appointment as I should have been. Furthermore you haven't been brought up to command.'

'You have made the mistake of overlooking my qualities just because I was basely born,' Wynnstan told him angrily, 'yet you were born a Viking and were a slave when you were young. Doesn't that make you a hypocrite?'

'Don't lecture me! It may be true that I've worked my way up since I was Lord Jørren's body servant but I've gained my present position the hard way over many years. You are scarcely more than a boy and one who's been promoted over the heads of more worthy men. You owe your position solely to Lady Cuthfleda's patronage, not to proven ability,' he said with a sneer.

Wynnstan took a step back as if he'd been hit. The barb was all the more telling because there was some truth in it. However, even if her support had played an important part in his preferment, he knew his own worth.

'If you don't value me, then I don't see how I can continue to act as your deputy.'

The words were out of his mouth without conscious thought. Wynnstan stood there quivering with fury and disappointment. A moment later his heart sank when he realised what he'd done in his anger. Arne wanted rid of Wynnstan and he'd just played into his hands. The look of triumph that crossed the man's face confirmed his fear.

'Very well then, I'll go and tell the Lady Æthelflæd that you wish to resign your appointment.'

Wynnstan watched Arne with dismay as he stalked angrily away. What would become of him now; more importantly, what future would he now be able to offer Astrid?'

Chapter Eleven

Autumn 906

Rain beat down on the roof of Lord Ywer's hall in Cæstir as Skarde entered the ealdorman's private chambers, shaking the rain from his oiled wool cloak.

'Well, we shan't run out of water,' he commented sardonically.

'Nor food with the harvest in,' Ywer added, inviting the Norseman to take a seat.

Having decided that Skarde wasn't likely to be the traitor, he'd enlisted his help to watch the other potential suspects. Although Godric seemed the most likely renegade, there were many other Norsemen and Danes living within the walls, mainly merchants and artisans.

A servant took Skarde's cloak away to dry it and Ywer waited for the man to close the door before speaking.

'Well, have you found out anything else?'

'I've had two street urchins take it in turns to watch Godric but he's done nothing suspicious. He's not met anyone in secret; when he leaves the warriors' hall it's always in the company of several other members of your warband. As they aren't always the same ones it doesn't seem likely that they are fellow conspirators; besides the boys said that none of the others looked like Danes or Norsemen.'

'So we're no further forward in finding out who the traitors are,' Ywer said bitterly, banging his fist on a table in frustration.

'All we can do is watch the gates and wait for whoever it is to make a move.'

'That doesn't help. We need to discover which of the gates will be opened so that we can lay a trap for the enemy.'

Skarde shrugged but said nothing.

'If it's not Godric, then who do you think our traitor is?' Ywer continued.

'My hunch is that it's Ødger the armourer. He's the most recent arrival, he's not got a family – at least not with him – and he's got three apprentices.'

'When did they arrive here?'

'Three months ago. I'm told that he bought the forge from an elderly Mercian blacksmith, paying for it in hack silver, and started to make weapons and chainmail.'

'I doubt that the four of them would be enough to overpower the guards on one of the gates.'

'They might if they waited for a rainy night when sentries would be huddled in whatever shelter they could find. They would be less alert and sound would be muffled by the falling rain.'

'Perhaps,' Ywer conceded. 'The weather is fine at the moment so we may have a little time before the attack. Let's question this Ødger and his apprentices and see what we can find out.'

Ødger stubbornly refused to talk, even when threatened with torture, but one of his apprentices wasn't as brave. He was the youngest of the three at barely fifteen, although he had the broad shoulders and muscles of someone a few years older. He might have a strong body from years of operating the bellows and wielding a hammer but his mind was still that of a child.

When Skarde came to question him away from the others it was obvious that the boy was terrified. He therefore decided to take a softer line rather than making threats.

'I just want to ask you a few questions. If you answer readily and truthfully you have nothing to fear,' he began.

'You, you'll not harm me? You'll spare my life?' the boy stammered.

'Yes, although you can't expect to return to your old life,' he answered him honestly. 'However, even as a thrall I'll make sure that you are treated well. I might even make you my body servant,' Skarde told him with a smile.

In fact he already had a perfectly satisfactory servant who was a Norse Christian like him. He had no intention of replacing him but the boy wasn't to know that. He'd only said it to gain the boy's co-operation.

'Where did you come from?' he asked the boy with an encouraging smile.

'Frodesham,' the apprentice said without a moment's hesitation. 'Ødger was the armourer there.'

'Why did he bring you here?'

'I'm not sure,' and then hastily added 'he said that Ingimund had told him to move here and had given

210

him silver to purchase a workshop here,' when he saw Skarde frown.

'Do you know the reason?'

'No, but,' he hesitated for a moment before rushing on, 'the other apprentices thought that it had something to do with helping Ingimund capture Cæstir.'

'Did they know how this was to be done?'

'Know? Not for certain but we discussed it endlessly when we were on our own. The other two thought that our task must be to open the gates.'

Skarde nodded encouragingly.

'Did you reach any conclusion as to which gates?'

'No, but we overheard Ødger give a youth a message to take to someone else in the settlement, so we thought that there must be others who would help us when the time came.'

The apprentice had nothing further to add that was of much use. However, he thought that the messenger's name might be Beadurof.

Skarde had the boy incarcerated on his own for the time being and sent for the two street urchins who he used as spies.

'Do you know anyone called Beadurof?' he asked them.

The two boys looked at one another before the elder replied.

'He leads a street gang of cutpurses known as the Sċeaduwe. He's not one to cross,' he said, licking his lips nervously.

Skarde sighed in frustration. Sċeaduwe meant shadows and everyone in Cæstir knew who they were.

They were the bane of Leofdæg's life as captain of the garrison. Merchants and wealthy artisans were forever complaining to him about stolen purses. Nobody ever saw one of the street urchins at work, even in broad daylight. The first the victim knew was when he went to pay and then realised that his purse straps had been cut.

One boy, or sometimes a girl, would distract the victim by bumping into him or shouting an obscenity at him whilst a second child took less than a second to cut the purse free with a sharp knife. So far none of the thieves had been caught, nor could Leofdæg find out where their base was.

Beadurof had a reputation for ruthlessness. One of his cutpurses had been tempted by a reward of twenty silver pennies and had gone to Leofdæg offering to show him where the Sċeaduwe operated from. Leofdæg arranged to meet the boy at dusk so that he could lead them to his base. However, before the day was out the boy had been found nailed to the palisade surrounding the ealdorman's hall complex by the hands and feet with his scrotum stuffed into his mouth. After that no-one had been willing to talk about the Sċeaduwe.

'Do you know where their base is?' Skarde asked, trying to hold the gaze of each boy in turn.

They wouldn't meet his eyes and dumbly shook their heads.

'I don't believe you. Unless you tell me I'll nail you to the door of this room myself and cut off your genitals.'

The two urchins looked scared but were still unwilling to talk.

'Very well. We'll see if one of you is prepared to change his mind after I've done what I threatened to the other. Now who shall I deal with first?'

His eyes fastened on the elder of the two and despite his futile attempts to wriggle free, two of Ywer's gesith grabbed the boy and held him against the door whilst a third drew his own dagger and took Skarde's in order to pinion both hands to the wood. The urchin wet himself and then fouled his bare legs as the man drew back his arm ready to plunge it into the boy's right hand.

'Stop! I'll tell you but only if you promise to protect us.'

'Co-operate with us and I'll train you both as scouts. As such you'll be members of Lord Ywer's warband. Mind you, after we've hanged Beadurof and his band of cutpurses you'll have nothing to fear in any case.'

Skarde had no intention of killing Beadurof, at least not until he'd named Ødger's accomplices. However, the two urchin's didn't need to know that.

'There's a store hut down by the jetty which had part of its roof blown off during the storm last year. It was never repaired and that's where the Sċeaduwe live.'

'When is the best time to find Beadurof at this hut?'

'It's said that he rarely leaves the place after dark.'

Skarde told his companions to take the boys, give them a good scrubbing and find them some fresh clothes. They could stay in the warriors' hall for now. Later he'd find out if they had the potential to become scouts. As soon as everybody had left the isolated hut he'd used to interrogate the two urchins he set off to talk to Ywer.

✝✝✝

Arne was worried by the silence with which Æthelflæd greeted the news that Wynnstan wished to stand down as his deputy.

'Why?' she asked.

'Why does he wish to do so? Perhaps he found the responsibility too great?'

'Nonsense! Do you feel threatened by him? Is that why you're so eager to get rid of him?'

Arne was staggered at her perspicacity. He'd told himself that Wynnstan was too young and inexperienced but, as soon as she suggested that he felt threatened by him, Arne realised that it was true. Arne was in his mid-thirties and he was still reasonably fit and the years didn't yet hang heavily on him. However, he was one of the oldest men in Æthelflæd's warband and it wouldn't be too many years before he would prefer the comfort of his own hearth to the rigour of campaigning. Consequently he was jealous of young men like Wynnstan who had their lives as warriors ahead of them.

'No, lady. We argued because he wanted to desert the vanguard and ride ahead to tell Lord Æðelred of our approach. When I wouldn't agree he told me he could no longer serve under me.'

'So this was said in the heat of the moment? If he really meant it I would have expected Wynnstan to

214

come and inform me of his reluctance to continue in my service himself.'

'I'm not sure he meant to break his oath and leave you, lady. I think he just wanted to resign as my deputy.'

'I have appointed him to his position. To abandon it without having the courtesy to come and discuss it with me first is to insult me, wouldn't you say? If so, he can hardly continue as one of my personal guards. However, we haven't heard Wynnstan's side of the story and I'm reluctant to reach any conclusions without doing so. Please send for him.'

Arne bowed and left her tent. His stomach felt as if it had a lead weight resting in it. Throughout the unpleasant interview Æthelflæd's demeanour had been cold and distant. Perhaps it wasn't only Cuthfleda who thought highly of the wretched youth. Although he had served her since Lord Jørren's death, she didn't know him well and his appointment as her captain had been so recent that he'd hardly had much of a chance to gain her trust.

'Lady Æthelflæd wants to see you,' he said curtly when he found Wynnstan.

Wynnstan had been grooming his horse, a task which a groom should have done but he found the task soothed him and dissipated his anger. He handed the brush to a stable boy and followed Arne back to the main camp without saying a word.

'Come in both of you,' Æthelflæd said a lot more warmly than when Arne had left. 'I understand that you suggested riding ahead to inform my husband of our imminent arrival?' she asked Wynnstan.

215

'Yes, lady.'

'What was your thinking? After all, as Arne has pointed out, the task I gave you was to command the army's vanguard, an important role.'

'We are still a few days away but, as far as I know, Lord Æðelred, is unaware of that. I realise that leading the army's advance is important but I suggested that I would be ideally placed to act as messenger. I know the country and, as the deputy commander of your hearth warriors, I felt that I had the necessary stature to brief him on the strength and other aspects of the relief force.'

'You didn't think to come to me with your suggestion?'

'No lady, not without first discussing it with my captain. Unfortunately I may have phrased my suggestion badly and I was slapped down. That led to a confrontation which I now bitterly regret and I crave Arne's pardon.'

'So you no longer wish to leave my service?'

The young man looked alarmed at the suggestion.

'I realise that I was hot headed and spoke out of turn but it was never my intention to break my oath to you. I hope that I may be forgiven but, if you feel that I have behaved in an unacceptable manner, I will naturally accept whatever punishment you deem appropriate.'

Arne could not but admire the way that Wynnstan had dealt with the matter. After that little speech he fully expected Æthelflæd to take a lenient view, which she did – confining herself to a verbal admonishment to show Arne more respect and keep his temper in check in future.

He would have to keep a close eye on his deputy. He was even more of a threat to his own position than he'd thought.

†††

Ywer had chosen Rinan, Bjørn and Skarde to lead the raid on the old store hut. Rinan's task was to throw a cordon around the landward side whilst Bjørn and his crew were to ensure that no one escaped along the river. Skarde was in charge of the twenty men who would enter the hut and seize Beadurof.

The night was illuminated by the pale silvery light of a new moon, giving them just enough light to see what they were doing. Once they had found the store hut the first problem Skarde encountered was the double doors, which were barred on the inside. No one was on watch as far as he could tell but his hopes of catching the band of thieves asleep would disappear if he tried to force an entrance.

'The roof has a large hole in it,' Acwel pointed out.

'Do you think you can climb up there and drop down inside without waking anyone?' Skarde whispered sarcastically.

'No, but the two boys could,' he replied, pointing at the two urchins who had guided them to the hut.

They looked a lot more respectable now that they were clean, had their wild hair trimmed and wore woollen trousers and tunics.

'You think we can trust them?'

'How else are we going to get in without alerting our quarry? I thought the idea was to catch them off guard so that Beadurof doesn't have the chance to slip away in the subsequent chaos. After all, we don't know how many of the young devils are inside.'

Skarde nodded. Acwel was one of the most experienced of Ywer's gesith and what he said made sense. He watched as his men gave the two boys a leg up onto the solid part of the roof. They crawled over to the gaping hole in the thatched roof and disappeared from view. It must have been a ten foot drop to the beaten earth floor below and there was every chance that one or other boy could have injured himself but no cry emerged so Skarde breathed a sigh of relief. A minute or so later one of the doors opened and a grinning face peered around it.

Skarde cautiously entered the hut, a seax in one hand and a dagger in the other. He waited to allow his eyes to adjust to the dimly lit interior and estimated that some two dozen children aged between eight and fourteen were sprawled all over the floor.

The embers of a fire glowed dimly in the centre, under the hole in the roof. He wondered what happened when it rained. Every hearth had a smoke hole above it but they were small affairs, often protected by a cover a foot or so above the ridge. The roof beams had rotted in places and the straw covering had disappeared. Consequently the smoke hole now measured some six feet across. He noted in passing that much of the daub had fallen away exposing the wattle beneath.

Beadurof was thought to be about sixteen or seventeen and so shouldn't be difficult to spot amongst the smaller bodies. At first he didn't see him but then he saw that there was a curtain across the far end of the hut. Presumably that was where he'd find the leader of the child thieves.

Beckoning Acwel and Wilfrid to follow him, he carefully made his way through the sleeping bodies to the tattered curtain. Meanwhile the rest of his men filed into the hut and waited just inside the doors. Easing aside the drapes that protected Beadurof's quarters from prying eyes he peered inside. The youth was sprawled naked on a bed of furs with a girl who couldn't have been more than eleven or twelve asleep beside him. An empty jug that had probably contained ale lay on the floor beside the pair.

He moved to the side of the makeshift bed and put the point of his dagger against Beadurof's throat before tapping him on the shoulder with the flat of his seax. The youth woke up with a start, lifting his head groggily as he did so. He immediately let his head flop back again when the point of the dagger cut into his throat, drawing blood.

Acwel moved forward and tied the girl's hands before she realised what was happening and Eafer did the same to Beadurof. The dagger at his throat didn't stop him cursing Skarde and the others to Hell and back so Skarde slapped him hard across the face and told him to shut up or he'd knock him out.

By now the children asleep in the main part of the hut had woken up. Most were secured without too much of a problem but a few produced the knives they used to cut through purse straps and tried to stab their captors. As the warriors all wore chainmail byrnies they did little damage but two were wounded in the leg. The courage of those responsible was foolhardy and they paid with their lives.

Once order was restored the children were taken away by Rinan's men. They would appear before Ywer in the morning charged with theft. There could be little doubt as to the verdict as two small chests were found containing stolen coins and other items such as jewellery burgled from various homes.

Beadurof was separated from the rest and taken to the hut Skarde had used to interrogate the two urchins. Perhaps now they would be able to find out who the other traitors were.

††††

Æðelred hadn't been idle whilst waiting for his wife to arrive with reinforcements. Supplies were running low which necessitated forage parties and on three occasions these had clashed with groups of Vikings bent on the same mission. On two occasions the Mercians had beaten off the Vikings and on the other they had given a good account of themselves before withdrawing. All of this, coupled with the knowledge that the Lady Æthelflæd was on her way with reinforcements improved morale. Wynnstan hadn't been sent himself but Æthelflæd had seen the sense in his suggestion and had dispatched a messenger. Once the news spread, desertions slowed to a trickle and then stopped altogether.

Many of those who had slunk away home previously now joined Æthelflæd with the new men she'd recruited on the road north. Those deserters who hadn't joined her would be found later and heavily fined.

Æðelred had also sent out scouts to watch Cæstir and its besiegers. One of these was a sixteen year old boy called Dægal from Wirecestre. He and three older men had been tasked to observe the Viking camp around the old Roman city and report back on any preparations that Ingimund might be making to assault the walls.

Once the four scouts had found a suitable spot in a copse on a small hill the men sat down to gamble and drink whilst Dægal kept watch. At first he spotted nothing out of the ordinary. However, as the day wore on everyone in the camp seemed intent on polishing chainmail and helmets and sharpening swords, axes and spears. Although this was a normal occupation for an army, the boy formed the impression that something was afoot.

He went back to the others and told them what he'd seen but they dismissed his intuition that something was going to happen as the imaginings of an inexperienced boy. Dægal was nothing if not persistent and eventually they gave way to his importuning and went to look for themselves.

By now it was late afternoon and the one thing they noticed straight away was the horses being brought in from the nearby pasture where they'd been tethered.

'There must be over three hundred horses there,' Dægal muttered. 'Where are they going?'

'Perhaps they're giving up and preparing to leave,' one of the others said hopefully.

Nothing further had happened before sunset and the scouts rode back to their camp. Dægal wanted to report what they'd seen but the others scoffed at the suggestion.

'What are you going to say?' the eldest of the group asked derisively. 'That we saw men sharpening weapons and the horses being brought into camp? We'd be a laughing stock.'

Dægal realised that it did sound as if he was jumping to conclusions. All the same he was certain that something was about to happen.

†††

'You won't get me to talk,' Beadurof said defiantly. 'Even if you threaten to kill me.'

'Oh, there is no question about your death,' Skarde replied with a grim smile. 'Your only choice is the manner. If you co-operate I'll give you a swift and relatively painless end to your worthless life. If you don't then you will die in a similar manner to that poor boy you nailed to the palisade. The only difference is your demise will be much slower and extremely painful. Now which is it to be?'

The youth licked his lips, a sure sign of nervousness however brave he tried to appear.

'What about the others?'

'Your band of thieves and cutpurses? That's up to Lord Ywer but I expect he'll hang them.'

Beadurof thought for a moment.

'If I tell you what you want to know can you promise me that you'll spare their lives?'

Despite himself, Skarde admired his concern for the urchins he'd led. Beadurof couldn't be completely evil if he had compassion. Perhaps, Skarde thought to himself, the life they led wasn't completely their fault. He could only imagine how difficult leading an honest life might be for a poor young orphan with no one to care for them and no way of earning a living. Beadurof was different, of course. At his age he could have found work at the port or as a labourer. However, he'd probably started his life of crime at a young age and merely carried on as he grew older.

'Very well. You carried messages to and from Ødger the armourer to someone else. Who was the other person?'

'Ødger?' Beadurof sounded surprised. 'There wasn't just one man, there were three. He handed me sealed cylinders and paid me to take them to Denisc, Heorot and Gifre the lame.'

Skarde knew Denisc; he was a goldsmith who had a Mercian father and a Danish mother. Gifre was a member of the night watch. He was an inveterate gambler but had no Norse or Danish connections as far as Skarde was aware. No doubt his co-operation had been bought with silver so that he could settle his debts. Heorot was not a man he had heard of so he asked Beadurof about him.

'He's a wheelwright; a Norseman but a Christian.'

'Thank you Beadurof, you've been most helpful.'

'You'll spare the lives of my people then?'

Skarde smiled. The boy spoke as if he was their lord.

'Lord Ywer has already decided to spare them, although they will be sold into slavery once this siege is over.'

Beadurof's eyes narrowed.

'Slaves? They'd be better off dead,' he spat.

'What did you imagine we'd do with them?'

'Feed and clothe them and teach them a trade. It's not their fault they're destitute,' he said angrily.

'Why would anyone take the trouble to do that? Street urchins exist in every settlement. It may not be fair but life is hard.'

'You could train the boys as scouts. I've heard that Lord Ywer's father often took boys in and many ended up as members of his warband. My boys are cunning and resourceful. They wouldn't last long if they weren't.'

'And the girls?'

Beadurof shrugged.

'There are only a few; I suppose they would have to be servants, but not slaves. They deserve better than to become the plaything of some fat old merchant.'

'I'll consider what you've suggested but I can't promise anything. It's the ealdorman's decision, not mine.'

'You promised me a quick...'

Before he could finish the sentence Skarde sliced his dagger across his neck, severing both carotid arteries.

As he wiped his dagger clean on the dead boy's filthy tunic he wondered how he could keep his promise not to see his band of child thieves sold as slaves. Suggesting that they might be trained as scouts wasn't an option. They were street urchins who had lived their whole lives inside the walls of Cæstir. Scouts needed to understand how to hide in open country and move silently through woods. These children simply didn't have the right background. He would have to think of something else.

☩☩☩

'What did you find out from the traitors,' Ywer asked Skarde the following day.

'Heorot wouldn't talk but the other two both told us the same story so I'm confident it's true as they had no opportunity to concoct a false one. Ingimund plans to attack tomorrow night. Ødger, his apprentices and the other three were to kill the sentries on the north-west gates and open them. They were to wave two torches from the ramparts as a signal to the mounted Norsemen waiting out of sight and they would then gallop in through the gates and prevent us retaking them. The rest of the Viking horde would then pour into the settlement.'

'How many horsemen? Did they know?'

'No, but we know that the heathens have some three hundred horses and all of them were brought in from the surrounding pastures a day ago.'

'Thank you Skarde, you've served me well. It'll not be forgotten.'

'I was hoping that, once my half-brother is disposed of, that I might be given his jarldom?' Skarde said tentatively, encouraged by the ealdorman's words.

Ywer nodded.

'You would naturally succeed him in any case. Is there no other reward you want?'

'Spare the lives of Beadurof's urchins. Eirik's lands will be short of people to work them when this is over. Children grow quickly and they can help re-populate Wirhealum.'

'You're going soft in your old age,' Ywer said with a smile. 'Very well; it's a neat solution. Children don't fetch much as slaves so it's not costing me much to let you have them.'

As soon as Skarde left Ywer sent for Edmund, Rinan and Bjørn to explain his plan to them.

'We don't have a lot of time so we will need everyone to work through the night,' he said in conclusion.

Chapter Twelve

Autumn 906

Ingimund mounted his horse in the darkest hour of the night, just before dawn, and led nearly three hundred mounted warriors towards a dip in the ground a few hundred yards from the north-eastern gate of the old Roman city. Once there he allowed his men to dismount and rest. His agents inside the walls were due to open the gates as the sun lightened the sky in the east. Once he saw the signal, their job was to gallop into Cæstir and secure the gates. The other twelve hundred Vikings would then enter the settlement on foot and the killing would begin.

He knew that Ywer only had a few hundred men with which to defend the place. The tall stone walls might be enough for the defenders to hold off an attack, although Ingimund was confident that his men could have got over the walls using scaling ladders if they had to. The trouble was, it would have cost him more casualties than he and his allies would be prepared to accept. This way the number of men he lost should be minimal.

He was only too well aware that the alliance between his own men, the Northumbrian Norse and the Danes from Mamecestre was fragile at best. They had joined him to gain land and plunder. They didn't trust him and if their losses outweighed the prospective gain they would desert him without a second thought. Some like Jarl Harald were only there because he had intimidated them. They would be the first to betray him if he failed to deliver what he'd promised. That was why Harald had been delegated to the rear of the attacking force.

He waited impatiently, the cold, dank night air seeping into his bones. The sky was full of leaden grey clouds when dawn eventually came. He looked towards the walls, anxiously waiting for the two waving torches that would signal the successful capture of the gates. At last the signal came; any longer and it would have been difficult to see at this distance in the growing daylight.

He vaulted into the saddle and dug his heels into his stallion's sides. Without waiting to see if the rest of the mounted Vikings were with him, he raced for the two gates as they slowly creaked open. He was a mere fifty yards away when he yanked savagely at the reins in an effort to bring his horse to a halt. Directly ahead of him the wide street that led to the centre was no longer visible. Instead there was a semi-circular wall some ten feet high. Evidentially it had been hastily built; only the bottom few courses had been roughly mortared in place. The top half was constructed of loose stones laid in the same manner as a dry stone wall. There must have been a timber walkway behind the parapet because the top of the wall was lined with archers and spearmen.

It only took him a couple of seconds to take all this in. He held up his hand to stop the mad dash for the gateway and yelled that it was a trap. It did no good. His men were driven by bloodlust and the prospect of

228

plunder. It's doubtful if few even heard him. Those that did were confused but ignored him. Only the slower riders at the rear paid Ingimund any heed but over two hundred charged through the gateway before the gates crashed shut behind them.

Ywer stood in the middle of the new wall. It had been a mammoth task to complete it in time, which is why he delayed giving the signal to lure the enemy into the trap until the last possible moment. Even then one of the outer ends of the semi-circular barricade, where it joined the old walls, was only two thirds the height of the rest.

He had manned the barricade with two hundred men but the walkway inside the original walls was also defended. He could spare few archers but the hundred warriors stationed there had bundles of spare spears and the rest – women, boys and men too old to fight – had rocks to roll down onto the enemy as well as barrels of oil and flaming torches with which to light the oil. Ywer had also sown the ground below with caltrops to maim the horses and any dismounted men who stepped on one.

The bewildered Vikings circled around the enclosure seeking an escape. There was none and the first volley of arrows and spears brought down horses and men alike. The defenders on the outer walls pushed the rocks and the oil barrels off the walkway crushing several and soaking more than a score in oil. Boys threw down their torches and those on whom the oil had splashed became living infernos. The nauseating smell of roasting human flesh filled the air. Other boys used slings to hurl stones at the enemy.

They did little damage but they added to the chaos and the Vikings' panic.

Godric was one of the archers on the walkway of the outer wall. Although his father had been Hæsten, the leader of the last serious invasion of Wessex and Mercia, he hadn't got on well with him. Hæsten was always comparing him unfavourably to his late brother and beat the boy for any minor misdemeanour. When Jørren had spared him after his father died, and even took him into his own household, his transfer of loyalty wasn't feigned.

Years ago, when he was a young boy, he'd been baptised as a Christian as part of the peace treaty agreed between King Ælfred and Hæsten – a treaty which his father had immediately broken once he had been allowed to leave the place in Cent where he'd been trapped. Godric had remained a pagan at heart at the time but more recently he had shown more of an interest in the teachings of the Nailed God – as Vikings called Christ. His interest had been encouraged by Abbot Æscwin and now he was as fervent a believer as any.

He drew back his bowstring to his ear and aimed at a horseman wearing a highly burnished helmet decorated with gold. The man was obviously a wealthy jarl and Godric gave a little whoop of joy when his arrow plunged into the Norseman's shoulder. A second later another arrow struck his mount's rump and it reared up in pain, depositing its rider in the churned up mud. The wounded jarl lay there for a moment; it was a moment too long. One of the other horses was stamping the ground in pain with a caltrop embedded in its hoof. The maddened animal brought its foreleg down, crushing the unfortunate man's ornamental helmet and squashing his head into a bloody mess of brains, bone and gore.

Like many others, Godric was repelled by the slaughter but he hardened his heart. This was a battle for survival and the more of the pagan enemy they could kill now the weaker the besiegers would become. He drew back his bowstring once more and his next arrow brought down another of the horsemen. Most had now dismounted or had their horses killed under them. They attacked the wall in a frenzy but the defenders repulsed them with ease. The Vikings were disorganised, frantic and in despair. Many grimly grasped their weapons and waited to be dispatched to Valhalla – Odin's hall of slain heroes - to join other Vikings who had died in battle and now, so they believed, lived a life of feasting, drinking and fighting whilst they waited for Ragnarök – the final battle.

A few brave souls tried to climb the stone barricade to get at their tormentors but those who reached the top were sent back to the bottom with a spear in their bodies. More arrows from the outer wall thudded into flesh but someone amongst the Norsemen had kept a cool head. He'd spotted the weakness where the barricade joined the old wall and he managed to clamber over the lower section and vanish into the streets beyond. Perhaps forty more managed to follow his lead but the remainder either perished or were seriously wounded in the confines of the killing zone.

By the time that the clouds cleared and the sun emerged one hundred and seventy of the besiegers had been killed. Those who were wounded didn't live for long. The women were only too well aware of the fate that would have befallen them had the Vikings managed to take Cæstir and they took a savage delight in killing off the survivors, often castrating them first.

Ywer was well satisfied with the success of his trap but now there were forty Norsemen loose in Cæstir and he needed to find them before they did too much damage.

†††

If Lord Æðelred was pleased to see his wife he hid it well.

'You've only managed to bring eight hundred men with you?' he stormed. 'What good is that? I can't tackle the Viking horde with scarcely more than two thousand men, and most of them poorly trained.'

He was exaggerating. The army now numbered nearer two and a half thousand but it was true that only five hundred of them were professional warriors.

'There is also the garrison of Cæstir, lord,' she pointed out calmly. 'Do we know what the situation is?'

He glared at her but grudgingly answered her question.

'The scouts reported no change two days ago.'

'Then, if you will permit it, I would like to send my own scouts to have a look. Things may have changed in two days.'

'If you wish,' he said waving his hand in dismissal.

Æthelflæd hadn't known what to do with Wynnstan after his reluctant rapprochement with Arne. Officially the young man remained as the deputy commander of her warband but the two men didn't like each other and, although they were careful to avoid any further conflict, the disharmony had become obvious to her warriors. Consequently they had started to take sides and that worried her.

Then she had an idea. Æthelstan had asked Æðelred for permission to form his own gesith. He'd agreed but, as yet, hadn't taken the matter any further. Wynnstan and Æthelstan had been close friends until the ætheling had returned to Glowecestre. What better person than Wynnstan to lead the boy's gesith?

However, before she put her plan into practice, she had one last task for her erstwhile deputy commander. She sent him with three others to Cæstir to spy on the Viking besiegers.

The four scouts looked at each other, worry etched on their faces. Although the besiegers' camp looked smaller than they had expected – containing perhaps twelve hundred warriors rather than the fifteen hundred Æthelred had mentioned – there were two developments that worried them. The Vikings had constructed a stout shelter beneath the south-eastern wall which so far had survived the attempts by the defenders to destroy it with rocks dropped from the walls. Wynnstan could only conclude that the Vikings were attempting to undermine the wall at that point.

However, he was just as worried by the approach of half a dozen ships being rowed upriver towards Cæstir. At this distance it was difficult to make out details but they didn't look like longships. As they drew closer Wynnstan thought that they might be birlinns of the type used by Ænglisc and Scots alike. However, these ships had a rudder rather than a steering oar which was characteristic of the galleys used by the Irish.

This was confirmed when the ships were close enough for him to make out the flag at the masthead of the leading galley. It depicted a red hand on a white background over a blue band with a fish embroidered in the band's centre. Neither Wynnstan nor any of his companions recognised the banner but it was that of Uí Néill clan from the north of Íralond. The new arrivals were led by Niall Glúndub mac Áedo, the brother of the King of Ailech.

The scouts watched as the crews disembarked on the north bank of the Dēvā a good five hundred yards from the walls of Cæstir. Wynnstan and the others counted as they did so and reached an approximation of three hundred lightly armed men similar to those who made up the fyrd but who wore nothing other than a length of saffron cloth wound around their waist and over one shoulder.

Most were armed with spear, dagger and a small round shield called a targe. About fifty of them were archers but their bows were of the hunting type, less powerful than a war bow. They were followed by a score of better dressed warriors in byrnies and

234

helmets equipped with swords, axes and larger circular shields.

'Come on,' Wynnstan said, 'we'd better get back and report what we've seen.'

'My guess is that the Vikings have lost a few hundred men in abortive attacks on the walls, or possibly through desertion,' Æthelflæd surmised. 'However, those losses have been negated by the arrival of the Irish.'

Unlike Wynnstan, she recognised the description of the banner as that of the Uí Néill, the dominant clan in the north of Íralond. What she didn't know was why on earth they would want to aid the Vikings who they had only recently driven out of Dyflin and the surrounding area.

'I'm less concerned about a few hairy-arsed Irishmen than I am about the Vikings mining under the walls. If they succeed in collapsing a section Ywer won't be able to stop them taking the place. Why on earth he allowed them to build a stout shelter against the walls like that is beyond me,' her husband grumbled.

'They probably pre-fabricated it and installed it at night; I'm less interested how they did it as I am in how we get men into Cæstir to reinforce the defenders.'

'You've abandoned the idea of attacking them, then?' her husband said with a sneer.

'No, but I suggest we need to give them more time to weaken themselves assaulting the walls before we offer battle. I also have an idea on how we might reduce their effective numbers.'

She went on to explain her plan. Æðelred was dubious about its chance of success but he reluctantly agreed that it was worth a try.

As a fluent Norse speaker, Wynnstan was the obvious choice to infiltrate the enemy camp. His first problem was locating Jarl Harald. He could be in any of the four encampments occupied by the besiegers. Three lay on the north bank opposite each of three of the gates whilst the fourth was on the south bank near the south-eastern end of the bridge.

Æthelstan had told him that Harald's banner depicted a black serpent on a brown background but he couldn't see any such banner in the two camps visible from his vantage point high in an oak tree on the south bank of the river. That probably meant that Harald and his men were in the camp opposite one of the northern gates.

To get there he would have to cross the river. The bridge was guarded at both ends and the next crossing point was a ford miles upriver. There was nothing for it but to try and find the ford. It would take time but he couldn't see any other option.

Dusk was falling by the time he'd made his way back along the northern bank and reached the woods to the north of Cæstir. He made for the north-eastern camp first as that was nearer but he was unable to make out the details of the various banners he could just see in the failing light. He settled down to spend an uncomfortable night in the woods. He daren't risk lighting a fire, even in a hollow, and so he dined on stale bread and hard cheese washed down by brackish water from a nearby stream. Even wrapped in his thick cloak he was cold and he slept fitfully.

He awoke when water splashed on his face. He sat upright with a jerk, his hand reaching for his sword but it was only raindrops. It must have started raining just before dawn and now rivulets of water were dripping down through the few brown leaves which remained on the trees. Soon they would be bare and the weather would turn even colder.

He ate a few mouthfuls of cheese and bread before jumping up and down to try and generate some warmth in his body. Leaving his horse where it was, he crept forward to the edge of the wood and climbed a large elm tree a few feet back from the tree line. From his perch some thirty feet up he had a good view down into the nearby Viking camp. It lay a good three hundred yards from both the nearest gates and the fortified amphitheatre, well out of range from the bowmen manning both Cæstir's walls and those of the redoubt.

He spotted Harald's banner almost immediately. Thankfully it flew outside a tent not far into the camp from where he was. He made a mental picture of the tent's location and climbed down. He could now look forward to a miserable day, cold, wet and hungry, before he could try and speak to Harald. To enter the camp during daylight was foolhardy. He would just have to wait until nightfall.

He had no problem getting into the camp. He was challenged but he replied that he'd been for a shit in the woods which seemed to satisfy the two sentries huddled under their cloaks around a spluttering fire. The rain hadn't let up all day and he was soaked to the skin. He was tempted to join them and take advantage of the fire to restore some warmth to his body but, although Frode had taught him to speak Norse like a native, he knew nothing of the personalities or anything else about the besiegers and would quickly give himself away.

He reached the tent with the serpent banner outside without any problems but there were two guards huddled under a makeshift shelter stationed at the entrance.

'I have an urgent message from Ingimund for Jarl Harald,' he told them, trying to sound more confident than he felt.

'Wait here,' one of them said gruffly and entered the tent.

'Bloody awful weather,' he commented to the other sentry.

He'd only said something because he felt uncomfortable standing in a puddle of water whilst the other man scrutinised him.'

'You look as if you've been for a swim in the river,' the other man said with a grin and Wynnstan relaxed.

'Jarl Harald will see you but leave your cloak here. He won't want it dripping all over his nice dry tent,' the other sentry told him when he came back out.

Wynnstan hesitated. He had done his best to look like a Norseman but his hairstyle, especially his clean shaven face, looked distinctly Anglo-Saxon. At the moment it was hidden under his hood.

He quickly whipped off the hooded cloak and handed it to the surprised sentry before pulling aside the entrance flap and stepping inside. He could only hope that neither man had the opportunity to see his face clearly in the gloom. There were no cries of alarm and so he thought that their suspicions hadn't been aroused. However, he hadn't got a clue how he was going to leave without them seeing him clearly.

Harald sat at a table laden with food, the sight of which made Wynnstan's mouth water. He had a goblet of ale in one hand and a knife in the other with which he was slicing a sliver of venison off a haunch.

He looked up as the Mercian entered but, much to Wynnstan's relief, he didn't immediately call for the sentries.

'I assume that you're a messenger from my son-in-law, not an assassin?' the jarl asked, looking the dripping stranger up and down.

'Not exactly, I'm a messenger but from the Lady Æthelflæd, not Lord Ywer.'

'Æthelflæd? We'd heard reports that Æðelred was somewhere nearby but not his wife.'

'She's joined him with another army,' Wynnstan, implying that her reinforcements were more numerous than was the reality.

'What are they up to? The Mercians have been harrying our foraging parties but they don't seem that keen to come to the relief of my son-in-law in Cæstir.'

'They want to make sure that they can inflict sufficient casualties on Ingimund and his allies so that he can never pose a threat to northern Mercia again.'

'You presumably don't count me amongst his allies?' Harald said with an amused smile.

'No, lord. Æthelflæd assumes that you are here because Ingimund pressured you to join him.'

'Æthelflæd assumes correctly. The same goes for several other jarls from north of the Mǣresēa.' He gave a resigned sigh. 'Ingimund has stationed his least trustworthy elements here in the north-eastern camp. He has ordered us to attack and capture the redoubt but the amphitheatre is almost impregnable. Of course, he doesn't care how many men we lose. We're expendable as far as he's concerned.'

It was exactly what Wynnstan was hoping to hear and he swiftly explained Æthelflæd's plan to him.

After leaving the Viking camp he made his way stealthily towards the amphitheatre's only set of gates. Thankfully the rain had stopped whilst he was with Harald. The sky was still cloudy but the moon occasionally made a brief appearance. When it did Wynnstan froze where he was until it went behind the next cloud. Although the ground was illuminated by the silvery light he knew that it was movement that attracted the eye at night.

'Who's there?' a voice suddenly called down from the top of the archway over the gates.

A moment later he heard the same voice tell someone to go and rouse the garrison.

'Stop! I've been sent by Lord Æðelred and Lady Æthelflæd. I need to speak to your commander.'

'How do I know you're not some Norse pagan trying to trick me?' the voice asked after telling his companion to wait a moment.

'My name is Wynnstan. I was here...'

'I know who you are, lad. I'm Wilfrid.'

Wynnstan knew him from the time he'd been at Cæstir with Lady Æthelflæd; he was one of Lord Ywer's gesith. He was surprised that someone so senior was on sentry duty but he later found out that he commanded the redoubt and had been called when a sharp-eyed sentry had seen movement between the Norse camp and the old amphitheatre.

Five minutes later Wynnstan was sitting in Wilfrid's tent explaining the plan to him.

'Will you be able to brief Lord Ywer?' Wynnstan asked before leaving.

'Yes, I'll make sure he knows what's going on. We've devised a simple method of signalling between us. I can't go into too much detail but I can tell him the gist of it.'

Wynnstan breathed a sigh of relief. He'd feared that he'd have to go into the old city and brief Ywer as well. It was already well after midnight and he was becoming concerned about time. He needed to creep back to where he'd left his horse and get well clear of the Viking camp before dawn.

He was tempted by Wilfrid's offer of a bed for the night but he needed to get back and make his report.

✝✝✝

Ywer stood on the walkway with Gyda and Irwyn staring despondently at the Viking camp across the other side of the river. Their son was now seven and was the image of his father at that age except for his

241

startling blond hair; something he'd inherited from his Norse grandfather.

They were now forced to live in a hut, a place which was overcrowded as it was shared with others who used to live in the hall complex. It was therefore good to escape the smoky, fetid atmosphere in the hut, even if only for a while, and breathe clean air. However, Ywer couldn't stop brooding about what had happened, even if the message that Eafer had sent him last night had lightened his mood somewhat.

The forty Vikings who had evaded the slaughter by the gates had managed to capture the compound which housed the ealdorman's hall and the monastery. Ywer had taken everyone capable of bearing arms to defend the walls and only old men and women, a few monks and several young children had remained in the hall complex. The Vikings had scaled the palisade and, according to the few who'd managed to escape, they'd killed everyone left there.

Tragically Eadwyn - Ywer and Gyda's baby son - and his wet nurse had been left in the hall. Ywer had frantically searched amongst those who'd managed to get away but they weren't there. He was forced to the conclusion that they too had perished.

Thankfully Gyda and Irwyn weren't with them. His wife was proficient with a hunting bow and had been one of those defending the hastily improvised wall around the killing zone. He had intended to leave the seven year old Irwyn in the supposed safety of the hall with his younger brother but the boy had asked his father if he could accompany him. Ywer was about to refuse his request but he had second thoughts and decided that it was time for the boy to see what warfare was all about.

The other member of Ywer's family, his uncle Abbot Æscwin, had also escaped being killed. He was helping to treat the wounded along with many of his monks.

As soon as he'd heard that the hall and monastery had been captured Ywer's first reaction was to storm the place and wreak a terrible vengeance on the Vikings inside. However, Edmund had objected.

'We've few enough men as it is, Lord Ywer,' the captain of his gesith had pointed out in as calm a tone as he could manage. 'If we assault the hall we'll lose dozens of men; men we need to defend Cæstir. We might have killed nearly two hundred of the bastard Vikings but that still leaves four times as many of the heathens out there as we have.'

'They may have spared the children in the hall, even if they killed all the adults,' Gyda added, more in hope than expectation.

She knew in her heart that the Norsemen would have taken their vengeance for the slaughter inflected on their comrades on everyone but, despite that, she continued to pray that Eadwyn might have been spared.

Ywer didn't reply. Instead he abruptly left them and paced along the walls in brooding silence until well after dark; then he came and found the hut that Gyda had appropriated for their use. He still said nothing to her, merely climbing into bed and turning his back on her to sleep. That made her grief for her lost son even worse. At a time when she needed her husband to comfort her he had spurned her. She thought that he probably hated all Norse people at that moment, including her. That hurt more than anything.

She slept fitfully, wondering what the future held. Even if they survived the siege, she was concerned that her marriage might not do the same. She had fallen in love with Ywer when he'd first come to her father's hall. That feeling had changed over the years that they'd been together, but only to become more profound. However, rejection was hard to take and grief coupled with bitterness could corrode even the deepest love. Ultimately it could turn into hate.

When she awoke the next morning it was to feel his lips on hers as he caressed her.

'I'm an idiot,' he whispered in her ear. 'It was unfair and selfish of me to ignore you in my sorrow. You deserved my support, not to be abandoned in your time of need. Can you forgive me?'

Despite her anxiety over her baby's fate, she felt as if a heavy weight had been lifted from her and she responded eagerly to his touch. She felt a pang of guilt about making love at such a time but her relief and his passion overcame her scruples. Later, as she lay sated, her remorse returned. She could only hope that it would lessen over time.

†††

'You can't put Æthelstan in command of the reinforcements!' Æthelflæd said in disbelief. 'He's barely fourteen.'

'An age when all free Mercians take up arms against our enemies,' Æðelred replied, barely keeping his temper in check. 'You are far too overprotective of your nephew. He's an ætheling and heir to the throne of Wessex. It's time he gained experience as a leader. Besides I'm sending some of my gesith with him and he's got Wynnstan, who you seem to rate so highly, as his captain.'

'We don't know that Harald can be trusted or that he's been able to convince his fellow jarls in his camp to change sides.'

'So you don't trust Wynnstan then? You don't think he's really managed to persuade Harald to let the reinforcements I'm sending into Cæstir to pass?' he scoffed.

'I didn't say that,' she snapped. 'I'm sure that Harald was convinced; I'm just not sure that his fellow jarls will follow his lead.'

He thumped the table.

'We don't have a choice. Any day now the enemy will finish undermining the walls. All they have to do then is light a fire to burn through the tunnel's supports and that section of the wall will come crashing down. When that happens the defenders won't stand a chance and the place will fall, closely followed by the rest of the shire. We need to reinforce them if they are to be able to repulse an attack through the breach.'

'Yes, yes; I understand all that, but why does Æthelstan have to lead it? Why not one of the ealdormen or senior thegns?'

'Because Æthelstan begged me to put him in command of the relief force and I said yes.'

✝✝✝

Wynnstan had been overjoyed to be appointed as Æthelstan's captain. They had been close friends the last time that they were together so he anticipated a return to that close relationship. However, Æthelstan was no longer a somewhat lonely young boy who looked up to Wynnstan and relished his friendship. He was now very much the ætheling who was eager to prove himself as his father's heir; not that King Eadweard had ever acknowledged his eldest son as such.

Æthelstan had grown up knowing that his father was embarrassed by his existence and wanted nothing to do with him. It sapped the boy's self-confidence and conversely made him bitterly determined to win Eadweard's approval. That resolve now ruled everything he did.

Of course, Æthelstan was pleased to have someone he liked and trusted as his captain but he deliberately kept him at a distance. That didn't mean he didn't consult his new captain and listen to his advice but he was wary of letting him get close again. He knew deep down that Wynnstan would never take advantage of their friendship but nevertheless the ætheling was determined to prove himself without relying on others.

Wynnstan had risen far and had done so quickly for one from such humble origins. He therefore put

Æthelstan's unexpected aloofness down to their very different circumstances. It was like a slap in the face. He felt rejected and believed that the ætheling was now ashamed of their former friendship. His initial delight at his new appointment turned to dust. If Æthelstan had been older and wiser he'd have realised how much he'd hurt a man who could have proved to be invaluable in the challenging times that lay ahead of him.

'Can I suggest that I go into Harald's camp first and confirm that they won't oppose our entry into Cæstir?' Wynnstan whispered to Æthelstan.

They stood just back from the treeline waiting for the sun to set. It had taken all day to lead the five hundred warriors and archers across the river and around to this spot. At one time Æthelstan feared that they might not make it before dark descended. If that happened his men might well get lost. However, Wynnstan reassured him that they would make it in daylight.

The ætheling was understandably nervous. This was his first opportunity to lead a sizeable force. Whilst he was grateful for the trust that Lord Æðelred had placed in him, he was conscious of his inexperience. He never imagined that such responsibility could weigh so heavily on his young shoulders.

Wynnstan did his best to encourage whilst not acting in any way that might seem to threaten the boy's position as commander. He found it a difficult path to walk.   To him the mission seemed straightforward as did its execution.

'What happens if you're discovered? They would learn that we are nearby and could attack us in the darkness,' Æthelstan objected.

'If I fall into the wrong hands I will claim to be a spy trying to find out about the Vikings' strength and morale. Don't worry, I would rather die in agony than let you down, lord,' Wynnstan replied tersely, resenting the implication that he could be forced to betray Æthelstan.

Æthelstan nodded his agreement after a moment's thought and Wynnstan melted into the shadows. He was troubled by Æthelstan's excessive caution. It wasn't like him. In the past Wynnstan thought that Æthelstan had verged on the reckless. It seemed odd but he eventually came to the conclusion that the boy's former bravado masked an innate insecurity. No doubt he would grow in confidence with experience. Wynnstan hoped so for all their sakes if he ever became king. He thrust his worries to the back of his mind. He needed all his wits about him as he approached the Vikings' camp.

Harald looked at Wynnstan in surprise when he entered his tent.

'Why are you here? Don't you trust me?'

'It's not that, lord. We wanted to make sure that your fellow jarls had supported you.'

'One or two took some persuading and I worried that they might betray me to Ingimund. I had them watched but none did so. Then yesterday Ingimund ordered us to attack the amphitheatre. It was a disaster and we lost over fifty men. That stoked the resentment we all felt towards him and you can rest assured that there is nothing all of us would like more than to see Ingimund brought low.'

'Will you help us then?'

Harald shook his head.

'We won't fight fellow Norsemen but we will remain neutral.'

Wynnstan had to be satisfied with that. He made his way cautiously out of the camp but evidently not cautiously enough. One of the men sitting by a fire wished him luck against Ingimund. He breathed a sigh of relief. That was better proof than Harald's word that these Norsemen were prepared to allow them to pass and enter Cæstir unopposed.

Chapter Thirteen

Autumn 906

Ywer stood on the walkway with Edmund, Æthelstan and Wynnstan watching the mining work in progress beneath them. So far the stout roof that the Norsemen had constructed over the tunnelling works had withstood the rocks that the defenders had thrown down. Work was progressing slowly because the miners could only dispose of the earth they'd dug out at night. The Mercians had thrown torches down to illuminate the disposal of the soil so that the archers could send a few arrows their way. The Vikings had suffered a few casualties in consequence. However, it didn't seriously impeded their work.

'Our other problem is the forty or so heathens who have captured my hall and the monastery,' Ywer was saying. 'Now we have more men I'd like to eliminate them.'

'We will still suffer significant casualties assaulting the palisade, lord,' Edmund pointed out, 'however many men we have.'

'They are contained I take it?' Æthelstan asked.

When Ywer nodded he continued, 'then I suggest we wait until Ingimund is dealt with and then we can negotiate their surrender.'

Wynnstan was impressed. There had been no indication of the ætheling's self-doubt and innate cautiousness since they'd entered Cæstir. Indeed, he seemed to have taken charge and Ywer deferred to him. However, Wynnstan suspected that his lord was putting on an act and deep down he was as doubtful of his own ability as a leader as ever.

The four listened gloomily to the faint sound of pick and shovel coming from underground.

'May I make a suggestion,' Wynnstan asked, glancing at Æthelstan. 'Do you have mead and bee hives?'

'Yes, but only in the grounds of the monastery,' Ywer replied.

'A pity.'

'Why, what were you thinking, Wynnstan?' Æthelstan asked curiously.

'The covering over the mining works is made up of thick tree trunks, lord, but there are gaps between them. If we could pour mead down and then throw the bee hives after it the angry creatures might force the miners to flee and our archers could pick them off as they emerged.

The other three grinned at each other.

'That might make an attack on the hall complex worthwhile,' Ywer said thoughtfully, 'but we still need to minimise our casualties.'

'I have an idea how we might be able to do that,' Æthelstan said tentatively.

That night a hundred men led by Edmund cautiously approached the hall compound. Heavy rain was falling and the night was cold. There was no sign of Viking sentries on top of the palisade. Hopefully they were huddled around a brazier somewhere. Four of the strongest Mercians hoisted two of their fellows up onto their shoulders and a boy of fifteen climbed up

251

until he was standing on the shoulders of the two men. From there he could see over the palisade and along the walkway that ran inside the top of it.

Satisfied that there was no one in sight, he hauled himself up and dropped down onto the walkway. Three more young warriors followed him before Æthelstan joined them. Ywer and Wynnstan had tried to dissuade him but the ætheling had insisted. It was proving to be a failure as a leader that worried the young ætheling, not embarking on a dangerous mission. Seeing the eagerness with which he swarmed up the bodies that formed the human ladder Wynnstan was reminded, not without with a pang of regret, of the impetuous boy he was once close to.

Æthelstan peered into the gloom from the bottom of the steps that led up to the walkway. He could see the flickering light of a fire behind the guard hut sited just inside the gateway and was willing to wager that was where the sentries were gathered on a night like this. He and his four companions crept closer to the gate using the shadows whenever possible. Only three men sat around the brazier, two had their back to the Mercians and the other one was looking into the fire.

With a nod to the others, Æthelstan drew his dagger silently from its sheath and the others did likewise. They poised themselves ready to rush forward and slit the sentries' throats from behind when a Norse voice stopped them.

'Well, well, if it isn't the pretty little prince. Did you think my men were so indolent that they wouldn't spot you climbing over the palisade?'

For a moment Æthelstan couldn't place the voice, then he realised who it was – Ingimund's son, Gunnar. He must have been amongst those who had escaped the killing ground in front of the gates and had then taken refuge in the ealdorman's hall.

He slowly turned to face Gunnar and the group of Vikings who stood at his back. The arrogant young boy of three or four years ago now had the wispy beginnings of a beard typical of a youth. The derisive look on his face, clearly visible in the flickering light of the fire, hadn't changed though.

'I said I'd get even with you for embarrassing me in front of my father when we first came to this miserable country, so don't think your death will be either quick or painless.'

Æthelstan cursed himself for being a fool. He should have known that recapturing the hall wouldn't be that easy. He determined to sell his life dearly but then he remembered that he was responsible for his companions' lives as well.

'If you let my men go, I'll fight you one to one,' he offered.

'Why should I do that? You're in no position to bargain. They'll die a warrior's death, quick and clean, but we'll keep you alive for a while whilst I think about how best to end your miserable existence. Perhaps the blood eagle might satisfy me?'

Although he'd heard reference to the blood eagle as a particularly gruesome way to die, Æthelstan didn't know what it meant. Had he done so he might not have remained so calm. It was barbaric and a practice that even the most bloodthirsty Vikings rarely resorted to.

The victim was held face down in a prone position whilst their ribs were cut from their spine with a sharp knife, then their lungs were dragged through the gory opening to resemble a pair of wings.

Even Gunnar's warriors were appalled at the suggestion and several began to remonstrate with him. It hadn't been a serious threat on Gunnar's part, just something intended to terrorise the boy. However, he hated to be thwarted and his men's opposition to the idea changed what was only intended to intimidate the boy into a firm intention in Gunnar's mind.

'Kill the others but make sure Æthelstan stays alive,' he ordered.

'You may be Ingimund's son but you seem to have forgotten that I'm in command here,' one of the men who had been standing watching the confrontation butted in.

Æthelstan vaguely recognised the man who'd spoken as one of those who'd been in the tent when Æthelflæd and Ingimund had first met. He couldn't remember his name but he evidently felt powerful enough to override Gunnar.

'You'll regret this,' the youth muttered, giving the man a vicious look.

'Enough! Kill the Mercian pigs, then we can get out of this accursed rain.'

✝✝✝

Wynnstan was getting worried. He and the rest of Edmund's warriors huddled in what shelter they could find opposite the main entrance to the compound surrounding the hall and the monastery. Æthelstan and his group should have secured and opened the gates by now. He went and had a quiet word with Edmund who nodded his agreement so Wynnstan gestured to half a dozen of Æthelstan's gesith and they followed him across a section of the palisade ten yards or so from the gates. The lightest amongst the group was Hengist, now the ætheling's body servant once more. He wrapped a length of knotted rope over his shoulder and between them they heaved Hengist high enough so he could haul himself over the top.

Once there the youth checked the walkway for sentries but all the Vikings seemed to have gathered in a circle around Æthelstan. He swiftly tied one end of the rope to the pointed top of the palisade and threw the other end to Wynnstan. Three minutes later the latter and two more men had joined him. All three had bows strapped to their backs but the bowstrings were kept in oiled leather pouches at their waists.

As soon as Wynnstan realised what was about to happen below him he strung his bow. The bowstring should be dry enough for the first few arrows to strike the Norsemen with full force; after that the bow would lose power as the string stretched in the rain but, at this range, it should still be able to do enough damage.

Wynnstan drew the bowstring back to his ear and let fly. His arrow struck a man who was about to deliver a killing blow to Æthelstan. It had been aimed hastily but it punched through the chainmail over his right shoulder and the Viking dropped his sword with a howl of pain.

He didn't pause to see where his arrow had gone but quickly sent two more arrows into the men crowded around the small group of Mercians. His companions did the same and in less than a minute eight of the enemy had been killed or wounded. Gunnar and his men had been taken completely by surprise and turned from attacking the small group of Mercians and sought to locate this new threat. By then two of Æthelstan's companions had been killed but the others seized the opportunity to attack the distracted Norsemen and managed to fight their way to the gateway. Once they had the gates at their back and with their flanks protected in the confined space between the two towers they had a much better chance of defending themselves.

Although the damp bowstrings were losing power, four more of the enemy were hit before the rest reached cover. Wynnstan realised that they themselves would be vulnerable if the Norse warriors managed to get up onto the walkway where they stood.

'Quick, we need to stop the bastards climbing through the hatchways onto the walkway,' Wynnstan yelled.

Whilst he and Hengist ran for the top of the stairs in one direction the other three hared along to the other access point. Wynnstan was beaten to it by Hengist who wasn't hampered by the weight of a mail byrnie or a helmet. The boy got there just as the trapdoor crashed back and the first head appeared. He thrust his knife into the right eye of the surprised Norseman who fell back on top of the men climbing behind him. Wynnstan shut the trapdoor and rammed the bolt across before the next man could try to get through it.

The other three had further to go and didn't make it before the first two Norsemen appeared on the walkway. However, three against two was good odds and the Mercians managed to kill their two opponents in short order; not before more Vikings had clambered through the trapdoor however. Although they were now seriously outnumbered, the walkway was quite narrow and the three Mercians conducted a fighting retreat back towards Wynnstan and Hengist.

Meanwhile the withdrawal of most of the Vikings to attack the Mercians on the walkway gave Æthelstan and the survivors from his group a respite and they sucked in great lungfuls of air whilst they recovered. Thankfully, the few Norsemen who remained before them seemed content to wait until their comrades returned. This didn't suit Gunnar at all who screamed at them to attack the four Mercians. The small group of Vikings looked at Gunnar as if he was mad.

'Why should we risk our lives when all we have to do is wait for our comrades to return?' one of them, a Dane, asked Gunnar belligerently.

For a moment the Dane thought that the furious boy was about to attack him and he raised his sword threateningly. Whilst the others were watching the little drama unfold Æthelstan took advantage of the distraction and seized his chance. The four of them lifted the heavy bar out of its brackets and pulled the gates open.

✝✝✝

Æthelflæd was getting increasingly frustrated by her husband's inertia. She wasn't alone; the army was equally exasperated at the lack of action. Apart from skirmishes with a few Viking forage parties, they had done nothing which would help those besieged in Cæstir. She and the ealdormen had remonstrated with Æðelred but met with the same response: he wasn't about to risk men's lives needlessly.

'He's turned into a coward,' one of the more senior thegns was heard to mutter at yet another meeting of the war council which achieved nothing.

Æðelred flushed with anger so he'd obviously heard the sotto voce comment but he didn't respond. The next day his body servant came to find Æthelflæd in evident distress.

'My master is ill, lady,' he said, wringing his hands. 'I don't know what's wrong but he just lies unmoving in his bed. I've checked he's breathing and he's warm to the touch but I can't seem to wake him up.'

When she entered her husband's tent she found several monks and Bishop Wirfrith clustered around the bed arguing noisily. It seemed that there was a difference of opinion about Æðelred's malady. Some thought he'd had a relapse and his old illness had returned, whereas others maintained that his brain no longer functioned, although his body still lived.

'Please be quiet,' Æthelflæd said above the hubbub. 'Whatever is wrong with my husband isn't going to be helped by this unseemly squabbling. Bishop, do you have an opinion on the matter?'

Wirfrith licked his lips nervously. Although he was the senior clergyman present, he wasn't a trained infirmarian, unlike most of the monks, and had no idea what was wrong with Æðelred.

'He's suffering from some form of sleeping sickness, lady,' he muttered uncertainly.

'Yes, I can see that but what has caused it and will he recover?'

At that moment Æðelred opened his eyes and tried to speak. However, his eyes were unfocused and only a few grunts and moans escaped his lips. Æthelflæd knelt by the bedside and put her ear to his lips but she couldn't make out what he was trying to say. After a while she got back to her feet and ordered all but the bishop to leave.

'Whatever is wrong with my lord it's plain that he's in no fit state to govern Mercia at the moment. Do you agree?'

'Sadly I do,' he said nodding. 'The most senior ealdorman is...' he started to say but Æthelflæd held up her hand to stop him continuing.

'Until he recovers I shall act in his stead.'

'I know that you governed Mercia when Lord Æðelred was ill before, lady, but this is different. We need a military leader, not an administrator.'

'Does that mean that you think that sitting here doing nothing whilst a heathen horde attacks Cæstir is going to give us victory; because that was what my husband was doing.'

'No, of course not; nor do any of the nobles approve of inaction.'

'Then I want your support at today's meeting of the war council. I have a plan to defeat the Vikings which is more than any of the ealdorman do; they just think we should be doing something. If they had their way we'd charge in and fight the Vikings shieldwall to shieldwall. That way lays carnage and probable defeat.'

'What's your plan, lady?'

So she told him.

†††

Edmund peered through the downpour as the gates creaked open.

'They've done it,' he cried triumphantly and ran across the space between the alley where he'd been sheltering and the half-open gates.

With a roar the rest of his men followed him, only to see the gates closing as they approached. As soon as the Vikings with Gunnar saw the gates open they attacked Æthelstan and his three companions with a ferocity born of desperation. They knew that once the Mercians outside the palisade got into the compound they were doomed.

The four Mercians defended themselves equally fiercely, determined to keep the gates open. However, they were forced back against the stout wooden gates and in giving ground they pushed them shut again.

However the bar wasn't in place and, when Edmund and his men put their shoulders against the gates, their numbers forced them apart again and men began to slip through the gap.

Æthelstan had been lucky to escape with a few minor flesh wounds so far but, as the pressure of the Mercians outside pushed him towards his attackers, one of the Norsemen thrust his sword into the young æthelings thigh. For a moment he felt nothing then the intense pain hit him as blood spurted from one of the minor arteries in his upper leg. He was lucky that the main femoral artery itself hadn't been cut but, as it was, he would bleed to death unless something was done to stem the bleeding.

Seeing the boy fall inspired Gunnar to greater efforts. He cut Edmund down as the captain of Ywer's warband stood over Æthelstan to protect him. Now his quarry lay unprotected and helpless at his feet. A feral grin lit up Gunnar's face as he thrust the point of his sword towards the boy's right eye.

The blow never landed. As Hengist watched in amazement Wynnstan launched himself from the walkway. The drop was over ten feet but it was twice as far from where he'd jumped to where Gunnar stood. He was never going to make it. Hengist imagined that he heard the crack as Wynnstan hit the ground, breaking his leg as he landed, but he couldn't have done so above the din of combat.

Agonising pain shot through Wynnstan's leg but he gritted his teeth and used his momentum to topple sideways. His head and right shoulder cannoned into the calf of Gunnar's left leg and the Viking's aim was spoilt. Instead of piercing Æthelstan's eye the blade scored across his cheek leaving a deep cut. When the scar healed no one would ever call the boy pretty again.

A second later Gunnar was knocked from his feet as the Viking defenders were overcome and someone hauled the ætheling to his feet before he could be trampled underfoot by Edmund's men, eager to wreak their revenge on the Vikings for the death of their captain. Wynnstan wasn't so lucky. By the time that Hengist reached him he had added three cracked ribs and a broken left arm to his list of injuries. Thankfully he felt no pain as he lapsed into unconsciousness.

†††

Wynnstan awoke feeling as if he was on fire. His broken leg and arm had been set and splinted but there was little the monks could do about his ribs. They would mend themselves in time. He didn't try to move but his eyes darted about him. He was in a tent and, by the smell of blood, puss and faeces, he was in the infirmary of the monastery.

He was conscious of someone dribbling water onto his lips and he opened his mouth, gulping the welcome liquid down his parched throat. His vision cleared and he saw to his surprise that the person with the water jug wasn't one of the monks but Æthelstan himself.

The ætheling had a livid puckered scar across his cheek which someone had sewn together with catgut. Not only did it spoil his good looks but it made him appear as if he had a permanent leer. Wynnstan thought that it would probably correct itself when the flesh healed and the stitches were removed. He certainly hoped so because the boy's present look was somewhat disconcerting.

He glanced down at Æthelstan's bare legs. Someone had evidently cauterised the cut to the artery and bandaged it. Obviously the boy should still be in bed himself and Wynnstan realised that the fact that he was administering to his captain instead of resting spoke volumes about Æthelstan's character.

'Stay where you are,' the latter told him firmly when Wynnstan tried to sit up. 'I'm told by Uhtric that it will be at least a month before the splints can be removed and you can start exercising to replace the wasted muscle.'

Uhtric was one of two brothers who had served Jørren as physicians since they were boys. The younger one, Leofric had died a few years ago but Uhtric continued to serve Ywer.

'I gather that I owe you my life,' Æthelstan added with a smile. 'I'll never forget that. Ask anything of me and, if it's within my power, I'll grant it.'

'My only wish is to continue to serve you as your captain, lord. I'll pray every hour that God will mend my body so that I can continue to fight at your side.'

'Well said. Even if your bones don't mend as they should, I'll still want you as my counsellor and my friend.'

Wynnstan lay back feeling elated. It seemed that the close relationship the two of them had enjoyed several years before had been restored. Furthermore, he detected a self-confidence in the boy that had been somewhat lacking before the attack on the compound.

'What happened after I lost consciousness?'

'Your idea worked a treat. Ywer's men poured mead down on top of the canopy protecting the miners and then threw the hives down. The angry bees swarmed out of the broken hives and, attracted by the mead dripping through the minor's shelter, they flew into the tunnel. The miners fled pursued by the bees. Those that weren't stung to death were slain by our archers. They won't try breaking into Cæstir that way again.'

Suddenly Wynnstan thought of Gunnar and asked if he'd been killed.

'No, he was wounded and captured. I had his right hand chopped off and cauterised in the flames of the brazier. You should have heard him scream! He passed out but survived the ordeal. I've kept him as a hostage for now but he'll never fight against us again.'

Æthelstan's pious hope was misplaced and he would live to regret his clemency.

✝✝✝

'Well? What did they say?' Æthelflæd asked the nervous Irishman standing in front of her.

He'd been bought as a boy from the slave market in Glowecestre by one of the thegns from Hwicce and had been promised his freedom if he took a message from Æthelflæd to Niall Glúndub mac Áedo, the leader of the Irish warriors who'd joined Ingimund.

'He's only here for the plunder that the Vikings have promised him, lady. He needs silver to ransom his brother who's been captured by Clann Cholmáin, their rivals for dominance of the north.'

264

'Yes, yes,' she said impatiently before the man could witter on about the complex political situation in Íralond. 'Will he do what I ask?'

'Yes, but he wants six barrels of silver, not the three you offered, lady.'

She contemplated sending the man back to offer four. Six barrels of hack silver was a lot to pay but she was impatient to end the siege of Cæstir.

'Very well, go back and promise him six. Tell him to wait until he sees the two red banners waving before he acts. If he gets the timing wrong we could all be in deep trouble.'

Now all she had to do was to sneak someone into Cæstir to tell Ywer about her plan.

Two days later, just after dawn on a cold and frosty morning in early November, Æthelflæd led the Mercian army out of the woods to confront the largest of the Norse camps outside the walls of Cæstir. The Viking camp looked like an ants' nest after it had been kicked over by a small boy but in a remarkably short time the enemy had formed a shieldwall to face the Mercian threat.

From her vantage point on a small hill behind her army she could see the Danes and Vikings in two of the other three camps racing to join their comrades. Somewhat tardily, Niall Glúndub's Irish contingent followed on. The warriors in the camp near the amphitheatre made no move to join the other Vikings and she smiled with relief. It seemed that Harald had persuaded his fellow jarls from north of the Mæresēa to remain neutral.

The warriors on both sides stamped their feet to try and generate some warmth in them as they stood facing each other on ground still covered by hoar frost. Æthelflæd ordered her archers to pepper the enemy ranks with arrows, not so much as to cause casualties – although that would be a bonus – but to goad the Vikings into attacking first.

With a roar the enemy charged towards their tormentors after enduring the hail of arrows for less than ten minutes. In that time perhaps fifty arrows had found a gap in the barrier of shields and struck men in the face or in the lower legs. More seriously for the enemy, some of them stumbled into the pits laced with pointed stakes dug by Ywer. However, that didn't seem to deter the rest.

Æthelflæd waited until the two sides were fully engaged and then she ordered the two flag bearers to wave their red flags vigorously to and fro. The Irish had belatedly arrived on the battlefield just as the signal was given and they raced to attack the Vikings in the flank. At the same time Ywer led the garrison out to take the enemy in the other flank. Now hemmed in on three sides, the Vikings found themselves unable to manoeuvre and they were gradually forced back against the walls of Cæstir. The semi-circle of ground they held grew smaller and smaller as the Mercians and their Irish allies pushed them back.

Æthelstan and Wynnstan had been carried up to the battlements from where they sat watching the battle unfold. As the Vikings were driven into a smaller and smaller area all except those in the front rank were unable to use their weapons. They fought bravely but the outcome was never in doubt. Nevertheless, Ingimund wasn't about to surrender and it wasn't until after he was killed that small groups began to throw down their weapons and plead for mercy.

Some fought on, secure in the belief that a place in Odin's Hall in Valhalla awaited them but the majority preferred to live. Unfortunately, the Mercians didn't differentiate between those trying to surrender and those determined to die. It meant that a significant number of those who wanted to submit were also killed.

When the din of battle died away and both sides stood too exhausted to fight on, a mere one hundred and fifty Vikings remained alive and unwounded. They, together with those who would recover from their wounds, were destined for the slave markets. Those too badly wounded were finished off.

Æthelflæd sent for Harald to thank him and his fellow jarls for their neutrality and to reward them but they had already left for their homeland. She paid the six barrels of hacksilver to Niall Glúndub, as they'd agreed, but even so there was enough other plunder recovered from the Vikings to pay each Mercian warrior a significant sum.

Naturally Æthelflæd took the lion's share, as was her right as commander, but it wasn't to replenish Mercia's coffers. In order to thank God for her victory she had promised to build a new and larger stone church on the site of the old desecrated one. She decided to dedicate it to Saint Werburgh, an abbess of

Ely and the daughter of the first Christian king of Mercia.

Æthelflæd would have stayed to help Ywer repair the havoc wreaked by the Vikings on his shire - and to exploit her victory by driving back the border with the Norse and the Danes further into Northumbria - but it wasn't to be. Three days after the battle she was summoned south. Her brother Eadweard had repulsed a Danish raid across the Themes and had chased the Danes as far north at a place called Tiddingforde.

It was a trap and Eadweard was forced into negotiations with the Danes of East Anglia and Northumbria. He requested his sister's presence during the talks. Her heart sank when she found out that he also wanted a contribution to the Danegeld being demanded to avoid all-out war. There wouldn't be much left in her war chest after building Saint Werburgh's church and paying Danegeld for her brother's folly.

Chapter Fourteen

Spring 909

Eadweard had been furious when he'd been forced to pay off the Danes so that he could escape unscathed from Tiddingforde. His sister's obvious but unspoken criticism of him when she'd arrived hadn't helped. That said, it wasn't all bad news. After hard negotiation, a pact had been agreed and both sides had kept the truce for nearly three years now. There were minor raids of course but that was to be expected. Archbishop Plegmund had played a major part in the negotiations and he'd insisted on including one clause in the treaty which was yet to be fulfilled.

'We were promised that the Danes would return the relics of Saint Oswald but as far as we know they still lie in the ruins of the monastery at Bardenai,' Æthelflæd told her council.

They looked at her expectantly, wondering where this was leading. Everyone present knew the story of Oswald who, together with Saint Aidan, had brought Christianity to the kingdom of Northumbria. Oswald had recovered his throne after being driven into exile when he was a boy but he'd been killed by Penda, the last pagan king of Mercia. His body had been nailed to a tree but had been recovered during a daring raid into the heart of Mercia by his brother. Ever since then a number of miracles had been attributed to him.

'I intend to recover Saint Oswald's remains,' she announced.

Æthelflæd's desire to obtain them was motivated by her outrage that the Danes had failed to honour their agreement to hand over such important religious artefacts but there was another reason: the prestige that possession of Oswald's bones would confer on Mercia.

Much to her annoyance her statement was greeted by a stunned silence rather than by enthusiasm for the mission that she'd anticipated. Their stupefaction was understandable; Bardenai lay in southern Northumbria a hundred and fifty miles north-east of Glowecestre and a good twenty five miles inland from the coast. Whoever was sent on such a foolhardy assignment would either have to ride over a hundred miles through hostile territory or sail to the nearest landing place in Northumbria – in itself a hazardous voyage – and then make their way through land controlled by the Danes to Bardenai.

'Lady, such a perilous undertaking is doomed to fail,' Bishop Wirfrith protested.

'Why? King Oswiu managed a similar feat when he recovered his brother's body from the heart of Mercia. I would have thought that a senior clergyman such as yourself would have supported such a venture wholeheartedly.'

Wirfrith looked suitably abashed and she thought that his lukewarm attitude had much to do with the status that the monastery at Glowecestre would gain at the expense of his own establishment at Wirecestre. He wasn't the only one to display scepticism. Although

Oswiu was reputed to have led a raid deep into hostile Mercia two and a half centuries before to recover his brother's body no-one was aware of how exactly he'd managed to do so.

'Unfortunately we don't have an Oswiu available to pull off such a daring exploit, lady,' one of the ealdormen pointed out with an insincere smile.

Æthelflæd glared at him and the man wondered when, if ever, Æðelred would recover sufficiently to take back the reins of government. He was a lot easier to deal with than his demanding wife. Æðelred had moments of lucidity that could last for several days but then he would have another relapse.

'No, but we do have someone who has a good chance of success.'

'Who? I can't think of anyone stupid enough to take this one, or with enough skill to pass undetected through both the Danelaw and Northumbria,' another ealdorman said as if that was an end to the matter.

'Wynnstan,' she replied. 'He's already agreed and Æthelstan has given permission for his captain to undertake the mission.'

†††

Astrid had been furious when Wynnstan told her. It had taken time but he'd made a good recovery from his injuries and they had married shortly after his return from Cæstir. They'd happily settled down to married life together, although she continued to run Deorwine and Cuthfleda's hall and he was busy recruiting and training Æthelstan's gesith.

The ætheling no longer looked like a boy. At sixteen he towered over most other men by a good few inches and he had broad, powerful shoulders. In the practice yard he could beat most of his hearth warriors with sword and shield without raising a sweat. Unlike most Anglo-Saxons, he didn't grow any facial hair but had it shaved off every few days.

Æthelstan spent his time training with his men and hunting but, although he enjoyed a boar or stag hunt as much as the next man, he preferred to hunt his prey stealthily on foot accompanied by Wynnstan. Stalking game was something that his captain excelled at. He'd never forgotten the skills he'd learned as a boy living with his father and Frode in the woods and it was a rare day when the two didn't return with several hares, a brace of pheasants or a deer.

Whilst Wynnstan only supervised the military training of new recruits, leaving the day-to-day instruction to others, he liked to be personally involved in passing his skills as a woodsman and hunter on to his small group of young scouts. It would be some time before they were as proficient as he was but he decided to take the most promising three with him to retrieve Saint Oswald's relics. Æthelstan had pestered his aunt to be allowed to go with them but Æthelflæd was adamant that it was too dangerous for the heir to the throne of Wessex.

It wasn't an argument that he readily accepted. Ælfweard, the eldest son of King Eadweard and Lady Ælfflæd, would be five in a few months' time and his father had already nominated him as his heir. Not that it meant that he would succeed; the choice of king lay with the Witenaġemot of Wessex. However, Æthelstan was now seen as more of a Mercian than a West Saxon. Ælfflæd had recently presented Eadweard with a daughter and she was now pregnant again. If it was another boy there would be even less chance of Æthelstan becoming King of Wessex.

Nevertheless, Æthelflæd always regarded him as her brother's heir and wasn't about to risk his life unnecessarily. She disliked Ælfflæd and her family intensely, regarding them as scheming opportunists. Eadweard had already made a number of sizeable grants of land to his wife and to her brother, Osfirth, which made them the richest family in Wessex after the king. Æthelflæd loved and supported Eadweard but she disagreed with many of his actions, not least his infatuation with his wife which blinded him to her true character. The thought of one of Ælfflæd's brats robbing Æthelstan of his inheritance enraged her.

✝✝✝

Wynnstan tried to calm Astrid down, refusing to rise to her accusations that he wouldn't leave her if he loved her.

'Are you so careless of your family that you would leave Wealhmær and the baby fatherless,' she stormed.

Wealhmær was their eighteen month old son. Astrid was pregnant again but the goodwife said that she was still in the early stages.

'I have no intention of dying,' he said soothingly. 'Besides, you still have your place at Cuthfleda's side should anything happen to me.'

It was the wrong thing to say and Astrid burst into tears. Wynnstan was well aware that it was a ploy to get him to change his mind. She wasn't the sort of woman to break down and cry, whatever the circumstances. He took her in his arms but she pulled away and rushed from the room.

He had hoped that they might be reconciled before he left but she deliberately avoided him, sleeping at Deorwine's and Cuthfleda's hall rather than in their bed.

He left with a heavy heart, still hoping that she would come down to the port to see them off. He had decided to travel to the coast of Lindsey on a trading knarr posing as a merchant selling bales of fine woollen cloth. The knarr would be travelling in convoy with other knarrs and two birlinns as escort and so he hoped that they would escape the attentions of the Viking and Flemish pirates who preyed on shipping.

The voyage was uneventful until they reached the south coast of Cent. At one point they were no more than twenty miles from the coast of Frankia and that was a favourite spot for Viking longships to wait for merchantmen. The King of the Franks should have patrolled these waters and kept them safe but his kingdom was infested with Danish and Norse invaders and it was left to the small fleet created by King Ælfred - with the help of Ywer's late father Jørren, then the Sæ Hereræswa of Wessex - to keep watch along the coast. However, they couldn't be everywhere.

As Wynnstan's convoy rounded the eastern extremity of Cent and turned north they ran into a contrary wind and had to tack to and fro to make any progress. Unlike fighting ships, knarrs couldn't be propelled by oars on the open sea. They didn't carry enough of a crew and they weren't designed to be rowed. They did have a few oars but they were only for manoeuvring in port.

As they beat to windward, three drekar – the largest type of Viking longship –appeared over the horizon from the east. The much smaller birlinns were outnumbered and stood no chance of defeating the pirates. There was only one course of action they could take and that was for the convoy to turn tail and head for safety in the port of Dofras.

Thankfully, the knarr on which Wynnstan and his companions had embarked was one of the fastest in the fleet. They made it to Dofras but two of the slower knarrs were caught and boarded.

Dofras was the base for Wessex's eastern fleet of longships but, as luck would have it, they were all out on patrol. The old Roman fort high above the port was well manned so the possibility of an attack by the pirates on the ships in port was remote. Nevertheless it caused Wynnstan to re-examine his plan to reach Lindsey by sea. Perhaps it would be better to travel overland to Lundenburg and board another merchantman there? At least he would be travelling through friendly territory for the initial part of the journey and Æthelflæd had given him a letter requesting safe passage for him and his companions; although he didn't want to use it unless absolutely necessary. His mission was clandestine and the fewer people who knew about it the better.

They slept on board that night. The captain of the knarr chafed at the delay as it was costing him money and some of his cargo was perishable. Nevertheless, it would be foolish to put to sea again until a stronger escort was available. Wynnstan was equally impatient but for a quite different reason. He was determined to return to Astrid's side long before the baby was due.

In the end the decision was taken out of his hands. A storm blew up which the experienced sailors said was likely to last for several days. By that time he and his three companions could be in Lundenburg from where they could take passage on a merchantman heading up the east coast.

✝✝✝

Algar and Eadling were two Angles; brothers who were ceorls in a vill owned by a Dane called Aksel, known as the Hold of Lincolia. Both their parents had died just after Algar reached fourteen; the age at which a boy became an adult according to the law and could inherit the land tenanted by their father. However, Algar had to pay his lord a tax before he could inherit. He had neither enough silver nor goods and produce in lieu to pay the tax and in due course Leif, one of Aksel's hearth warriors, was sent to confiscate their land.

Algar had the brawn whereas Eadling was the one with the brains. Algar had a reputation for losing his temper easily so Leif should have expected trouble when he came to evict the two brothers. However, he was a Dane who regarded the Angles who lived in his lord's domain as beneath contempt. Algar wisely let his brother do the talking at first and Eadling put forward an argument for granting them more time to find the tax or, better still, allow the brothers to pay what was due over a year instead of all at once.

Unbeknown to the two boys, Aksel had already given the brothers' land to a distant cousin. Consequently Leif wasn't interested in anything that Eadling had to say and impatiently demanded that they leave.

When it dawned on Algar that Eadling had failed to persuade Leif to let them keep the land he lost his temper. Inevitably a furious argument ensued which Algar ended by punching the intractable Leif in the face. Although a warrior, the Dane wasn't expecting trouble and the blow took him by surprise. Leif's nose was broken and he lost two front teeth. Although he was a powerful man the sudden and unexpected pain took him off guard and he stepped back in surprise.

Algar had been chopping logs when Leif arrived and not all had been stacked. The Dane caught one with his heel, lost his balance and fell on his back. He hadn't bothered to don his helmet and his bare head struck a rock. Had he not done so he would doubtless have quickly recovered and killed the two boys. Even if Algar could have reached his axe, he would've been no match for an experienced warrior armed with sword and dagger. As it was the, Dane died instantly.

Had Algar killed a fellow Angle he would have had to pay weregeld to the man's family and, if he didn't have it, the only solution open to him would have been to sell himself and the twelve year old Eadling into slavery.

However, he had killed a Dane and he suspected that Aksel wouldn't be satisfied with enslaving them as thralls. The man would want his head and that of his brother. There was only one option open to them - to flee and become robbers - wolfs heads outside the law. They quickly packed anything of value they possessed and added Leif's purse, silver arm rings and weapons. With Eadling riding the Dane's horse and his brother herding their solitary cow, their few sheep and two pigs, they fled into the woods.

Over the next two years they were joined by three more outlaws and together they managed to survive by using what they'd brought with them sparingly and supplementing it by preying on small groups of travellers on the road from Lincolia to Malberthorp.

†††

Wynnstan had chosen his three scouts to accompany him because of their ability to move undetected through the countryside and their proficiency with the bow. The eldest was called Sawin. At eighteen he was four years younger than Wynnstan but old enough to pose as a fellow merchant. The other two, Wardric and Tidhelm, were both fifteen and were cast in the role of servants.

Malberthorp served as the local port but there was no harbour, merely a long stretch of golden beach. Knarrs had to run up onto the beach to unload and many of the local inhabitants made their living by dealing with cargoes quickly before the tide could either strand the ship or float it off the beach. That meant that each merchantmen had to wait its turn for a crew of labourers to become available.

Wynnstan fretted impatiently as the knarr that he and his scouts had taken passage on at Lundenburg lay at anchor. The captain had nothing to unload apart from his passengers and no cargo to take aboard and so, if anything, he was even more exasperated by the delay than Wynnstan.

If it was only a question of disembarking the passengers he could have done that without the help of the men on shore but Wynnstan had bought some fine woollen cloth dyed in rich colours in Lundenburg to support the pretence that he was a merchant. The bolts of cloth also contained their byrnies, helmets, bows, quivers and swords. Although the material was wrapped in oiled covers to protect it, the bales needed to be carried ashore carefully to avoid any risk of them getting spoiled by sea water.

Wynnstan had purchased four riding horses and two pack animals in Dofras for the journey as far as Lundenburg. He had contemplated taking them on board but the captain had pointed out that it would be difficult to disembark them at Malberthorp. There was no wharf or hoist at Malberthorp, nor any other means of getting them out of the hold and putting them ashore safely, and so he'd been compelled to sell them before they'd embarked. He only hoped that he could buy suitable replacements on arrival.

However, it was now too late in the day to seek out fresh mounts and, although he wasn't keen on staying the night in the settlement, without horses he and his companions had no alternative. The only tavern offering accommodation was already full and they were forced to share with two other travellers. As the pair had arrived first and taken the only bed, Wynnstan and the others would have to sleep on the floor. It was an inauspicious start to their mission, especially as the other occupants were Danes.

Whilst he was a proficient Norse speaker Wynnstan couldn't speak Danish well enough to pass as a Dane and his scouts only spoke Ænglisc. Thankfully the two Danes accepted him as a Norseman and showed little curiosity about the others, assuming that they were Norse as well. That was a relief but it showed how fraught with danger their mission could be.

The next morning dawned wet and miserable. Their failure to find suitable horses added to their depression. Thankfully they did eventually find two sorry looking nags to carry the bales of cloth with their hidden contents. Wynnstan was told that there was a horse breeder's farmstead some five miles inland and so they set off into the downpour on foot.

Mindful that they were now in enemy territory, Wynnstan and Tidhelm led the two packhorses whilst the other two moved cautiously through the trees on either side of the road to ensure that they weren't about to be ambushed. Normally traders would travel these roads in a group for greater safety but Wynnstan knew that their pretence to be merchants wouldn't last long if they joined proper traders.

They reached the horse farm without incident and Wynnstan managed to purchase four riding horses. They were all mares and compared unfavourably to the stallions they were used to riding in Mercia. To make matters worse their owner had demanded far more than they were worth but at least they were all mounted now.

The detour to the horse farm had taken them out of their way and so they were still fifteen miles from their destination when darkness fell and they made camp for the night. Thankfully the rain had let up but dark clouds obscured the moon.

As there were only four of them, Wynnstan took his turn as sentry and, having relieved Wardric, he took his post standing behind a large tree. He was practically invisible in the darkness. The fact that he could see little, and certainly nothing the other side of the tree, didn't matter. He relied on his ears to warn him of danger.

Being a woodsman since he was a young boy, he ignored the scuttling of small animals and other natural sounds made by nocturnal creatures. He enjoyed these moments of solitude in the middle of the night and allowed himself time for reflection. He knew how fortunate he'd been to join Æthelstan's gesith, let alone become its captain. Given his lowly birth there was no way that he could have become the right hand man of an ætheling. Normally the companions of a son of the king would be the relatives of ealdormen and rich thegns. However, Æthelstan's status as an ætheling was debateable. His aunt treated him as if he was Eadweard's legitimate first-born son but it was a claim repudiated by Eadweard and his wife - the ambitious Ælfflæd – who kept alive the fiction that Æthelstan was a bastard. Everyone was well aware that she would do everything in her power to ensure that her eldest son, Ælfweard, became king after Eadweard.

Now that she had produced a daughter as well and was said to be pregnant again, her influence over Eadweard was increasing and Æthelstan's position was consequently weakened.

His thoughts were interrupted when he heard the unmistakable sound of leaves rustling. It could have been an animal but his instinct told him that a human was close by. He listened intently for further sounds that would help him locate the stranger but there were no more sounds for a while. Then he heard another sound. Someone had brushed past a bush and he or she wasn't far away. He waited looking to one side of where he expected whoever it was to appear. It was always easier to spot someone in the darkness using peripheral vision.

A slight figure, almost indistinguishable from the surrounding vegetation, came into sight and crouched down studying the three sleeping figures around the embers of the campfire. Whoever the intruder was he seemed to be alone and he wasn't that old. The figure moved towards where the horses were tethered. One of them whickered softly when it smelt the approaching boy and he froze.

It gave Wynnstan the opportunity to edge closer to him. By the time the boy moved again he was only two yards behind him. When the lad reached the horses they pulled away from him, straining against the ropes that tied them to posts driven into the ground. The intruder stroked the neck of the first horse he came to, whispering softly in its ear. That calmed the animal enough for him to draw his knife and bend down to cut the rope that secured it.

As he did so Wynnstan made his move and brought the pommel of his dagger down on the boy's head. As he did so he sensed a second person behind him and he ducked as a sword whistled over his head. If he hadn't moved so quickly he would have been killed. He rolled on the ground and grabbed his assailant's lower legs, bringing him crashing down and knocking the wind out of him. It was only then that Wynnstan realised that there were several other intruders.

Thankfully his scouts had been awoken by the noise of the scuffle and came running towards him sword in hand. The other robbers took one look and melted back into the trees, leaving Wynnstan free to concentrate on subduing the one who had tried to take his head off. It would have been easy to kill the attacker who had tried to decapitate him whilst he was on the ground but Wynnstan allowed him to regain his feet in the hope that he'd surrender.

However, the outlaw made a wild cut at Wynnstan's chest as he rose up. The latter knocked the rusty sword away with ease and stabbed his opponent in the right arm. It wasn't a deep wound - Wynnstan hadn't intended it to be – but it was enough to make his attacker drop his blade. By this time the other boy had got to his feet groaning and holding his head.

Posting Wardric and Tidhelm to ensure the other robbers didn't return, Sawin and Wynnstan took the other two back to the camp and coaxed the fire into life again. By its light they could see that the two were youths clad in tattered clothes and looking half starved. They looked so similar in appearance that they had to be brothers.

'Are you Danes,' Wynnstan asked the two boys, although they didn't dress like Danes.

The older one just glowered at him but the younger shook his head.

'Angles then?'

The lad nodded.

'What are your names?'

For a moment he didn't think the youngster was going to reply but then, after a nod from the older boy, he did so, albeit reluctantly.

'I'm Eadling and my brother is called Algar.'

Eadling looked at Wynnstan warily before asking 'what are you going to do with us?'

'That rather depends on you. I'm guessing that two boys like you didn't become outlaws out of choice.'

So he told them their tale. Unfortunately, it wasn't that uncommon, even in Mercia. Wynnstan studied Eadling by the light of the flickering flames and liked what he saw.

'Do you know Bardenai?' he asked.

'The old monastery?' the boy replied looking puzzled. 'We know where it is but we haven't been there; there's no reason to. It's just ruins. We do know the area though.'

'Could you guide us there avoiding the road and Danish settlements?'

'Of course, but why? There's nothing there.'

'That's not your concern. Just do as I ask and I'll spare your lives. However, I'm not so foolish as to trust you so your brother will remain bound and tied across one of the packhorses. If you even think about betraying us he dies. Understood?'

Eadling looked at Algar but his brother was looking at the ground sulkily and evidently wasn't going to reply. The younger boy regarded Wynnstan thoughtfully, wondering if he could trust his word not to kill them eventually; but then, what other choice did they have? He nodded.

††††

Edith, the daughter of the late ætheling Æðelwold and Ecgwynna, was now six. She knew nothing except life in the convent where her mother was a nun until a messenger arrived. Now she was to leave her mother and join her aunt, the redoubtable Lady Æthelflæd of the Mercians, and the lady's nephew, Æthelstan, who it seemed was her half-brother. She hadn't known that she had any other family and initially it was all rather unsettling. However, the more she thought about it the more excited she became.

The messenger introduced himself as Deorwine and introduced Edith to Cuthfleda who would look after the little girl during the long journey back to Glowecestre.

285

Edith couldn't understand why she was suddenly being uprooted and parted from her mother but it was Ecgwynna who had arranged for her daughter to be fostered by Æthelflæd. She had known for some months that she was dying of the wasting sickness and, quite apart from sparing her daughter the agony of watching her mother's health deteriorate, she was anxious to make arrangements for her future. Of course, Edith could have always become a nun but she was an adventurous child - much like her half-brother - and Ecgwynna was realistic enough to realise that the cloistered life wouldn't suit her daughter.

For his part, the discovery that he had a sister had surprised Æthelstan and he was curious about her. He prayed that she wasn't going to be as vapid and self-centred as his cousin Ælfwynn. A year ago there had been some talk of a betrothal between the two of them but Ælfwynn had been as opposed to the idea just as much as he was and the idea had been dropped.

When Edith arrived her brother was delighted to find that she was nothing like Ælfwynn. Even at six, she was a witty companion and had an intellect that promised to be as clever as her brother's. The two siblings got on from the start. Of course, Æthelstan had been well aware that he also had a half-brother and another half-sister in Wessex but he regarded them as impediments to his rightful inheritance, not relatives.

Æthelflæd had always been like a mother to him but he had always wanted a sibling to make him feel as if he was part of a proper family. Now he had his sister he felt more complete, especially as she looked up to him in a way that massaged his ego. He thanked God for sending him Edith.

The only cloud on his personal horizon now was his concern for Wynnstan's safe return.

Chapter Fifteen

Late Spring 909

The two Northumbrian boys seemed to be cooperating but Wynnstan had learned long ago that appearances can be deceptive. He therefore continued to keep the older boy bound to his horse during the day and tied the two brothers up at night. He knew that they resented this, especially Algar. During the day when Eadling led the way under the watchful eye of his scouts he had no sense that the boy was looking for a way to betray him but at night he heard the two of them whispering together and he suspected that they were plotting something.

After two days of circuitously approaching Bardenai Eadling told him that they were close to their destination. They had encountered nobody on the way there but then they had been following paths made by animals and little used pathways.

'What happens to us now, lord?' Eadling asked him nervously.

Wynnstan was conscious that Algar was watching the pair of them and could sense his animosity. No doubt he feared that Wynnstan would dispose of them now that their usefulness was at an end. However, finding the ruined monastery was only part of the task. Even if the relics were still there, he and his companions still had to get back to Mercia. He hadn't yet decided how best to do that.

They could return to Malberthorp and seek passage on a merchantman heading south or they could try and make it overland. Both alternatives held risks. If he opted to travel back to Malberthorp he would need the services of the young outlaw as a guide but if they headed south on land the two brothers wouldn't be of any use once they left the area that they were familiar with.

He had a feeling that he could trust Eadling and he had the makings of a good woodsman. He would be prepared to recruit him as a scout after they returned to Mercia but the problem was Algar. He didn't like the older boy and he didn't trust him. His instincts about people were seldom wrong. Ideally he would dispense with his services now but there were two problems with that. He didn't think Eadling would want to be parted from his sibling and, more importantly, Algar could betray them hoping for a reward as soon as he was released. He decided to temporise.

'I haven't decided but I'll probably want to keep you both with us for now. When I do let you go I'll reward you for your help.'

Eadling nodded thoughtfully and went over to speak to his brother. Wynnstan could see that they were arguing but they were doing so quietly and he couldn't hear what it was about.

'I don't trust them,' Sawin told him quietly later that evening. 'They're plotting something.'

'Yes, I know but what? We still need them for now so we'll just have to keep a close eye on them.'

The next day they broke camp before the early morning mist had cleared and set off on the last mile to their destination. The wood took on an eerie stillness, the trees looming out of the gloom looking bigger than they were in reality and the normal sounds of birds and small animals were blanketed by the fog.

Wynnstan was worried in case Eadling got lost but the boy seemed to know where he was going. He could have waited for the mist to burn off but he wanted to reach the place early. It was said to be deserted but he couldn't be certain that was the case. They therefore approached with the utmost caution.

One minute they were in open ground surrounded by nothing but impenetrable whiteness and the next buildings loomed out of the gloom. The huts in which the monks had lived were no more than burnt out shells but the small stone church had more or less survived. The thatched roof was gone and only charred rafters remained but the walls still stood.

As they entered, the peaceful atmosphere was disturbed by birds taking to the air on panicked wings. Leaving Wardric and Sawin to watch the door and the two outlaws, Wynnstan and Tidhelm made their way to the stone table that had served as the altar. Someone had tried to smash it up but had only succeeded in breaking off a corner of the top. According to Æthelflæd's information Saint Oswald's remains were hidden under a flagstone behind it.

Someone had been there before them. The roughly hewn stone flags had been lifted and cast aside. There were piles of earth beside numerous holes in the soil where looters had searched the area in the hope of finding buried treasure. He couldn't imagine that the heathen Danes had been searching for Oswald's bones.

290

He looked around in despair and then he noticed a coffer in a corner. It had been smashed open and then discarded. Scattered around it were several bones. One looked like a thigh bone and others were from an arm and a hand. However, the most important was the skull. Many religious sites boasted that they had parts of Oswald's skeleton but only Bardenai was said to have his skull. The jaw was missing but otherwise it was intact.

Tidhelm rushed outside to the horses and came back with a leather sack into which he and Wynnstan reverently loaded the bones and the skull. Satisfied that they had collected all that there was, the two returned to join the others.

'Quiet, captain,' Sawin whispered, putting a restraining hand on Wynnstan's arm as he emerged from the church. 'Danes.'

The mist was clearing a little but not enough to see any distance. However, they could hear the sound of hooves on the hard earth and the distinctive noise made by men riding in chainmail. Everyone remained stock still not making a sound; everyone that is except Algar.

'Over here,' he called out suddenly in Danish. 'There are armed Mercians outside the old church. Rescue us before they kill us.'

†††

Æthelflæd did her best to look pleased at the progress her husband was making with his recovery. After being bedridden for so long his muscles were wasted and, although he felt stronger every day, he could only move about with the aid of a stick and the shoulder of one of his gesith to lean on.

She found it galling to resume her role as consort after governing Anglian Mercia for so long. Æðelred had been consulted, as was his right, when he'd been lucid but there was little in practical terms that he could do to interfere from his bed. Now that he was able to sit in a chair and preside over the regular meetings of the inner council and the occasional assembly of the Witenaġemot things were very different.

She knew that he hadn't approved of her choice of Deorwine as Ealdorman of Hwicce but what she hadn't expected was his resolve to remove him. He had informed her of his decision prior to raising it at the Witenaġemot and she had been appalled. Not only was it unfair to Deorwine, who had been doing an excellent job as ealdorman, but it would enrage Cuthfleda.

It wasn't as if she could restore Deorwine to his position as her captain. That wouldn't have been fair on Acwel but in any case even he was to be demoted. Æðelred had decided, as once before, that his wife didn't need a separate warband of hearth warriors. They would be merged with his and he would provide her with an escort when necessary.

'The other ealdormen won't approve of your proposal to take Hwicce away from Deorwine,' she said in a last attempt to get Æðelred to change his mind.

'Ah, but I'm not. I agree that my nobles would become unsettled if I merely demoted one of their number but I have a legitimate reason for doing so. Hwicce was once a kingdom before it became a shire within Mercia and it remains by far the most powerful part of my territory. I've decided that it would be better - and more equable to the other ealdormen who govern much smaller areas – to divide it into three new shires.'

'Divide and conquer, you mean' she muttered under her breath.

'Which are these new shires to be, lord?' she asked out loud.

'Glowecestre will remain the centre of a smaller shire consisting of the southern part of Hwicce. The northern part will be divided into two, one shire centred on Wirecestre and the other around Waruwic.'

'Waruwic? But that's only a small settlement, and one that is close to the border with the Danelaw.'

'Which is why it needs expanding and turning into a burh on the pattern developed by Wessex.'

'Surely the Danes will see that as provocative.'

'Precisely. Your brother had encouraged me to do just that. He feels strong enough to start to expand into the territory captured from us during your father's time as king but he needs an excuse.'

'He hasn't shared any of this with me,' she exclaimed, surprised by this revelation.

'Why should he? His emissary came to me, the Lord of Mercia, not my wife,' he said scornfully.

She thought it more likely that on arrival at the Mercian capital the emissary had intended to speak to

293

her but had been intercepted and shown into Æðelred's presence. It could hardly be otherwise. Her husband's recovery was too recent for tidings of it to have reached Wintanceaster yet.

Like her brother, she was keen to embark on the re-conquest of that part of Mercia controlled by the Danes, especially as they were divided with no one able to unite them at the moment. However, her infirm husband was hardly the man to lead the Mercian army into battle.

'If you are intent on pursuing this course of action you need to appoint a Hereræswa. What better man for the role than Deorwine?'

Æðelred's first reaction was to dismiss the idea out of hand but he hesitated. It was true he did need someone to command the army and Deorwine would normally be a strong candidate. The problem was the man and his wife were loyal to Æthelflæd, rather than to him. However, the appointment would be acceptable to the Witenaġemot and make it easier for them to accept the division of the powerful shire of Hwicce into three.

'I'll think about it,' he said before dismissing her.

†††

'We need to get out of here,' Tidhelm yelled as he saw the figure of a mounted Dane materialise out of the thinning mist. Wynnstan paused only to cut the treacherous boy's throat before following Tidhelm into the cluster of burnt out huts around the church. Wardric ran after them a moment later dragging

Eadling with him, his seax pressed against the boy's side to ensure his silence.

'Where's Sawin?' Wynnstan asked once they were in the woods and clear of the Danes who were scouring the settlement for them.

'I don't know,' Tidhelm said with a frown. 'I thought he was behind me.'

'Damn; they must have captured him and, nearly as bad, they have our horses,' Wynnstan said with a curse.

'At least we are armed and still have the saint's relics,' Tidhelm said, holding up the leather sack.

'Not much good without the means of escaping Northumbria and returning to Mercia,' Wardric muttered.

'Right, we need to follow those Danes when they leave.'

'But we're on foot and they're mounted,' Wardric pointed out.

'They're probably going at walking pace and, if we hide our byrnies and helmets here to lighten our load, we shouldn't have any problem tracking them.'

'What about him?' Wardric said, pointing at Eadling who was sobbing over the death of his brother.

Wynnstan thought for a minute before addressing the weeping boy.

'You have a choice. You can join your brother in Hell,' he said brutally, 'or you can give me your oath and join us. However, one step out of line and you're dead. Understand?'

The boy wiped the tears away with a filthy sleeve and made an effort to pull himself together.

'Yes, lord. My brother was an impetuous fool and it often got him into trouble. I'll miss him dreadfully but I cannot blame you for killing him.'

The boy took a deep breath and Wynnstan knew instinctively that what he was about to say was spoken with reluctance.

'I'm all alone in the world now and, if you'll give me food and your protection, I'll become your sworn man; if you'll have me that is.'

'I'm not a lord; you call me captain. I've said that I'll give you the opportunity to prove your loyalty but there'll be no second chances. Right, enough talking; let's move.'

It wasn't difficult to find where the Danes had camped for the night. They had stuck to the main road through the woods and, as darkness descended, the faint flicker from a couple of fires was visible in the trees off to the right. Wynnstan left the others and crept forward until he could see the campsite more clearly. At first he couldn't locate Sawin and he worried that they had killed him but then he saw him sitting in the shadow of a tree to which he was tied. It was too dark to see if he was injured but he moved his legs and so at least he was alive and conscious.

He counted some thirty Danes – far too many for comfort. He waited until he was certain that they hadn't bothered to post any sentries before making his way back to the others.

'Sawin is tied to a tree to the north of their campsite and our horses are tethered to the east of it, together with theirs. I'm going to cut Sawin free and, hoping that he's able to walk, we'll make our way to the horse lines where we'll meet you. As the horses are all tied to a long rope line it shouldn't be too difficult to undo the ends of the rope and lead them away. Once clear, we can select the best animals for ourselves and a couple of packhorses for our kit and scatter the rest. All happy?'

'What happens if he's been beaten and can't walk?' Wardric asked with a frown.

'Then I'll have to carry him,' Wynnstan snapped impatiently.

'Wouldn't it be better if one of us came with you?' the boy persisted.

Wynnstan didn't reply for a moment. He wanted the two of them to stay with Eadling just in case his oath of loyalty proved to be worthless. After all, his brother had obviously thought he could gain favour with the Danes by betraying their presence. He glanced at the Northumbrian lad. His instinct was to trust him and he decided that he should go with his gut feeling.

'Very well, you can come with me; Tidhelm you and Eadling go to the horses and wait for us there. Good, let's go.'

The moon put in infrequent appearances through the patchy cloud cover. However, even when it did illuminate the sky, the new leaves on the trees prevented too much light reaching the ground over which the small group made their cautious way. After a while they were guided by the glow given off by the Danes' dying campfires otherwise they might well have missed their way. Travelling at night through

297

dense woodlands was never easy, even for a skilled tracker like Wynnstan.

When they neared the camp they split into pairs. Eadling might not be a trained scout but he had learned to move silently during his time as an outlaw. At each step he moved his leading foot around to make sure he wasn't about to step on a dry twig. The sound of one breaking with a sharp crack could alert an experienced warrior, even if he were asleep.

Wynnstan reached Sawin and put his hand over his mouth to stop him making a sound as he woke him. At the same time Wardric cut the ropes around his chest that bound him to the tree. Seconds later he sawed through those that tied his hands together.

'The bastards broke my leg so that I couldn't run away,' Sawin wheezed in pain when Wynnstan took his hand away.

It was obvious that even carrying him would be impossible in his present condition. However hard he tried, Sawin would cry out in agony with every step.

'Keep an eye on the Danes,' Wynnstan whispered in Wardric's ear as he cast around for some wood to use as splints.

It took him ten minutes before they were ready to move. He'd got Sawin to bite down on his own belt and gagged him with a piece of cloth torn from his tunic to make sure he didn't cry out. Then he splinted the broken tibia as best he could before hoisting Sawin onto his back.

Wardric went ahead carefully moving anything out of the way that might trip Wynnstan up or make a noise. At one point they froze when one of the Danes got up and went for a piss at the edge of the clearing not ten yards from where they were standing. Thankfully he didn't detect their presence and stumbled back to his blanket none the wiser.

Their progress was painstakingly slow and Tidhelm was panicking by the time that they reached him. As they approached the horses a number started to whinny and neigh. Wynnstan could hear the sounds of several Danes getting up and making their way towards them to investigate. Hopefully, they thought that the horses were just reacting to the presence of foxes or other animals. That seemed likely as they were walking towards them, not running.

'The rope ends are undone,' Tidhelm said in a horse whisper.

Wynstann hoisted the injured Sawin onto the bare back of the nearest horse and, pulling the whole herd with them by the ends of the rope to which their halters were tied, he and Tidhelm led them into the woods.

The moon chose that time to put in one of its sporadic appearances and it bathed the clearing in its soft silvery glow. The Danes could see their horses being stolen and, with shouts of rage, they charged after them.

There had been no time to retrieve their saddles but thankfully Wardric had the presence of mind to pick up the bales of cloth which had been offloaded from the pack animals and left lying on the ground. Tidhelm threw one to Eadling and picked up the other, still clutching the leather sack containing Saint Oswald's bones, before darting after the others.

Wynnstan tugged at one end of the rope urging the reluctant horses to a faster pace but he could clearly hear the Danes gaining on them. Thankfully the moon disappeared behind a dark cloud again and darkness descended once more.

'Stay still!' Wynnstan hissed at the others after heading off at right angles to their previous direction.

In the intense darkness the only clue the Danes had was sound. Wynnstan was frightened that one of the horses would make a noise and betray their whereabouts but they remained quiet, content to munch at the new grass at their feet. The Danes could be heard blundering about less than a hundred yards away but the sound faded away as they continued to head in the original direction taken by Wynnstan and his companions.

It wouldn't be long before the Danes realised that they were chasing shadows so they quickly selected a horse each and another to carry the bolts of cloth. They would have to ride bareback but that couldn't be helped. After leading the rest of the horses further into the woods they tied the ends of the rope to two trees. By now they could hear the Danes retracing their steps and they lost no time in riding away. Half an hour later they had retrieved their byrnies and other discarded equipment and were heading east to put as much distance between themselves and the Danes as possible.

They kept going through the night. It wouldn't take the enemy long to find their horses in daylight, if they hadn't already done so, and therefore Wynnstan led them away from the road and along a stream to cover their tracks. After that Eadling took over as their guide and they headed into the hilly country known as the Wolds.

When they camped that night Wynnstan took off the temporary splint on Sawin's leg and reset the bone so that it would mend properly. The boy fainted with the pain and remained unconscious for the rest of the night so it wasn't until they broke camp at dawn the next day that he told Wynnstan what he'd overheard the Danes discussing.

'The three brothers who rule Northumbria jointly have recently been reinforced by more Norsemen from Dyflin,' he said through teeth gritted against the pain from his broken leg. 'As a result they feel strong enough to invade Mercia. Some Danes in the other parts of the Danelaw are willing to join them and so they intend to try and push their southern border down to the River Temes.'

Sawin's statement was greeted by stunned silence. Not only would their part of Mercia lose its independence but, once the three Norse Kings of Northumbria - Ingwær, Eowils and Halfdan – ruled all of the land between the Temes in the south and the Tes in the north, Wessex stood little chance of surviving as the sole remaining Anglo-Saxon kingdom.

Chapter Sixteen

Summer and Autumn 909

'So all you have to support this supposed plot by the Northumbrian kings is some Danish tittle tattle overheard whilst your scout was delirious having had his leg broken?' Æðelred asked incredulously. 'If I went to King Eadweard with this tale and put Mercia on a war footing I would look like the biggest fool in Christendom.'

Wynnstan squirmed uncomfortably as he suffered Æðelred's ridicule in silence. He'd made his report and there was nothing further he could say. He was dismissed and left the hall feeling angry and humiliated. The Lord of Mercia hadn't even congratulated him on the safe retrieval of Saint Oswald's relics.

He paused outside the hall, unsure where he should report next. As the Lady Æthelflæd had sent him on the mission he had intended to go to her hall first but Æðelred's chamberlain had intercepted him en route and told him to report to his master. Now he debated whether to go and see her next, go to the hall occupied by the Ealdorman of Hwicce and see his wife, something he wasn't sure he wanted to do straight away, or go and let Æthelstan know of his return. In the end the decision was taken out of his hands.

Astrid came running across the courtyard towards him, her beaming face banishing any doubts he might have had about a frosty reception. Really she shouldn't be running he thought, noticing the size of her belly which made her haste more than a little ungainly.

'Husband, you're back safely,' she cried, throwing her arms around him and giving him a kiss on the cheek in front of the grinning sentries on the gate.

'Hush, Astrid; everyone is looking at us.'

His wife had the grace to blush but her exuberance at seeing him again was undiminished and she dragged him off towards their hut.

'I want to know all about it. The rumour is that you've brought back Saint Oswald's relics,' she chattered.

He stopped suddenly, reminded that Tidhelm was waiting for him with the leather sack containing the precious bones. On arrival back at Glowecestre they had taken Sawin straight to the monastery so that the infirmarian could check his leg. Wardric had stayed with him whilst the others had made their way to what was now being called the palace where both Æðelred and Æthelflæd had their private chambers. He'd left Tidhelm and Eadling near the gate when the chamberlain had intercepted him.

'That may have to wait,' he told her, stopping suddenly. 'There's someone I want you to meet.'

During the thankfully uneventful return from Malberthorp by sea he'd got to know Eadling and the more time he spent with him the more he liked him. He'd bought the boy new clothes in Malberthorp

303

before embarking on a knarr heading for Lundenburg and, with proper food, the boy had begun to fill out. He still looked as thin as a rake but the gaunt look caused by hunger had gone.

Wynnstan had never had a body servant, although as a captain he was entitled to one, and so he offered Eadling the job. He would still train as a scout but, as a member of his household, he hoped that it would be better for the boy than living in the warriors' hall. Eadling had been grateful, even though it was still a servant's post when all was said and done. Wynnstan suspected that to some extent the boy saw him as a replacement for his elder brother.

'This is Eadling, who has become my body servant. Eadling, this is my wife and your mistress, Astrid.'

Astrid took one look at the nervous waif and took pity on him.

'Welcome Eadling. It's about time my husband had someone else to look after him instead of relying on me the whole time,' she said, giving him a broad smile.

'I'll see you later, wife. Tidhelm and I should report to the Lady Æthelflæd then I must go and see Lord Æthelstan.'

She nodded and took Eadling under her wing like a mother hen as the two made their way out of the gates towards her hut.

The reception he received from Æthelflæd was in marked contrast to her husband's. She was full of gratitude for the retrieval of the saint's relics and pressed a bulging purse on him. Tidhelm smiled broadly as he handed over the precious leather bag knowing that he and the others would get a share of Wynnstan's reward.

Æthelflæd wasn't dismissive of what Sawin had overheard either. Unbeknownst to her husband, she had several agents in both the Danelaw and in Eforwic, which the Vikings called Yorvik. They too had reported that the Norse kings were gathering men but they didn't know to what purpose.

'I'll write to King Eadweard again. This supports what we already suspect. We didn't know where they intended to strike but this indicates that it's probably into Mercia. My husband refuses to believe that there is any threat, which will make it difficult for us to prepare for an invasion.'

She banged her hand on the table in frustration.

'I shouldn't wish illness on anyone but now would be a good time for my husband to have another relapse.'

She gave Wynnstan a penetrating stare.

'I know you have more sense than to repeat that. Please would you go and find my nephew and tell him I'd be grateful if he could attend me as soon as convenient. Come with him,' she added. 'We need to decide what to do now.'

†††

'What do you mean by writing to Eadweard behind my back?' Æðelred stormed at his wife. 'He wants me to assemble an army and join him in an invasion of Northumbria. This is plain madness and your interference in matters that don't concern you are to blame. No doubt Cuthfleda and your damned nephew are in the plot too. Well, you are all to be arrested as traitors.'

Æthelflæd stepped back, not because she was afraid of Æðelred but to avoid the foaming spittle that shot out of his furious mouth.

'Calm yourself husband,' she replied soothingly. 'You don't want to bring on another of your attacks, do you?'

'Oh, you'd like that wouldn't you? Then you could take over Mercia again. Well, no more. I've decided to make Bishop Wirfrith my regent if I ever fall ill again.'

'Wirfrith? What does he know about warfare, or how to govern come to that? Besides, he's old and frail now.'

Then a thought occurred to her.

'Has this been put to the Witenaġemot? If so, I've not heard of it.'

'No. I'm calling a meeting at the end of the month to implement my plan to split Hwicce into three and to discuss our response to Eadweard's demands. It's time your brother learned that Mercia is not part of Wessex. I'm fed up with him treating me as some sort of vassal.'

'But you are. There is a treaty between Wessex and Mercia that obliges us to support him when required and, in return, my brother will come to our aid when necessary. The treaty made it clear that Mercia is the junior party in this alliance.'

'Damn the bloody treaty. The threat is imaginary and, if it isn't, it's Wessex they'll invade, not Mercia.'

'That's not what we've discovered. The target is definitely Mercia. That would put the Vikings all along the north bank of the Temes. It's obvious when you think about it. They'll want to consolidate their hold on Mercia before embarking on any attack into Wessex. They've invaded and lost too many times in the past not to eliminate the threat to their west first.'

'We've learned? What do you mean *we*? I assume that Eadweard has agents in the Danelaw but we implies that you do as well.'

'Of course, it's the job of any ruler to know what his potential enemies are up to.'

'You've set up a network of spies without my permission?' he said incredulously.

'You were ill, lord. I thought it was sensible to do so to protect the interests of Mercia.'

'That's for me to decide, not you. You'll hand over details of all these agents to me immediately and confine yourself to your bedchamber. You aren't to leave it for any reason, do you understand? I'll confine Deorwine, Cuthfleda and Æthelstan as well, just in case they try something stupid.'

'You are making the biggest mistake of your life,' she warned him, her eyes flashing dangerously. 'What do you think Eadweard will do when he finds out?'

'Do? He'll do nothing. I rule in Mercia, not him.'

'If you think that, husband dear, you're an even bigger fool than I thought you were.'

†††

The Witenaġemot was in uproar. Far from supporting Æðelred, many of his ealdormen and thegns openly told him that he was wrong to imprison his wife, and mad not to join Eadweard in a pre-emptive attack on Northumbria. It was plain that many saw inaction as condemning Mercia to an invasion they would have to face on their own. Some even advocated approaching the Welsh to make common cause against the Vikings.

It was whilst Bishop Wirfrith, who was presiding, was trying to restore order that a harassed looking sentry came running into the hall.

'Lord, King Eadweard is at the gates,' he cried out above the din.

Immediately the hall fell silent.

'What!' Æðelred boomed, his furious face turning a vivid shade of red. 'Has he brought his army to invade Mercia?'

'Nnno, lord,' the man stuttered. 'Just his gesith.'

'Hadn't we better see what he wants, lord,' Deorwine said calmly.

He was no longer an ealdorman. At the meeting of the Witenaġemot the nobles and senior churchmen had supported the division of Hwicce into three new shires – especially the Ealdorman of Herefordscīr across the Sæfern from Hwicce who had long been jealous of his neighbour's wealth and power. However, they had insisted on making Deorwine the Hereræswa of Mercia, despite Æðelred's objections. That made him the second most important person in the hall.

For a moment it looked as if Æðelred would let his rage overcome his common sense, then he relaxed.

'Open the gates. I'd better go and see what he wants.'

If Æðelred was prone to hot anger, Eadweard's wrath was ice cold. He ignored Æðelred's false words of welcome and strode into the palace complex before telling a bemused servant to go and fetch his sister.

'Is there somewhere that the three of us can talk in private,' he demanded curtly, addressing Æðelred for the first time.

The latter was cowed by the king's presence and by his domineering personality. Gone were Æðelred's pompous claims not to be a vassal. It was clear to all exactly what the relationship between the two men was. Eadweard didn't need an army at his back. He probably didn't even need his gesith. He could have ridden into Glowecestre on his own and taken command.

'Sister, it's good to see you again. I trust that you're well, despite being imprisoned against your will?' Eadweard said, with an angry glance at her husband.

'Greetings brother; yes, I've been well treated during my captivity, thank you.'

'I've not come just to release you from incarceration, although I couldn't have allowed that to continue, of course. My main reason for visiting is to find out why Mercia has made no preparations for the invasion of Northumbria, or do you want to lose your land and turn your people into thralls, Æðelred.'

'I've seen no evidence that the Danes intend to attack us, Eadweard,' Æðelred retorted, displaying some of his former belligerence. 'Are you sure that this isn't a fabrication to give you an excuse to invade them?'

'You have my word that it is so; is that not good enough for you? I understand that you've been ill for a long time. Perhaps you're still suffering from paralysis of the brain?' he suggested with a chilling smile.

'I'm perfectly well, Eadweard, thank you.'

'I can't recall giving you permission to address me by name, Lord Æðelred. My title is cyning; please use it.'

Æðelred opened and closed his mouth like a fish, his face turning red once more.

'Very well, cyning,' he said at last, making it sound like an insult.

'Good. Well you had better tell your servants to pack.'

'Pack, er cyning?'

'Yes, I'm desirous of your company on my journey to the muster point at Scirburne. My sister and your hereræswa are more than capable of mobilising your nobles and the fyrd, I'm sure. They are to meet us at Evesham on our way north through Mercia to attack Northumbria from the west.'

☩☩☩

Æthelstan rode towards Evesham with Wynnstan by his side feeling nervous at the prospect of meeting his father. When he was a boy Eadweard had wanted his first-born son to become a monk. Had he done so there would have been no prospect of him becoming the heir to the throne of Wessex, which had obviously been Eadweard's intention. He wanted no challenger to the æthelings born to his second wife.

Although he was always presented to the world as a bastard, Æthelstan was well aware that Abbot Æscwin held the original marriage certificate between Eadweard and Ecgwynna safe in his coffers in Cæstir. Knowing that he was legitimate only served to stoke his anger with his father. Now that he was legally an adult Eadweard could no longer force him to become a monk but he worried that his father might exile him or find some other way of removing him as a threat to his sons by his second wife - Ælfweard and the newly-born Edwin.

He needn't have worried. When Æthelflæd introduced him to Eadweard the latter looked startled at first. Doubtless he hadn't expected to be confronted by a tall, muscular young man who looked several years older than his actual age of nineteen. Æthelflæd smiled to herself; there was no doubt that the king was impressed by his eldest son. He looked every inch the warrior and carried himself like the ætheling he was.

Eadweard surprised everyone present by gripping his estranged son's shoulders and giving him the kiss of kinship on his cheek.

'Let's hope you fight as well as I'm told,' were the only words Eadweard addressed to his son but Æthelstan had been publicly acknowledged by his father and that would suffice for now.

311

He smiled to himself when he thought how furious the Lady Ælfflæd would be when she heard.

The combined armies of Wessex and Mercia totalled some four thousand men. Had he chosen to, Eadweard could have carved a path north through the Danelaw to Northumbria with such a force but his intention was to dissuade the three kings of Northumbria from flexing their muscles, not antagonise the Danes in the Five Boroughs and along the north bank of the Temes.

It meant that Mercia had to find provisions for the host; the alternative would have been to allow them to forage. Wessex and Mercia were long standing rivals who'd vied for supremacy in the land of the Anglo-Saxons – now coming to be called Englaland - and only the invasion of the Great Heathen Army half a century ago had united them in a common cause. Consequently the West Saxons would have had no qualms about raiding and pillaging their way north given half an excuse to do so.

When they reached Cæstir Ywer and the fyrd of his shire joined the army, including the Norsemen of Wirhealum under Skarde's leadership. Eadweard was all for striking across the River Mæresēa and devastating the lands of the Northumbrian Norsemen before swinging eastwards and heading for the Viking capital which they called Yorvik. However, Ywer had persuaded his father-in-law to bring the Norsemen who lived there to join him. As he pointed out to Eadweard, he could hardly start by attacking his allies.

Instead the mighty host headed along the south bank of the Mǽresēa towards Mamecestre.

Although the Norse who had settled along the west coast of Northumbria owed nominal allegiance to the brothers - Ingwær, Eowils and Halfdan – who ruled in Jorvik, the easternmost stronghold of the three kings was in reality Mamecestre which had been a Roman fort centuries ago. Eadweard had no intention of getting bogged down in a siege; his intention was to ravage the land and kill as many Northumbrian Danes and Norsemen as he could. That way he hoped to disrupt their plans to invade Mercia and ultimately Wessex. However, when he arrived the Dane who called himself the Hold of Mamecestre came out and surrendered his stronghold to Eadweard.

'This is a great opportunity to establish a fortress to protect Cæstirscīr from the Northumbrians,' Æthelflæd told the war council that evening.

'Who do you have in mind to command it?' Eadweard asked after nodding his agreement to the proposal.

'I thought perhaps your son Æthelstan?' she suggested.

It wasn't that she wanted to give her nephew what might prove to be a dangerous appointment but she was mindful that Ælfflæd would have been alarmed by Eadweard's recognition of his son. At least he should be well out of the way of her possible vengeance at the furthest extremity of Mercia.

Wynnstan was dismayed when he heard. Æthelstan was a bachelor and showed no inclination

313

to get married as yet but Wynnstan had a family and he'd be stranded hundreds of miles away from them. Besides, Astrid hadn't yet been delivered of their baby and he'd promised to be back in Glowecestre in time for the birth.

However, as Æthelstan's captain he had no option but to stay by his side in the former Northumbrian stronghold. He stood beside his lord on the ramparts to watch Eadweard and Æthelflæd's army march away to the east. It took some time for the thousands of warriors to disappear over the horizon. Several groups of mounted warriors rode away from the main column as they marched, some were scouts but the larger groups were forage parties. Now Mercia was free of the burden to feed the host, they would need to raid for food as they carved their way through Northumbria.

†††

Halfdan glared at his two brothers. Each ruled a different part of Northumbria but it was Halfdan's realm through which the Ænglisc horde were pillaging their way at the moment.

'We are unprepared to meet them in the field,' Eowils insisted. 'We haven't yet mustered enough of our own men, let alone called on our friends in East Anglia and the Five Boroughs to join us.'

'Then we must abandon Yorvik and retreat to the north to give us time to assemble an army strong enough to oppose them,' Ingwær stated.

'You seem very happy to surrender my lands to the bastards whilst gathering our forces to defend yours,' Eowils sneered.

Whilst Halfdan ruled the eastern part of what used to be called Deira, Ingwær had taken the western half together with Lindsay south of the Humbre. That left the wild moorland region as far north as the River Tes for the youngest of the brothers – Eowils.

Despite his brother's objections Ingwær did have a point. The terrain was ideal for small groups of Vikings to make a series of pinprick attacks against the invaders. The region was largely uninhabited with few large settlements; should Eadweard be foolish enough to pursue the Vikings that far, the enemy might well be able to force him to make a humiliating withdrawal. However, Halfdan didn't agree.

'We cannot abandon Yorvik. Ever since Ragnar's sons captured it the place has been our most important settlement and stronghold,' he maintained. 'Our men would never forgive us; we'd lose their support and perhaps even our lives.'

Viking leaders had often been killed in the past after they'd lost the confidence of their men.

'What do you suggest we do then? Ingwær demanded. 'Fight a pitched battle which we're bound to lose?'

'No, withdraw behind Yorvik's strong walls and challenge Eadweard to do his worst,' Halfdan said.

'But it's harvest time,' Ingwær said with concern. 'We sit here like trapped rats whilst they eat our winter grain.'

'Not if we gather what we can now and burn the rest in the fields,' Halfdan said grimly.

As Eadweard marched eastwards he was confronted by smouldering fields and a land bereft of people and livestock. He glared impotently at the walls of Yorvik when he got there and gave in to the demands of his men to return home; they had their own crops to harvest. By the middle of September he was back in Wessex wondering what exactly he'd achieved.

Meanwhile in the outpost that was Mamecestre Æthelstan gathered in stores for the coming winter and waited for the inevitable attack by the Northumbrians.

Chapter Seventeen

Early 910

Winter had been unusually cold and snow had blanketed the ground for much of the time between Yuletide and the middle of March when a thaw eventually set in. As the accumulated snow melted, the land became flooded and travel was impossible. Stocks of food in Mamecestre were running low, as they were elsewhere, and Æthelstan worried about supplies in case they were besieged.

As soon as the land began to dry out he sent out hunting parties to gather as much meat as possible which was then smoked or salted. Some grain remained in store but not enough to last until the next harvest was in. Life was going to be hard whether or not they were attacked by the Vikings.

The fortress was as well prepared as it could be. During the winter the residents had been far from idle. The Roman fort had been a stone one - as was the case at Cæstir - but many of the sandstone walls had crumbled away over time. Most of them had therefore been repaired with timber with a wooden walkway below the parapet.

Like most Roman forts, there was a double gate in the middle of each wall; one for entry and the other for exiting traffic. These were largely intact and the defenders repaired any damage there was. Three of the gates, whilst still outwardly appearing unchanged and therefore capable of being breached by a battering ram, had in fact also been reinforced behind by a stone wall, as had one of the two remaining double gates, leaving just one access point to the fort.

It had been sited on a bluff by its original builders and that made it difficult to assault except from the east. This meant that the defenders could concentrate their strength there. Wynnstan had supervised the building of a timber tower on each corner where the original Roman stone towers had collapsed. From there the archers could command the approaches to each wall.

The inhabitants had produced barrels full of arrows, spare throwing spears and had placed rocks all along the walkways ready to lob down on those trying to scale the palisade. By the start of May Æthelstan was satisfied that they were as ready as they could be for any attack.

Wynnstan was out hunting with Eadling and Sawin in late May when they spotted a group of Danish mounted scouts. He immediately abandoned all thoughts of hunting and raced back to Mamecestre, sending Sawin off to warn Rinan who patrolled the south coast of the Mæresēa to the west. He in turn would inform Ywer.

Two days later the besiegers set up camp outside the fortress' four gates. There weren't as many as they had expected; no more than five hundred Danes. Æthelstan had his own gesith numbering thirty five, another twenty professional warriors, the watch numbering two score more and the fyrd made up of the freemen of the settlement and the ceorls from the surrounding farmsteads who had taken refuge.

The latter two groups were a mixture of Danes, Northumbria Angles, Norsemen and several of mixed background. He didn't know how far he could trust some of them but even those of Scandinavian origin were Christians and so he hoped their faith was stronger than their Viking heritage.

All told, Æthelstan had some two hundred and fifty men and boys old enough to fight. The problem was that, whilst most of the attackers would be experienced warriors, two thirds of the defenders had some weapon training but no actual battle experience.

The Vikings had split into four groups and camped three hundred yards back from each of the gates, no doubt thinking they had caught the inhabitants by surprise. If they thought that they had prevented Æthelstan from sending for help they were mistaken.

Nothing happened that morning. The Northumbrians were busy setting up their tents, watering their horses and posting pickets to watch the gates. Parties also disappeared into the woods to cut wood and make scaling ladders. Then, just after midday, the first attack came.

The first wave consisted of two hundred who concentrated their attack on the east wall. The first rank held their shields in front of them to protect the second who carried the ladders. Behind them came the men who would be first up onto the parapet. Wynnstan had placed the weakest bowmen on the walkway, siting his best archers in the towers. Their task was to kill the men carrying the ladders.

They had to wait until the ladder carriers were close to the wall where they weren't protected by the shield bearers from the flanks. Once they were able to target them they sent volley after volley their way and killed them in droves. Only those in the centre of the line were safe at first but, as they neared the palisade and erected their ladders they too were exposed. The Vikings had set out with forty ladders but less than half reached the wall.

As the enemy swarmed up them they were hit by more arrows from the towers whilst the defenders hurled down rocks and spears at those climbing towards them. A few did manage to reach the top but not enough to form a bridgehead. The few that did manage to get onto the walkway were swiftly killed and their bodies thrown down onto their comrades. It soon became obvious to the enemy that they were losing men to no good purpose and they beat a hasty retreat leaving the ladders behind.

'How many do you make it?' Æthelstan asked Wynnstan as the two surveyed the carnage in front of the east wall.

'About four score, lord,' the latter replied with a grim smile. 'What about the wounded?'

'Send men out to cut the throats of those near the palisade, otherwise their cries of agony will depress the fyrd. We haven't much alternative but to allow them to collect their dead and wounded further out.'

The Vikings shouted insults and protests as Æthelstan's warriors cut off the cries of the wounded and robbed the bodies of the dead of armour, weapons, silver arm rings and any other valuables. A few brave Vikings, incensed by what was happening, rushed forward to attack the looters but a volley of arrows soon dissuaded them.

As darkness fell Æthelstan felt satisfied at the way the day had gone. The besiegers had lost a sixth of their number whilst his casualties were two dead and three with minor wounds from the brief fight on the walkway. All the same he was puzzled why the Northumbrians had sent so few men to try and retake Mamecestre.

The answer came the next day. Those already besieging the stronghold were merely an advance party. No doubt their leader had thought to gain glory and loot by taking the place before the main body could arrive. If so, he was hardly likely to be popular with whoever was in overall command.

'I make it well over a thousand,' Wynnstan said gloomily.

Æthelstan nodded his agreement, staring at the new arrivals thoughtfully.

'I believe their leader might be Ingwær who calls himself one of the Kings of Northumbria. I've heard that his banner is a white horse's head,' he said pointing towards the black flag with its white embroidery flying outside the largest tent in the camp opposite the east gate.

'Let's hope that Lord Ywer can raise enough men to defeat that lot,' Wynnstan said morosely.

His captain hadn't been in the best of moods ever since they'd taken over the fortress but Æthelstan was well aware of the reason. He was worried about Astrid. She was due to have given birth several months ago but no word had reached them from Glowecestre. The harsh winter had prevented travel, of course, but the roads had been open for a couple of months now. Many women died in childbirth and that thought preyed on Wynnstan's mind. The longer time went by with no news the more convinced he was that she had died and no-one wanted to break the news to him.

He shook himself out of his sombre mood and studied the enemy.

'They're up to something in the woods. Perhaps it's more scaling ladders but I have a feeling that they won't be in a hurry to try a direct assault again. I think it's more likely that they're making a battering ram.'

'If so I pray to God that they use it against any gate except the south one,' Æthelstan replied.

That was the one place where they hadn't constructed a stone wall across one of the gates.

Nothing happened for the rest of the day and Wynnstan returned to the hut which he'd appropriated for his use and which he shared with Eadling and two other servants. Normally the boy would be waiting for him with a tankard of ale and some bread and cheese but there was no sign of him. Instead, the girl who did his laundry brought his ale and the platter with the refreshments.

'Where's Eadling?' he asked with a frown. 'Is he ill?'

The girl looked at the ground unwilling to meet her master's eyes.

'I don't know, lord. He went out sometime this morning and hasn't returned,' she replied hesitantly.

Wynnstan was puzzled. He didn't think the boy would have run off to join the enemy, although he spoke Danish well enough to pass as one. He didn't have time to speculate further as one of his men came to tell him that Lord Æthelstan wanted to see him. Ingwær had approached the palisade with a small party asking to negotiate.

'What do you want Ingwær? Have you come to offer me your surrender?' Æthelstan called down to the rather fat Norseman sitting on a horse that appeared to be suffering under the weight of its rider.

'You address me as konungr,' the fat man replied, using the Norse word for king. 'I'll give you until nightfall to surrender. If you do and promise to pay me a thousand silver pennies as compensation I'll allow you and your warriors to depart in peace. You'll leave your weapons behind, of course.'

'And the inhabitants?' he asked, ignoring the demand that he address Ingwær as konungr.

'They stay so that I can root out the traitors and hang them.'

'You're not considering it, lord?' one of the leading merchants asked him in a panic.

'No, of course not. Quite apart from the fact that I've no intention of abandoning you, the bloody Vikings would slaughter us once we were out in the open and unarmed,' Æthelstan replied quietly before turning back to the Vikings outside the walls.

'That's not acceptable, Ingwær, you've already lost a significant number of your warriors. Try and assault

323

us again and you'll lose a lot more. I suggest you go home with your tail between your legs like the cur that you are.'

'You'll regret that, Æthelstan. I'm going to skin you alive and hang your mangy pelt in my hall.'

'You are in arrow range, Ingwær. You have one minute to get the hell away from here before my archers kill you.'

The defenders cheered as the king turned tail and kicked his reluctant horse into a canter back to his camp.

Two days later the Vikings wheeled their ram towards the east gate. It consisted of a tree trunk some three feet in diameter suspended on several stout ropes in a cage mounted on four pairs of wooden wheels. The cage was roofed in thick timbers to withstand rocks from above and several smaller tree trunks jutted out at right angles to the sides of the cage so that men could propel it forwards.

Warriors with shields did their best to protect those pushing the ram but still a dozen or more were hit and had to be replaced. Eventually the ram reached the gates and the men inside the cage swung the ram to and fro slowly gathering momentum until the pointed end of the ram crashed against the gates.

The timber gates shuddered under the impact as time and time again the ram struck the place where the two gates met. Normally each blow would weaken the baulks of timber used to bar the gates but in this case the gates were held shut by the wall behind them. This was constructed using two skins of stone, each over a foot thick, mortared in place and then the gap between them had been filled with stones and rubble. Repeated blows of a heavy ram could weaken stone walls in time but the timber gates acted as a cushion reducing the impact on the stonework.

'It's time I think,' Æthelstan told Wynnstan who nodded and signalled to four of his men standing on the platform above the gates.

They tipped a large barrel of oil over the edge so that it crashed onto the roof of the ram. The barrel broke on impact, spilling its contents all over the roof. Some oil landed on the gates but that couldn't be helped.

One of the warriors threw a torch down and the oil ignited with a whoosh. In less than a minute the roof was ablaze and, as flaming oil dripped down through the slats of the roof onto the men below, human torches ran away from the ram screaming and beating frantically at their burning clothes and skin.

A few minutes later there was nothing left of the ram except for scorched timbers surrounded by charred corpses. The archers on the palisade had ended the agony of the men who ran away before they burnt to death. The smell of roasting human flesh caused several of those watching to vomit. Æthelstan had hated doing it but he needed to dissuade them from using a ram again as the next time they might attack the one set of gates without a stone wall.

✝✝✝

Eadling stank to high heaven. The only way he could leave the fortress was via the latrines. There was a set of these in the middle of each wall. They protruded so that urine and faeces dropped straight down into a deep pit dug at the base of the palisade. Normally night soil, as it was euphemistically called, would be collected each morning and carted out of the fortress to a midden situated some way away. Obviously this wouldn't be possible during a siege and so Wynnstan had come up with this way of disposing of human waste.

Eadling was slight enough to squeeze through the hole on which posteriors normally sat to relieve themselves and he dropped down into the fetid pit below. He panicked as his head sunk below the surface but he had the presence of mind to close his mouth and stop breathing as he tried to reach the surface. He needn't have worried; when he straightened his legs he found he was only shoulders deep in the filth.

He hauled himself out of the pit and rolled on the ground to try and free himself of most of the muck. It was only when he looked up that he realised that a sentry was staring down at him open mouthed. A second later an archer joined him and hastily strung his bow, thinking he was a spy trying to escape to the Viking camp.

Eadling ran as fast as he could, zigzagging until he reached a dip in the ground out of sight of the archer. Two arrows had come close to hitting him and, as he lay in the depression to get his breath back, he found himself wondering if he'd made a mistake. After a few minutes he crawled away in the direction of a stream hoping that the Vikings hadn't spotted him.

He washed himself as best he could and lay on the bank letting the late May sunshine dry him. Once it was dark he took a long drink, wishing he'd thought to bring some food with him, and set off towards the enemy camp. Thankfully he managed to evade the sentries on the periphery of the camp who were more interested in chatting together than in watching the area between them and the fortress.

Once in the camp he strode purposefully hither and thither listening to what the Vikings, who seemed to be mostly Danes, were saying. He saw a helmet lying outside a tent which someone had recently scrubbed the rust off. He picked it up and carried it around trying to look as if he was a servant who'd scoured it with sand and was now taking it to his master. It seemed to work because no one challenged him.

'When are we going to get out of here and join the rest on the ships?' he overheard one man say as he and his companions sat around a fire eating something out of a cauldron suspended over their fire.

Eadling's stomach rumbled with hunger but he ignored it.

'I've heard that twenty more longships have come from Man and Íralond to join us. With the ships we're building that'll give us a fleet of two hundred or more, enough to defeat the poxy Mercians at any rate.'

'Aye, but the Cumbrian Norse are building the ships and theirs aren't as good as our Danish drekar,' another moaned.

'As long as they get us down to the mouth of the Sæfern they can be damned knarrs for all I care.'

At that moment one of the Danes looked up and gave Eadling a suspicious look. He moved away hurriedly before he could be challenged. So the Vikings were building a fleet along the coast to the north to take them down to near Glowecestre he mused. He suspected that Wynnstan would be pleased with such information. Hopefully it was worth getting covered in shit for.

Wynnstan was restless and couldn't get to sleep. He was getting more and more worried about Eadling's disappearance when the guard on the south gate sent for him. It appeared that someone claiming to be his body servant was trying to gain admittance.

It took several minutes for the guard to remove the bracing timbers and the three bars that held the right gate shut during which time Wynnstan was wondering what dire punishment would be appropriate. However, when he heard the boy's tale he decided that any reprimand for leaving the fortress without permission could wait.

The boy still reeked of the shit pit and so he had him wash again and don fresh clothes before taking him to see Æthelstan. Eadling felt sorry for the laundry maid, a girl who he fancied himself in love with. She would have the devil of a job to get his old clothes clean again.

The ætheling listened to Eadling's tale but he didn't know whether to believe the boy or not until Wynnstan assured him that he could trust him. Once convinced of its veracity, it was obviously vital to get the information to Æthelflæd, but how? In the end he decided that it would have to wait until Ywer arrived with the relief force.

†††

Rinan was away visiting one of his other vills when Sawin arrived at Apletune with the news that the Vikings were on their way to lay siege to Mamecestre but thankfully Bjørn Frami's longship was there. Sawin told him what he knew and Bjørn debated whether he should send out scouts to find out more about the invaders. However, he was more at home on the sea than he was on land and decided that the priority was to sail to Cæstir and inform Ealdorman Ywer.

When he landed with Sawin in tow it was only to find that Ywer was also away touring his estates. It wasn't surprising; after such a harsh winter he would naturally want to know how everyone had fared.

He was received by the Lady Gyda in the main hall. She was seated on a small chair to one side of the one normally occupied by Ywer whilst her ten year-old son, Irwyn, stood on her other side. When he'd finished speaking Gyda pursed her lips, deep in thought.

'I'll send a messenger to my husband at once, of course, but to save time I'll send out a summons for the fyrd to muster. The question is where?'

'Cedde might be a good place, lady,' Sawin suggested with a nervous look at Bjørn in case he'd spoken out of turn. 'It's six miles south of Mamecestre and on the south side of the River Mæresēa so it's near enough to reach there in one day's march but far enough away for them to remain undetected by the Northumbrians.'

'Does the Mǣresēa not flow past Mamecestre then? Surely that would be too close to the Danes for a muster point?' Irwyn asked.

'No, that's a tributary of the Mǣresēa called the Irwell, er...'

He hesitated not sure what to call the ealdorman's son. You didn't call a boy with an unbroken voice lord, however highly born, and it seemed impertinent to call him by name. He was saved by Gyda.

'You know the area so Cedde it is, unless you want to comment Bjørn?' she said with a smile to put Sawin at ease.

'No, lady. I know the Mǣresēa though and there are shallows upstream and downstream from Cedde. Our forces could cross at either point and so approach Mamecestre from either the west or the east.'

It was three days before Ywer returned to Cæstir. The messenger had trouble finding him and when he did he was a good day's ride south of Cæstir.

'Thank you, wife,' he told Gyda after embracing and kissing her in their private chamber. 'You did the right thing. I'll change and have something to eat before setting off for Cedde. When is the muster called for?'

'Two days hence, so there is no rush. At least stay tonight.'

'I fear not. I need to get there and send out scouts to establish the exact location and strength of the Viking army. Then I have to decide what to do.'

'Can I come with you, father?' Irwyn asked eagerly.

'I don't see why not,' his father started to say.

'He's far too young,' Gyda protested.

'I was abducted and enslaved by the Culdees when I was a year younger than Irwyn is now. The experience taught me to be resilient and to stand up for myself. You can't mollycoddle the boy for ever, Gyda. Don't Norse boys leave their mother's side before they are ten?'

Gyda bit her lip and glowered at her husband but raised no further objections. High born Vikings were fostered away from home from the age of seven or eight until they reached fourteen and became warriors. However, Ywer did postpone his departure until dawn the next day so that she could spend a last evening with her son. Ywer had secretly had a byrnie and helmet made to fit Irwyn's small frame and he also presented him with a dagger with a hilt bound in gold wire and a jewel encrusted belt. He didn't think he'd ever seen his son look so pleased.

When he reached the muster point he found that just over a thousand men had arrived, most members of the fyrd from northern Cæstirscīr but over a hundred of them were thegns and their hearth warriors. With Ywer's own gesith and warband he had just under thirteen hundred men available so far. However, judging by the reports from the scouts who'd already been to reconnoitre the land around Mamecestre, they faced a slightly superior number of Vikings who would be more than a match for his fyrd. He'd need to think of some way of improving the odds.

Chapter Eighteen

Late May – June 910

Ywer had been hesitant about appointing Godric - the son of the last Viking leader to have invaded Wessex and Mercia - to become his captain after Edmund's death but all the other members of his father's original warband were either dead or had become too old to lead men in battle. Despite his father's history, Godric had proved his loyalty and was respected by the somewhat diverse group of men who made up Ywer's gesith.

Some were Norse who had joined him because his wife was the daughter of Jarl Harald, an influential leader of the settlers who had crossed the Íralandes Sæ to settle on the eastern seaboard of Northumbria north of the Mæresēa.

One of the most prominent of these Norsemen was a man called Birger Njal. Njal meant giant and was a name given to the man in jest because of his small stature. Despite his height, or lack of it, he was a doughty fighter with arms and legs like tree trunks. He was the man Ywer chose as his emissary to travel to see Jarl Harald and the other jarls who inhabited the area immediately north of the Mæresēa.

Whilst he was waiting for what he hoped would be reinforcements from Harald, he decided to liven things up with a night time raid on one of the four Viking camps. He chose Godric to lead the raid and gave him fifty men who were of either Norse or Danish descent. Their task was to infiltrate the camp and cause as much damage as they could. As soon as the alarm was raised Godric's men were to beat a hasty retreat which Ywer would cover with his archers. They would shoot fire arrows into the camp with the intention of setting the oiled leather tents alight and stampeding the Vikings' horses.

Godric led his men towards the camp in small groups. Each pretended to the sentries that they had been in the woods to defecate and at first all went well. However, when a second group tried to enter the camp via the same route someone smelled a rat.

One of Godric's men cut the throat of the suspicious sentry and the rest quickly killed his companions. However, the damage had been done and someone nearby raised the alarm.

By this time some thirty of Ywer's men were inside the camp. The discovery that the camp had been invaded caused chaos. The Vikings didn't know friend from foe as they all spoke Norse or Danish therefore the besiegers resorted to asking for the identity of each group's jarl. This quickly revealed who was who but by this time most of the infiltrators had managed to escape. Only one group of five were cornered; they sold their lives dearly and succeeded in killing eight of their assailants before the last one was killed.

Once Ywer realised that the raid had been a failure he ordered his archers to light the oiled rags tied to the tips of their arrows and a rain of fire cascaded down on the Viking encampment. Many struck the ground where they did no damage but many landed on the tents which burst into flame. One or two hit men causing serious burns.

However, little real damage was done. There was one modest achievement. The Vikings allowed their horses to graze on nearby pasture during the day but brought them into the camp at dusk. Fire panicked them and they stampeded away from the blazing tents, trampling other tents and men underfoot as they went. One of those who got in their way inadvertently was King Ingwær. He wasn't killed but he suffered a broken leg, arm and collarbone.

Vikings from the other camps began arriving on the scene. Ywer's body servant gave three blasts on a horn and his men melted away into the darkness. A few came across wide-eyed horses and managed to calm them and took the animals with them to Cedde. Others managed to get lost during the retreat but they eventually found their way back the next day.

Ywer wasn't aware of the injuries suffered by Ingwær of course, but he estimated that they had caused more than a score of casualties and had gained fifteen horses for the loss of five warriors. It would have caused little but inconvenience to the Vikings but it did boost the morale of his own men.

Æthelstan and Wynnstan had watched the fires spring up and had heard the shouts and the clash of weapons from their vantage point on the top of the gateway opposite the camp.

'What do you make of that?' the ætheling asked his captain.

'I'm not entirely sure. I can only presume that Ywer has arrived. However, why launch a small scale night-time raid rather than relieve the siege?'

'I suspect because he doesn't have enough men to confront the Vikings in the open,' Æthelstan replied gloomily. 'How are our supplies holding up?'

'Not well. So many have taken refuge in the fortress that we've probably only got enough food for another fortnight. Perhaps it's time to think about going onto half-rations,' he suggested.

'Let's see what the next couple of days bring.'

†††

'So my son-in-law expects me to haul his arse out of the fire once again does he?' Harald asked Birger Njal.

The jarl sat in his oversized chair on a raised dais glaring down at the man who stood in front of him. Harald didn't need the added height of the dais to tower over Birger, even seated.

'If Ingwær regains Mamecestre he'll become the dominant power in this part of the country,' Birger pointed out. 'He might not be sympathetic to those Christian jarls who helped Lady Æthelflæd defeat Ingimund, who I'm led to believe was a distant cousin of the three kings of Northumbria.'

'By Thor's hammer, you're asking a lot, boy. If we don't interfere Ingwær might well leave us alone; I suspect he's got other things on his mind judging by the reports of frenetic boat building to the north. However, if we side with Lord Ywer we'd better win or

Ingwær will probably inflict the blood eagle on me and my fellow jarls. It's not a way I'd wish to die, believe me.'

If Birger had noted the reference to the old gods by a man who professed to be a Christian now he didn't say so.

'Irwyn is with Lord Ywer, jarl,' Birger said apropos of nothing.

'Is he,' Harald said thoughtfully.

He was devoted to his only child and to his grandson.

'I can't promise the other jarls will join me but I'll do as Lord Ywer asks,' he said eventually.

†††

Despite the considerable pain he was in, Ingwær insisted on being lifted onto his horse. The reports of an army approaching from the west alarmed him but, when he saw them for himself he grinned in anticipation. As they formed their shieldwall their numbers seemed even less than his own and most of them were farmers and artisans, not warriors.

Ingwær had many faults and one of them was being overconfident. When one of his jarls suggested sending some scouts to check the woods to the right of their position he scoffed at the idea. It was just as well as Ywer had stationed two hundred archers in the wood. He also had another surprise in store for the Viking king.

The one unknown was what Æthelstan would do. There had been no way to get a message to him and he prayed that the ætheling would use his common sense when he saw what was happening. He didn't want to just win this battle, he wanted to annihilate the Viking army and remove the major threat to his shire for a decade to come.

There wasn't a cloud in the sky and the sun beat down on the two opposing armies. Boys ran along the lines with water skins amidst the stench of urine as men relieved themselves where they stood. There were several priests and monks with Ywer's army including his elder brother, Abbot Æscwin. They were there to treat the wounded and to care for the spiritual needs of the men. They passed along the rows of warriors and the fyrd saying mass and dispensing the sacrament.

Opposite them the Vikings fingered the mjolnirs or other talismans of the old gods that they wore around their necks and prayed to Odin and Thor for victory. A few of the Danes were Christians but there were no priests with Ingwær' army. They looked on enviously as their opponents were blessed and absolved of their sins.

Ywer's army occupied the higher ground and Ingwær was hoping that he'd be foolish enough to charge downhill and attack his shieldwall. When it became apparent that wasn't going to happen the Viking king reluctantly gave the order for his men to advance. They'd been impatient to do so for some time and the ordered ranks lost some of their cohesion as men raced forward at different speeds. As they drew level with the woods a hail of arrows struck their right flank. It was the side that men held their swords, axes and spears; their shields being on the other side.

The Mercian archers got several volleys away before the Vikings realised what was happening. When they did several hundred of them broke away and charged towards the woods where the archers were hiding. Now the arrows were having less of an effect as the enemy could hold their shields in front of them. The archers hurriedly withdrew further into the trees chased by the furious Norsemen and Danes.

It was only then that they realised they had run into a trap. Jarl Harald and his allies had joined Ywer with three hundred warriors. They had arranged themselves in a formation called the bull's horns in the woods into which many of the Vikings charged before they realised. Confronted by the unexpected semi-circular shieldwall the disorganised enemy panicked and tried to retreat. However, the semicircle closed around them and they found themselves hemmed in.

The slower ones and those outside the trap beat a hasty retreat but Harald had caught over a hundred within the bull's horns. Few escaped. Even those outside the trap fell prey to the archers who hid behind trees and attacked them from the rear with daggers and seaxes as the Vikings passed them.

Meanwhile Ingwær, cursing the men who'd broken away from the advance, continued towards Ywer's shieldwall with the remaining thousand or so. The Mercian front rank consisted of well-trained thegns and hearth warriors supported by the more experienced men of the fyrd in the second rank. These were all armed with spears. Behind them stood another three ranks of the fyrd whose job it was to push their shields against the backs of the row in front to prevent them from giving ground.

Ywer had stationed himself in the centre of the front rank with Rinan on one side of him and Godric on the other. He waited for the first of the Vikings to reach him and swallowed nervously. He was far from a coward but the huge Dane facing him carried an axe that most men would have had difficulty in lifting. The Dane waved it around as if it weighed nothing. He lifted it above his head and Ywer raised his shield instinctively, although he knew such a formidable weapon would smash through it as if it was made of parchment.

It was the job of the man on the right to protect the one to the left and as the giant lifted his axe high Godric stabbed him in the armpit. It seemed as if the Dane hadn't even felt it so Godric dragged his blade out and jabbed it up under the giant's chin. As the axe descended Ywer stabbed his sword into the Dane's thigh causing his leg to buckle. This in turn meant that his head dropped, forcing Godric's sword further into the man's skull until it penetrated his brain.

Godric felt his sword being dragged out of his hand as the Dane collapsed onto the ground in front of him and he hastily pulled his seax out just as another Dane swung his sword at his neck. For a moment Godric thought he was a dead man but someone in the second rank thrust his spear through one of the eyeholes in the Dane's helmet and into his brain. He joined the giant and together their bodies made a barrier in front of Ywer and his companions.

Similar fights were taking place all along the line. Some of the Mercians were killed and the men in the second row stepped forward to take their place. In some cases some of those who'd started in the third row soon found themselves in the front rank. The battle had been joined for twenty minutes and the Mercians were in danger of being overwhelmed in places when two things happened. Harald's Norsemen erupted from the woods and charged towards the rear ranks of the Vikings and Æthelstan appeared at the base of the hill with the garrison from Mamecestre.

Those in the rear few ranks of the Vikings turned to face the new threat which weakened the pressure on the Viking front ranks. They stepped back to gain a breather which was an error because Ywer immediately gave the order to advance. Once having moved back it was difficult for the enemy to hold their ground and they were forced further and further down the hill.

Suddenly Ingwær and his hearth warriors broke away from the fight in a wedge formation and attempted to get back to where they'd left their horses. Ywer's archers had remained at the edge of the wood with instructions to kill any Vikings who fled the field and they now peppered the retreating king and his followers with arrows. Hearth warriors were sworn to protect their lord and Ingwær's were no exception. A score of the fifty bodyguards were killed or wounded but the rest remained clustered around their king, protecting him with their bodies. More continued to fall but eventually a dozen or so reached the horses at the bottom of the hill and helped Ingwær into the saddle.

Beorhtsige was Ywer's best archer and although the range was about three hundred yards he took careful aim at the king as he settled in the saddle. For the first time Ingwær was unprotected by his surrounding warriors and Beorhtsige sighted on him, drew back his bowstring to his ear and released. He watched the flight of the arrow and cursed as the wind took it off course.

However, Ingwær dug his heels into his horse and it moved forward taking the unfortunate man into the path of the arrow. The arrow didn't hit him but it did lodge in the animal's buttocks. It reared up and deposited its rider on the ground. Ingwær yelled in pain as his broken bones were jarred by the impact but then fell silent as one of the injured horse's rear hooves crushed his helmet and his skull.

Half an hour later it was all over. They had watched as their king had deserted them and now word spread that he was dead. The heart went out of the Vikings. When the count was done Ywer had lost just under a hundred dead or so seriously wounded that they wouldn't survive but three hundred and sixty Vikings had been killed and another two hundred or so were wounded and had their throats cut. All told the siege of Mamecestre had cost the Northumbrians over seven hundred of their best fighting men.

†††

Wynnstan had suffered a couple of minor flesh wounds and it was whilst these were being dealt with that Ywer came to find him.

'I have a letter for you from Glowecestre which arrived just as we were about to set out,' he said, handing him a sealed leather pouch.

Wynnstan thanked him and exchanged a few words whilst he waited patiently for Ywer to leave so that he could read it. He'd assumed it was from Astrid –at long last – but his heart sank when he saw that the seal was Cuthfleda's. He feared the worst as he broke it and unwrapped the covering.

To my esteemed friend Wynnstan, greetings,

I should have written before this but I wanted to wait until I had some definite news to tell you. There was no point in worrying you unnecessarily.

He grunted. He'd been worried to death at the deafening silence from Astrid as it was. He would rather have known what was happening, even if the news was bad. He scanned the rest of the missive seeking mention of Astrid and the baby.

I'm pleased to tell you that at long last Astrid is showing signs of recovery. She hovered near death for some time having lost a lot of blood during the birth and I feared for her life. As I write this letter she is awake and is making sense. For a long time she was delirious and drifted in and out of consciousness. I'm delighted to tell you that the infirmarian sees no reason why she should not now make a full recovery.

However, there is bad news I fear. He doesn't think it wise for her to bear another child. She had suffered internal injuries and he says it would kill her if she tried to give birth again.

I'm sorry to have to tell you also that the baby was born dead.

I know that you are sworn to serve Lord Æthelstan but I think at this moment your wife has the greater need of you. Please come as soon as you can.

God be with you always,

Cuthfleda.

Wynnstan lay there feeling numb after reading through the letter a second time. The monk who was sewing up the two flesh wounds he'd suffered bandaged them and moved on to the next patient. Wynnstan continued to lie there until someone asked him to move so that another wounded man could take his place and be treated.

He stumbled out of the infirmary and stood in the sunshine thinking about Astrid and wondering if she would ever forgive him for not being with her when he'd promised to be back in time for the birth. It wasn't his fault that he couldn't be, of course, but he doubted that she'd see it that way, especially after what had happened to her and the baby.

One or two people passing by gave him a curious look and he eventually realised that he wasn't achieving anything by standing in the sunshine in a sort of stupor, so he set off to find Æthelstan.

The ætheling readily gave him permission to visit his wife and, as he was headed for Glowecestre, Ywer asked him to take his report on Northumbria's ship building programme to Lady Æthelflæd and warn her of the impending invasion of Mercia. He addressed the message to her because, as far as he knew, her husband was still the guest of King Eadweard - no doubt to keep him from interfering in the governance of Mercia.

It was a hundred and forty miles to Glowecestre by land and it would have taken four or five days overland, even taking a change of horses. As it was, Ywer asked Bjørn Frami to take Wynnstan there by sea. The prevailing wind was from the west and, given good conditions, the longship should be able to get there in two, or at the most three, days.

As soon as he reached Glowecestre he made for the hut he shared with Astrid but she wasn't there. A servant told him nervously that his wife was in the hereræswa's chambers in the palace. For a moment he had to think what the man meant. Apparently the Lord of Mercia's hall complex was now commonly referred to as a palace – a Frankish term – but hereræswa stumped him until he remembered that was Deorwine's new appointment. Lady Cuthfleda had evidently taken Astrid to her own chambers to recover.

He cursed in frustration. If he went to the palace he would have to report to Æthelflæd before he went

345

to see his wife. There was nothing for it and he went to find Æthelflæd's chamberlain.

When he was shown into her presence he found that both she and Cuthfleda were deep in conversation. However, Æthelflæd broke off what she'd been saying as soon as she saw her nephew's captain.

'Have you brought news from the north or have you just come to see your wife?' she asked.

Her critical tone and hard face told him she blamed him for not coming to see Astrid long before this.

'Both, lady. We have been besieged in Mamecestre by the Northumbrians and I only learned of Astrid's illness when Lord Ywer came to our rescue bringing with him a letter from Lady Cuthfleda.'

Immediately she heard his explanation Æthelflæd's face softened.

'I see. Well, have you seen her? No? Well what are you standing here for,' she asked with a smile. 'Go and see your wife and son and come back here to eat with me at noon. You can tell me your news then.'

Wynnstan gave her a grateful look, bowed and left the chamber.

He made his way to the area of the palace occupied by Deorwine and Cuthfleda. The hereræswa wasn't a sensitive soul and, forgetting the man hadn't yet seen his wife, eagerly asked Wynnstan for his news as soon as he saw him.

'Lord, may I see Astrid first?' he asked, trying not to let his irritation show.

'What, yes, of course. My apologies,' Deorwine replied, feeling a fool.

'Thank you, lord. Lady Æthelflæd has invited me to join her to eat at noon. If you're there perhaps I can tell you what has been happening then?'

'Yes, fine. Off you go; the boy here will show you where Astrid is.'

Wynnstan turned round expecting to see a servant standing behind him but instead it was a two year old boy. It took a moment but the eager look on the child's face and the similarity to his mother told him it had to be his son, Wealhmær.

'Father?' the toddler said uncertainly.

It had been some time since he'd seen the boy and Wynnstan realised that someone must have told him that his father was here.

'Yes, Wealhmær, it's your father,' he confirmed, leaning down and picking the boy up.

He hugged him briefly and lifted him above his head, much to the delight of the small child who squealed with delight.

'Come on, let's go and see your mother,' he said, putting the boy down and taking his hand.

The excited toddler pulled him along the corridor to the end and into a small bedchamber. Astrid was still in bed but she was sitting up doing some embroidery. Her face was thinner and she had rings under her eyes. He thought she had aged since he'd last seen her as well.

'Wynnstan!' she cried in delight, trying to get out of bed but her husband pushed her gently back down again.

'I'm so sorry I didn't come earlier but I only found out what happened a few days ago,' he said contritely.

347

'How are you? You look better,' he added gamely, although in truth she didn't look well at all.

'I needed you but instead you remained with your friend,' she accused him. 'You promised me you'd be here for the birth. She died, Wynnstan,' she cried, breaking into sobs, 'she died and you weren't here!'

'I know my love. It is to my eternal regret that I couldn't be with you when you needed me most. Æthelstan was given command of a fortress as a buttress against the heathen Danes and, as his captain, I had no option but to stay with him.'

'I sometimes think that you care for him more than you do for me,' she said petulantly.

Wealhmær sensed there was something wrong between his mother and father and burst into tears.

'Now look what you've done,' Astrid accused him. 'You've upset my son.'

'I think you mean we've upset our son,' he said with emphasis on the *we* and the *our*. 'I'll leave you to rest,' he said, trying not to let his anger show. 'I'm to dine with Æthelflæd so that I can make my report about the siege by the Northumbrians and the battle that followed.'

For the first time Astrid noticed the bandages around her husband's upper arm and his thigh.

'You're wounded,' she exclaimed, instantly contrite.

'They're just minor flesh wounds, nothing to worry about.' His anger disappeared as quickly as it had flared up. 'It really is good to see you on the road to recovery after your ordeal,' he said with a smile. 'I'll come and tell you all about it after I've dined. For now, get some rest.'

He kissed her and his son and headed for the main hall concentrating on what to say about events at Mamecestre. It was only after he'd left the room that he recalled that he hadn't commiserated with Astrid over the death of their baby girl.

Chapter Nineteen

July / August 910

Wynnstan and Astrid glared at each other.

'It's far too soon for you to think of returning to your duties,' he said when she told him of her intention.

Although Cuthfleda and Deorwine didn't have their own hall they had a separate section of the palace with their own servants. Before the still-birth and her subsequent illness Astrid had continued to run the household and act as Cuthfleda's companion. Whilst she was bedridden things seemed to have run smoothly without her supervision and he couldn't understand why she needed to rush back and serve her mistress.

Over the past month Astrid had continued to make a good recovery; the bags had gone from under her eyes, she no longer looked gaunt and much of her former vigour had returned. Nevertheless she tired quickly and Wynnstan worried that she was rushing things.

His other concern was his absence from Æthelstan's side. The longer he stayed in Glowecestre the more he worried about what was happening on Mercia's northern border. Word had reached Æthelflæd that the Northumbrians now had a fleet of well over a hundred ships up and down their west coast. Some would be drekar and others the smaller snekkjur but, with crews ranging from as little as thirty to over seventy, a fleet that size could carry an army of perhaps five or six thousand.

'If you are well enough to resume your duties then I have no excuse for staying here,' he pointed out, hoping that would dissuade Astrid.

'Well, don't let me keep you from rushing back up north,' she flashed back, thinking he was looking for an excuse to do so.

'Don't let's argue,' he said with a sigh. 'You know the last thing I want is to be parted from you and Wealhmær. Why don't you both come with me?'

'We've been over this,' she said wearily. 'My place is here. Lady Cuthfleda needs me.'

'Why? She has Æthelflæd for female companionship and her own family. Surely I need you more and I want to be there to watch my son grow up.'

'Well then, you should have stayed as a member of Æthelflæd's gesith then, shouldn't you?'

And that was the nub of it, Wynnstan thought. He almost believed that she was jealous of his relationship with Æthelstan. They seemed to have reached an impasse – again. He made preparations for his return north overland but then something happened to change his plans.

Everyone had expected the Northumbrians to invade up the estuary of the Sæfern and were therefore surprised when they heard that they had landed on the north coast of Somersaete in Wessex. Whether their fleet had been driven too far south by contrary winds, or perhaps their navigation was at fault, wasn't known. The local ealdorman had immediately called out the fyrd but when he learned that the enemy numbered some six thousand he didn't dare engage them on his own.

Consequently they ravaged much of the shire unopposed before reinforcements arrived from Dyfneintscīr and Wiltunscīr. Rather than engage them, the Northumbrian Vikings retreated to their ships. Not that they were afraid of being beaten but there was no point in incurring casualties in a battle when they had already gained so much plunder and hundreds of Saxon captives destined for the slave markets. They set sail once more, this time for the Mercian shire of Herefordscīr on the other side of the River Sæfern from Glowecestre.

Æthelflæd was hot and bothered by the flies that sought refuge from the sun in the shade of the tree canopy that met overhead as she rode the last few miles to Theocsbury, the place chosen by her brother for their meeting.

Eadweard had been in Cent when he first heard of the initial raids in Somersaete and immediately set out from Dofras with twenty longships. He'd mobilised the western shires of his kingdom and marched into Mercia to meet up with his sister's forces.

When Æthelflæd reached Theocsbury she greeted her brother and welcomed the goblet of ale one of his servants offered her. It was only after she'd slaked her thirst that she noticed someone with Eadweard whom she hadn't expected to see. Hywel Dda was the King of Brycheiniog, a minor Welsh realm which bordered Herefordscīr to the west. The Wealas were more accustomed to raiding Mercia than becoming its allies and she wondered what had happened.

'You know of King Hywel of course,' Eadweard said smoothly as he introduced him to Æthelflæd. 'The damned Vikings have raided his lands as well and he's prepared to join with us to defeat them. He's confident that he can persuade Brochfael ap Meurig of Gwent to join us as well.'

'King Hywel, it's good to meet you at last,' Æthelflæd said smoothly, trying to hide her distaste for a man whose raiders had been a thorn in her side for decades.

No doubt Hywel's response, professing admiration for her and wishing her a long life, was as insincere as her greeting.

It was only then that Æthelflæd spotted her husband amongst those standing behind Eadweard.

'I hope that you have brought enough warriors to join me, wife,' Æðelred barked at her.

'Shall we go inside to discuss our strategy, brother,' she asked, ignoring her husband who gave her a furious look.

'So, we're all agreed then?' Eadweard asked an hour and a half later.

'I assume you'll allow me to lead my own army,' Æðelred asked sarcastically.

'I'm worried that you haven't yet fully recovered from your illness, Lord Æðelred,' Eadweard replied with a smile. 'Besides, I need you beside me to advise me. I'm sure that your heræswa, Deorwine, can lead them adequately.'

He turned away from Æðelred to address the assembled war council.

'All we need now is to track the Vikings and pick the ground on which to attack them. That will be your job, Wynnstan.'

The latter would have preferred to use his own scouts but he couldn't wait until Æthelstan had joined them with Ywer and the fyrd from Cæstirscīr. As it was, he would be leading men provided by Eadweard and Æthelflæd, few of whom he knew and few knew him. It was hardly satisfactory but he'd have to make the best of it.

He looked at the seventeen men allocated to him and was pleased to see that he recognised five of the Mercians. He talked to each of them individually and then picked the best two. The three of them would each lead a group of six scouts. He sent the other two to search for and then shadow the Northumbrian horde while he chose the five scouts with whom he was moderately familiar to help him locate the Viking fleet.

If the Vikings were raiding to the west of the Sæfern it made sense for their fleet to be somewhere along the far bank of the river. He crossed over the old Roman bridge at Theocsbury and turned south west following the river bank. The terrain varied from open pastureland to scrubland interspersed by small woods. It would be easy to stumble across the enemy encampment without warning and so Wynnstan sent two scouts forward to act as a screen. They passed Glowecestre on the far bank without encountering anyone but half an hour later the two scouts came racing back.

'The Viking ships are half a mile away, Wynnstan,' one of them – a fifteen year old called Swiðhun – called out excitedly.

'Thank you, Swiðhun, but keep your voice down. We don't want to tell the Vikings we've found them, do we?' his captain said with a brief smile.

'No, I'm sorry,' the boy said contritely.

'Where exactly are they and in what strength?'

'We counted ninety longships but there might be more beyond the bend in the river,' his older and wiser companion reported with a derisive glance at Swiðhun. 'Some were beached but the majority were anchored midstream. There were several small camps along the bank where the longships were beached. We estimated that the total guard force left behind with the ships numbered perhaps four or five hundred; mainly ships boys between eleven and fourteen but there were quite a few greybeards as well.'

'Thank you; that was a very concise report.'

Wynnstan tried to recall of the older scout's name but it escaped him. He didn't like to confess he'd forgotten it so he'd have to wait until one of the others addressed the man by name.

Leaving the others to watch the enemy fleet in case they moved, he took Swiðhun and returned to Theocsbury to report to Eadweard and Æthelflæd. The only others present for the meeting were Deorwine, Cuthfleda and the Wessex hereræswa, Osfirth, who was the Ealdorman of Wiltunscīr and the king's brother-in-law.

'Cyning, Lady Æthelflæd, we've located the enemy ships,' he began, launching into his report without preamble. 'They're on the other bank some three miles south of Glowecestre. Forty ships are moored or have been beached whilst another seventy are anchored in the river. The Vikings have left some five hundred to guard their fleet but they are mainly boys and old men.'

'I thought your task was to locate the main body of Vikings, not empty ships,' Osfirth sneered.

Eadweard seemed embarrassed but said nothing whilst Æthelflæd and the others glared at him.

'I think Wynnstan was reporting to your king and his sister,' Cuthfleda said mildly.

Just at that moment the door opened to admit a flustered looking Æðelred.

'I've just heard that two of the scouts have returned; why was I not informed?' he said looking agitated.

'Ah, Lord Æðelred,' Eadweard said with a false smile. 'Good of you to join us; Wynnstan was just telling us that he's found the Viking ships.'

'And the Vikings themselves? Has he found them?'

'Why don't you ask him yourself?' his wife snapped, annoyed that Æðelred was treating Wynnstan as if he wasn't there.

'Well?'

'I have two parties of scouts out looking for them but...'

'So you haven't done what you were told to do, which was to find the Northumbrian army' Osfirth said triumphantly.

'No, Lord Osfirth, not yet,' he replied frostily. 'I thought it more important to return and report first; this is a golden opportunity to burn or capture their longships.'

'What good will that do? It'll merely trap them in Mercia where they can wreak havoc,' Æðelred said, looking at Wynnstan as if he were mad.

'Not so,' Eadweard cut in. 'With their fleet destroyed or captured they've no option but to strike out for Northumbria overland. We can harry them as they go and then face them in battle. We need to annihilate them, not just get rid of them for now. That way Northumbria won't be in a position to come to the aid of the Five Boroughs and East Anglia.'

'I'm sorry, I don't follow your logic, Eadweard,' Æðelred said looking puzzled.

'It was always our father's dream to unite the Anglo-Saxon peoples into one kingdom,' Æthelflæd explained. 'If we can eliminate Northumbria as a fighting force for a decade it would give us a chance to re-conquer the Danelaw.'

'But first we need not just to defeat the Northumbrians - and hopefully kill the two kings who are left - Eowils and Halfdan – but slaughter their warriors,' Eadweard added. 'To do that we need to lure them into a trap. The first step is to deprive them of their means of escape by sea. Wynnstan, thank you. You have done exactly as I wanted. You can leave the destruction of the ships to us. Return now and bring me the location of the main Viking force.'

✝✝✝

Wynnstan crouched beside a bush near the summit of a low hill overlooking a sizeable settlement called Liedeberge midway between Hereford and the River Sæfern. The huts and halls on fire but the large stone-built church seemed to have survived. As he watched, the enemy slowly made their way eastwards, driving a herd of two hundred cattle and three times as many sheep ahead of them. To the north of the burning buildings a few hundred warriors guarded the captives they had taken so far. A hundred more had evidently been captured in Liedeberge and were being taken to join the others.

'Bastards,' Swiðhun muttered as he and four other scouts watched.

'They'll pay for it, believe me,' Wynnstan whispered. 'They appear to be heading for where they left their fleet. Obviously they don't know it isn't there anymore.'

Deorwine had led a force of a thousand Mercians against the fleet two nights previously, killing most of those left to guard it. He'd selected forty of the best ships to be taken upriver to the docks at Glowecestre for division between Wessex and Mercia and had burnt or sunk the rest. Some Vikings had escaped the slaughter but evidently they hadn't yet found the main body.

Wynnstan and his five scouts trailed the main group of Northumbrians for the rest of the day. The other two parties of scouts were shadowing smaller groups of raiders, all of whom were heading south towards where they'd left the fleet.

Early the next morning a small group of riders arrived just as the Vikings were breaking camp. They brought with them two boys who looked to be thirteen or fourteen who were dressed in the trousers and heavy woollen tunics typically worn by ships' boys. It looked as if the Northumbrians had found out about the loss of their fleet.

When they eventually set off they headed due east.

'They're heading for the bridge at Theocsbury,' Swiðhun concluded.

'Looks like it,' Wynnstan agreed with a smile.

'But that's where our army is,' Swiðhun exclaimed.

'Yes, but I wonder whether that's where Eadweard will want to offer battle,' one of the others said. 'If they find the bridge defended they could just head north along the river. There are other bridges and several ferries.'

'But it would take them time to cross and they'd be vulnerable whilst doing so, especially with all those captives and the livestock,' Wynnstan pointed out. 'However, that's not our problem. We need to get back and report.'

When the Northumbrians reached the bridge they found it only lightly defended by fifty archers and a few spearmen. They took some casualties but eventually the defenders beat a hasty retreat and the enemy started to pour over the narrow bridge.

Eadweard waited until about a thousand Vikings had crossed before he acted. Suddenly several thousand men surrounded those who had already reached the east bank and archers drove back those trying to join them. Someone drove a cart forward so that it blocked the exit from the bridge. The horses pulling it were killed but that didn't matter. Men heaved the cart over on its side and clambered up to defend it from the Vikings.

The thousand or so on the east bank were surrounded by many times their number and, although they fought valiantly, their numbers were whittled down until they were all either dead, wounded or captives.

As dusk fell the Vikings gave up trying to cross the bridge and withdrew. By now they had lost a quarter of their original number, including those who'd died guarding the fleet, and their morale had suffered a severe shock.

☩☩☩

Swiðhun watched from the east bank as thousands of Vikings poured down the steep slope above the western end of the bridge at Brigge on the Sæfern. It took a long time for the warriors, their captives and the herds of sheep and cattle to cross and the scout and his companions didn't wait for them to do so. Once they saw the vanguard head due north they left their observation post, mounted their horses and cantered away to inform King Eadweard.

Wynnstan was no longer with the scouts. As soon as the Cæstirscīr contingent had arrived, bringing Æthelstan with it, he'd re-joined him and took over command of his gesith.   Æthelstan had been welcomed by his father and the others but Osfirth pointedly ignored him. Wynnstan had caught the look of hatred on the Wessex hereræswa's face when he thought no one was looking and he decided that the man needed watching. He wouldn't put it past him to have Æthelstan assassinated.

Eadweard seemed reconciled with his eldest son but he failed to acknowledge him as an ætheling which meant the king had decided to maintain the fiction that Æthelstan was a bastard. He was included in the war council, along with the two hereræswas, the ealdormen, Æthelflæd and Æðelred. The latter had objected to the presence of his wife, saying that Mercia didn't need two leaders; he was sufficient. However, Eadweard countered by saying that she was there as his sister.

The place chosen as the battlefield was a slope between Wōdnesfeld and Totenhale. The problem was making sure the Vikings took that route. It lay more easterly than the direct way back to Northumbria.

'I suggest we raid their camp one night and drive off their cattle,' Æthelstan suggested. 'They won't want to lose hundreds of the stolen animals and they'll pursue us.'

'It's the best hope that we have of drawing them in,' Æthelflæd agreed.

'It's too risky,' her husband countered. 'The raid could go wrong and they might just send a few men to recover them whilst the rest continue north-east.'

'What do you suggest then, Æðelred?' Eadweard asked but the Lord of the Mercians had no alternative suggestion. 'Anyone else? No? Then it's worth trying.'

Æthelstan and Wynnstan studied the Viking camp for some time. Somehow Swiðhun seemed to have got himself transferred from Æthelflæd's warband to the ætheling's and had attached himself to Wynnstan like a limpet. Æthelstan teased Wynnstan that he'd got himself a new puppy but his captain refused to rise to the jibe and didn't reply. In truth he was flattered by the lad's hero-worship and found him useful as a sort of assistant and messenger. He suspected that Eadling was a little jealous of Swiðhun as a result but he had other things to worry about.

The camp stretched for half a mile along the bank of a tributary of the Sæfern called the Worfe. It was neither wide nor deep and was easily crossed. The encampment was on the east bank whilst the livestock were allowed to graze on the other side guarded by a hundred warriors and the fifty boys who acted as drovers on the march. Æthelstan had a problem; he needed the livestock to cross to the other bank in order to drive them in the direction of Totenhale.

He'd been given five hundred men; two hundred archers, the same number of warriors and a mixture of farmers who were members of the fyrd and boys who knew how to drive animals. In addition he had his gesith, who were the only ones who were mounted.

'We need to cause a diversion in the main camp, whilst we kill the guards and drive the livestock north,' Wynnstan whispered to Æthelstan. 'The archers and your gesith will have to delay pursuit until we can get them across the river.'

Æthelstan nodded his agreement and they decided that dawn would be the best time to launch the raid. Meanwhile he sent Wynnstan to pick twenty men and organise the diversion.

'Go and fetch Sawin, Wardric and Tidhelm,' Wynnstan told Swiðhun. 'Tell them to pick fifteen good archers and meet me in the woods at the southern end of the enemy camp. Oh, and tell them we'll need to start fires.'

The boy scampered away leaving a scowling Eadling with Wynnstan.

'He's like a love-sick girl,' the younger boy growled with a scowl.

'He's useful,' Wynnstan snapped. 'Now go and fetch the bow and quiver from my horse.'

Twenty minutes later Wynnstan was ready. Sawin lit a small fire hidden from sight behind a hastily constructed stone wall using the flint and shavings he always carried with him. As the first of the sun's rays illuminated the horizon the archers prepared fire arrows and the rest lit torches.

Whilst the fire arrows rained down on the Vikings oiled leather tents the tinder dry brushwood ignited with a whoosh, sending smoke towards the enemy encampment. The breeze from the south blew the smoke a fair way into the camp and, at the same time, it spread the fire along the ground. Shouts of alarm were followed by men running to put out the fires. After sending another two volleys of fire arrows blindly into the smoke Wynnstan and his men quietly withdrew, retrieved their horses, crossed the river and made their way through the woods on the far bank to the pasture where the livestock had been.

By the time they reached it the only signs that any animals had been there were the piles of cow dung and sheep droppings. There were also numerous dead bodies; all appeared to be Vikings. Evidently Æthelstan's tactics had worked and he was now on his way north.

Suddenly he heard fresh cries of alarm coming from the Viking camp. He assumed that some of those looking after the livestock had escaped and any minute now hundreds of Vikings would be crossing the river towards him and his men. Thankfully, whilst the water was shallow enough for horses to cross it was more than waist deep for men and whilst the Northumbrians waded furiously through the water to reach Wynnstan's men, their progress was painfully slow. Long before the first man had reached the west bank the Mercians had disappeared into the woods heading north after Æthelstan.

✝✝✝

They soon caught up with him as his boys slowly drove the cumbersome herd of cattle and large flock of sheep along the narrow road. The boys were kept on their toes trying to prevent strays heading off into the woods on either side but eventually they emerged from the trees onto open grassland. They could see the sun glinting off the River Worfe away to their right and Æthelstan decided that it was time to cross over to the east bank.

Fifty archers were sent back to ambush the pursuing Vikings in the woods whilst the rest drove the animals downhill towards the river. They didn't need much urging. As soon as they smelt the water the cattle changed gait from amble to a lumbering run whilst the sheep positively rushed down to the river.

The problem was trying to get the animals to stop drinking and cross over. This was achieved by a mixture of prodding with sharp spears and using ropes to pull the leaders across. The last few had just reached the far bank when the archers galloped out of the wood and headed down to join them. Mounted Vikings weren't far behind.

Æthelstan pushed on with the animals whilst Wynnstan remained behind with the archers. As soon as the Vikings came within range he gave the order and the first volley emptied over forty saddles and brought another score of horses down, spilling their riders in the process. They were aided by the fact that few Vikings had been up and about at dawn and, in their eagerness to set off in pursuit, few had bothered to don byrnies, helmets or even collect their shields. Therefore they were more vulnerable to arrows than would have otherwise been the case.

By the time that the leading riders had reached the far bank they had suffered another fifty casualties and the remainder hesitated. That changed when hundreds more Vikings arrived. They were also mounted and the new arrivals were dressed for war. A man in a helmet inlaid with gold led the way into the river and, despite the hail of arrows unleashed at them, several made it to the far bank.

Wynnstan ordered his men to drop their bows and pick up their spears. As the horsemen emerged from the water the Mercians drove spears into the chests of the horses and the exit from the river was soon a churned up mess of mud and blood. Horses thrashed about in their death throes, forming an obstacle to those behind. Meanwhile those unhorsed tried to attack the spearmen on foot. Many had lost their shields and, trying to attack the Mercians from below, they were at a serious disadvantage.

Two horsemen erupted from the water just in front of Wynnstan. He thrust his gore covered spear into the first and the horse fell back into the river throwing its rider into the water. Wynnstan didn't have time to recover his spear before the other horse got its forelegs onto the bank and heaved itself up beside him. The man to his right, who would normally have covered him, fell wounded at that moment and Wynnstan saw the Viking's axe descending towards his head.

He knew his helmet wouldn't save him and his shield was still on his back so that he could wield his spear properly. He saw death facing him but, in the instant before the axe could cleave his skull in two, someone leaped up and grabbed the horseman's arm, deflecting the axe so that it whistled harmlessly past his shoulder. However, in doing so it embedded itself in his saviour's stomach.

It wasn't until someone else had stepped forward and gutted the axeman with his spear and Wynnstan had pulled his own spear clear of the first horse that he had a chance to glance down at to see who had

366

sacrificed himself to save him. With shock he realised that it had been Swiðhun. He wasn't dead yet; stomach wounds are usually fatal but it takes the wounded man time to die. Wynnstan pulled Swiðhun behind the front ranks and tried to comfort him as the boy writhed in agony. At last it was over and someone put his hand on his shoulder. He looked up to see Eadling standing beside him.

'I'll look after his body, captain. They need you in the front rank.'

Wynnstan nodded gratefully and, trying to ignore the hollow feeling in his stomach, he took his place on the river bank once more. He realised that he'd rather taken Swiðhun's loyalty for granted, even made light of it, but he felt incredibly moved by the boy's sacrifice.

It took some time but eventually the Vikings had had enough and withdrew. As they made their way back across the river, many up to their waists in water, the Mercians picked up their bows and sent a few volleys after them. All in all the enemy had suffered nearly two hundred casualties in the skirmish.

Wynnstan's men had losses as well. Nearly fifty men had died or were so seriously wounded that they were unlikely to survive. Another sixty had minor wounds. Thankfully Uhtric, one of Ywer's best physicians, was with them and he and his assistants would do their best to patch the wounded up.

Between them Wynnstan and Eadling carried Swiðhun's body up to where the wounded were being loaded into carts taken from a deserted settlement half a mile away. Regrettably the rest of the Mercian dead would have to stay where they fell; there was no alternative as there was only room on the carts for the wounded, but they tied Swiðhun's body to Eadling's packhorse so that he could be given a proper Christian burial. Wynnstan couldn't remember the last time he'd cried but he wept as he mourned the death of a boy he'd only known for a short while. If he'd stayed with Æthelflæd's warband he'd still be alive.

†††

Eadweard sat on his horse behind the assembled ranks of the armies of Wessex and Mercia, Lord Æðelred by his side. Soon they would dismount and go to join their men in the front rank of the shieldwall which stretched for one thousand yards between two woods. The slope in front of them was far from steep but it was long and the ground around the stream at the bottom was boggy. The combination of the two should ensure that the Northumbrians were exhausted by the time they reached the Anglo-Saxon army.

Much to their annoyance Æthelflæd and Cuthfleda had been sent to the baggage train in the rear with the livestock and the boys who minded them. The other person who wasn't with the main army was Æthelstan. He, together with Ywer and the Cæstirscīr fyrd, had been given the most important task of the day.

The slope was lined by two woods where over five hundred archers were stationed, the majority on the enemy's right flank. A further two hundred archers – the most inexperienced – stood behind the shieldwall ready to send arrows at high trajectory into the mass of the enemy. They probably wouldn't cause too many casualties but it would cause the Vikings to raise their shields above their heads. Not only would that slow them down – it's difficult to run uphill holding a heavy shield above your head – but it would give the bowmen in the woods a better chance of scoring a hit.

As the enemy floundered through the marshy ground the king and the Lord of the Mercians dismounted and their horses were taken to the rear. The two men pushed their way through the ranks to take up their places as priests and monks went along the ranks saying mass and dispensing the sacrament. Boys followed them giving the parched warriors a much needed drink. Although there was a fair breeze the sun was hot.

Archbishop Plegmund walked along in front of the serried ranks with Bishop Wirfrith and several other senior churchmen. One of the priests was carrying the relics of Saint Oswald, brought from Glowecestre for the occasion. Today was the fifth of August, his feast day, and the men were assured that the long dead saint would give them victory. The irony that Oswald had been King of the Northumbrians, against whom they were fighting, escaped them.

As the weary Vikings ascended the slope the archers commenced shooting but this time none of the enemy were foolish enough to charge into the woods in pursuit of their tormentors. Instead the men of the left flank lowered their shields and those on the right changed their shields over to the other arm. Consequently the Northumbrians didn't suffer nearly as many casualties as Eadweard was counting on.

Meanwhile, two miles to the rear of the Northumbrians Æthelstan and Ywer waited nervously for the reinforcements they had been promised. If Hywel Dda and the men of Brycheiniog and Gwent didn't turn up as promised King Eadweard's strategic plan would be in tatters.

†††

Despite their inferior numbers the Northumbrian Vikings forced the Anglo-Saxon shieldwall back several paces during their initial assault. They weren't about to be prevented from returning to their homes with the plunder they had taken and many behaved like the legendary berserkers, attacking with no thought to their personal survival.

The shieldwall was in danger of collapsing in a number of places as the Norsemen and Danes carved their way through the first two rows of warriors to the nervous men of the fyrd in the rear three ranks. It was then that Æðelred acted. He drove the Vikings in front of him back as if he were demented, yelling indecipherable curses. He'd discarded his shield and used a seax in one hand and his sword in the other, cutting and thrusting as he made his way into the ranks of the enemy.

After he'd advanced five yards the Vikings began to close around him, hacking at his body, arms and head. He should have been killed but his men, seeing their lord in danger, surged after him and formed a wedge which pushed the enemy away from Æðelred. They had almost rescued him when a Dane with a hand axe brought it down on the Mercian leader's right forearm, breaking both bones and partially severing it.

Any normal man would have collapsed but Æðelred was so fired up that he ignored the searing agony for a moment and gutted the axeman with his seax. As the Dane fell at his feet, his men dragged their lord to the rear and into the care of the infirmarian monks. When they stripped off his clothes and his armour they were amazed that he wasn't already dead from loss of blood. By now Æðelred had lapsed into unconsciousness and he didn't feel the probing instruments that pulled bits of chainmail and clothing from his wounds before cleaning them and sewing him back together. Then the monks applied honey poultices to speed the healing process.

Æðelred's foray into the Northumbrian ranks may have been folly but it rallied his men who now pushed the enemy back down the hill. The men of Wessex weren't in a position to witness the Mercian lord's act of heroism but word spread and they attacked with renewed vigour.

Both sides were exhausted and had suffered significant casualties. The Vikings withdrew to regroup and boys ran along the Anglo-Saxon ranks dispensing water to the parched men.

Up to that point the sky had been cloudless and the summer sun had shone down relentlessly on both sides. Men's sight was hampered as they sweltered under their leather arming caps and steel helmets, the salty sweat running down into their eyes. The Vikings suffered most as they were some way from their baggage train and their water skins.

Eadweard gave thanks to the Lord as a few fluffy white clouds scudded across the sky, obscuring the sun for several minutes at a time and bringing some relief from the unbearable heat. Gradually the clouds became more prevalent and, by the time the Vikings launched their second attack, patches of blue sky were becoming a rarity.

†††

Not all the Northumbrians were engaged in the battle. Eowils, one of the two remaining kings, had sent three hundred men off to the flank to circle around the woods and attack the Anglo-Saxon baggage train in the rear. He reasoned that, once the men of Wessex and Mercia saw the smoke from their burning wagons, many would race back to salvage what they could of their possessions and rescue the women and children travelling with the army. However, Eowils had reckoned without Æthelflæd.

There were several hundred women – laundry maids, some wives and rather more whores – as well as hundreds of boys under the age of fourteen. The latter acted as water carriers and looked after the multitude of horses, oxen to pull the wagons and livestock on the hoof to feed the army. The rest consisted of the clergy, the wounded, the drivers of the wagons and various servants and artisans such as blacksmiths, armourers and wheelwrights.

Æthelflæd was well aware of the vulnerability of baggage trains and she and Cuthfleda had chivvied the drivers to drive their wagons into a large circle. The encampment for the non-combatants was thus protected, at least to some extent, from attack.

She had a rudimentary fence constructed of cut branches to act as an enclosure for the horses but allowed the oxen and the livestock to graze on open pasture under the watchful eye of some of the boys. Cuthfleda briefed them on what they were to do in case of an attack.

The least seriously wounded, some of the more resourceful women, the servants, artisans and the oldest of the boys were detailed to act as defenders and everyone, the clergy excepted, found something to use as a weapon.

Waldemar, the Danish jarl chosen by Eowils to lead the raid on the baggage train, was surprised to see the wagons drawn up in a circle instead of the usual haphazard layout. However, he had hundreds of experienced warriors and he didn't expect any resistance from women, boys and the wounded. He dismounted and led his men towards the wagons.

The first surprise was a score of arrows shot by Æthelflæd herself, Cuthfelda, a few women who were hunters and the older boys. Not all were well aimed, far from it, and many were using hunting bows, not war bows. Nevertheless, a few Vikings were wounded and three men were killed, including the one next to Waldemar.

As they neared the wagons he could see a determined line of defenders wielding spears, axes, long gutting knives used for butchery, daggers and even a couple of blacksmiths' hammers. He still didn't think that he had anything to worry about until some of his men off to the right cried out in alarm. A large group of animals – oxen, cattle and sheep – were stampeding towards the attackers.

The herd, maddened and panicking, avoided the circle of wagons and ploughed into the line of Vikings. Many were trampled to death whilst others suffered broken legs, smashed ribcages and dislocated shoulders. Few escaped completely unscathed.

Waldemar had a broken right forearm and a horn had torn through his byrnie, scoring a long shallow cut across his abdomen. He had scarcely recovered and was looking about him to see what had happened to his men when a screaming mob leaped down from the wagons and ran towards him. Somehow he had lost his shield, spear and sword but he still had a long dagger hanging from his belt. He pulled it out with his left hand and turned to face them.

Cuthfleda was the first to reach him. She had a sword in her hand and, to Waldemar's surprise, she knew how to use it. He parried her first lunge with difficulty and then she feinted at his head. He jerked back out of the way but she diverted her attack to his belly at the last moment. His byrnie and leather liner were in tatters and her blade sliced easily into his guts. He knew he was a dead man but he was determined to take his attacker with him.

He brought up his dagger to strike her under her chin but she was too quick for him, moving her head out of the way at the last minute. He was surprised at the agility of a woman who appeared to be approaching old age. His last thought as he collapsed in agony was that he didn't know that the Anglo-Saxons had shield maidens.

Æthelflæd looked around her in satisfaction. Not a single one of the attackers had survived. Her husband might have banished her to the rear for safety – or more likely to prevent her adding to her military reputation – but she was glad that he'd done so. The outcome would have been so very different if she hadn't been there; of that she was in no doubt. Furthermore, she had secured her own victory – albeit a small one.

After she had congratulated everyone she turned to the grinning boys who had stampeded the herd in the right direction just in time.

'Well done boys, I'll ensure you each receive a silver penny as a reward,' she smiled. Their grins quickly faded when she added 'now you had better go and round our livestock back up again.'

†††

As the Northumbrian Vikings readied themselves for another attack on the Anglo-Saxon shieldwall those in the rear turned in consternation as they heard war cries coming from their rear. They turned to see hundreds of Mercian reinforcements together with thousands of yelling Welshmen pounding up the slope behind them.

Ywer and Æthelstan had decided to keep their gesiths mounted and so ninety horsemen led the charge as they emerged from struggling through the bog at the base of the slope. Those in the rear rank of the Vikings were the youngest and least experienced warriors and none had faced a charge by armoured horsemen before. Indeed few on either side had; it wasn't a tactic that was usually employed. Warriors normally dismounted to fight.

The horses bared their teeth with the effort of cantering uphill before breaking into a gallop for the last hundred yards or so. That sight, plus that of warriors aiming long spears at them from behind helmets and shields inspired terror in the young Northumbrians and they broke even before the mounted Mercians reached them.

Ignoring them, the ætheling and the Ealdorman of Cæstirscīr aimed for the backs of the Vikings still engaged with the Anglo-Saxon shieldwall. They spitted the remaining rear rank with their spears as if they were on a boar hunt. Most then obeyed their orders and turned their horses to withdrew but battle-lust drove some of them to discard their spears and draw their swords before attacking the next rank. It was a mistake. Surrounded by the enemy, they were pulled from their horses and slaughtered.

However, it did achieve one thing. Whilst they were dealing with the score or so horsemen the line was weakened and the Saxons facing them were able to break the enemy shieldwall. Once the breach was achieved Eadweard's men flooded through the gap and began to roll the Viking line up in both directions.

Meanwhile the men of Cæstirscīr and their Welsh allies had reached the rear of the Northumbrians facing the Mercians. When the cry went up that King Eowils had been killed the heart went out of them and the remainder of the Vikings were routed. They tried to flee but they had difficulty in escaping. The archers from the woods joined the men of the shieldwall and together they formed the bull's horn formation, enveloping the Northumbrians on three sides. When the Cæstirscīr fyrd and the men of Brycheiniog and Gwent closed the circle they had nowhere to run.

'No mercy,' Eadweard cried, 'no mercy! Kill them now and your women and children will be safe for a generation.'

Wynnstan felt the slaughter of men who were trying to surrender was wrong and he paused for an instant. Then he saw the banner of King Halfdan being held aloft as a rallying point a few yards from where he stood. He was the last of the three brothers who had jointly ruled Northumbria. None had sons; if he could kill Halfdan a struggle over the throne would ensue and the Northumbrian warriors who survived would be too busy fighting each other to bother with Mercia or Wessex.

He gripped his sword and his shield more tightly and laid into the nearest Viking. The youth was inexperienced and it took Wynnstan no more than a few seconds to kill him. He stepped forward and realised that he had reached the circle of hearth warriors who guarded Halfdan. There weren't many of them left and two minutes later he'd defeated the last of them and stood within feet of the last of the Northumbrian kings.

Halfdan was the tallest of the three brothers and towered above Wynnstan. Unlike the rotund Ingwær, this brother was fit and slim. Wynnstan just managed to take this in before Halfdan swung an axe at his head. He barely had time to raise his shield before the axe thudded into it, jarring his arm and numbing it. The king tried to drag the axe out but, so forceful had the blow been, it was wedged fast in the lime wood shield.

Halfdan let go of the axe and reached for his sword. Wynnstan dropped his shield, which was now more of a hindrance than a help, and thrust his own sword towards Halfdan's throat. The Viking king had only half drawn his sword from its scabbard but he managed to duck and the thrust went over his head, scraping the back of his helmet on the way.

Wynnstan saw his chance and brought his knee up smashing it into the king's nose and mouth. Halfdan straightened up spitting out teeth and blood as he finally managed to drag his sword free. However, his nose was squashed like an overripe tomato and he'd been temporarily blinded by the blow. He swung his sword at where he thought Wynnstan was standing but it sang through empty air. Wynnstan had sidestepped and brought his own sword up as he did so. He thrust it into the king's neck and bright red arterial blood spurted out. Moments later Halfdan crashed to the ground and lay still.

Wynnstan looked around in case he was about to be attacked by another enemy but all he could see was a circle of grinning Saxons, Mercians and Welshmen cheering and shouting his name. The battle hadn't just been won. Eadweard had his wish; the Northumbrian Vikings had been annihilated.

Epilogue

February 911

The coffin sat in front of the altar as the mourners filed in behind King Eadweard and his sister, Lady Æthelflæd. Ywer walked with the other ealdormen but Æthelstan processed on his own immediately behind his father and aunt. All were glad to be inside the walls of the monastery church, now renamed Saint Oswald's in honour of the relics now housed there.

Outside a blizzard raged obliterating the footsteps of those attending the funeral of Æðelred, Lord of the Mercians. He had lingered on after being severely wounded at the Battle of Totenhale but he'd remained weak and delirious for seven months before he finally succumbed at the end of January. Two weeks had passed since that day to give the ealdormen and the senior clergy time to reach Glowecestre along the snow covered roads.

It wasn't so much as to be present at the entombment of Æðelred in a stone sarcophagus in the church but to attend the Witenaġemot, which would be held the following day. There was only one item on the agenda – electing Æðelred's successor.

It was a matter that preyed on Æthelflæd's mind to the exclusion of everything else. When her father, King Ælfred, had died, her mother, the Lady Ealhswith, had retired to a convent; this was normal practice for the widow of a king. Æðelred hadn't officially been called a king because he had no royal blood in his veins, nor would Ælfred or Eadweard have permitted it, but he had been King of Western Mercia in all but name. Although Æthelflæd had governed the land on and off for the past few years, that had been in her husband's name. Now he was dead the lords spiritual and temporal would probably choose one of their number to rule them.

One obvious candidate was the ætheling Æthelstan. Although he could claim no royal Mercian heritage, he'd been brought up there, his grandmother had been a Mercian and both his father and grandfather had royal blood, albeit from Wessex.

Had Hwiice not been taken from him and sub-divided, Deorwine might have been another. As it was, he was no longer an ealdorman and the others wouldn't accept him. Ywer would have been a strong contender if it wasn't for the fact that he wasn't a Mercian, not even an Anglian. He'd been born of Jutish parents in Cent; furthermore he'd married a Norse woman and even Norse Christians were distrusted.

Æðelred had left behind a child – the Lady Ælfwynn. She was his heir but few thought she would make a good ruler. There was always the possibility that one of the ealdormen would seek to gain power through marriage. All of them had wives – not always an insurmountable problem – but it was more likely that one would seek to make a son or nephew her husband and gain power that way.

The final option would be to recognise Eadweard as King of Mercia as well as of Wessex. He would dearly love that but Mercians hadn't yet overcome their deep-seated distrust and loathing of the West

Saxons. It might happen in time but a union of Mercia and Wessex wouldn't be accepted by the Witenaġemot and, if her brother tried to force them to accept him, it was likely to lead to conflict. A few months ago self-preservation decreed that the two should be allies but, with the threat from Northumbria eliminated, that was no longer necessary.

The more she thought about it and the more she discussed it with Cuthfleda the more she was convinced that there was only one obvious choice: she was the ideal candidate. However, she doubted that the exclusively male Witenaġemot would ever entertain the idea. She was well aware that some of the ealdormen had resented her leadership when her husband was alive but incapacitated. Now that he was dead they were almost certain to oppose her.

That evening Eadweard asked to see her privately. What he had to say came as something of a shock.

'I need someone as the ruler of Mercia who will ally themselves to me and help me to conquer the Danelaw. As far as I can see, there is no better person for that role than you, dear sister. Together we can realise our father's dream of a united Englaland through the union of all the Anglo-Saxon peoples and the subjugation of the Danes and the Norse invaders.'

'That's a dream, Eadweard, as you well know. Even if we conquer the rest of Mercia there is still East Anglia and Northumbria, not to mention the independent Anglian Earldom of Bernicia between the River Tes and the Firth of Forth.'

'Does that mean you won't help me to even recover the rest of Mercia?'

'No, of course not. Nothing is closer to my heart, but the Witenaġemot would never accept me, a woman, as their queen.'

'Queen no,' he frowned. 'But as Lady of the Mercians.'

No, she thought, of course my brother would never make me queen, even if he could – which she doubted. He wanted to portray Mercia not as an equal partner in an alliance, but as a vassal of Wessex. He always had. Well, she could accept not having a royal title if it meant hanging onto power, but he needn't think she would meekly do as she was told. They would rule as partners or not at all. But it was all a dream wasn't it?

'The ealdormen won't accept me as their leader,' she objected.

'Ah, but the Witenaġemot will. The clergy revere you for your piety and for the recovery of Saint Oswald's bones and I have secured the votes of enough of the ealdormen to ensure they elect you. I didn't even have to bribe Ywer,' he said with a grin.

She looked at her brother in surprise. It wasn't like him to spend his money to help others. There had to be something more in it besides Mercia's support in attacking the Danelaw. She soon found out what it was.

'There are a couple of small favours I'd like in return,' he continued smoothly. 'Lundenburg is at the extreme eastern end of Mercia and lies between Cent and Ēast Seaxna Rīce, part of Wessex before it fell to

382

the Danes. It would make sense for it to revert to my control, don't you think?'

It was logical, she supposed, and it was a small price to pay for not entering a convent.

'One more thing. Oxenafordascīr lies where Wessex and Mercia meet. I have plans to build burhs there as an initial step in recovering the Danelaw. However, I'm unwilling to invest men and money there unless it becomes part of Wessex.'

She thought of refusing but Oxenafordascīr had not really been part of Mercia for some years. Its inhabitants were more Saxon than they were Anglian and their ealdorman hadn't come to the funeral and wouldn't be attending the Witenagemot. Of all the shires in Mercia it was the one whose loss was one that the other ealdormen might accept if handled correctly. They'd object, of course, but that would just be for form's sake.

'Very well, I agree; but I suggest we leave announcing these two concessions until after I'm installed by the bishops as Lady of the Mercians and the ealdormen have sworn fealty to me.'

Accompanied by Cuthfleda, Æthelflæd set off the next morning to trudge through the swirling snow to the monastery church where the meeting of the Witenagemot was being held. Her feet in her dainty red leather shoes were freezing but she was feeling more uncomfortable about the meeting to come. Eadweard wasn't a Mercian, of course, and so wouldn't be attending. She only hoped that he'd been as clever in procuring her election as he thought he'd been.

THE BIRTH OF ENGLAND SERIES WILL
CONTINUE WITH

THE CONQUEST OF THE DANELAW

DUE OUT LATER IN 2021

Historical Note

900 to 910 AD (or CE if you prefer) is a decade for which there are few written records but in the years after King Ælfred's death the two Anglo-Saxon realms which remained free of Danish or Norse control – Wessex and Mercia – moved from the brink of survival to a position from where they could embark on the reconquest of the rest of the country that would become known as England.

I have used the term Viking to refer to Danish and Norse warriors. Strictly speaking it is incorrect as it refers to those undertaking an activity – i.e. sea borne raids and piracy – but saying Danes and Norsemen where both were involved would be cumbersome.

The various sources which are available often offer conflicting accounts of the same event. For example the Battle of the Holme is recorded at taking place on 13th December 902 in the Anglo-Saxon Chronicles and in 904 in other records.

Whilst something is known of the events in and concerning Wessex, far less is known about this period in Mercia. The Mercian Register is a series of brief insertions included as part of the Wessex-orientated Anglo-Saxon Chronicles. It scarcely mentions Æthelflæd until after the death of her husband and, although we know he was prone to bouts of illness, we know very little about what part his wife played in the government of Anglian Mercia until she became the Lady of the Mercians.

Some important events are largely missing from Anglo-Saxon records. For example we are reliant on Welsh and Irish chronicles for the arrival of Ingimund and his subsequent attack on Chester.

Evidently there was much more extensive written information about this period at one time because historians in the later medieval period refer to documentation which has since been lost. I have therefore had to rely on a somewhat patchy history on which to base the main events depicted in the book.

If the sequence of events – or even their existence – are debateable even less is known about the individuals who shaped those events, their appearance or their characters. Here I have to confess I have given my imagination free reign.

What is certain is that the achievements of Æthelflæd and Edward paved the way for her nephew and his eldest son, Æthelstan, to complete the unification of Wessex, Mercia, (both the Anglian half and that part in the Danelaw), East Anglia and Northumbria into one kingdom initially called Englaland – the Land of the Angles.

After Æthelstan's death the kingdom fractured from time to time but the foundations were there and setbacks to the unification of Anglo-Saxon England proved temporary.

I am particularly indebted to the following sources:

- Ælfred's Britain – War and Peace in the Viking Age by Max Adams

- Alfred, Warrior King by John Peddie

- Pauli's The Life and Works of King Alfred translated by B Thorpe

- The Warrior Queen – The Life and Legend of Æthelflæd by Joanna Arman

- Edward the Elder and the Making of England by Harriet Harvey Wood

- Æthelstan by Sarah Foot

- Anglo-Saxon England by Sir Frank Stenton

- The Anglo Saxons edited by James Campbell

Printed in Great Britain
by Amazon

18199255R00220